THE STYX Patricia Holland

THE STYX

Patricia Holland

The Styx is a work of fiction. Names, characters, businesses, institutions, places, events and incidents are either the products of the author's imagination or used in a fictitious manner. Any resemblance to actual persons, living or dead, or actual events is purely coincidental, or as stated in the Acknowledgements.

Published in 2017 by Lacuna in Armidale, New South Wales, Australia
www.lacunapublishing.com

Lacuna is an imprint of Golden Orb Creative
PO Box 428, Armidale, NSW 2350, Australia
www.goldenorbcreative.com

© Copyright Patricia Holland 2017

All rights reserved. No part of this publication may be reproduced, stored in a retrievals system, or transmitted in any form or by any means, electronic or mechanical, including photocopying, recording, scanning or otherwise, except under the terms of the Australian *Copyright Act 1968*, without the permission of the publisher.

All enquiries to the publisher: general@lacunapublishing.com

Cover design by Golden Orb Creative
Cover image "Muscinae" from Ernst Haeckel's *Art Forms of Nature* (1904)
Author photograph © Glenn Adamus

Text design and production by Golden Orb Creative
Typeset in 12pt Adobe Caslon Pro

A National Library of Australia Cataloguing-in-Publication entry has been created for this title.

Foreword

A movingly-great read! A great story teller. After reading the first chapter I found myself laughing along with the main character's wonderfully silent sense of humour which comes through easily and naturally. I loved her powerfully hungry take on life and the environment.

Aboriginal Australians and Torres Strait Islander people need to be represented by more voices in fiction. I know children in similar situations who have hardly had a whisper of life, let alone a voice.

In this wonderfully drawn protagonist, the author's unique style caused this sardonic Murri to read the entire book in a sitting. I cheered for both the author and the resilient, eccentric character who will live long in both heart and memory.

John Wenitong (Pemulwuy Weeatunga)

Contents

Foreword by John Wenitong — v

Shadows of the Wuku — 1

Prologue — 2

Part I: Disempowered — 1990s — 5

Part II: Empowerment — 2001–2004 — 73

Part III: Power Wars — 2004 — 225

Part IV: Surrender — 2014–2016 — 255

Epilogue — 260

Author's notes — 263

Acknowledgements — 266

About the author — 267

for Sophie

The villainy you teach me,
I will execute, …
but I will better the instruction.

William Shakespeare, *The Merchant of Venice,* III.i.65–66

Shadows of the Wuku

If you stay still long enough, and listen, you will hear the shadows. You can hear the stormbirds call them. They call them "Wuku Wuku". They keep me safe. The stormbirds and these shadows keep me safe.

The stormbirds watch over me all day, and in the evening they call "Wuku Wuku". I hear their call and I breathe in the night; I breathe in the shadows of the night.

The shadows stay all night to watch over me. In the morning, the stormbirds greet us both. "Wuku Wuku," they call to me. "Wuku Wuku," they tell the shadows. I breathe in the day; I breathe in the wild air.

Prologue

January 16, 2016

The shadows in The Wall have voices that never go away. When no one's there, they don't lie dormant, but travel, seeking out safe passage with any Wuku, young, old, sick or well, near and far. For the first 50,000 years, the songlines bounced happily in and around the maze of basalt walls. But for the last hundred or so, they have echoed the world, searching, searching, rarely finding a place to rest; and as far as I know, these days, they pretty much have to settle for me.

To help them rest back home, I mind-travel my way behind the main homestead and follow the track around to where the trees start to meet overhead. I love this part where the air turns cool and leopard trees puff breezes at each other. Around a few bends, the trees turn into paperbarks, tempting you to follow them downhill to the creek. But if you take the track north, through the gate and skirt Styx Lake, Burdekin plums promise sweet treats and lure you up a pretty sandstone rise and straight into the clutches of our endemic can't-go-back-bush. These days, this clump is mostly hacked away from the path, so you can travel freely. But it heralds the start of basalt land and the lava tubes that 190 millennia ago collapsed to form God's own country for the Wuku, and Hell on earth for everyone else.

You are the only one I can trust with this. I'm so full of a weird mixture of self-doubt imbued with an arrogance in the belief that so few have the capacity to understand, appreciate really. But I know if there's something there to be understood, something to be found out, you will help me find it, and you will judge me kindly; not condemn, at least.

So many memories implore me to start with them. There's the memory of first light every day touching the mint green walls. The memory of travelling through time with my mother, learning about The Wall, learning about the shadows and my wallabies, my very own bridled nailtail wallabies. I remember the feeling of water, so much water, deliciously touching me all over, selflessly.

Then there's the memory of his sweat, the smell of his sweat—sweet rancid cow manure caught in synthetic trousers. And of the dust, lingering a long time after he drives down to the road, and warning long before his return. And the chorus of floorboards from the kitchen promising a lot, but always veering to another agenda. And fear, always fear. The latter isn't an isolated memory, more a general permeation, flavouring everything, for me; distorting perhaps, shaping definitely.

Memoirs are really stepping stones of our lives. They pinpoint our journey down to a few isolated events, occasions, reflections. But I've never felt that any few of these or even a million can tell it properly. There are always too many people involved: too many tangents, too many perspectives. All the pivotal points in our lives involve others—in some cases involving their pivotal points too; in others, some mundane decision about some random thing equates to a pivotal point for us.

After she left The Styx, after my mother Rose left home, in the earliest of early days before I could type, I saved her life through my thoughts, remembering as much as I could of her every day, of our life together. But that wasn't enough. Just in case I forgot something, I dreamt my memories too, and I swallowed my dreams. Then I was sure I'd done all I could to save her.

Since then, I've spent years, more than a decade now, mulling over what to use, what to say, what not to say, how much damage the truth will cause, how much I really care, or why I should. It's become a mire of shifting uncertainty. I'm determined to publish this memoir, but in terms of facing the world with it, you are the only one I feel I can trust. You know what you'll be dealing with. I feel you are the only one who would be prepared to let my truth speak—but I will understand if you'd rather not.

Thank you again for your flowers. I think of you often,

Love, Sophie

Part I
Disempowered – 1990s

… when did he regard
The stamp of nobleness in any person
Out of himself?

William Shakespeare, *Henry VIII*, III.ii.11–13

Chapter 1

Rememory 1

He said my mother was a drunk, addicted to amphetamines, and suffering from bipolar II. He said she had gone back to her community to drink herself to death in peace. He said she had forgotten me, and was most probably already dead. He said she preferred men to me; that she changed them like she was the official Aboriginal taste tester. He was pretty sozzled at the time, but the venom he spat was sober hatred.

His rejection of my mother seeped into a rejection of me too. My soul withered. Life held no laughter for me. It was lonely and stark. There wasn't even a routine to take energy from. I existed, waiting for someone to notice I stank. Waiting for someone to notice I was hungry, thirsty, hot, cold, mosquito bitten, wasp stung.

We live on a cattle station, Styx River Cattle Station, fronting a heap of beaches and beside the Great Basalt Wall. The Styx River runs around behind our homestead and, from my favourite verandah, I can watch it roll in and out every day, twice usually. It is never apologetic in its appearance.

The name of our cattle property meant something once, said something to everyone around here. Now I suppose it still does say something—whatever the tourist brochures tell it to. In my mind, I usually just call it The Styx.

It's pretty quiet out here a lot of the time; and since my mother left, there's not a lot of joy. But there is always plenty of laughter to be heard around the place when outsiders are involved. "Going outback," they say—must be some conceptualistic coastal outback, hey. For a taste of life on a cattle station, they think—well, they mostly all definitely make it to the cattle yards. My father sheds limitless laughter in greeting tourists. You'd probably like him. Most people do. Most people appreciate the social ease he generously, freely, gives. I often recognise the relief people feel at social gatherings, in the easy and safe social harbour he offers. He is often kind, thoughtful, to them. A few short moments of time can add a great deal to a person's perception. Hail fellow well met, that's my father. Back then in the early days, they lapped it all up and he glowed in their light. When guests—paying guests—came to stay on the property, some evenings he would introduce the bar hangers-on to revolting parlour games, such as swinging potatoes in a stocking, simulating baggy balls, playing verandah bowls.

I'm just picking one random night now, in about 1993 when I was sixish, sevenish. The moon shone an almond sliver onto my face. They had forgotten to close the curtains again and the window was open in case a breeze shuffled in. My nappy was pretty much at capacity, but it was on the way to summer, so if anything, the wetness offered relief from the remains of the day's heat. My cot bed had embedded scum on the getting-out side—some remains of vomit, no longer smelling too much, stains of chloral hydrate, and saliva, lots of saliva.

This night the rail was up and the putting-Sophie-to-bed job had been done. It was silent in my bedroom if I didn't rattle the rail, and I could hear shrieks of laughter—some casually raucous, others salacious—from the bar, twenty metres from my bedroom window.

"Okay, June, show us what you can do with your balls," I heard my father say. Shrieks of laughter drowned him out for a while.

"I love a woman with balls," another wit joined in.

"Come on, Sid, your turn, grow another set," June called out.

I think there are sound grooves in the bar walls of this exchange. Every time, with each new group of tourists, he acts like it's the first time for such fun. Almost equally as ridiculous, every time, with every new group of them, they seem to actually believe that it is funny. From every tourist bus—easily one every week—he has them ball-bowling in the bar well into the night while I lie alone, scared: scared of being alone, scared of not.

In so many other ways these early years were silent ones, for me. Not that I couldn't hear, just that I had no voice. My disability gave me a part-time brain, with no-way communication. I couldn't meaningfully speak. I could shriek and scream with frustration, pain and fear, but had no ability to form coherent words. I looked basically normal, albeit very thin and frail, but I could not toilet myself or feed myself, couldn't even effectively scratch myself. I had little ability to walk. Sometimes I could totter a few steps, then randomly fall one way or another. I couldn't use my hands in any purposeful way. I could flail my arms wildly around, grab and never let go, but could not hold a cup. Or even a hand.

Rememory 2

Everyone seems to think the worst of disabled people. If they don't get normal feedback, they think you're dumb. Mentally, I can process information fast—far faster than other kids, I reckon. And I can read minds. Faces tell me what people are thinking. Faces jump from their skin and bones and shout every tiny emotion at me.

"How are you today, darling?" The voice is usually jaunty, but the eyes are always dead. The smile is dead.

"Have you been a good girl?" A self-conscious laugh, sometimes a pat of my head, and they feel satisfied: they take pleasure in their kindness.

"Thank God that part is done," they think.

"How totally revolting, ugghhh," the slight pursing and micro twitch of the lips says.

Then the dead smile swings to someone else and a light switches on. Their eyes dance in the relief of someone normal. At least I increase the joy they feel with each other's company.

I can read it all. The most miniscule flicker of malice, contempt, lust, love is written in bold capitals across their faces. These things scream at me, and sometimes make me scream. Inside.

It's called Rett Syndrome, my syndrome. Back then, when I was little, some people considered it the most extreme form of autism. It's got to be one of the worst disabilities to have. It makes Asperger's or even the most dysfunctional alphabet disorder seem mild in comparison. Rett is severely physically debilitating and painful. If you're lucky it leads to death, usually suffocation during a bout of pneumonia; but if you're unlucky, you live on and on and on and on. Interminable days of suffering. Interminable days of neglect, boredom, frustration, despair.

Some people get lucky and get drugged. If you scream and flail enough, you can get them to drug you; usually to shut you up, sometimes to put you out of your misery. Rett Syndrome means mental and physical torture for everyone involved. And it grows.

Regresses you further and further, every moment, every day, every year until your teens. Then it stops, slows at least. Sometimes reverses. A bit. If you live long enough. Boys with Rett are lucky. They never get born.

Rememory 3

"What a good man looking after that poor little creature," they all say. "He is so unselfish, doesn't put her in a home. He's devoted to her."

My father loved this idea of himself. He'd cultivated it for so long that I think he actually believed it. It had grown onto his skin, only flaking off in the privacy of his own home. Just for me.

My mother became a burden. At first it was okay, more than okay. It was only shortly before the cachet of mixed-marriage days. He was the centre of everyone's gossip, and he glowed. In those early days, she was who he thought she should be. Grateful, he thought she should be, and I think he believed she was. At the start.

It was good then, up until she left, up until I was five and a half. She made pancakes for breakfast every Sunday. And I had a birthday party every year; so did he. Even though I didn't have any friends, she'd find some. She made it such an occasion to dress up—she always made me a new dress—and bring presents and have fun, around me, in the name of me. She'd make a special cake and he'd help me blow out the candles. And she'd take photos—some of him and me, mostly just of me. This happened every year she was here. But then, when she strayed from his agenda and developed ideas and wants and loves, he really had no option but to lose her. And she would have to suffer because of it. Never to benefit from her life with him, he told her. And showed her.

Rememory 4

After my mother left Styx River Station, my father didn't really need anyone. He liked being the token single father, someone all the mothers fêted and simpered at. He liked making a show at school events of being the devoted father.

I can see him now, pushing me up the path to school from the car park. He, the picture of an RM Williams rural bloke. Me, skinny, legs and arms undersized and always askew, pushed in an undersized pastel-pink wheelchair that, from its very nature, could never be cute.

He always had something slightly skew-whiff to match me: rumpled hair, shirt-tail hanging out, sleeves rolled too high, uneven. Something for everyone to latch onto to pity, to offset the endless well of pity they couldn't allow themselves to properly begin to negotiate towards me. It could almost comfortably be displaced onto him. He would only have to turn up three or four times a year at most, to attract the tag of devoted father.

It wasn't a big deal for him to no longer have my mother around. He always liked going to social functions alone or with a wingman or two. He attracted more attention that way. For him, the chase for attention was sublime. He walked differently, dressed differently, stood taller. And smelt of going out.

Rememory 5

My father always had so much to do, he said. Dozing with a book in a squatter's chair was research, he'd say. Reading *Country Life* magazine was keeping abreast of things. Apart from going to sales and conferences, in the early days, he didn't seem to do much in the cattle side of things—plenty of staff to do that—but he always had some project in the offing, some scheme to roll out, some way to big-note himself—mostly to himself. And to his cronies.

He has—had—three main cronies: Silas, Dominic and Warren. Creepy crony number one, Psycho Silas, is ace wingman and the master manipulator, with money to invest from his very lucrative psychiatric practice in Leichhardt, a town with the highest mental health problems per capita in the country. His greatest joy is in seeing the impact of his manipulations—usually to the detriment of others involved, and not always for his own personal gain. The pain of others is sufficient joy for him. His patients, especially those underage or in government care facilities, are frequent targets, often involving inappropriate sexual behaviours—sometimes on his part, but by no means necessarily.

Crony number two, Dodgy Dom, is a bit of a wingman too, a small-town lawyer, a minor investor with major free legal advice who, at nineteen and still at uni, married the wrong woman for the wrong, but then socially pragmatic, reasons. He is tall, not bad looking in a rugby union way, with a resulting mutual magnetism towards women—pretty well any women—which generally turns to petulance on his part if they don't continue to show sufficient interest in him; and contempt when they do.

The third crony, generally an afterthought and only included when they need him, is Warren, the fixer. Rabbit Warren is on the bottom of the pecking order and crony social hierarchy, and definitely not an investor in terms of cash. He used to manage his parents' gift shop, but when that went broke, he has worked on and off at Styx River, calling himself head stockman, manager, overseer—whichever title takes his fancy at the time. The highlight of his life always involves something dodgy, more often than not borderline illegal, and in many cases straight out illegal. When it suits, especially when travelling overseas, thus limiting the chance of being sprung, he'll claim to be a police officer—always a sergeant; significant that it's never inspector. These days he's a communications officer for the police. Still not a real policeman.

The four cronies have always been a tight group. Even when one of them drinks too much and abuses one or the other of them, the rift is only ever temporary. They always have a plan to hatch, and I think they love the togetherness of hatching plans, probably more than the plan itself.

You'd think this sort of stuff would wash over me. Especially when I was five, and even when I was ten. But not much happened to me, ever, and while my syndrome limited me physically, my mental faculties were intensified, so anything, everything was noticed. And noted for future rememories.

Rememory 6

Rett Syndrome does lots of bad things to me, inside me. Some days are bad, often the days are bad. Some days the pain in my head, in my bones, in my everywhere, comes on and I scream. And scream till blood comes into my throat.

In the early days, my mother gave me medicine—red mercy medicine—but it took a while to work. I screamed in her face, my hands wrapped in her hair, wrapped in mine, twined, twisted in crazy-girl fists grabbing, dragging, ripping the pain away—hers and mine—my face in her face, noses smashed together, me screaming in her face, she screaming inside, weeping outside, her tears washing the red medicine stains from my chin down my neck, soaking our clothes. Until the pain stilled. Fist nests of black and gold hair stilled. Then I'd sleep. But she wouldn't.

After she left, the hair was only gold.

Rememory 7

They call us the halo children. For some cruel parody of life, we have a sort of ethereal beauty. You can see the veins under our skin even though it feels all smooth. We're like that while we're young—before puberty—even though most of us don't live that long. But if we do, when our hormones go ultra-haywire, we mostly seem to grow fat and ugly. Because of neglect, I reckon. Disabled kids rarely get braces. No one worries too much about diet and exercise for us. We don't get bought Proactiv face wash, or cute little eyeshadow packs for Christmas. We don't get put on hormones for our skin. We don't have boys chasing us. Well actually sometimes we do, but only the real warpos, not in the will-you-go-out-with me way.

I didn't get fat. After my mother left, I didn't get enough food to get fat. If I had usable arms I could have raided the freezer for out-of-date frozen fish fingers or frozen peas. But I'd need usable legs too. If I had hands that could hold things, I could have fed myself. If I had a voice, I could have demanded food. But my hunger was no one's main priority. Of course I got fed, but I couldn't eat quickly. Everyone thinks eating slowly equates to not being hungry. So I suppose I stayed in the ethereal stage, a bit shrivelled ethereal.

At home, I was trapped in a second-rate wheelchair—when I was lucky. Other times I was left in my cot soaking in excrement with stale urine blistering my skin. Shame I was blessed with exceptional olfactory senses. This is the life many of us lead, hidden from outside scrutiny. Even more so for me, hidden in out-in-the-sticks-Australia, a place of romantic wonder under the golden sun.

Rememory 8

The stormbirds endlessly plead for the day to begin. It's still and quiet. This is the time of day when I am most aware of being alone. I'm most scared at this time of the day. The stormbirds scream my fear, my silence.

No one else is awake and I'm hungry and wet and *stinkin'*. Believe me, no one's in a hurry to wake up and face that. Everyone's sick of having to change my *stinkin'* nappies. Mum never worried, but. Every morning, she always jumped up and said, "Hey, Soph, let's sort this *stinkin'* nappy." I love the word *stinkin'*.

Everyone's sick of having to spoon-feed and clean up after me too. You can see it in their eyes. Hovering on the edge of the horror of imagining what it's like to be me. Even good people hover on that edge of horror—good, bad, everyone hovers—no one really goes there. They may glimpse, but never visit waking up inside a dead person's body, trying to move limbs you're not really connected to, beating on the smeared Perspex willing someone to let you out. No one does. No one finds you. No one is looking.

Hours after I woke, before I saw anyone, I could hear voices. My father must have made the call. I didn't hear the phone ring and believe me, I would have. Station phones have this ear-piercing phone projector bell ringing thing and it has no mercy.

"G'day, maayt, how goes it?"

On the other end of the phone, I could vaguely hear some bloke say my father's name—or maybe I just inserted the usual sub-text. No introduction necessary.

"Yes, it's me, how did you know?" My father always says that.

He's always surprised when people recognise his phone-bellow. The bellow is honed from when the phone lines were very dodgy party-lines. He learnt to phone-talk over the crackle and lots of other background voices. My father likes to make sure he's heard.

"There's about two hundred and fifty empty greys, and a hundred and fifty pregnant. ... No, no brindles, just a hint of gold on some. ... Yep, all white tails, no white faces. What are they paying? ... Mmmm, they'll need to do a bit better than that. No point in keeping them in the yard for that. ... Let me know if they come to the party. If I don't hear from you by smoko, I'll open the gate."

Stomp, stomp, stomp to the kitchen to make coffee. If he hears Sharon, "the nanny", banging around, he'll yell to her, "How about a cuppa, darl." It is never a question. And there is rarely an answer. Sharon bangs a few cupboards, then stomp, stomp, stomps out to the verandah with his coffee.

"Have you got Soph up yet?" He has asked her that every single day of her existence at The Styx. "She'll need changing, and breakfast." He says it as if they go together like tea and scones, bread and butter, surf and sand.

There's a newsreel of the world I see and hear in my head. I watch and record everyone out there having a good time, having a bad time, wasting their options, talking about me, arguing over who has to "look after" me, planning things that scare me. I am alone, waiting for others to do what they want to me, to this discounted mind and rotting carcass of a body. I've not been allowed to completely rot away, but it is very clear to me that it is not necessary to have depression to crave death.

Chapter 2

Rememory 9

It's a wild place, my place.

Every morning, and at various times during the day, I'm plonked on the verandah.

"There you go, Soph," a jaunty voice (on a good day) says.

"I'll be back in a sec, just have to …" That's Sharon who gives me reasons—she feels she has to justify her actions because she's on the payroll. Her voice has that, "I'm a diligent and very, very busy person," ring to it.

My father, however, rarely gives a reason. With him it's almost always just, "There you go, Soph."

I love mind-chatting and passing the time of day with the view. I can see out beyond the islands. I can see the start of the basalt wall and the rainforest, and I can even see the town of Lilian Bay, way into the distance on the other side of Lilian Bay. Both the town and the whole bay have the same name, weird, hey. It should be Lilian Bay Bay, I reckon. Strange calling a town Lilian Bay, but, hey.

"Good morning, sea; good morning, sand," I mind-say.

"Good morning, Sophie," they both say back. Very well-mannered in terms of small talk, the sea and the sand.

Nothing is ever the same through my verandah rails and out over the cliff. The beach changes its mind at least four times each day. My eyes walk from my house to the sea, and the sand is never the same twice. One day it throws prickles and greying moondust, the next crunching salt and quicksand. Sometimes smooth, sometimes rippled, seabeds peel a kilometre out to sea.

The nearest beach that I can see is Pandanus Beach. On its southern end, the beach forms a creek that feeds into an inlet where people paddle-board and putt-putt around in small boats, and pelicans stand in ankle-deep water watching people fish really badly. It's called Lilian Bay Causeway Lake; well that's what the sign says, even though it's not really a lake. Everyone just calls it The Causeway. The creek's got a proper name too. Officially it's

Basalt Creek, but no one calls it that. They just call it The Creek. It doesn't have a sign, but.

Pandanus Beach is a really tidal beach. It has a bore tide on a king tide. It's scary way out there where the low water mark shrinks. When the tide turns, people try not to panic. They try not to rush to out-walk it back to the high tide mark, but they do. I do too, in my mind, for them.

During the week, there's virtually no one walking along The Causeway. At weekends, it's a fisherman's fishing place. Cars creep in at all times of the night spilling out to their own closely guarded secret spots. It's all to do with the tide and generations of passed-down knowledge. I've never seen anyone actually catch anything, but there's always plenty of blood on the ground when we go over that way, and the fisherers, they keep coming.

My mother said the people over at Pandanus Beach are different. It's where she grew up.

"They are united by their difference," she said. "No one chooses to live there if they have other options. The place claims its inhabitants. They move in as a last financial resort," she said.

"It's too tidal for most people, not really a swimming beach, but you'll never get cheaper beachfront land. That's the main reason they come," she told me.

Apart from the few houses in The Causeway bowl, Pandanus Beach is all beachfront: one long, lonely, mixed strip of community history. They are mostly 1950s original beach shacks, a smattering of 1980s monuments to the socio-economic rise of the tradesperson, and now two or three testaments of the 2000s—the monuments to hard-won financial comfort. The people who come rarely leave, even when they can afford to leave. They can never explain what keeps them there.

My mother told me that Pandanus Beach taught her to live in the present.

"It's taught us all to live with little and to expect lots from life," she said.

Every weekend that we drove over The Causeway—even still, even these days—kids are fishing, old men are fishing, there's always an Islander woman in a long flowing, blue flowery dress fishing. There are those who just sit, those who just think.

"They're not waiting," my mother said, "they're just living."

From where I sit now, I can see countless islands, some floating into shore wearing petticoats, some misting into the horizon. The coastline sprouts the oddest foliage, tufts of surprised crazy-man hair along the ridges, stunted pandanus with funky branches frozen in sashaying dervishes. On the northern end of the causeway inflow, mangrove swamps seep into columns of hexagonal rock, lifting fifty metres up from the sea. Thousands of these shapes fold neatly into each other, perfect fit, perfect six-sided shards. There's a geological theory to all of this, but most don't need to know.

My mother's old house where she grew up is on the northern strip that separates The Causeway Lake from the sea. It looks empty now when we drive past, though sometimes the lawn has been mowed, but the house has never been painted. Perched on the strip like that, it seems a tenuous existence at the mercy of the elements, at risk of dissolving into the water table.

She told me that the locals knew their stuff back then in the 1950s.

"In Cyclone David we had one hundred and fifty-five kilometre gusts, but our skillion-roofed shack stood proudly in its path. Louvres screamed, but lived. Fibro walls strained, but stood firm. The old asbestos roof levitated, but soaked back to rest. Just down the coast a bit, massive brick monstrosities exploded. Nature's retribution, we strip-dwellers smugly thought," my mother said.

That's the sort of stuff she told me.

Her old place is the closest settlement to Styx River Station where I live, but it takes the longest to get there. It's so, so close across the basalt maze walls. But, by the only road in, it's a three-hour drive through town, circling two vast corporation-owned cattle stations. As the crow flies, Styx River is a mere ten kilometres from my mother's old house. As the crow flies, for me, it's a universe apart.

My mother loved that place growing up. She'd get so excited at times, she'd gush at me.

"I love the retirees on bandy-legs who smile and aren't in a hurry. I love The Causeway melting pot of inhabitants, living in jaunty-roofed shacks nestled around the caravan park. I love The Causeway pride and joy—the fish and chip shop. I love their display of framed certificates wallpapering the shop declaring 'Best Fish and Chips on the Coast'." I counted 12 frames.

"I love the fifth Sunday of the month markets," she said every time they were on.

"I love the pink and blue paddle-boats," she'd say every time we passed them.

She loved lots of things, and she loved me. I know she did.

I loved it when she was like this—she was so happy. I hate what I've lost. I hate what I've been cheated out of. I hate her for her weakness in allowing it all to happen. *How could you let it happen? You forgot me. How could you forget me?*

I hate, I hate, I hate. I hate who I am. I hate me.

Rememory 10

It's wild out there today. The sea is going sideways fast. It looks like a wall again, higher than the person standing on the sand. The tide rushes the water in, the wind rushes it sideways, and the sand's sweeping sideways too. I feel in the midst of ethereality. Grains of sand float, fleet, sideways across the tidal flats, across the bay almost to me. A time-release video sped up. It's beautiful. Also, freaky.

My parents told me things I shouldn't have heard. People often forget, not realise, not care maybe, that I can hear, understand. And I can hear what people say on the other end of the phone. My hearing is that good.

My father was away in Thailand with his chief crony, Psycho Silas. My mother rang their Bangkok hotel suite, and Silas answered. While she was small-talking the "hello, how are things" to him, I saw her face freeze, her eyes shrink to dead. I could hear her heart, and then I couldn't. I think it stopped too.

"He's in the other room doing naughty, naughty things to a little brown-skinned girl we picked up in a bar," Silas told my mother. He was obviously high, drunk, excited, all three probably.

My mother had been lonely I think, and only rang to see how things were going; for a chat.

My father was on a "fact-finding" mission into the live cattle export trade, and a few weeks before, when he started planning it, he said to my mother, "Do you want to come too?"

Her face lost energy, just slightly; her eyes shrank, hollowed, just slightly. She looked a bit taken aback, hurt that he hadn't taken it for granted they would go together—like other couples.

"I'm sure we'll be able to find someone to look after things here," my father continued, "but it's just the program …" He was referring to the artificial insemination program. "We'll have to get someone who understands cycling heifers, they're so touchy. And there's the issue of what to do with Soph."

My mother had been such an easy mark. He had known she'd offer to stay behind, to take care of things so he could go without the drama and worry of finding someone suitable to take over. I don't think she would have left me anyway. I know she wouldn't have.

They had gone through so much, finding out about my disability. The horror of such a horror is too much for anyone. Too much for her, too much for him, and so beyond too much for me. Fortunately, at the time of finding out about my Rett, no one told me about it, and I didn't have enough knowledge at that time to put what I heard into context. Back then, I hadn't put it all together. About Rett Syndrome that is.

"You deserve a break," my mother said to my father about the trip. "I'll stay and look after things here."

My father replied quickly, far too quickly. "I'll ask Si to come with me then."

As soon as he spoke, my mother stared at nothing. I could tell she knew she'd been stage-managed. Her eyes had looked bruised.

Over the phone, in Bangkok, Silas's voice rose with an excited, spiteful tinge. It smacked of how he resented my mother. "He's always been a little too smitten with the dusky, Rose."

Silas cackled more than a laugh's worth, as we both heard my father splutter at him, "Don't tell her that!"

Although I only heard my father faintly, and I certainly wasn't fully aware of it then, to my mother, his response said so much. It said it was true. It said there was collusion against her. It said that their doing something like that was a normalised situation. It said her marriage was a sham and that she was not a credible entity. It said she should be careful. And it said that he knew he would have to be too. It was a game-changer, my mother's diaries told me, years later when I accessed them.

Rememory II

The sea has given up its tempest. It is lying dormant, dark, drinking in my thoughts, refusing to offer me acknowledgement. I awoke with spiders in my hair. They are just hanging out, popped from white sacs. This is not an unexpected visitation. In some spidery breeding cycle, they regularly pop out, daily, nightly, visit in groups, then if no one notices and squashes them, the spiderlings begin to disperse gradually away, hopping from pillow to mosquito net, to wall. They mean no harm. They say hello, never to return. I am sad and feel lonely to see them go. Devastated if they are squashed.

When my father accused my mother of attempting to kill me, a new lowness of soul was born. I overheard him brag of the court case, brag of how she lost me. I know what happened, yet I still can't fathom how it could have happened.

"Yes perhaps," the judge said in the custody hearing, "but an attempted mercy killing."

My father hardly drew a fabricating breath; he wasn't fazed by this.

"Oh no, she wanted to get rid of her because she was sick of looking after her. She did it for her own selfish needs. And she drinks. Unstable. Not a fit mother," my father said he said in court.

This woman who painstakingly sewed me party dresses in Laura Ashley fabric with the softest silk voile collars.

"She's mad, the bitch; dresses her up like a doll. She's off her tree. Unstable. She wears cheesecloth and hangs 'round with hippies. She drinks and spends too much money—bipolar two. And I have proof. See these pictures? Year after year, she's parading her around in new dress after new dress. She treats her like a show pony. Unstable. Not a fit mother," my father said. And so did his cronies, and so did their wives, and so did their friends.

And he bought it. The judge bought it. The judge had judged and had bought into this woven and patched fabrication. The judge who was judged to have the wisdom. Judged fit to wield the power.

In court, you could see the judge and my father instantly bonded. Over the six and a half days of divorce proceedings they reminisced together. Initially when he was called, and later when he gave evidence, my father glowed the confidence of a fifth-generation rural empire hand-me-down. The judge, keen to vicariously escape his own solitary confinements, showed off his rural knowledge, his affinity, looked pleased at being able to drop a term or two in validation of his rural industry-ness. Soul mates. Romancing the bush. Both salt of the earth. Together, salt in my mother's bloody soul.

"Sole custody," the judge said. "Safer for her to stay in the comfort and security that she knows, with the nanny. And her father," he added almost as an afterthought.

"Can't make the property unviable," the judge said, "for the child's sake—a child with special needs."

"But some financial provision for the wife's education; should she choose to take it up. Perhaps when, if, she finishes, sorts her life out, the contact could be reviewed. Supervised until then," the judge said.

My mother's friend was a barrister. Even she couldn't crash through my father and the judge's bond.

My mother's barrister friend knew the gossip. The judge's wife was a drunk.

"He is a good man," my mother's barrister friend mimicked the sycophants.

"With all he had to put up with. He never complains. Does all the shopping, stocks the fridge," my mother's barrister friend said.

"He organises and pays for the housework, the washing."

"He says nothing as every night she drinks her way through the evening game shows."

"He says nothing as her head droops, slumped, spinning into her unwashed stench."

"He says nothing as he nightly picks her up and puts her to bed—carrying her."

My mother's barrister friend said she extrapolated the next bit. Imaginative, barristers are.

"He returns for a dropped slipper, a solitary glass, silently gathers the bottles and even more silently places them wrapped in newspaper in the bin. A soliloquy to tolerance and devotion. He supports her soddened soul. She will never leave."

"There is never a mention of rehab," my mother's barrister friend said.

Rememory 12

My father drove me home after my custody hearing. A ten-hour drive, speeding on a cloud of cigarette smoke and fast food. A couple of hours into the trip he rang my mother.

"I can't stop her screaming. Do something will you. Say something. You are so manipulative. You've brainwashed her. I'm her father. Tell her she's going home with me. Tell her she belongs with me now. Tell her she has to, that's how it is. Tell her to be happy. With me. Now."

At first my mother was granted fortnightly access. "Supervised."

"Three hours on the second Saturday, and three and a half on the adjacent Sunday. No overnight stays," the access order said. Too risky. Too unstable, it implied.

To supervise, my father chose a woman both he and my mother knew. My mother's mother wasn't to be trusted: too weak and under her power. His mother couldn't face it: too weak and under his power.

He chose a social worker, an ex-girlfriend of Psycho Silas's. The previous girlfriend of a previous boyfriend of my mother's. She had never liked my mother. She always avoided looking into my mother's eyes. My eyes, too. During these access visits, my mother looked like a labrador trying to please. The other woman plumped in the power of the rejected.

The social worker ex-girlfriend of Silas's called the shots of when and where we met, and my mother complied. Anything, anywhere, anytime.

The social worker ex-girlfriend of Silas's judged the trinkets my mother brought me. She judged the conversations my mother had with me (pretty one-sided obviously).

The social worker ex-girlfriend of Silas's wrote it all down— professional value judgments for the court.

The social worker ex-girlfriend of Silas's judged my grandmother's love of her daughter and granddaughter. This fortnightly visit was my grandmother, Lila's, only contact with me too. Supervised.

My mother graduated to fortnightly overnight weekend visits. Supervised of course, and this time by a friend of hers from way back.

The novelty had worn off. The social worker ex-girlfriend of Silas's was getting sick of spending her weekends watching my mother. The new regime was supervised by a friend from my mother's teenage days—Martha, a welfare worker and part-time artist. My mother and she had drifted apart, but stayed connected through their past.

My father knew Martha's drinking habits. He knew her dope-smoking habits. Martha was a suitable supervisor, my father's affidavit said, and the judge had ordered it be so.

My mother was allowed to speak to me twice a week for no more than five minutes each time on the phone. Those two calls had to also cover any family member of hers. If my grandmother rang, that was one of my mother's phone calls gone. Often I knew my mother had rung, that she was on the end of the phone talking, but my father didn't even bother to put it to my ear. Many of these times I was too far away to hear what she said, but I knew what she was saying.

"You forgot me," my silence screamed down the phone at her. "You forgot me!"

If my mother rang five minutes early, "You're too early," my father would say. "Ring back on time," he'd say and the phone would slam.

He was his happiest at these times.

If my mother rang five minutes late, "You're too late," he'd say. "Ring on time." The phone would slam with glee.

The conceited confidence of victory. Judged fit. Endorsed.

After she left Styx River, my mother found work in North Queensland. During their marriage, she had wanted to finish the six months left of her studies and become a journalist. My father had poo-poohed the idea. "What do you need a degree for," he'd scoff. After all he didn't have one, he'd be really saying.

"I suppose you think you'll get a job with Fairfax," my father's crony Dodgy Dominic had sneered at my mother straight after the court case. He begrudged the small amount of maintenance money set by the judge. "Yes, a life in the sticks is definitely the credential for great things." He said this just out of range of my father's hearing.

For Rural Press, however, my mother's rural knowledge was credential enough. She became the next in a series of try-too-hard exploitees sent from Brisbane with a car, camera and notebook to North Queensland, and an expectation to file too many far-flung stories and too many pictures every week. My father'd try to hide her published stories from me, but when he forgot, sometimes I'd see her picture as a photo byline on the front cover of *Country Life*.

One allocated-phone-contact-night, when my mother was travelling for a story, she rang too early. I was in my wheelchair, right next to the phone when my father answered it. Mum was driving up the Atherton range from north of Innisfail, where public phones were scarce. She rang at the bottom of the range. It was five fifty-six pm.

"You're too early," he said. His slam of the phone stabbed through my mother's ear, through my mother's heart.

She drove so fast up that road, she later told me. It was raining and her tears blinded her around the ridiculously tight bends twirling the mountain. She couldn't drive faster. Gravel became ball-bearings impossible to see in the dark. Impossible to disregard. The guardrails were only meant as guides, not second chances. It was further than she realised to the next phone. She was never going to make it. Halfway up, still no phones, nowhere to pull over at all. Then a caravan park motel glowed at the next bend. Gravel delivered her to the "Enquiries" door.

"Please, please can I use your phone, it's urgent," she said. They looked shocked. She looked like a crazy woman, a desperate woman.

"It's past six. You're too late." He slammed the phone down again. It was six oh-three pm.

A few months later, it was my fortnightly weekend with my mother and opening night of Martha's art exhibition. The affidavit stipulated pick-up time was ten am Saturday at McDonalds in Leichhardt. My father had dictated the pick-up and handover times and location. It needed to fit in with the operations of the cattle station, the judge had said. My father was always scrupulously rigid with these times. He never allowed me to leave his car before ten am, even if he arrived early and my mother was there waiting. He'd sit in his car, smoking a cigarette with his country music blaring, waiting for that ten am to arrive.

Leichhardt is almost fifty kilometres away from Lilian Bay, where Martha lived, and on this occasion because of her art exhibition, it had been tight time-wise and headspace-wise for her. But Martha was generous.

"Of course I will supervise the handover," she said.

My father and I stayed at Lancer's Savoy Hotel in Leichhardt on the Friday night. The cattle trucks had been late picking up cattle from Styx River, and we drove into town straight after, arriving well after dark. Soon after we arrived in Leichhardt, my father's stock agent rang him.

"Maaaayyyyt, we've got some Indonesians interested in a few more heifers. Doesn't matter if they're pregnant, but they have to be greys and no black tails, no white faces. Definitely no brindles. They want two-fifty and they've got good money. Can you get them in by lunchtime?"

My father rang my mother the next morning at seven-thirty am.

"You can have her now, I have to get back," he said.

He was snappy and of course my mother had no idea of what was going on.

"But we're at the gallery still hanging pictures," I overheard my mother say. "We were working on ten o'clock." She was never good with change.

"Well do you want her or not?" my father said. "What sort of mother are you? You've got till eight fifteen to get here."

My mother's voice was panicked, desperate to comply. Scared he'd use it to say: "Bad luck, you're too late."

But he had weekend plans that didn't involve any adhesions.

"Can I come by myself?" my mother asked. Her voice was quiet.

"As long as you don't tell anyone," he said. "I don't want to see this in an affidavit or anything."

Rememory 13

Sometimes the sea reminds me that I have no life. It tells me how perfect the world is. Perfectly calm turquoise sea. Perfectly blue cloudless sky. Perfectly perfect weekend. Inhabited by perfectly perfect peaceful lives living perfectly perfect existences. All perfect except mine. The windless air whips me in the face, slaps me until I'm senseless with loneliness; a lonely, wasted existence. Sometimes the sea is just too perfect to bear.

Two weeks after Martha's art exhibition, on handover, my mother asked to see me on Mothers' Day, the following Sunday. The court order said that this was allowed, but he'd forgotten, hadn't factored in that he had to bring me into town the next weekend as well. My mother was never allowed to pick me up from Styx River homestead, my father had insisted in the custody hearing. "Too disruptive to the cattle station operation," he'd said to the judge. The judge had nodded, knowingly nodded.

"Never to set foot on the place again," my father had said to my mother.

My father said to my mother, "Get out of my face. No more playing this game. You're only doing it to spite me. You know you're making it harder on her. You're pathetic. Insisting on carting her around from pillar to post. Insisting on ringing her, talking to a silent phone. How do you know she's even there listening? You're just so pathetic," my father said to my mother.

"You are dead to me," he said to my mother. "You are not going to benefit in any way from your life with me," he said. Again.

"She's a pain in the arse every time she comes back from you," he said when my mother rang to confirm the Mothers' Day access.

"She screams for hours every time. I'm so sick of it," he said. "I'm so sick of the sight of you. What about my needs? You're so selfish. You haven't changed. It's all about you. She doesn't care who looks after her. I give her everything she needs."

"I'm sick of all this messing around. It's too disturbing, distressing," my father said to my mother. "You're not seeing her anymore. At all. Full stop. I will put a stop to this access nonsense," he said.

My mother had thought she was on track for access to be reviewed. She was right.

Rememory 14

I was still only five years old when my mother found out she had lost all contact with me in a fifty-minute judge judgment.

My mother had run out of money. The custody case had sucked up more than all her settlement money. Legal Aid wasn't an option, she was told. She defended herself. She failed.

I was in the Family Court childcare centre with Sharon "the nanny" for precisely sixty-five minutes. After the hearing, my father stuck his face in the door and said, "Ready," to Sharon. There was no need to make eye contact.

He picked me up and shoved me in my wheelchair, didn't bother to strap me in, and wheeled me into the lift, then along the street a bit, to a coffee shop. Sharon happily trotted after. Food was sure to be on the agenda.

The coffee shop was tight space-wise, so he backed my chair into a corner where the trays were kept.

"Don't bother taking her out of the chair, just give her a bottle," he said to Sharon.

When we were out, he usually had Sharon add a double dose of chloral hydrate to my bottles of milk; strawberry milk, he called it. "To keep her comfortable," he said.

To keep me quiet and him comfortable, he meant. But I often complied and drank the sickly stuff. Oblivion was my favourite place to visit.

Sharon ate her vanilla slice with her right hand while holding the babies' bottle to my mouth with her left. She was concentrating on her vanilla slice, and didn't notice I'd slipped to the side and was falling out of my wheelchair. Milky pink dribble dribbled from the bottle into my hair, into my eyes, up my nose.

My father didn't notice either. He was talking to Psycho Silas on the café's payphone. "Hi, yep, we won. We covered everything, I think. All the same mantra," my father said.

He spoke fast, animated, triumphant, oblivious to everyone in the coffee shop. "Yep, Yep. Unfit mother. Depression. Drugs. Is seeing a psychiatrist. ... Yep, yep, the one you said. His report was good. It said she spoke of multiple partners, often talks of life having no meaning, history of taking anti-depressants."

Silas must have been commenting, because my father paused. Not for long though.

"Yes, yep he read that part of the psych report twice; how she talked often about how her whole family were devastated by what happened to her when she was in grade eleven. How she never really got over it. How it changed them all—her mother, her brother, herself—turned them all even more dysfunctional. That bit seemed to be pivotal, I reckon. Made them all out to be soaks, druggies. Damaged."

Silas must have got another few words in.

"Yep, yep," my father yepped back. "Yep, we argued mentally unstable. Yep, yep, everything you said. A danger. Sexually promiscuous. Abo alco—we didn't say the Abo bit, but it was understood."

Silas's cackling cackled down the phone and onto the vanilla slices, but my father was on a roll, and hardly paused.

"Yep, yep, we said everything you said. Rose keeps changing jobs, a drifter. The access is causing the child stress. Every time she returns, the child is distraught. Too much carting around. Causing everyone stress. Too confronting, too disrupting. Preferable under the circumstances of the severe disability, for the child to stay in the comfort and security that she knows. With the nanny. And her father. Without any contact, until further notice. Until she sorts herself out—yeah, big joke, you could see even the judge knew that wouldn't happen. ... Yep, he acknowledged Rose's 'little job'. Said let's see if she can stick with it. ... Yep, everything you said. I think we included everything, yep, yep," my father yepped to Silas on the phone.

There was a short silence this end.

"No, she represented herself. It was embarrassing. So pathetic. She tried to do the legal speak thing. People were trying not to laugh. She had no idea. Really, totally pathetic. I felt sorry for her," my father said.

"Yep, Yep. The judge agreed," my father continued. "More stable for the child, and safer, to stop the contact temporarily, the judge said. To be reviewed, he said, when—if—the mother sorts her life out. Yep, yep, that's what the judge said," my father said. "Yep, she's gorn for good."

I slithered to the floor and my head bounced off the last bit. Sharon had to put her fork full of vanilla slice back on the plate. She dragged me up into my chair and did up the straps.

People watched and their faces said, "What a good man with all he has to put up with."

My father rang my mother soon after that last court case, very soon after, that night in fact. There was a simplicity, a calmness in how he spoke. He had a kindly voice almost.

"It must be very hard for you," he said. Then hung up.

Chapter 3

Rememory 15

After my mother left, my life was shit. Survival shit. Sad shit. Sick shit. But when I started school, some things at least, started to change. That first bus trip into school began the trudge of undeathing. My father hated that I went, that he had no say in it. Losing control. It was like history repeating itself one generation along.

My mother had organised it all. Before she left, she had me registered with the Education Department and, back then, failing death—my death—or protracted medical appointments he'd never bother to make or attend, it was too late for him to change anything. Once I was "on the books" Education Department-wise, I was in the system. I was mainstream. He had to send me. He must have been livid—under the surface, and a bit above.

My mother had fought and made many enemies in insisting that I get to go to school. She was pretty determined. Quietly. She would probably have even pulled out the racist card if she'd needed it. Every card, if she'd needed it.

The occupational therapist and special-ed teacher she'd been taking me to were not supportive of me going to school. Or of me having access to an electronic communication board. People always thought I was dumb—less than dumb really—virtually vegetative. They refused point-blank to fill in any of the necessary forms. They were pretty toxic, and very patronising.

"Hello, Sophie," they'd over-enunciate as if my hearing had Rett.

They'd talk the same way to my mother. "Hello, Rose, and how is Sophie today?"

They said "Rose" in a drawn-out manner, especially the "o" elongated into an "owww" and a downward intonation of superiority.

They used to say, "Hello, Rose, and how are we today?"

But my mother replied, "You look much the same as usual, fairly fresh really, government job I suppose …" and on she rambled.

They weren't impressed. My mother was getting uppity, they thought. And they were being so nice to her. Nice in an as-long-as-you-keep-to-the-rules way. Social rules, I mean, their social rules, run by "people like them". All was well as long as Mum knew her place within the racial tolerance dance.

The occupational therapist and special-ed teacher had been initially a little too welcoming to us—instant best friends. Progressive, small "l" liberal types, glowing in showing indigenosityship—as long as my mother was who she should be, and grateful for their patronage.

But Mum strayed. When she didn't agree with them, brought up the subject of communication boards, schools for me—proper schools, where you learn things schools—their eyes rolled. And their words were more carefully enunciated and stretched and went down at the end of the sentences. As if they were statements of what would be.

Mum stopped lifting the ends of her sentences too. And didn't flinch—well not much—at their exchange of contemptuous looks. The volley of looks that said, "these sorts of mothers will never face the fact that their child is simply retarded." But eventually their voices went up at the end of their sentences, squeakily up—a fair while later though, after Mum wrote to the Minister.

She would never have written to him but, if she hadn't run out of options. If they hadn't kyboshed all her suggestions, hadn't been dodgy, Mum would never have done it. But they really gave her no option. Just after I turned five, my mother again brought up the subject of communication boards and schools. We were at the special-ed unit in Heathwood, the nearest biggish town to Styx River. Heathwood lost its country charm as it started to service the local coal mines, and developed into supermarkets, McDonalds, Kentucky Fried Chicken, endless takeaway outlets and rockblock motels designed for driving into and not staying long.

The special-ed unit was in an upmarket donga, a little way off the main drag, down a newly bitumened road, and positioned just before and beside the flash new Heathwood State School. Mum parked at the back of the car park under the only tree, a sad and lonely specimen, and walked fast, wheeling me up the ramp, eager to get me into the air-conditioning. Instead of going straight into the big "school" room, Mum stopped at the office marked "Director".

"Hello, Kourtney," Mum said. "I'd like to talk to you about a communication board for Sophie."

"Yeeeessss?" Miss Kourtney enunciated the word into a question loaded with surprise that it was an issue, and that it wouldn't be for long. I was nervous. I knew there was going to be an "issue" issue, and my repetitive back-of-hand to mouth flapping-slapping increased speed and intensity. The dribble started dribbling. My mother automatically leant over and held my slapping hand gently to stop it getting damaged by my teeth. Her touch was cool, and I relaxed. She let my hand sit in my lap, and the flapping-slapping slowed to a gentle pinching then slowish flap-slap.

My mother's voice was very pleasant, as if it was the first time she'd said it. "I would like Sophie to have a chance to communicate. For her to get an education. A communication board might allow her to communicate, to make choices. Then next year, I'd like her to attend a proper school just like other children. She should be given an opportunity to learn."

My mother took a breath, almost a sigh. Miss Kourtney's mouth turned into one much older in response to the "proper" comment—a mistake on my mother's part perhaps, but in hindsight I think intentional.

"Yes, Rowwwse, I received your written request—on both accounts; and I have written back, yesterday," Miss Kourtney said.

That meant she hadn't sent it yet. She didn't poke her chest out, and she would have, to award her own pious diligence, if she'd already sent it. But I think she'd written it. Her words were like written words.

"I don't think that sort of equipment would be suitable for Sophie," Miss Director Kourtney pompoused.

"And furthermore, my professional opinion is that I don't believe it is appropriate for Sophie to attend a mainstream school."

Miss Kourtney spoke from the back of her throat, with assumed authority. Then the look of superior "professional" wisdom crossed her face, setting her eyes, followed by the lingering silent sneer of "mothers like you …".

Miss Kourtney always made out that everyone should feel grateful for being allowed to attend "her" school. Especially so after the sign "Director" appeared on her donga office door. And her breasts looked larger after that too. There were limited places in the unit, she'd intimate. Total crap—she was always watching her arse and making sure that she maximised her numbers, to maximise her pay scale. It simply wasn't in her interest for anyone to "graduate". It was a small town, limited catchment area.

"Kourtney, Sophie needs to be given a chance." My mother's voice was still pleasant and reasonable, but quite definite, especially the first and last words.

She felt it was my chance for an education. All the other kids my age at our playgroup had already started pre-school at the schools they would be going to the following year. I was going to a "special" pre-school, and there wasn't any grade one progression planned—it didn't have a grade one. In those days it wasn't automatic to integrate students with severe disabilities into regular schools. Jesus, I couldn't even graduate from pre-school in those days.

"I want her to be given a chance to learn. I want her to have a communication board. A young boy in Leichhardt suddenly became 'intelligent' when he was given access to a communication board," Mum said, doing the finger inverted commas. "I want the same for Sophie."

"Sophie is a very different situation," Miss Kourtney said.

"I'm a situation now?" I thought.

"She has a different skill set from that Leichhardt boy," Miss Kourtney said.

"Yeah right, Miss Missy, say what you really mean. I don't have any skills is what you really mean." But Miss Director Kourtney wasn't listening to my thoughts.

"I have considered it," Miss Kourtney continued, "but after discussions with Kittie (occupational therapist), we decided against it."

K-Kourtney and K-Kittie—the two Ks, just need another one, hey.

As far as Director Kourtney was concerned, that was the end of the discussion. She stood up, stretched her mouth into double white lines and as she walked past us said, "We'd better start our lesson session now."

So far, my education "lesson sessions" had consisted of Miss Kourtney sticking fluffy toys and her face in my face saying, "This feels soft, soft." Enunciating extra clearly and loudly and slowly. It was a sort of chewing motion with her mouth.

I quite liked having the outing, but I agreed with Mum. I was so over the fluffy toy and face-in-my-face thing, and I didn't like the way she dissed my mother and dismissed her concerns.

"Ahhh-owwwwwwwww-gedddoffff-owww," Miss Kourtney said.

My mother has such self-control. She didn't laugh once as she untangled my fists from Miss Kourtney's hair. Mum had her lips close to her teeth—her determined look—but when she determined her next step, she probably didn't think Miss Director Kourtney would get sacked.

Rememory 16

The shells have all gone. Usually there are gazillions of them patterned up and down and across the beach, but this morning, they're all gone. Just a sparse spattering of the odd one here and there, but basically gone.

The Government made my mother cry. When she answered the phone, at first I thought something really bad had happened. But they were tears of gratitude, the deepest, deepest gratitude. My mother said it was unfortunate two local allied health workers—the two Ks—became casualties, but I don't think she really meant it.

"I'm telling a big fib," was written across my mother's face in sparkly gold letters, and her lip service words slipped to the floor.

She had, I later read in her diary, naïvely written to our local state member, who also happened to be the new Minister for Education, and told him everything. She even sent a picture of me—a snatch of time without drool or hand slapping. The halo effect can be quite a powerful persuader. It didn't occur to my mother that her letter would spark official enquiries across two departments. She didn't know the OT and special-ed director would be sent copies of her letter (I wonder if they sent a copy of the photo too?). She didn't know they would be publicly shamed and humiliated; both of them eventually dismissed, sacked.

Would she still have done it all, if she had? Yes, I think so. Definitely. I knew when she watched Miss Director Kourtney walk past her, ignoring her, after refusing to apply for even the communication board, it wasn't the end of "the issue". My mother was driven with the imperative to make sure I had an opportunity to be educated. She was a woman obsessed. "No" was not an option.

These allied health and education workers hold keys to the quagmire of options available to injured and disabled people. They know how the system works. They write the recommendations for special equipment, assistance and all sorts of facilities, options and opportunities. This local crew carefully kept the big picture stuff to themselves and dealt out the options piecemeal, as it suited them.

Another of the catalysts for my mother's letter was the other K, the OT, Kittie. K-Kittie rang my mother, telling her that there were visiting specialists to the city, Leichhardt, one and a half hours away, that I could take advantage of. It didn't dawn on Mum at first that the visits were arranged to fit in with OT Kittie's shopping needs—government vehicle, government fuel, government paying her a day's wages. My mother said she had fleetingly thought that the connection between the suggested therapist appointments and my needs was at times tenuous, but she had still been naïve. She thought it was all about helping me.

The suggested visits weren't weekly—maybe monthly. OT Kittie would meet Mum and me in Leichhardt at whichever clinic's turn it was that time. She would briefly smile at us and pat Mum on the shoulder and me on the head—carefully avoiding any risk of spittle contamination. Then she would disappear, and reappear a few hours later with a car full of shopping. We'd get another pat and we'd see her again next clinic visit.

What was going on only dawned on Mum when she—we (I was there too)—overheard OT Kittie on the phone discussing picking up sheet music one of her friends had ordered.

"Don't worry; if they're not there this week, I'll be back the week before Christmas," OT Kittie said to her phone friend.

When she later happened to mention another specialist who coincidentally coincided with this same week, Mum twigged to the pattern. How did she feel? She didn't realise anyone could be so tight with money to twiddle the system for free transport and a day's wages. Hurt, disbelief, anguish that anyone would use—exploit—a little girl so cruelly disabled. So when the special-ed director refused to apply for communication equipment, my mother got doubly angry.

Mum included an outline of K-Kittie's therapy visit practice in her letter to our local member—it's probably still on the Department file—and kept a copy in her computer diary folder. Resulting action—suspension, inquiry, termination. Miss Director Kourtney met a similar fate, but in her case for continually failing to follow educational standard protocols. It included her dealings with other kids too, a number of them.

Director Kourtney actually resigned; she didn't wait for the formal termination letter. She couldn't handle being around the scrutiny of the ministerial investigation of her implementation of educational requirements. It was basically a case of too many fluffy toys, too little accountability.

You'd think educated people would accept they had erred. You'd think they'd be shamed, repentant, humiliated. But some people—probably the sort who'd exploit the disabled in the first place—simply hate. They store their hate and allow it to swell with a growing indignity of the injustice. The indignity of losing out to a frickin' boong and retard. How dare they be treated so shabbily? How dare their status not be insulation?

Revenge brews, gurgles, waiting. And I guess OT Kittie didn't have to wait too long for her revenge. Her husband Dominic is the crony solicitor who won my father's custody hearing against my mother.

Rememory 17

I can hear the tide raging against the sand dunes. These are modern dunes, only five years old, and the sea isn't happy. You think you can appease the gods by dredging a channel? You think you can cover up a hundred years of people-abuse by a week of sand dredging? Think again. You'll get away with it for a short time, then just when you think it's worked, just when you think those brick and tile monuments are safe, the real gods of the universe will chuck a hissy fit and change it all back—and more.

All those years ago, not long before Mum left, the phone rang right on nine am. Mum was reading me a book in the air-conditioning. We were sitting right next to the phone, so when she answered, I could easily hear both sides.

"Good morning," the phone said. "Elizabeth Ellis here. I'm the Department of Education regional manager, based in Leichhardt.

Our psychologist and I would like to discuss with you the school you'd prefer for Sophie to attend. As I see it, you have five equidistant options …"

It took a while for it to sink in. My mother's body initially stiffened into auto-defence hostility response reaction to government departments, then a cloud of incredulity puffed through her. Her letter had worked. Beyond anything imaginable.

"Sophie is required to undergo assessment of her current achievement level," Miss Ellis said. "All students attending Queensland state schools undergo this testing, but in light of Sophie's disability, unfortunately the only people with the skills to assess her are in Brisbane. Would it be possible for Sophie and yourself to attend an assessment in Brisbane? It is of course fully funded."

I watched my mother's brain jump way, way ahead of where she thought even remotely possible. All the "ifs" had been bypassed. I was mainstream.

Rememory 18

The flight to Brisbane for my assessment was a nightmare. My mother sounded like she was weeping when she wrote in her diary about the trip.

The major airline pilots were on strike, and the only option—one of those ill-fated Beechcraft Barons—fluttered insignificantly for four hours each way. Unmodified altitudinal pressure changes played havoc with my brain, repeatedly triggering epileptic fits, triggering hours and hours of screaming. Mum seriously questioned what she was doing.

"Does education warrant such torture?" she wrote in her diary.

"If I'd known this was the cost, probably not. But there are no specialist assessors locally who have the skills to test someone with the extent of Sophie's disabilities," my mother wrote.

In the Brisbane office of Anne Sorenson, testing someone like me didn't seem to be a problem. The day before, when we arrived at Brisbane airport, we took a stinkin' taxi to the city and stayed at Lennons Hotel. Lennons is a bit old-world flash, and Mum liked it because it was on street level and she could wheel me straight into the Queen Street Mall. When we walked into the hotel lobby, the man at the desk knew us and spoke to me by name. I liked him.

"Hello, young Lady Sophie, and how are you this fine afternoon?" He's called me Lady Sophie forever—I can't remember when he started.

We had spent quite a bit of time in Brisbane over the past few years, when they were trying to find out what was wrong with me, when I was diagnosed with Rett Syndrome.

"Put her in a home," the diagnosing paediatrician advised. "Get on with your life. She will never be older than ten months of age mentally, less probably."

I was there, fully mentally functioning at three years old when he said this. I reckon I was more like mentally five years old. I'm way smarter than most kids. Modest too. The specialist was old and meant well, but I had to do something, so I spat on him, screamed and flailed my arms and legs. He didn't understand what I was trying to say, and he gave Mum some medicine to keep me "comfortable".

It was a horrendous trip, that diagnosis trip. It was just Mum and me and we took a taxi from the specialist's rooms at Wickham Terrace back to near Jimmi's on The Mall Cafe. It isn't far—only a few blocks, but the hill is very steep and Mum was scared she wouldn't be able to hold the chair, wheeling down.

The taxi driver was mightily pissed off—because it was just a short trip, I think. When he stopped in Edward Street, he didn't bother to get out to help Mum. He popped the boot, and left Mum with me in one arm to drag the wheelchair out onto the road. It was one of those old heavy wheelchairs. As soon as she closed the boot, the driver accelerated off leaving Mum, me and my chair in a heap, crumpled in the gutter, bruised, spluttering in exhaust stink.

But on this later get-into-school visit, fortunately for us, the Education Department building was on the flat in Ann Street, just two blocks from Lennons Hotel. The government building was what you would call "serviceable". Nothing fancy, and very grey. But the lift worked and pinged us to the tenth floor. Anne Sorrenson was youngish, thirtyish, and had a lovely smile. Good teeth. To her, my disabilities weren't a problem and she talked to me and Mum equally, as if we were equal in every way, except I was a bit more important. My mother's confessions about setting the Government onto the Heathwood therapists was a story she'd heard before.

"Other towns, other children, same thing, it is a very sad reality," she said. "I've got no idea why things are still like that. You did the right thing. It's their job to know this sort of stuff. We all need to be able to stand up to scrutiny. Does us good, keeps us on our toes. It's tragic that so many kids miss out, and that so many people like yourself have to feel guilty about wanting what you're entitled to. Therapists like them deserve everything they get and more. Feel outraged that you were forced to write to the Minister. Sophie has a right to be educated. You have a duty to make that happen. It just shouldn't be that hard for you," Angel Anne said.

"Sophie, are you okay with staying with me to do some assessment activities? Just look at the 'Yes' on this side, or 'No' over there, to tell me." She pointed in turn to the two A3-size signs on either side of the wall behind her head.

I looked at the A3 sheet of paper on the right "Yes" side of the wall. Ann validated my response with another question.

"Sophie, did you enjoy the flight down?" My eyes snapped to the left "No" side of the wall.

"Difficult trip, was it?" Ann asked. Both Mum and I flicked our eyes to the "Yes".

My mother's face reflected a million thoughts and regrets. It couldn't be that easy. All it took was believing, two pieces of paper, and I was talking! There was no over-enunciating, no raising of volume, no itsy-bitsy baby talk, just normal conversational dialogue, no different from how she was speaking to Mum.

"It'll probably take an hour or so. Sophie, do you need your mum to stay?" Angel Anne asked.

My gaze had an added confidence. I set my eyes to the left A3 "No" side. My first independent decision. And my mother couldn't have been happier being ditched.

Rememory 19

My mother was nervous. She had put me on the front verandah and was fussing, tidying the house, wiping paintwork with a cloth, fiddling with cushions. I found it irritating, so just watched a catamaran sail north, probably to Pearl Bay, I figured.

Miss Ellis and Phillip Mosely, an Education Department psychologist, drove up to the front of the homestead in a brand new, white Toyota LandCruiser. It was school inspection day and they were going to take my mother and me around all the five schools to see which we liked best. Mum could choose any of them, Miss Ellis said.

"I thought we'd go to Barrunda first, then Amulla, Giangurra via the back road, then Minbun and finish with Mango Downs," Miss Ellis said. "The principals are all expecting us."

Miss Ellis was extremely efficient. Phillip just smiled and nodded. He obviously knew Miss Ellis well. My mother was still in shock I think. So she just nodded too.

The two first schools were very welcoming. One principal, especially so. "We have other disabled students, a Downs, an ADD and a CP," he said. He pointed to a young teenager wildly racing around the schoolyard chasing other boys.

"That's Timmy, our Downs. He's a lovely boy; very happy. The others are really good with him."

Everyone was so friendly and I imagine he meant well, but by the look of Mum's tightening lips, I was sure his school dropped to the bottom of her list.

Another principal, while welcoming, was rather vague. Miss Ellis called her an acting principal. I thought so too.

"Lovely to meet you both," she said, and proceeded to tell us about her sister's husband's brother's child who was disabled. "Cerebral palsy I think, or a syndrome …." Her words tailed off into the wasteland of syndromes.

She was an associate and supporter of the inclusive club, she wanted us all to know. Mum smiled sweetly, and that school dropped down to the bottom of her list too.

The third and fourth school principals did not want me there, in any way, whatsoever, no way. They both had suspiciously similar prepared lists of obstacles justifying why it was impossible to have someone so disabled attend.

The Giangurra principal didn't look at me once. I sort of felt sorry for him, for his discomfort. He wasn't acting. "We don't have appropriate toilet facilities," he said.

"Not a problem," Miss Ellis said, "we have funding to overcome that."

"As you can see, our classrooms are high-set and we have no ramp," he said.

"It's only one flight. We can fund a ramp or a lift. That will not be a problem." Miss Ellis's serenity was scary, and he should have known when he was beaten.

Small doorways, small classrooms, untrained teachers, no medical support, all were met with patience and the same response. As we drove away, Miss Ellis said to my mother, "Don't take any notice of his objections. It is your choice, and that school is one of your choices."

My mother said, "I don't want to send her where she's not going to be welcome." And those two schools dropped off her list too.

Miss Ellis was ambivalent, I could see. Sensible point of view, she silently agreed with my mother, but the challenge of battle was sweet.

The school my mother bullied into taking me was the least equipped of the five equidistant from Styx River Station. Mango Downs State School had a husband and wife principal–teacher team, Mr and Mrs Stephens—he was the principal, she was the teacher (of course). They both walked out to meet us when we pulled up under gigantic poinciana trees. The car was air-conditioned, but the town was blistering. I waited for the heat to sear my face as my mother strapped me into my wheelchair. However, one hundred years ago, the school had prepared well for its environment. The air fluttered, cooled by a breeze caught and kept by the trees. Everything felt like it was where it should be.

"Good afternoon," we all exchanged. My legs and hand–mouth slappin' did the talking for me.

"We have afternoon tea ready near the tuckshop," Mr Stephens said. "Sophie, do you like scones?" He looked directly into my eyes and saw a student. "Would you like a cool drink?"

My hand flapped and drool drooled. I was nervous.

Mrs Stephens hadn't said a lot, but what she said was significant. As she gave us the classroom tour, she expressed the most insightful issues about having me, so she had no chance.

"I'm concerned about your expectation of academic outcomes," she blurted to my mother. "I'm concerned about whether, as Sophie's teacher, I'm going to be able to deliver the outcomes you want."

She was doomed.

"I just want you to offer Sophie the opportunity to learn," my mother said.

Mum's eyes were shining, her skin turned opal.

"Treat her just like the others. As much as you can. When it's her turn to be asked a question, ask her, then give her time to think of an answer. It doesn't matter that she can't say anything, and you may never know if she's right, but she will know. She'll learn internally."

With that, the two flights of stairs and no lift seemed no barrier.

Chapter 4

Rememory 20

Winter turns to summer without a thought for spring.

The jasmine mocked my father for at least nine months every year, twelve in a good season. My mother planted three different jasmine varieties all over the place, everywhere, in the 1980s as soon as she moved in, and even now when she's not here, bodily at least, he has no option but to remember her.

She taught me the proper names for each variety. Some aren't real jasmines, but they smell the same-ish. *Jasminium polyanthum*, or Pink Jasmine, flowers in winter. It wraps itself tightly through the lattice on every verandah on all four sides right around the house.

Then, when it has a rest, *Trachelospermum jasminoides*—she called it Starry Starry Night and Day Jasmine—takes over for the hotter times. Until it flowers, you don't realise it's there. It's just a general green, cooling the house, day in, day out, intertwined with the Pink Jasmine, but is much more steadfast, refusing to die down even if my father turns off the sprinkler system. Mum set it up so that in the hotter months, every hour, the sprinklers around under the eaves mist for three minutes, air-conditioning the entire homestead.

Then there's the third jasmine variety, *Cestrum nocturnum*. It's not a real jasmine, but Mum and me, we adopted it as part of the jasmine family because we loved it so. Virtually every night after the worst cold weather, and in high summer, and lots of other times of the year, *Cestrum nocturnum*, or—Mum's name for it—Nighty-Night Jasmine, visits on dusk to wish me goodnight, flooding the house and garden, insisting on acknowledgement.

It must choke him, to breathe her in, in every breeze wafting through the house. He must gag on her scent hitting the back of his throat when the air is heavy and still. For me, *Cestrum* smells like the end of cold nights. Even in summer, it smells like the sweetest spring.

At the end of October—it was after Mum had left, and just after I turned six—Mrs Stephens rang my father regarding my starting school in Term One, the next year.

"If we start Sophie on the first day with all the others, she will feel much more a part of her class," Mrs Stephens said.

It was simple. I was one of her students now, so I now needed to attend school. And she wasn't leaving it to chance that my father was on task. She's a bit like my mother. There is no stopping her when she's on a mission, and she even sent the local priest, Father Ryan, out to congratulate my father on supporting me so strongly in my education.

"You are a credit to your grandfather," Father Ryan told my father.

"When our gift from God, Mrs Stephens, told me you were sending Sophie to school next January, I literally fell to my knees and cried," Father Ryan said.

> "Though the mills of God grind slowly,
> they grind for one and all;
> With such patience He stands waiting,
> with your actions you stand tall."

That's almost sort of Henry Wadsworth Longfellow. Father Ryan's ability to misquote was legendary. He would never let the real words, or even the real sentiment, stand in his way.

"And I have uniforms for her," he went on without a breath, "courtesy of Mrs Stephens of course." Father Ryan would be a good didgeridoo player. He can breathe in with his nose, as his words are tumbling out of his mouth.

At that stage I wasn't sure if I really wanted to go to school. The unknown sours our thoughts, but with any whiff that my father was being "managed" by Father Ryan, my mood couldn't help but freshen. You have to admit it was a cute tactic, and for me it made me feel so very much less alone.

Rememory 21

The sea is still, the sky invisible—opaque, but invisible.

My school exercise books were all covered in poo-brown paper. My father's latest "friend" covered them all in one crinkled batch with her stinkin' horrible son's stinkin' school books. I am sooooooo glad he doesn't go to Mango Downs State School. He used to pinch me or flick up my skirt when my father wasn't looking. I swear his mother saw him do it, and did nothing. Her son is never ever at fault. I taunted him, she'd say. Or maybe she thinks I should feel grateful for his attention.

I didn't want poo-brown paper. I wanted the flying-unicorn contact covering and all the other school stuff my mother bought for me. I wanted the poppy pink pencil case with the letters S O P H I E in plastic slots. I wanted my cat, dog and bird exercise book labels. My father's latest "friend" knew I had this stuff.

"Ridiculous," she said to my father when he gave her Mum's bag of school stuff, to "help" me get ready.

"What is she going to do with that?" my father's latest "friend" said. "Contact covering is messy fiddly stuff. I had brown paper on my books at school. It's much easier to cover them with. That's all we ever use. Ridiculous nonsense turning books into a circus, and what's she going to use them for anyway? Rose always overdid everything. Never knew when to stop."

My father's latest "friend" had been my mother's closest friend. Or so my mother thought.

Rememory 22

Now I'm going to school, every school morning, Mum's jasmine screams at me, "Get up, get up!"

The bus leaves at seven fifteen am sharp from our boundary cattle grid, a few kilometres down and along the main road, and I hate being late. My father is always late. Sharon, "the nanny", was government-funded during school time as my full-time aide, but I may not talk about her much, as it makes me angry and she is irrelevant. I have to have an aide because of all my one-on-one contact needs: sitting on a chair, wiping of the nose, feeding of the food, getting on and off the school bus, the carting up and down the stairs, and all the unmentionable "toileting" aspects. But anything else, and it's not her job, she reckons. The rest of the time—admittedly there isn't too much of that—she sits around looking bored. She hasn't even got a driver's licence!

To get things rolling every weekday morning (except school holidays and days he was too hungover to make sure "the nanny" got up), I would march up and down the verandah—half a metre at a get-up-fall-down time—tottering from foot to foot, lurching from wall to chair, hanging on by leaning, desperately flappin' at anything, until everything dissolved, and I thumped on the floor, to start all over again. I'd scream until he got his act together to drive us to the bus stop. He'd tell people in a sweetly amazed voice, "It's amazing, she seems to know when it's time to go."

Derrrrr. There's a frickin' clock in the kitchen—you spastic.

My cousins—my father's brother's kids—were always at the bus stop on time. I spent a lot of time at their place over the years. They lived ten kilometres down the road—it was a dirt road back then—on the opposite side, on the rubbish-country side, my father called it. Their property was twenty thousand acres of undeveloped bush. It was a nightmare to muster, but carried a fair few head of cattle, a few thousand at least. Their house smelt of cats' piss and rats. Just about every day after school at the bus stop, their mother, Aunty Zeb, would bring little treats for them—Kinder Surprises, lollipops, gingerbread girls—but not for me, even though she knew she was picking me up too. She always, at least slightly, resented me—lots really. I was a non-person, and I think she didn't want to waste her money. I'm still not sure what hold he had over them. He probably paid them to have me after school, so he wasn't tied to the bus run. That's the only thing that makes sense.

I overheard Aunty Zeb once, talking to someone on the phone.

"It's a pain in the arse having to have her with us all the time," Aunty Zeb said. "But I have to admit, half the time I forget she's there—unless I can smell her. No, she isn't toilet trained at all. She just sits there, then if I forget her for too long she starts screaming and ripping out her hair. Then I have to feed her. It's all so messy. That fat slag Sharon, she just reads magazines and eats," Aunty Zeb said.

"Yep, she's the aide slash nanny. Government-funded because Sophie isn't toilet trained. I mean, how stupid can it be, sending her to school when she can't talk—it's just wasting the teacher's time, and what a waste of money."

Aunty Zeb flicked back her dyed-too-black hair that needed a wash, lit a cigarette and had a swig of wine to wash it down, while her friend had her talk turn.

Aunty Zeb's real name's is Debra. She has very dark black hair, dark black everywhere except for sometimes she's got a white stripe down the middle. Everyone calls her Deb. Except me. My mind calls her Zebra, Aunty Zeb.

"Yeah, too right, hey." It was Aunty Zeb's turn again now. She had a voice not unlike Fran in the US sitcom *The Nanny*. Same strangled-screechy voice, but Australian strangled-screechy.

"Rose was a total pain in the arse. She was a bloody boong for Christ's sake, and not a young one. She was older than him, you know. She was right up herself, thought she had some sort of God-given right to make extra demands for things just because she had a spastic daughter."

Aunty Zeb sucked and swigged again, while her friend had another turn. While she was suckin' and swiggin' she fiddled with her hair and didn't notice the blob of cream cheese she was rubbing into it, then "svsssssstttt" Aunty Zeb's cigarette said, as she dropped it in the almost empty milk container. It was her turn again.

"Yeah, thank God he got rid of her. His mother, yeah, you've met Aggie, hey? Yeah, she was shocked shitless when he said he was going to marry her. I mean, sure, sleep with her if you must—after all it's a family tradition—but marry her!"

A waft of fresh cigarette smoke floated my way. And a glug glug glug new glass of wine. Aunty Zeb was just warming up.

"Aggie didn't never acknowledge Rose, hey—her own daughter-in-law! Didn't go to the wedding. Hardly ever spoke to either of them again. Never invited them to Christmas do's, hey," Aunty Zeb said, not at all sadly, and she wasn't finished.

"Aggie doted on Sophie, but—our girls too—but she was totally gaga over Sophie. Never seemed anywhere near that keen on her own sons. First-hand knowledge of white male squattocracy with her father, I reckon. Yeah, well she married an outsider, too, hey."

Aunty Zeb always seemed particularly happy chatting on the phone. You could get a full family history, just listening in.

THE STYX 47

Rememory 23

I loved that bus ride to school. It was heaven. Hot. Stinking with boy sweat. Very bumpy because it was old—the bus I mean—and did I say hot? So *stinkin'* hot. But to me it was my rescue boat out, and people talked to me. Well they did eventually, after a few bus rides of gawking and talking about me.

"Mum says she's retarded."

"Mum said it's a waste of time sending her to school. One step away from a vegetable, Mum said."

"Spastic," they all said.

After they got all that out of their systems, the kids started looking at my eyes instead of my chair.

"Hi, Soph, what's going down today?" Gus was the coolest, hottest boy at the school. "You goin' to lead the march for sports day? I'll push your chair if you like?"

I mean how cool is that. He was probably the first kid, ever, to treat me normally. And I love it when he bends down to look me in the face. He never stinks, and he has very white teeth. It was his mother who made the vegetable comment—and they have an ultra-size Bible open on its own stand right inside their front door. Go figure.

At the start, Mrs Stephens, the teacher, always had a po-face about me being at the school. She always treated me well though, and precisely followed the Education Department's guidelines. She's a good person really. Just a bit stilted. And she should wear her hair out more often.

As a teacher, she often morphed into Mr Stephens's role, head-mastering things.

"Sophie's computer has arrived. When we get it set up, she's the only one who can touch it though. We'll need to make sure we keep the others right away, to keep it safe," she said.

Nooooooooooooooo. I don't want to be different, I thought. They'll all hate me, and all the parents will go on about it being a complete waste of money and special treatment for spastic boongs and not fair that their kids aren't treated equally.

Mean-wellers often divine wells of meanness.

Rememory 24

How did I feel back then? There's not a word for it. You'd have to have something like Rett Syndrome and have the pain thing and the epileptic thing happening, to have made up a word to reach that feeling. There are probably almost words for the people who died at Auschwitz. The survivors write about it. Do they find words that properly fit?

Are there words for when, every day in every country right now and forever ago, people are locked up for life, people are tortured, people have no say in anything they do or what happens to them? Are there enough words for that? People with Rett, people with other syndromes and diseases that lock them into an unconnected body—unconnected except to feel scared, panic, pain, horror and hopelessness. They know it will never end. No one's going to save the virtual vegetables. I don't think there are any survivors to write about that. I don't think enough words exist. Yet.

But I was saved. By that thing in the box sitting there for three weeks because no one knew how to use it, and as I was the only one allowed to use it, it was a waste of time and effort in working out how to set it all up. And it was taking up space.

Rememory 25

Miss Ellis, the Regional Education Director, was cruising the Mango Downs neighbourhood checking up on things. The town of Mango Downs was named in the 1880s after the chestnut racehorse, Go Mango, who lay down at the start of THE bush race of the season, and refused to budge until the race was over. The racetrack, originally on the edge of a cattle station, was dubbed Mango Downs, and the name still stuck when it grew into a town.

I'm not sure what it was like back then, but these days, Mango Downs isn't really the sort of town you cruise to for fun. When you drive into the outskirts, your brain is primed for relief after an hour of one paddock of cows after another, after another, after another. But the relief response dries up when you're faced with hot, dusty, scumbag-looking houses, shacks really. They look abandoned, but they're not. Lots of dead cars, lots of skinny dogs, mostly related. Lots of fat women, probably mostly related too, in stretched to cruelty dresses, too short, far, far too short (the dresses, not the women). The only other female dress option is the I've-given-up dress, the low socio-economic version of the filmy, hostess dress that has relaxation in mind. In this case, it simply has heaps of relaxation room in mind, for future expansion.

I can never understand the high pregnancy rate among the townswomen. But I suppose the blokes aren't much better—worse probably. Even more of them is on show. Gut-popping bellies flopping over stubby shorts, bra-less man-boobs, arse-crack lined with black and yellow cheesy bits. Sometimes, when they bend over, you're sure you get a glimpse of scrotum. And they all wear dirty thongs on their feet—heavy-duty double-plugged flip-flops. You get the picture. And they drink a lot. A lot, a lot. And don't smell nice.

Miss Ellis rang to let Mr Stephens know she was coming. Even good people need a watchdog to keep them honest (not in the pinching money sense). She would have her assistant, Brad Jenkins with her, she said. Brad was hot and young and ambitious and smart, and he was Miss Ellis's right-hand man. They both seemed to like it that way.

Miss Ellis had been around. She was in her early sixties, never married and looked as if she still wore the same well-cut, fine wool skirts and sensible shoes from back in the fifties. She had an aura of capable assertiveness, laced with compassion. Perfect for her job of ensuring things were done her way.

"How are you settling in, Sophie?" she quite genuinely asked me.

Miss Ellis was not patronisingly asking as if there was no way I could answer. She sought my answer in my eyes, and knew there was something wrong. She looked at Mrs Stephens.

"How are the students going? Learning the ropes of the computer?" Miss Ellis asked.

No kids had touched it, not even me. It was still in the box.

"We are going to set it up in the staffroom." Mr Stephens sounded a bit defensive.

"We will be very careful to make sure it stays safe," Mrs Stephens said.

Miss Ellis was having none of it.

"Don't be ridiculous," she said. "It belongs in the classroom. All the students should be using it, taught to use it. Sophie, of course, has priority, but the others need to be able to use it too, so they can share skills and enjoy it as a class—all the classes. There are drawing programs, games, quizzes, cartoons. The programs are exceptional, but some take considerable learning time."

By the look of her, you'd never have thought Miss Ellis was so groovy.

But she hadn't finished. "It's endless," Miss Ellis said, "and it will change the way we do things. When you get it set up, Brad will show Sophie and the aides how to be Sophie's hands and read her eyes. Then he'll run through a few things with some of the other students, and then with you and the remainder of staff. It's a resource primarily for Sophie, but one to assist in integrating and involving her with the others. It's imperative it's used to death. If anything breaks, the funding includes a provision for maintenance and updating. Just ring Brad. He'll sort you out."

And that's exactly how it happened. That's exactly what happened, how I went from vego victim to having freedom and friends and power. And the sweet, sweet taste of revenge.

Chapter 5

Rememory 26

All three whiffs of jasmine greet me on this first day of freedom.

Raylene, my favourite teacher's aide, unpacked the computer and set it all up. God, the energy expended to get the box opened and the computer thing up and running. She spent hours over the weekend working it all out. Her partner, Ruth, had parent interviews last Friday night, so Raylene stayed on, way past her assigned five and a half hours at $15.75 an hour remuneration (no sick leave, no holiday pay). She came back "in her own time", "for her own interest", I heard Mr Stephens say, on Saturday and Sunday.

Ray and Ruth are a perfect match. Raylene has huge boobs and a cowboy ringer's waist—reed-thin in a converging lines way, hey. Ruth has no boobs up top but heaps from the waist down, booby bulges bulging out just about everywhere. Even her feet have booby bulges. They are very nice to each other, Ruth and Ray, and to their two kids. Ruth is full of four-year trained teacherness, while Ray is the quiet teacher-aide-achiever. They're both lovely, but.

Miss Ellis's Brad came and gave everyone at the school the once-over computer-wise. He was very impressed that Ray managed to get it all set up and working. Ray was nice to him, but she didn't go all gaga in his close proximity like most of the other women did. Raylene is her own woman, and is real smart.

"Look at the keys, Soph," Ray said. "Then look at me when my finger is on the key you want. It's going to be slow, but let's try it. Okay?"

"Two blinks if I'm right."

"Okay?" Ray said.

"Blink, blink," my eyes said.

Sharon, "the nanny" Sharon, wasn't looking happy. She wasn't the patient type.

"There's no way I'm going to be able to do this," she said to Raylene. "It's ridiculous."

"It's tedious, but it's a link for her," Raylene said. "She can talk to us for Christ's sake; it's got to be worth it."

Ray ended up taking on the role as my scribe. Sharon didn't see it as her brief. It wasn't in her interest for me to become verbal.

Rememory 27

I hate being patted on the head. I hate people over-enunciating and peering into my face as if it's a window to see if anyone's home. I love it when people talk to me as if I'm a person. Gus always does that. He doesn't see twisted limbs, staccato movements and the drool dripping from my mouth. I don't know what he sees, but to him, I'm real.

It took a long time for the Education Department to get their act together ramp-wise. (This did not fall under Miss Ellis's control.) So, for the first couple of years, Mrs Stephens let Gus have the job of hauling my chair up and down the school steps. There are forty-five and a half of them, but to Gus it was not a chore.

"It'll be part of my day," he told Mrs Stephens when he volunteered for the job on my first day at school.

"And, as a bonus, I'll get extra muscles," he said, and included me in his smiley eyes.

Every school morning, after full-school (seventy-three students) morning parade, singing the national anthem on the tarmac beside the Australian flag and pledging hand on heart (Sharon would hold my hand over my heart for me) to love God and the Queen, Sharon carried me up to our classroom. For us it was normal, a ritual of dignity, this daily procession of us, Gus and the chair, the teachers, and then all the kids starting with the grade oners—all nine of them. Back then, I didn't realise how humiliating the chair and me carrying procession was, and that soon it would be legislatively and workplace health and safety-wise unacceptable. Political correctness floated through even our school, and on my third year there, we got a ramp—a long, long ramp.

At first I missed our routine of Gus carrying my chair; I just didn't feel as special when Sharon pushed me up the ramp. I love Gus for insisting I was important. For insisting I was part of the kids. Now I wonder how things would have been without him. Sooo different. Maybe I would have lost hope and conformed to vegetablism. Maybe none of this would have happened.

Rememory 28

Who would have thought that our teacher's aide Raylene would be such a total wiz with computers? It was a bit disconcerting for the computer illiterate "four-year trained" teachers who greedily sucked up her knowledge as she showed them how to work the programs and school email and Internet. She was so helpful to them, yet they seemed to resent that she knew more than them—which wasn't hard.

Ray helped me start a journal. I just added stuff each time we were at the computer. She had endless patience with me. She'd say, "Okay, Soph, would you like to do this, would you like to do that?" She never tried to boss me around. Everything was fresh and nothing too much trouble for Raylene. My disability issues were simply facts of life, nothing to get upset about, nothing to be made an issue of. For Ray, they were all part of life's rich tapestry, and to be taken in one's stride.

Raylene was under-appreciated. Her teacher's aide status stood in the way of the principal formally recognising her contribution. At least that's all I can think it could be. Everything she did was professional and full of flair.

One year, when I was about twelve I think—it was her first year producing and directing the school Christmas concert pirate play—she involved every student in a feature role. Jaden, a grade fiver with Downs Syndrome, had a major, major role where he wielded his sword and yelled, "Make 'em walk the plank."

Raylene made sure his lines had no "sss" because he was self-conscious of his lisp.

I was super-scary pirate Captain Long John Silver, and little Cindy Haddock, Ray and Ruth's daughter, was dressed as Captain Flint, my parrot, speaking for me. I had a big patch on my eye, one tooth blackened and a red bandanna around my head. We all had striped shirts, ripped denim shorts and bare feet. The whole cast sang the closing pirate song and it was obviously a huge hit with everyone's parents.

I looked around for my father, desperate to see him, drunk even, flirting even, asleep even, but of course he wasn't there. Everyone's came except mine—mine didn't come.

Rememory 29

Summer in Central Queensland burns Satan. This morning the sun had risen early looking for victims.

The school is huge on parent involvement—especially the Christmas concert. Many parents have to take time off work to be there. Everyone's parents wrap a Christmas gift for Santa to hand out. Everyone's, except mine.

I remember that "make 'em walk the plank" school concert year, when it came to the present handing-out, Santa (our principal, Mr Stephens) said to Santa's helper (my teacher, Mrs Stephens), "Oh he must have forgotten again, have we got the spare?"

Everyone was all happy and excited. It was stinkin' hot. I've already said that, haven't I? The kids changed into bathers and ate cheerios—mini sausages—or little boys' dicks, LBDs, as the kids called them. "LBDs, LBDs!" they were yelling, poking cheerios at each other (at crotch level when they were sure no adults were watching) while they were running around under sprinklers squealing and cackling. Sharon was mooning over someone's ringer brother, and everyone else was too busy with their own families to notice me.

Still in my chair, still dressed as a pirate, my black eye-patch had slipped down the left-hand side of my face, the top digging into my eye socket. The flies are super thirsty when it's hot, and swarmed in on the juice from my nose, making it hard for me to breathe without sucking them in. I was really thirsty too, super desperately thirsty. It was forty-two degrees Celsius and the sun had found me still tied in my ancient wheelchair, and I was weeping, hungry, parked on the outskirts of the throng, sitting on a steaming pile of splodgy excrement that stung the sores that were already raw; they were weeping too.

It's a wonder someone hadn't noticed the smell.

Rememory 30

My father didn't come to the school concert because he was away "on business" climbing Mount Kilimanjaro in Africa. He was a triple diamond in Amway, and told everyone he helped house the poor.

He bought old, really cheap, houses, did them up using cheap backpacker labour, and flogged them off to the lower end of the housing market. Some, about ten I think, he's kept and rents out to "help house the poor people" on a permanent basis. He ups the rent a few weeks into the "lease"—he writes his own—and as he is so nice and apologetic about it, and they can't afford to move after just having the expense of the bond and moving in, they cop it every time.

He has a way with people—especially the poor saps who are not real bright and not real educated. They seem to love him. They seem flattered that such a golden prince would be their "mate".

I'm not sure about the whole Amway thing, but he tells everyone it's a "gold mine", and plays "motivational" videos to anyone too stupid to walk away. All his friends, even the creepy cronies' wives, are in Amway.

He often travels overseas—about six or seven times a year. He's been hiking in Japan "on business", skiing in France and Switzerland "on business", kayaking down some famous rapids somewhere "on business".

He came back all fired up with another new scheme and eager to get together with his cronies—now promoted to his "business partners". They turned up a few days later and stayed. They were all very chummy, obviously in full bonding mode, and hung around in the bar laughing, drinking, smoking the night away.

Chapter 6

Rememory 31

Today the sea simply doesn't exist.

School holidays are lonely, but so are Sunday mornings. It hurts to tell you how it feels waking up to my father's hangover. The hours of waiting for his liver to process last night's alcohol. Then finally when the heat sweats him awake, his stinkin' breath splutters all over me, alone in my cot, alone in the house. No one wants to revisit that. But sustained hate is well fed.

Rememory 32

I haven't seen the sea for three days. My father has been away and Sharon diligently pops into my room three times each day to change my nappy, takes me to the kitchen to eat and drink, then puts me back in my cot in-between. Not even the delights of 90210 video reruns to pass the time. I feel I have missed so much.

This morning my father is expected back, so I'm verandah-ing at last, and the sky is pink, impossibly merging to blue, then falling behind an opaque and corrugated grey-green sea. Despite today's incandescence, foreboding breaths of wind float through.

When he told my mother she was dead to him, my mother didn't fight. Not enough. Every night I fight for her. But it counts as little in my dreams as it did for her. Perhaps it wasn't love or courage she lacked, merely a sense of self. Away from me, she shrank, withered, and was no more. He must have known how little fight she would have against him. He was grooming her for the end. The judgement of a person is by their treatment of the fragile and vulnerable. Some so strong, so large, are capable of acts so delicate, so humane, so humble. Some so greedy, so drowned in self, are capable of enjoying, crushing even—especially—the most delicate and vulnerable.

My mother told me of a man two metres high, weighing one hundred and forty kilograms, hard muscle encasing an invisible neck, who refused to swat a fly on the windscreen. His passenger wanted to squish the fly, but the man said, "No."

He said, "Wait," and stopped the car.

Two giant overstuffed fingers moved slowly, gently, closer parallel to the fly, mesmerising not just the fly, then closed on one wing drawing it safely to freedom.

"This man was Wuku," my mother said.

Rememory 33

The sea's blown up. Swamp green with white caps. The islands are withdrawing, sinking.

I remember when he sold her books. It was about six months after she left and a definitive action of a mean mind. The books were all I had of my great-grandfather who was nicknamed "Shakespeare" by the local grazier William Northampton.

"These men were both your great-grandfathers," my mother told me.

Every night when she put me to bed, my mother told me stories about her past—our past. She often repeated the stories, but I was never sick of them, not like *90210* re-runs.

My mother said Northampton settled Styx River Station in the late 1800s when he ventured north from Brisbane in search of adventure and the rumoured "promised land".

"Rumour had it that there were extensive holdings of lush pasture and abundant water gushing from the earth," she told me.

"The grass was always green and the water, that appeared like magic whenever needed, held healing and other magical properties. The rumours said no white man would ever be able to take these lands, as all who tried had perished—disappeared without trace."

"They were describing The Great Basalt Wall," my mother said. "It was known as The Wall to locals, and had magnetic properties that rendered all normal senses of direction useless. The diatomaceous earth, with underground water springing up seemingly at every clump of trees, earned its 'magic' tag by offering year-round livestock fattening opportunities regardless of drought conditions elsewhere. This land was a veritable nirvana, an actual Promised Land," she said.

"Rumour has it that Northampton listened to the rumours and, unlike most Europeans back then, respected their validity. He searched for the local people—the Wuku Wuku—and developed an initial rudimentary communication system. In time, he learnt to speak the Wuku dialects—three quite different language systems—but of course nothing is documented," my mother said.

"Northampton was presented with a Wuku bride—the greatest honour bestowed on a non-Wuku—which meant he was immune to The Wall's curse. They weren't too worried that he already had a Mrs Northampton. Perhaps he didn't tell them. What probably happened is that Northampton made sure he always had a Wuku companion, so he was never in danger of becoming lost. As he was recognised as a Wuku, he was also never in danger of being harmed, which is another possible explanation for the disappearance of everyone else. Wuku idolised and held all animal life sacred—all animal life, that is, except non-Wuku people."

Shakespeare (my great-grandfather, not the playwright, hey) would no doubt, these days, be diagnosed as being on the Autistic Spectrum, the previously named Asperger Syndrome. He learnt to read and write English in a very short time and his resulting speech was, even for the times, oldfashioned and formal. He could remember word for word everything he heard or read. To test him out, Northampton gave him some of the real Shakespeare to read. My Wuku grandfather had an obscure sense of humour and from then on, in retribution for being treated as an amusement, he forever more, until the day he died, regaled them at every opportunity with quote after Shakespearean quote. That's how he got his name, hey.

"Love looks not with the eyes but with the mind." "Cowards die many times before their deaths." "Nothing can come of nothing." Northampton loved this wicked side of Shakespeare, and bestowed on him a beautiful hand-tooled, leather-bound *Complete Works of William Shakespeare* and a set of huge historical dictionaries. Shakespeare cherished these books and passed them on to my grandmother, who gave them to my mother, and then on my eighteenth birthday, they were to go to me.

"The books are all I have to remember him by and are to be yours," my mother told me.

Until my father sold them after she left.

I overheard him organising the "surplus goods and chattels" auction, talking to the agents and auctioneer.

"Rose knows about the auction," I overheard the agent say to my father. "We've received letters—plural—from her, and she's left phone messages begging us to let her buy them. Shall I fax you the letters?"

"Bobby, my boy, naaar, just tell me the gist of what she's said." My father was not particularly that interested, but seemed amused it was causing distress—mildly to the agent, but especially to my mother.

"She explains the books' value to her—they were her grandfather's," Bob Moorehouse the agent said. "She says she will beat any bid."

My father laughed. "Just ignore her," he said. "I will not do business with her."

I couldn't quite catch what the agent replied.

My father had four beers' worth of intolerance. "Fuck her. Ignore her. She's not having them," my father said, and he slapped the phone down.

Later when I had access to the station computer, the auction manifest said the books were sold to "undisclosed" purchasers. My heart still weeps. Shame on you all, including you, auctioneer stock and station agent Bob Moorehouse. You're no better. Your heart is in a vacuum, your soul will seep. Cowards die many times before their deaths.

Rememory 34

This morning the beach is dark, the sand grimy. Black coral, lace-shaped, like super large brains, has become flotsam along the high-water mark. Creatures have also washed up. Some are bloated, some simply look as if the life has been sucked from them: dugongs, turtles, sea birds, stingrays, fish. The sun radiates a perfect new day oblivious to the genocide.

My mother told me she didn't see herself as a real Aboriginal person. I remember the day she told me this. There were so many dead things on the beach, and my mother was in a dark, dark mood.

She was very negative. It was so opposite—the deaths and her mood—from the mint green day. We were trudging through the station dump. It was rough and a bit boggy after a little tease of rain, and it was hard-going pushing my chair. She was strong, pushing with a hump back and her arms stretched out, going at a bit of a cracking pace for the conditions. My teeth were clacking together on the big bumps. Just as well I have the back-of-hand slapping to fall back on to keep my teeth apart.

Dumps on cattle stations aren't full of rubbish. Anything that is eatable goes to the chooks, and anything not usable-again is burned. Even plastics get burned, wafting smoke, black and stinky. Dumps on cattle stations are full of treasures for the future, museums of the past.

We trundled along the main dump drag, past five dead cars and four Toyota ute carcasses, all mostly with tyres removed. Car tyres are very handy in cattle yards for bouncing calf cradles down on, and for crafting into molasses troughs. My mother spun my chair left, and a whip-fast brown snake, with a yellowish belly and an evil sneer, fled from her presence. Bits of sticks flicked themselves away from her path. We cut hard right, through washing machine alley. The washing drums make great aerated holders hung from the shed roof by pulleys, away from the worst of the rats and mice. With the air-holes, things don't get so mouldy—on the remote chance it ever really rains properly again.

"I didn't grow up that way, as an Aboriginal person," my mother continued, rambling on as she trudged.

"In fact it was played down. I mean, I'm not really black black, just a bit more tanned really. I wasn't encouraged growing up to make a lot of that part of my heritage. I would never feel right ticking that box to get special consideration (unless absolutely necessary of course)." I added the last bracket bit.

I loved it when she rambled, I got to learn so much. It was like listening in, sneaking into her mind.

"Sure, I have a pretty solid splat of indigenosity from my mother, from the Wuku people," Mum continued.

"My mother—your grandmother—copped quite a bit of racism from both sides. She always totally refused to own up to who my father was, same with her mother before her, but they must have been white, I'd say. My mother wasn't really black in her home-life because she mostly lived at Styx River, working in the main homestead. She didn't have a whole mob of family on a day-to-day basis, or even in a lob-on-you sense."

"Lots of whites shunned her too. Just about everyone when she was growing up. It's less racist these days—especially in the cities. But in small Central Queensland towns in the fifties, sixties, seventies, even in the nineteen-eighties, rednecks ruled. To be really truthful, out bush, they still do."

"Regardless though, we're still it as far as Wuku goes," my mother said; then stopped, dead-stopped.

My chair was still. She was silent, looking up at the The Wall, listening intently. I listened too. The shadows spoke sternly, reminding us of who we are. Our wallabies breathed in the shadow talk. We should have too.

Rememory 35

Wuku land borders the town of Lilian Bay to the south, and spans thousands and thousands of hectares, including kilometres and kilometres of perfect coastline with the most perfect beaches and island group probably anywhere in Australia—maybe the world, I don't know. My mother said she knew very few Wuku. Her mother knew very few either. This area holds much pain going back to early European settlement. Somewhere in The Wall, high up along a ridge of basalt, an unofficial monument still stands—called Niggers Bounce.

These days about one third of Wuku country is National Park—The Great Basalt National Park. About one quarter is now controlled by the Army as part of their training ground; and the remainder, the largest proportion, is on Styx River Cattle Station. Apart from the town and a few hobby farms, Styx River is one of only a few generational family-owned properties left in the whole region, and by far the largest.

Most of the Great Basalt National Park is still, even today, only peripherally accessed by the public. People still don't really talk about it a lot, even these days. To the landholders, it's just understood, and everyday practice, not to go there. The Lilian Bay locals only go in as far as Styx Lake—a real lake, a freshwater lake that borders Styx River Station to the southwest—and the adjacent Red Falls waterfall and swimming hole. That's okay territory for non-Wuku, and a magnificent spot. It has a clear road in and out, for those willing to bounce or slip and slide (depending on the season) along the forty kilometres of dirt track from the main road.

Further north from Red Falls, Styx River Cattle Station uses the outer basalt pockets of grasslands to fatten easily a thousand bullocks on spring-fed grass throughout even the meanest, cruellest droughts. There are plenty more of these pockets of gold further into The Wall, but the access options for the inner range are far too inhospitable for cattle; people too. Studded throughout The Wall are infinity-drop cave holes. They are almost impossible to spot in the long grass. Some of the holes are person-fall-in size, others are larger—horse, bullock, motorbike, or car-fall-in size. Some of the holes are said to drop down more than half a kilometre. I've no idea how they worked that out, probably The Wall shadows told us, but no one's volunteering to test the theory. Definitely no running through fields of green in The Wall pockets, hey. That's one of the reasons why it's so dangerous taking cattle in. Even if you managed to walk them in, and even if you managed to find them again, there's a high chance you wouldn't be around to ever get them out again. Shakespeare's Pocket in the outer wall is a bit more civilised. All the cave holes are fenced off.

The inner range lies kilometres further in, beyond Shakespeare's Pocket, beyond a labyrinth of rugged basalt lava tubes, some hollow, some collapsed, some waiting to collapse. Many tubes are flooded with permanent spring water, others with salt. It's so weird. One pool can be the freshest water you could ever drink, then another, just three metres away, can be salt, tidal fed from a different underground watercourse.

The coastal area on the southern, Lilian Bay side of Styx River cattle station is also unsuitable for grazing. It is a messy, difficult to manage wasteland, infested with wild pigs, wild cattle, dingoes and—so the locals say—crocs. Even the pig shooters don't venture in. Too many lost dogs, they say.

This wildness in and around The Styx, however, has its own cachet. Effectively so isolated, with so many beaches, so much mystique, so unexplored and unspoilt, this all adds up to so much potential for wilderness tourism.

In Australia, traditional owners may be greatly affected by any significant land-use change or development such as tourism, but most culturally significant sites stand unmarked to the European eye and, unfortunately, unknowingly desecrating sacred sites is the norm, rather than the exception. It stands to reason that the most beautiful places for Europeans may well have also been appreciated sometime over the past forty to sixty thousand years by our Indigenous peoples. Australian government and even corporation awareness of Indigenous cultural heritage started to grow in the 1990s, and such matters, while mostly not supported by strong legislation, started to become significant issues for developers to address. To developers and mining corporations, community support—including Indigenous support—is gold. Mining companies and developers are well aware to try to avoid awakening the sleeping sacred-site serpent.

In this way, traditional owners can have, to some degree, power and bargaining tools. Groups of Indigenous peoples have very successfully lobbied the government or corporations—mostly for improvements in the health, education and living conditions of their people. Hopefully this will continue to build.

While Wuku numbers are few, our cultural sites are many; unfortunately, as yet, Wukus have no established power-base. There are just so few of us. My mother knows of me, herself and her brother cousin; but she has no idea where he is, and I don't think I've ever met him. There's also a small group of Wuku who also belong to other language groups, living amongst and identifying with the other groups, joining in with their community life.

Traditional belief says that to be a Wuku custodian, you have to live on Wuku land within the shadows of past Wuku. And they don't hold with dual citizenship—if you are another group, you're not Wuku. So, no wonder no one wants to hang onto our heritage, when there are more powerful, established lobbying groups nearby. Like most Indigenous groups, Wuku believe that the land, the body and the spirit are all one. Leave the land, you're no longer whole, your spirit is back living in your country forming the shadows. Without being a part of your country, you simply cannot be whole.

Traditionally, Wuku custodians are born, not elected. There's a very strict lineage of power, control and wisdom that flows through the family depending on the names given by the spirits. At birth, Wuku receive a totem. Mine is my wallaby, my bridled nailtail wallaby. We're also given a complex name that determines who we can and can't marry, and who is custodian. And we are given a bond word, a blood-word, that is kept strictly secret between mother and child; so, obviously, I can't tell you mine. It's a mother's responsibility to ensure her child knows this blood-word from birth. It is used as a mantra lullaby every night to float us to sleep.

If it all sounds complicated, that's because it is. Possibly too complicated for European mind-sets. But if you think this belief system is illogical, think of Christianity where the answer to every difficult question is: "We as mere human beings can't expect to understand the higher-level understandings of God". At least Wuku is earth-being logical, if pretty complicated.

When my mother lived at Styx River, she was Wuku custodian. Then, when I was born, she read me my Wuku name, Sophia Beatrice Noorgoo Wukuburri, which included bestowing on me the future caretaker role. So now, with my mother off the property, Wuku custodianship lives in me.

Wuku don't discriminate on gender, age or disability, but the real world does. In the eyes of the government, a minor's interests are managed by his or her parents. After my father got rid of my mother, as my sole custodial parent, he significantly influenced Indigenous interests on Styx River. When she left, effectively he became custodian of Wuku.

Fortunately, the shadows didn't see it that way.

Chapter 7

Rememory 36

Stormbirds always pop in to chat to me when they know I'm feeling especially lonely. Today, they have lots to say, but they mock, and bring broken promises.

It's best most people don't know everything about the drought. I'm certainly not going to tell you everything. It would make you feel too sad.

We've sold off more than half the herd and are feeding the rest. My father, or what's left of the station hands—there seem to be fewer every week—go out every day, several times a day, to pump water, check dams for bogged, weak cattle, fix windmills, and deliver molasses and urea to keep the cattle alive. The cattle won't get fat on it but, hopefully, it will keep them alive until it rains and some grass grows.

Everyone has a different way of transporting molasses and urea out to the paddocks for their cattle to slurp. The molasses is really only used to safely administer the urea, which helps the cattle's stomachs break down the dry grass. Some of the paddocks are thirty kilometres away and the property roads are barely tracks, so actually transporting the heavy molasses and urea mix is an exercise in itself.

For our sort of broadish-scale operation, this is the most economical form of drought feeding, but there are many pitfalls. If you don't mix the molasses and urea properly, if it still has chunky lumps, and an animal takes a big slurp of straight urea, then it's curtains for them.

We have a custom-made tank that's a bit like a cement mixer, and it mixes as we drive out to the paddocks. But, as the molasses is very heavy and the paddock roads are so rough, the molasses trailer is always falling apart, needing to be patched up.

There's not a lot of leeway in getting all of this done. You can't get around all the cattle and water points in one day or even two—so missing a full day in repairs to the trailer is not an option. In drought times, in the heat we get out here, cattle won't last much longer than twenty-four hours without water. So the paddocks relying on windmills to pump water have to be checked at least every second day. It's exhausting. A normal person would have cashed in droughts ago. Good job there's not many normal people around here, hey.

Of course, none of this watering–feeding drama relates to cattle in The Wall's pockets. Those cattle don't need people-managed watering of any sort, or any sort of drought feeding. They sup in the Garden of Eden. Unfortunately, we don't have enough accessible pockets for the whole herd—even the whole depleted herd.

Drought feeding and monitoring is also very expensive, and there's not as much money coming in when you've got mostly skinny cattle.

When my father goes on the molasses and water runs, he usually carts me along too. It seems everyone else is away in drought times, *gorn*, or doing something else. Quality father–daughter time together—not. He never has the Cruiser's air-conditioner on. I think he keeps the windows open so he can see everything. So, you're chewing dust all the way, and when something needs fixing, I'm parked under a tree for ages—and I mean ages, ages. Yep, I'm whingeing.

Cattle are also always breaking through fences in the drought, looking for food. We were careering along the public dirt road this day on our way back to the homestead, when we came across a mob of young steers. They'd escaped from Uncle Alex and Aunty Zeb's place over the road. I could tell by the brand. Without a word, and without even an ash-flick or a puff of the durry stuck in his mouth, my father chased them along towards a wire gate into Styx River country, opened it, herded them in, and shut the gate. We will eat them over the next few years. He can't sell them because, now that would be stealing.

There's no way he would do this to our western neighbour. She knows her cattle so well, she knows if one farts, probably has names for all ten thousand of them. But my uncle … his record keeping and attention to detail reflect his drinking habits. And probably, come to think of it, he at least half trusts his brother.

We sped back home. It would be a more accurate description to say we hover-crafted all the way back, in record time I think. When the dust cleared a bit, I could see we had arrived at our homestead front gate. Another car, a big flash shiny brand new one, was parked with the engine going. For the air-con, I suppose.

"G'day, g'day," my father said. "Just been drought feedin'. Had to drag a bogged cow out of a dam."

This of course was crap. We'd been out slopping molasses and stealing cattle, but his story sounded so much more heroic.

It turned out this bloke was from the mines, a white-collar gold miner. And he must have been important, because my father cracked open the Coronas. Me and my dust were plonked on the couch in front of *90210* Episode Two Trillion repeated, but I could hear quite a bit of what was going on.

"We are just prospecting at this stage of course," Mr Gold Mine said, spreading out his map. "Exploratory only."

"We plan to diamond drill along these identified seams over approximately six weeks. Depending on the outcome, we'll either leave it there, or will need to come back for more extensive drilling. We will, of course, compensate you for loss of income and significant inconvenience."

My father liked this bit. Dominic could help him determine the maximum extent of income loss and inconvenience, times two, times ten, times who knows what? Mr Gold Mine would be well and truly mined.

"What will your men do for accommodation?" my father asked.

Must be a male-only company.

"We of course could accommodate them here in our home-stay cottages." My father generously offered accommodation at $165 per person per night (including breakfast, a packed lunch, smokos, and dinner).

"That's our bulk rate of course," he said.

The conversation continued on these lines, and I drifted off to sleep in front of the telly, drooling the drool of the drooler.

Rememory 37

I still haven't been dusted off, but at least the new day is shiny.

The creepy cronies rocked up soon after breakfast. There must be some juicy plot to hatch.

Psycho Silas brought petit fours for morning tea. He even gave me one—a strawberry one—and I carefully smeared it on as many surfaces as I could, including myself.

Dodgy Dominic cringed at the mess, but my father and Rabbit Warren didn't notice, and I think Silas liked adding to the chaos.

"Newstar Mining seem pretty keen," my father said. "I think they're underplaying what they expect to find." Ever the optimist, hey.

"They're talking about compensation, what d'ya think, Dom?"

Dominic took his time. It was his time to star. He ruminated for a full slurp of tea time, then glanced at me before speaking.

"You know, if you played the Wuku indigi-cultural card, you could probably triple or quadruple or even put a nought on the end of the compensation. Especially now Rose isn't in the way to put the kybosh on it any more. It could well be a goer. We wouldn't call it compensation, we'd call it something else, but it could well be a nice little drought earner."

Silas gobbled down his second, then third, chocolate petit four. Any sort of quasi-legal underhand manipulation excited him.

Warren sat smoking just outside the room, and at intelligent intervals nodded.

"Leave it with me, maaayyytte, and I'll see what we can do," Dominic said. "I'll get the cultural heritage thing started, then contact Newstar. This could get interesting."

Interesting to Dominic meant he was going to make a shitload of money.

Silas loved the intrigue of bleeding some poor sap—well maybe not so poor in this case—but it still gave him his jollies.

Warren said he knew some off-duty cops if Newstar needed pilot vehicles for their heavy machinery.

My father saw the glorious possibility of a drought bailout plan, so all was right in the world of creepy cronies. For a while at least.

Rememory 38

I really don't like weekends. Sometimes, when there are tourists or cattle buyers or other visitors here, I get trotted out for show and tell.

"He's such a good man. He's on his own you know, and copes with looking after that poor little thing; that pathetic thing," they all think.

"He does everything for her, devoted."

That's not quite how it all generally plays out. On Saturday mornings, I'm left to wallow in urine-soaked nappies until ten or eleven o'clock. It smells just as putrid to me as it does to normal people. My sense of smell hasn't got Rett Syndrome. The urine stings and feels like acid. In winter, it's freezing.

They've still got me in a cot-like bed. People in wheelchairs obviously don't notice or worry about things like dignity and pride. It's all about expediency. And really, I don't blame them at all. It's a hard slog looking after me. I'm skinny, but still big in terms of lifting, changing, bathing, dressing.

Have you ever noticed how people with disabilities never have braces on their teeth? I know I've gone on about this before, but people with disabilities have often the most shocking looking teeth—bucked, gappy—but I don't think I've ever seen them with braces. Even in families where the other kids do.

Can you see how we feel like non-entities and unworthy? It's like because we are so much trouble in other ways, we shouldn't expect the orthodontic work, trendy clothes, cool haircuts, makeup, teenage magazines, funky music, and the list goes on. It's no one's fault. We do take enormous energy to maintain in any semblance of day-to-day existence. But it doesn't mean we don't feel inequities, and it doesn't mean we don't feel unworthy and hurt by being overlooked. Hollowed by a void of rights and choices, our souls are gouged by reality.

I'm being negative, sour and cynical. I'll think of all the positive sides to Rett, all the things I should be grateful for. I'm creative; I'll think of some. Give me time.

Rememory 39

Holidays are the worst.

I wish he'd set up a computer at home that I could use. I heard about a woman called Tessa from a property way, way out west, Western Australia west. She is almost as physically disabled as I am, and studied at university from home with a head pointer—a stick attached to her head. She can control her head enough for that, and she can speak. Not well. But just enough to ensure she doesn't live totally at the whim of others. I can't imagine her ever being dominated. But apparently, she once was.

Up until she was in her thirties, Tess was treated by everyone—including her family—as if she was both deaf and permanently five years old. Her web diary talks about how people would peer into her face, pat her on the head, and ask her if she'd been a good girl. Like she had a chance not to be!

She writes about her thirtieth birthday, when she was still a captive on the property, and everyone was sitting around drinking wine, beer, rum, champagne. But not her. Tess'd been parked in her wheelchair on a rutty bit of ground, so even though she had a motorised chair that she could operate with a joystick, her wheels were stuck in ruts and there was no way it would move.

No one was talking to her. No one noticed there was anything odd about it, until a visiting journalist arrived with a bottle of bubbly and a packet of straws. She was writing a story about Tessa completing her master's degree in Australian literature, a thirty-thousand-word thesis. That means God knows how many million letters all tapped one head nod at a time.

"Wanna drink, Tessa?" the journo asked. Tess nodded big time, and the journo set up a wine glass with a straw, on a table that she could reach.

The surrounding disapproval was unanimously instant. Silent, but piercing. Like it's not as if Tess was driving anywhere on a public road. Not as if she was going to fall over—she was strapped in. Not as if she was going to say anything intelligible she'd later regret. How terrible Tess might get sloshed on her birthday. People just don't realise the extent to which they fracture our rights. We are disabled, so our rights must be too, proportionately to our level of disability.

Rememory 40

My life is school. I'm getting better, faster at eye-pointing. Raylene virtually reads my mind she's so fast at typing. For about one hour each day we explore the Internet. It seems to be growing in size—noticeably—every day. We came across a new sort of communication tool for people with very limited motor control. It reads eyes. It's only in the prototype stage, but Ray's asked if I could be a guinea pig for its scope of application. School is so exciting. I can sniff the possibility of freedom.

Part II
Empowerment – 2001-2004

Let me embrace thee, sour adversity,
for wise men say it is the wisest course.

William Shakespeare, *Henry VI Part 3*, III.i.24–25

Chapter 8

Rememory 41

My liberator has arrived. The trial Raylene applied for me to be part of is starting. It's not the same trial, it's another one, a more advanced one, still with eye-reading software, but even more unbelievably amazing. The box with the new computer and all the bits arrived at the school this morning, and Ray has just put it all together and installed it. All I have to do is sit in front of the screen and eye-reader cam, and look at the letter I want. Just stare at it one micro-second longer than a glance and voila! Like magic, it registers on the screen. Suggested words pop into another box, and if I glance at them a microsecond and a bit, they're selected. There's even a spell check, but I won't worry about that until I've got all the rest really sorted.

It's like the computer reads my thoughts. Unbe-frickin-lievable. So much faster, and all on my own. There's even a vocalisation option where it actually says what I've written—and I can turn it on and off all by myself. At the moment, I'll leave it off—far too scary-scary, and maybe not a good idea. But wow! I may almost become independent. If it works, I will certainly be able to write without having someone i-scribing. I'll write differently if I don't have to edit my thoughts. Until this, Raylene or someone else has had to be so close I taste their breath. So close, they second-guess my words, judge me, even if like Ray they judge kindly. If my liberator works, it will be the closest thing to privacy I've ever experienced. If it works.

Rememory 42

This computer set-up is amazing. It's reading my eyes seamlessly, and I get an eerie feeling it's reading my mind. Ray set up my email account, and my disability is melting. The Internet has turned me into a proper person—almost—at least for the time I'm at school. She's applied for a new computer for home, so she can install it there too. That would be soooooo cool.

"You know more about the Internet than me now, Soph," Ray said.

"Just think, not long ago we were spoon-feeding you your life. Now you know more than almost everyone. As long as you have this computer set-up, you're going to be able to talk and do stuff, have freedom, heaps of stuff. Soph, it's going to be so different for you."

"Yep," my eyes typed.

Rememory 43

The thing about being in a wheelchair and everyone thinking you're retarded is that they all talk in front of you, forgetting you're there. It was Saturday and all the "house staff"—i.e. Sharon—had the weekend off. My father and the cronies spent the day with the air-conditioning at full tilt in the office, smoking, drinking coffee and snacking on my favourite—vanilla puff-pastry cream cakes—looking over plans and writing stuff down. I was there, parked in the corner sans cream cake.

"What you should do here, my dear fellow, is timeshare units like at the Gold Coast." You might have noticed Psycho Silas is prone to pomposity.

"It's all been done before," my father said. "Who'd buy a timeshare out here, when they could go down to the Goldy where it's all happening?"

My father was in an awkward mood. I'd heard his red wine ramblings on rural paradise tourism, a taste of the outback, in touch with Australia's heritage (meaning Cattle-station-time not Dreamtime).

"My dear chap, I mean eco-timeshare," Silas said. "You'd have a resort and a camping ground too, an up-market one. Sell the timeshares as owning a piece of ancient Australia, five-star wilderness tourism for self-funded retirees, and enviro-wanker cashed-up yuppies."

"It could work," Rabbit Warren said. Always the practical one. "If you blast and bulldoze a track in from The Causeway, so grey nomads can do the round trip—they hate doubling back." He learnt a lot from managing his parents' gift shop. "Doesn't have to be a wide track, just enough to get a five-wheeler mobile home and a coach in."

"The greenies would never let that happen." My father's comment of course. But his face had contracted, withdrawn into itself. He wasn't just being awkward, he was bucking against change.

Yaaayyy, strike one for us. But I yaaayyyed too soon.

"Your place here is on several titles, right?" Dodgy Dominic said. "If you sold all the surrounding ones, this block would be land-locked right? Except for fronting The Causeway, right? Council have to let you have some sort of do-able access. Well, maybe not 'have to', but they would be well justified in granting it, if you play your cards right. You'd have to get some sort of change of use approval too, but again, they could be persuaded. You're right though, it's the enviro-impact report that's going to be the main issue. You've got the blackfella side a things sorted, now."

They all laughed, and at least they all had the decency to acknowledge me with a glance. Even a shutter-second, each, made me feel acknowledged.

My father swung back on his chair, stretching, yawning, raking his fingers through what was left of his hair.

"Well I've got to do something, doesn't look like the season's going to break in a hurry. There's still an El Nino up there. I can't afford the molasses forever, and with the mining downturn … that's likely going to dry up soon too."

"You'll make a killing." It was easy for Silas to be optimistic. His psychiatric practice grew as the drought worsened.

"You'll make a killing," he repeated as if his saying it twice made it far more true.

"My dear fellow, just imagine all those single mothers coming for holidays. I'll have the mother and you can have the daughter," my father said in a higher pitched voice, mocking the crap Psycho Silas is always sprouting.

Silas threw his head back, laughing. His eyes grew sparkly moist, brighter. "Très amusee," he said, not disagreeing. The quality of his French is inversely proportional to his pretentiousness.

He's such a dick. He shot the odd glance my way, looking to see if I was paying any attention. The back-of-hand swatting is useful that way. I can fixedly concentrate on accurate back-of-hand–mouth coordination, and releasing extra drool is extremely effective in moving attention away from me.

The breaks of silence reflected the idea growing in each of their minds. I could hear change. The rattling air-conditioner mantra-ed change.

"Beer o'clock?" My father opened the double-sided fridge that linked the office and lounge-room bar area. There were four snap pssssts and numerous clinks. At last he remembered me, and held up my sippy cup of red cordial for me to drink. I almost felt like one of the gang.

"You will need investors of course," Silas said, pointing to his own chest then looking over to Dominic.

Dodgy Dom's hands waved at nothing. "We're not in a position, I'm afraid. Four kids in private schools ..." He forgot to mention: "plus the one on the side, the long long-term bit on the side and her kid"—his secretary, don't you know.

"But I could contribute my time in lieu; for a share in the enterprise." Dominic was ultra-good at always wangling an angle for himself.

My father's thoughts conveyor-belted across his face in a downward serpentine, then reversed back up. He hadn't been to uni, but he was just as smart—and devious—as Dom.

"Yeeess, that could be possible ..." He was in his thinking-very-carefully mode. Dominic having an interest would ensure extra legal effort, but they would have to keep track of the costs.

"We could make it on a percentage basis. Over the course of the enterprise, your continued input would equate to a set percentage share," my father said.

Everyone took it for granted Rabbit Warren wasn't a contender. Don't mention the parents' gift shop.

My father continued with his hair wisp raking, this time with beery fingers. "Why don't we all work on some figures, then each bring them to the table to discuss."

There was of course no table. But it lent an air of formality, businesslikeness, that they all sagely nodded at. At this stage, they were all splayed on squatter's chairs on the verandah, the long-legged squatter's chair variety. All four cronies were sitting in a row, all looking out, Corona in one hand, cigar in the other, eight socked feet waving at the pool that needed cleaning. The business was done so the discussion turned back to "The Development" in a general billowing of reality sense. It was certainly getting them very animated. They cleaned up the vanilla slices, Silas cutting the last one into three. Rabbit Warren missed out. Me too. I may have mostly been ignored, and didn't get a share of the vanilla slice, but at least my father did the responsible parent bit and put my chair next to his. He didn't leave me parked outside alone. This time.

He did once. I was about five or six then, and he parked me on the front verandah while he made a cup of coffee, but the phone rang, and he settled in for the long yack: sippin', puffin' 'n' yackin', 'n' sippin', puffin' 'n' yackin'. I was parked right next to a paper-wasps' nest. About a million wasps attacked me just because I was there. The pain. I can still feel every sting. Screamingful pain. Strapped in. My legs locked in pain, my arms locked in agony. Every panic. Every terror at not being able to get away or do anything to brush them off. Trying to scream, wasps flying into my mouth, stinging my insides. Choking in my throat, drowning in my vomit.

Rememory 44

The jasmine is warning me that it isn't going to be a good day. There was no smell to wake me this morning.

The change-of-use application is one of the many formalities my father has to go through for his tourist development application. He didn't ask me if I wanted to go to the big-wigs' meeting to discuss the idea. Why would he? He doesn't ask the dog if it wants to go mustering. It was a school day, and the first I knew about not going to school was when he turned left out of the house paddock gateway down towards the road, instead of turning right to the school bus. I yelled, screamed, flailed, but the seatbelt had me pinned. If he noticed my weeping, he didn't say anything, just silently pulled over on the dirt track.

Rememory 45

Wild shadows flicker on my face as we drive off the property.

He drugged me. Again. Force-fed me the red medicine. There's no law against it. He's my carer. He has half a dozen bottles of chloral hydrate all lined up waiting. Psycho Silas gives him the scripts. "To keep her comfortable," he always says at every signature flourish.

I hate my father's smell. Sweaty synthetic trousers, old sweat, new sweat, cow dung, spray-on starch, and too much expensive cologne. He doses me with the medicine when I'm strapped in the car. I knew it was coming when he put the towel around my neck: filthy, stiff in parts, kept stuffed under the seat. He tilted the seat back, right back, held my head down, pinched off my nose and jammed a horse syringe of chloral hydrate down my throat. It's all happened before, innumerable times. Panic, gagging, weeping in frustration, knowing I will eventually crumble into sleep. Then he took off the towel, scraped it across my face, and stuffed it back under the seat.

Rememory 46

Leichhardt was still hot after baking in Central Queensland's summer. The rush from car to freezing lobby made me feel just for an instant like a grilled chop—a pretty mingy one with the blood sucked dry from too much handling.

My father was pumped. The other three cronies met him in the lobby as we arrived, and together they whispered confirmation of game plan, battle strategy, not sure which, probably both.

You have to experience flash Central Queensland hotels first-hand. And you probably have to suspend your disbelief of how much gossiping cow cockies and their cronies do over such trivial subjects—such as wallpaper. Also, please forgive me if my descriptions fall far short of the real aura of authenticity built into the hotel.

Lancer's Savoy Hotel has been the epicentre of Friday and weekend cattle-sale landed gentry for at least four generations, and the décor has barely changed. Who knows where red-flocked wallpaper with subtle hints of gold can be sourced? But the four generations of Lionel George Lancers have managed to track it down. Expensively, but relatively easily for LG Lancer I in his prime, in red flock prime. He was forward thinking and bought enough for two revamps. Thirty years later, the same red flock was purchased with pride, one final time, by the geriatric, but still in total control, LGL I.

Then, only a few years later, but after the late LGL I coffin hand-over, the breath of fresh air—Lionel George Lancer II—twirled life into the décor, still with the highly elegant red flock, but this time with gold spiralling grape vines and bold trim—all rumoured to contain real gold, a monument to the booming beef industry. He kept this up for a few revamps but, unfortunately, LGL II topped himself when beef prices crashed, making way for ultra conservative Lionel George Lancer III to re-flock with a suitably muted tone. No flamboyant gold trim, no gold interwoven leaves and not even the regal red flock, rather a brownish beige flock, tastefully understated—or so I imagine LGL III thought. (Before going into the family business, he dreamed of being an accountant.)

Complaints poured in. Beige was simply not acceptable. Cow cockies love writing letters of protest.

> Dear Mr Lancer,
>
> On my recent trip to the Annual Leichhardt Gala Beef Bull Sales, I had once again occasion to be accommodated at your highly-respected establishment. Both my dear wife, Mrs Donaldson-Nobb, and I were appalled to experience your lack of respect to our temporary industry downturn with the removal of the traditional red and gold flock! Your esteemed father must be turning in his grave! [Exclamation marks are big in the cattle industry.]
>
> The Savoy has always been a grazier's solace from God in His Wisdom's variants of weather and economic fluctuations. It is no exaggeration to state that my wife and I were devastated, as was every other grazier with whom we had the good fortune to come into contact, during the course of the Leichhardt Gala Bull Sales.
>
> On behalf of many, we implore you to reconsider and replace the depressing and plain beige flock, with the Lancer tradition of red gold interlacing. I beg you, return to us our oasis in the desert!
>
> Your faithful servant in God's Blessing,
> William (Bill) Elliot Edward Donaldson-Nobb
> "Innisfree" Via Black Gin Creek.

Hence the resplendent and glorious glory of red flock, interlaced with gold leaves and urns, returned.

Rememory 47

Lancer's Executive Meeting Room Oasis Suite blasts ice from its air-conditioner.

My father's face twitched after he finished talking. He had that relaxed but sincere look. Leaning back, one leg crossed over the other, ankle on knee. I don't know how people don't see right through him. He's a caricature of the lying, cheating, wheeling, dealing conman. Everyone who sits like that, and everyone whose face twitches like that, is lying, cheating and wheeling to get someone to do, or believe, something. I feel embarrassed by him, for him.

But no one else seemed to notice. No one seemed to notice the whole dramatisation. Him, his slime-ball spiel, his D-grade acting of devoted father, his careful positioning, then ignoring of, the starring prop—*moi*. Certainly no one else noticed me either, except for the wheelchair, odd hand movements, drooling, and skinny, wasted body. I'm viewed via peripheral vision, and represent more a symbol, than a real, live person. A symbol of pity. Today I'm a symbol of Indigenous clout. And a symbol of the untouchable. I think he might just get away with it.

The mayor was quiet for a moment as the discussion sank in.

"We, as a community, need development, and I'm very excited at what I'm hearing from you, but as you are aware, there are a few complex issues that Council needs to consider—namely land use, environmental, and cultural heritage issues," the mayor said.

"Our hands are tied in these matters unless we can get clearance from all three."

"From the Indigenous side of things, I understand, as your daughter's guardian, you have that covered in terms of cultural sensitivities," the mayor said.

"We will of course have to carry out independent enquiries for confirmation, but I can't see a problem there. Most of the property is freehold at any rate."

"There's the change of use issue," he continued. "We'll have to advertise and invite objections and comments, but frankly, we see that community support on the whole should fall in our favour. It doesn't really bother anyone else in any significant—direct—way, so if there are objections, they'll be irrelevant as far as I can see."

"We have a very active environmental action group, who may cause some problems in that area. As a council, we have no objections that can't be voted out, but I can guarantee you, the greenies will scream blue murder—because of the nailtails predominantly. And because of them, everything will have to be done by the book, and you'll have to foot for an enviro study.

"If you go through the Department of Enviro, after you submit the application—and that in itself will take a good few months or so to get together—it will take another twelve months at least, maybe eighteen, probably more, depending on departmental timelines. You could go independent, which will undoubtedly be faster and will be just as effective as long as it's a reputable outfit. Either way, the costs are much the same, and either will work equally well; as long as you haven't got anything to hide, of course." (The last point was said as a joke, in case you didn't pick up on it.)

None of this could have been news to my father. He had entertained the mayor and many councillors "FOC" (free of charge) on many occasions in the station bar. Many free drinks, and letting them win the potato-sacking game many times.

"If I may summarise, from Council's point of view," the mayor said. "Your main stumbling block is environmental. From the State side of things, how do you see matters, Minister?"

Everyone looked over to the then Queensland Minister for Environment and Economic Development. Interesting portfolio bedfellows.

The minister was not shy to take the floor.

"The problem, specifically, is the issue of the nailtails. If there's nailtails involved, it's a no-go zone I'm afraid. Our hands are tied. Even if we could get around the Nature Conservation Act, the federal Environment Protection Act overrides all State considerations. We've asked Dr Andrew Martin to join us today. He should be here shortly. I imagine you are familiar with his legislative work on endangered species, mining claims, native title, and general land management issues. Andrew is considered to be the last word in these matters. He spans both State and the Feds. If he says it's alright, it's no doubt alright. If he says there's significant risk to significant colonies of nailtails, then that could well be the end of the matter, I'm afraid. As a government agency, we're not prepared to deviate from his recommendations. The Commonwealth could simply override us on any account, if we did."

"This must be Andrew now."

The minister, the mayor, my father and all the cronies (except Rabbit Warren) whipped their heads to the door as Andrew walked in.

The cronies (other than Rabbit Warren) had blanched as soon as Andrew's name was mentioned, and now sprang to their feet. The local government pollie was clearly intimidated and felt out of his social comfort zone, so he stood too, as did the minister. My father is rarely, if ever, intimidated, but the relaxed confident conman body language snapped to the "I'm your humble servant" one. Underneath his bluster and forced smile, he must have been very worried.

This Dr Andrew Martin must have been smart and not easily swayed by dollars or the whiff of power, and definitely not intimidated by the Central Queensland squattocracy. He probably wasn't into potato-sacking parlour games either. This was not going to be as plain sailing as they thought.

Part of me relished their discomfort, but mostly, I was nervous for the remaining nailtails.

"Andrew," the mayor said as a way of both greeting and acknowledgement.

The one word sounded like a question. Like a statement. Like a reverence. Like an introduction. Like a nervous expectation. He introduced everyone else, then for the first time turned to me. For the first time in the hour and a half we'd already been there, the mayor acknowledged my existence.

"This is Sophie," the mayor said loudly, enunciating carefully.

Like, how did he know who I was? No one had introduced us. Like, I have a surname, don't you know, Mr Mayor?

But he wasn't talking to me. He wasn't even looking at me at that stage—still. He actually patted me on the head—no joke! Christ! I was fifteen years old!

Then the mayor forced himself to look at me. Confronting, aren't I? Odd, random jerky hand movements, a fair bit of slobber, and my emaciated teenage body. I was having a bad day. I was pissed off with missing school. I was pissed off with my father for pretending to include me. I was pissed off with him for using me as his token for entry to Indigenosity. I was pissed off with him for drugging me. I was pissed off with him using me as bait for his money-making venture. I was pissed off with him for planning to destroy my country. And, majorly, I was pissed off with what I was sure were his plans to eradicate the nailtails. The mayor had no chance.

"Fuck! Let go!" He actually screamed. A proper girl's scream. I had a fistful of greasy comb-over wisps—sparse, extremely revolting, product-coated hair. I've no doubt he was ultra-protective of what little remained, so perhaps screaming wasn't extreme. He had bent down to peer into my face. Looking at me, seeing only pathetic disability, refusing to allow empathy to sully his comfort zone, blind to the existence of a life in there, looking for the reflection of his public perception.

My father was furious with me. I know he didn't think of me as being "all there", so anger was hardly an appropriate emotion for a father to feel towards his grossly disabled daughter. I was banking on that to ensure he'd calm down before we got out of the public domain buffer—it doesn't always work.

"I'm so sorry, Mayor." My father was always obsequious when he wanted something. "She has a lot of pain and grabs at whatever's nearest."

The mayor spluttered, but managed to get a grip on things—really quite quickly. I almost felt a tincture of guilt. He wisely retreated to his tub chair and re-drained his empty coffee cup. My father tried to usher Andrew to the safety of a tub chair too—to a comfortable distance from me, and to the more comfortable ground of manipulative bullshit chitchat. But Andrew would have none of it.

Andrew's nose twitched with amusement. No one ever notices, because of the hand flappin' 'n' everything, but I have exactly the same nose twitchin' mannerism, so I knew exactly what it meant. Andrew appreciated the sentiment behind my comb-over grabbin' foray. He thought it was hilarious.

"Sophie, I'm so pleased to meet you." He looked into my eyes for a response, then picked up my hand and shook it.

Not a limp fish shake. Not a pretend end of fingers shake. He shook my hand properly, gently, but with a respectful pressure. He didn't seem to notice that my hand was covered in sores from my constant hand-biting. He seemed oblivious to the nose slime and dribble coating the back of my hand and stringing from my wrist. He didn't seem to care that he ended up with a heap of it in his hand. He must have felt the fragility of my useless chicken-like bones. He must have perfectly judged the lack of muscle tone. He must have been aware of the pure impotence of my physical being. I don't know what he saw. But I saw no revulsion. I saw only acceptance and compassion. He offered me acknowledgement that I was a person. For him, I existed.

Andrew didn't stay long, but long enough to confirm that the federal environmental policy required a developer to apply for approval where endangered species were involved.

"It's a part of the world that interests me greatly," Andrew said. "I'm very happy to be involved in the on-site inspection. It easily falls within my remit."

The cronies (even Rabbit Warren) were fairly quiet for a few moments after he left. I could see they all thought, "Holy shit!" "No way!" "How can we stop that happening?" Or words to that effect.

Dodgy Dominic was the first to break the silence. "But of course, if there's no nailtails, the federal government wouldn't need to be involved." He was earning his share-value already.

"Well that's right," the state minister said. "There's no requirement for federal approval per se. If there's no nailtails, we wouldn't have to bring the federal side of things in. But now they've been mooted—and it is reasonably common knowledge that Styx River was at least once nailtail country. I mean, there's a stuffed one in the national museum, with a plaque beside it naming The Great Basalt Wall as its endemic habitat. We'd need federal approval, or some sort of university or other credible report that there aren't any current colonies in, or closely adjacent to, the development location."

"An independent report? Commissioned by us?" Dominic's brain was scheming overtime.

"Yes, but with a reputable commercial research agency, a government-approved agency, or a university. If they reported that there was no evidence of a current population of nailtails, that would justify our approval, on the basis of there being no endangered species to be an issue. With that, we wouldn't have to insist you receive federal approval first."

My father was thoughtful rather than angry on the drive home. While he was within phone service, he spoke to one of the cronies. Dominic, I think. Something about him looking into an environmental consulting group. It seemed such a long drive back. For the whole time we were there, since that morning when we left home, he had forgotten to change my nappy, and the acid was eating my flesh.

Chapter 9

Rememory 48

I think the jasmine plants have procreated, because the scent is getting stronger and stronger. Strong enough to last for hours, regardless of where you go.

I didn't find my mother's diary until I was sixteen, but I had access to the computer months before. The home computer Raylene applied for arrived and she offered to install it and the eye-reading software, so I had access on weekends and holidays. She is so generous—I mean, no one pays her for this sort of stuff. She just offers and people accept. Some people attract oodles of gratitude—usually people who do nothing of an altruistic nature. Others, like Ray, never seem to attract gratitude—and they are always doing generous, kind things. Usually their kindness is just absorbed: chewed up and shat out. I thought she was a bit overly optimistic that my father would let me use it, and for ages he didn't. Reruns of *90210* and *SeaChange* Season Two were entertainment enough, I guess he thought. But then the video player packed it in while Sharon was on leave, so he had no option.

He had hit the port and cigars the night before and was extra seedy that morning. He didn't pick me up from my cot until almost midday. His hands are very large and strong so it doesn't hurt as much as Sharon's grabby reaching clutching as she drags me out of my cot bed. She always changes my nappy pants before she gets me out, so she doesn't get any splodge or wet patches on her clothes. She's a bit adverse to urine smell on her own person. But my father still uses the change table that I'm twice as long as, and always gets splodge or squish on his shirt. He forgets every time to avoid it. This time my nappy pants were really heavy—well beyond capacity—and just fell off my snake hips as he lifted me out. One leg hole momentarily got hooked on my foot, and crap splattered on me and my striped flannelette sheets. I think this time he escaped splodge contamination.

"Oh shit," he said. It was involuntary; I thought it too. "These bloody nappies. Okay, Soph, maybe we'll do the bath thing."

He was a bit reluctant to do too much cleaning of my bits now I was older. And looked positively ashen when I had the rags. Fortunately for him, this was not one of those days. He dressed me in mismatched pants and top, and forgot to put knickers over my fresh nappy pants—they help keep them in place. But hey, at least the urine wasn't stinging.

"Soph, which will it be? *90210* or *SeaChange*?" He wasn't looking at me, so wasn't really asking me, but I think he felt he was, which was some comfort. To both of us.

He shoved a *SeaChange* video in the player and turned it on, but the machine was a goner. Its time was up. The light wasn't on, no one was home. The player was kaput.

"Shit! Fuck!" he said, still fiddling with the on–off switch as if repeated snappier action might be more effective.

"Okay, it's going to have to be the computer. I hope you know how to work it, Soph. I haven't a clue."

The computer was smiling at me, beaming actually. I was dying to explore it. Ray said she'd transferred over everything from my mother's old one—hopefully all my mother's stuff. My father hardly ever used it, well not that I saw. But he knew where the on button was, so that was a good start. His computer interaction was extremely annoying. Every time he touched any moving part, he snatched his hand back. He touched every key and surface as if they were hot and seemed astonished when anything responded appropriately. Fortunately, it wasn't hard for him to set it up for me. Raylene had installed my eye-reading camera to start automatically with the software via an icon shortcut on the deskop screen. My father's face screwed into a fist while his stubby fingers stabbed up and down and he swivelled in his chair, rolling slightly to the right, blocking my view. I noticed a darkening of his shirt where it stretched tight across his back bulge, and heard fevered key stabbing. Then his shoulders relaxed, and he angled to allow me to see.

"There you go, Soph," he said, almost triumphantly.

Super Mario and Donkey Kong were back on, muted, but there were lots of visual things happening on the screen. I'd loved it seven years ago at school when I first learnt how to move Mario around the maze, and it seemed, according to my father, I still did. He wheeled me into the desk, and for a few moments watched me watching the screen. I heard his stomp to the kitchen and the kettle filling. A few minutes later his squatter's chair breathed out as his body hit the canvas, and his feet automatically found the leg arms. The chair valiantly supported its charge and together they followed their daily ritual of sharing coffee re-rings and *Queensland Country Life* newsprint.

I was all alone with my new toy.

Rememory 49

I think jasmine has a soporific function. Well it certainly seemed to, by the sound of my father's snores.

The files from Mum's old computer that Ray uploaded onto my new one were a mixed bag. Up until the end of March, 1992, documents were organised into meaningfully labelled folders. After then, it was chaos. Most of the chaos files were stored in two folders named "work" and "stuff"—these were my father's. I started methodically sorting through each folder, copying all of my mother's files and deleting all the content of each original folder. I hid all of my mother's files in a password-protected folder labelled "Gardening". He would definitely never look there.

Threading through each folder and document, treading in my mother's footsteps, and letting her hold my hand through the garbage my father collected, made me happy, connected. Just because I could, I checked out what he was punching and scrabbling at before he handed the screen over to me. His "stuff" folder was empty, but in the trash sat oodles of "deleted" files, all featuring women in very uncomfortable poses. I helpfully deleted them properly.

The phone rang. I flipped the screen back to Super Mario. Stomp stomp stomp, to the kitchen phone. I could hear my father talking and the clash of the kettle on the tap, then the scrape of a breezeway chair. It must be one of his cronies. He was there for the long haul.

Flipping back to my stuff, I found that one of my mother's folders labelled "Odds and ends" was password-protected. Nothing else on the whole computer had had any sort of security. I tried

"Sophie". *Incorrect password.* "14 10 1986". *Incorrect password.* "Styx River". *Incorrect password.* "Red Falls". *Incorrect password.* "Noorgoo Wukuburri". *Incorrect password.* Maybe I didn't get the spelling right … this was not going to be quick.

Rememory 50

The sea is totally lonely today. Even with me watching, and with the dogs Xavier and Harry and the woman on the beach. I don't really know the dogs' names, but I see them so often on the beach with the woman, that I have to name them—with the names of my mother's old dogs. I haven't named the woman on the beach though. She and Xav and Hazza braved the one kilometre of sand to the water's edge, and it engulfed them on their return. It is only shallow and of no danger really, but to the eye, it wraps them in its vast lake-ness. She wasn't enough to offer the sea solace from its tidal life of loneliness, and I could see she was spooked. But the dogs didn't care.

It took me almost eight months. I had just turned sixteen when I worked out the password and found my mother's diary. It was frustrating to have to wait for my father to give me access to the computer each time I had a new possible password inspiration. I really only had about one or two opportunities a month. After I cracked it, I still couldn't email myself the files for ages, because at home we only had dial-up and he would hear me connecting. Not a good idea to tempt fate.

It was so obvious, when I worked her password out. "You fuckin' idiot," I said to myself, "fuckwit, fuckwit, fuckwit." It was our blood word—not fuckwit—I mean fuckwit isn't our blood word. I typed our secret bond word in, and there was my mother.

Chapter 10

Rememory 51

The last time I saw my mother was back in 1992, on a Friday, July 10, at Lancer's Savoy Hotel in Leichhardt, when I was five and three-quarter years old. My mother was so excited. After she lost all access rights, I hadn't seen her or heard her voice for two weeks, and the only contact she was allowed was in writing, via Dodgy Dominic. I gleaned from my father's ranting to Dominic, and anyone else who would pretend to listen, that my mother was contesting the contact decision, maybe even the custody decision. Then out of the blue, my father rang her. He suggested they meet for a drink—the three of us: him, Mum and me—and have dinner afterwards.

"Meet us at lunchtime and take Sophie shopping for the afternoon, if you like," he said in his super sleazy nice conman voice. "She'll need things for school. She's starting next term." I knew this wasn't true. I was supposedly starting the next year—at the earliest.

My mother's voice, over the phone, sounded surprised-hopeful-excited, all virtually at the same time, as if perhaps life wasn't heading into such a black hole. Perhaps they could come to some civilised arrangement, I think she thought. Like other people do, I think she thought. Something fair that didn't need months and years of court drama and legal fees for him, anguish and at best Legal Aid for her. My memories from that night—for a long time, I haven't understood them all. Memories the survival part of me told me to forget.

We met my mother at Lancer's Savoy Hotel. My father and I booked into a huge flash room with lots of sofas and two separate bedrooms and two massive bathrooms, and I mean massive. It all smelt a bit—a lot—mouldy, but. Flash, though.

We checked in, picked up the key, wheeled into the lift, and zoomed up to the top floor. The lift sign said "Penthouse". We actually had our very own lift! It went all the way down to the car park too, and we had our own special sort of drive-in garage room in the basement. Soooo cool, I thought. I was soooo excited.

"Be back by five," my father said, when he handed me over to Mum in the lobby of the hotel. "We'll meet in the room at five sharp. Come straight up." He pointed to the lift with the sign "Penthouse" next to the buttons. "Then we'll all go downstairs for dinner, if you like."

"Sophie so loves going to swanky restaurants," my mother said to my father. She was in labrador dog mode. "She loves choosing from the menu. Hey, Soph, school's just around the corner! EXCITING!"

My father grunted.

"Don't be late," he said to the air in front of him as he walked away from us.

Mum and I spent the afternoon shopping for school things. They were the school things I mentioned previously. I'd probably never be able to properly use them, but they were on the school book list, so Mum said I had to have them. I got to choose the colours. I got to choose everything. I got everything pink, even though blue was my favourite colour. I didn't want anyone to think I was a boy, hey.

We went to the biggest newsagency in Leichhardt—the one in the West Street Mall.

"It has the best school stuff," Mum said as we wheel-chaired from Casuarina Arcade Car Park, steamrollering over chewing gum splodges, dodging drivers with their heads on backwards, whooshing past the derro durry munchers—one of them coughed big time as we passed and Mum sped up.

"We don't want to breathe in their filthy slag spit particles," Mum said.

A touch overprotective perhaps, but she had a point. We wheeled past, around and through all this, then straight into the newsagent.

"I checked them all," Mum said. She meant the newsagencies. "And this is the best one. Especially it's got the best contact designs," Mum said. Mum loved contact-covered school books. So did I.

There were twenty-seven different contact designs: stars, birds, footballs, motorbikes, dogs, cats, and heaps more. And there was one with unicorns.

"Soph, how about we get a different design for each book?" We had seven exercise books.

We did the eyes-right-for-yes, eyes-left-for-no eye thing.

"No," my eyes-left said.

Mum looked a bit confused. "Don't you want lots of different pictures?" Mum asked.

"No," my eyes-left said.

She went through the options one by one.

The girl behind the counter was watching us, staring at us really, and her bottom lip was longer than her top one.

I won't bore you with the million choices of eyes-left we went through, then she pointed to the unicorns.

"Yes," my eyes-right said. And my legs flapped, and my hand–mouth swatting got going.

We bought seven rolls of unicorns. "Just to make sure we have enough," Mum said.

We also got name labels. I chose dogs and cats and birds for them.

My pencil case was a rectangle of poppy pink, with a zip and plastic slots for little card letters. We put S O P H I E in mine while the lady with the long bottom lip was adding everything up.

On our roundabout way back to Lancer's, we stopped at McDonald's. "Afternoon tea," Mum called it. If you can call a Happy Meal afternoon tea.

I had an ice cream too. Mum had an apple pie and a cup of tea. I think all four of our legs were flappin', it all tasted so good.

I had a go on all the kids' play area things. Mum took me through the tunnels, bounced me in the bouncy area thing, and we slid down the slides, I don't know, at least a million times each, I'd say.

"We probably should go back, now." Mum sounded reluctant, but it was quarter to five, so we went back.

Mum was super chipper though. "We are going out to dinner," she said. "Like a proper family," I expect she thought.

Mum seemed so happy wheeling me and all our shopping into the special penthouse lift. She spoke into holes in the wall, and then the lift door opened. I think she was nervous, because she was super chatty, then silent, then super chatty, then silent.

The lift opened straight into our hotel room, and Mum and I breezed into the lounge. Then she stopped almost dead. I could feel the air freeze around us. Psycho Silas was there. My father looked nervous for some reason. Silas looked hyper, like he was on uppers or something. He probably does cocaine, I'd say, or some similar prescription substance. He probably writes some upper up for some poor loony sap, then snaffles it all for himself. Probably gives the patient salt tablets, or lots of aspirin to help him/her bleed to death.

I didn't think all of this at the time of course, but as I got older, I started to think about things in my adultish brain, rather than my almost-turning-six-year-old brain.

In her still frozen state, my father offered Mum a drink, but she said she wanted to give me a snack first.

"To tide her over till dinner," Mum said. She said it like she was asking for permission.

My father nodded his head towards my bedroom. He and Silas exchanged glances, but Mum didn't notice. She had turned into my room to put our shopping away.

She gave me some yummy quiche she'd brought with her from her home. I was full from the Happy Meal, but ate it anyway. It made her happy. Then she gave me a bath and dressed me in my brand new red dress. My definitely very favourite ever dress. We'd bought it from Russell's Department Store, the expensive shop.

While she was doing all this, my father yelled, "Wanna drink? Wine?" It wasn't really an asking-her yell. It was more a "hurry up and get out here" yell. She didn't look towards him, and she swallowed a lot, but she said, "Yes". A quiet, "Yes", but he didn't need to hear it. It was understood.

She put me on the bed surrounded by pillows in front of the telly. *Bill and Ben the Flower Pot Men* was playing on one of the trillion channels the hotel offered. She must have been extremely stressed and distracted to leave me in front of that, hey!

Mum went into the other room to join my father and Silas. She didn't seem in any hurry, but had run out of jobs to do. I think she would have much rather stayed watching Bill and Ben with me, or even more rathered we had just gone down for dinner—just the three of us, sans Silas.

From my TV-propped-up-in-front-of position, about half of the penthouse lounge was visible. Silas was in my line of sight as he handed my mother a glass of wine. I was on a bit of an angle, but could sort of see them all through the bedroom door. Mum glanced at Silas for a second, reluctantly, a very uneasy glance, and her hand was shaking as she took the glass. She didn't want to take it, but she did.

As her lips took their first sip, her eyes looked over to me, to check on me, and our eyes met. Our faces saw each other's faces for just a second, one fraught second before she sat down, out of my sight. That was the last time I ever saw my mother's face.

Rememory 52

Silas was droning on, pompousing about God knows what, with my father interjecting at intervals. Then their voices dropped. I hadn't been listening until their voices became gluey. From the bed in that room, if I stretched a bit sideways, basically flopping, stretching over the pillow, I could see flashes of Silas and my father. Silas was half turned away from my doorway, bent over, fiddling with a syringe. Without a word, my father took it, wrapped it in a thick wad of newspaper and stuffed it in a black garbage bag.

Then the attention turned to me. My father came into my room and shoved through my teeth the teat of a bottle of pink milk. He held my nose, snot and all, until I had no option but to gasp for air. He virtually forced the pink milk down me, because I certainly didn't want to fill up anymore, when a scrumptious dinner was supposed to be in the offing. My crying over the pink milk dribbling down the front of my new red dress is the last I can remember of Lancer's Savoy Hotel that night.

Next I knew, I was back in my cot bed at Styx River, waking up to the sun rising over Lilian Bay, listening to stormbirds screaming until the sun disappeared from the sky.

Chapter 11

Rememory 53

I don't know what to say about my mother's diaries, Rose's diaries. I was hungry to read them, but now I've read them, they can't be unknown. Some of it is impossible for me to process right now. All of a sudden being sixteen years old feels so young, so ineffectual, and at the same time so old, so protective. She was only sixteen years old when she was raped. So many times they degraded her, soiled her, before finishing with her and sneering, "Let's go, fuckin' prawn's gone off." As they laughed, her soul trickled into the sand. A person with no soul has no resilience against intimidation. It explains so much, but also leaves so much bare.

She wanted me to know. She used my bond word. She wanted me to know. I think she knew her diaries might be my only way for me to know things about her that at some stage I needed to know, more grown-up things than you could ever tell a little girl.

Her later entries—written after I was born, but before she left—are vignettes of her past, her younger days. Writing it down, hiding it, was her insurance policy in case … just in case. "These are for you, Sophie," she wrote in one entry. "I don't want you to read them, but I hope against hope that one day you will."

Accepting my mother's absence as normal crept up on me. Where the fuck is she? What the fuck happened?

There's really nothing I can do right now. I have Googled her, but have found nothing except some very old stories from her journalist days, from up to about a year after she left. Then nothing. If she died, she didn't die straight away, and there was no funeral notice in Ms Google. I won't feel complete without knowing, but the shadows aren't talking. They still won't tell me. They tell me I'm not ready to know everything. Yet.

My mother's diaries are private. They are too painful, too private to share, but some need sharing, some shed light into the present. I thought my mother was an innocent. In so many ways, she probably was, but certainly not in every way.

Gardening\Odds and Ends.doc

Back in the almost mid 1970s, when I just finished grade 12, things were still not that great for me. I was still living in the same house with my mother and my brother cousin Valentine. Lila was there physically, but not always in a functional way. She was an artist, quite successful. Dynamic, I think you'd say; sometimes, often, booze boosted dynamic. In our house growing up, Lila's agenda was the only agenda. And she'd flirt with a lamppost if it smiled at her; leered at her. A leer was validation of her attractiveness and, of course, her worth.

Valentine, my Valentine, I loved so much growing up. He was the diamond in my life, at least when we were young. But not now. Not since that "party" at the reservoir when I was a discarded receptacle for male self-love, a used and discarded receptacle reviled, ridiculed, with even my victimhood, my suffering, denounced. That night of my life, that section of that night of my life did not happen, they said. After their rewind of that tape, Valentine was never okay again. He was 17 when it happened, and I was in grade 11, and ever since he has just seemed angry all the time. Angry that he had been banging my new best friend, my one day and night best friend, while her best friends' boyfriends were all banging me, banging poor bristle-head me. Since that event-that-didn't-happen, Valentine has been an angry stinkin' cocktail of dope, booze, cigarettes and petrol. And somehow, I know it's my fault.

In the year or two after that party, to escape my life, I spent a lot of time at a rented share house known as South Camp, an old outstation of Styx River perched on a basalt outcrop overlooking Lilian Bay and the strip where we lived. In my first year at college, I moved into South Camp full-time.

Nobody derided me at South Camp. No one tried to feel me up when my mother wasn't looking. No one wanted anything of me. They were happy that I just was. There. Whenever I liked.

The matriarch at South Camp was 18, just six months older than me. She had long skinny legs. Long, long, skinny legs, a hook nose and a jive arse attitude. She had the sometimes tricky combination of high self-importance and low self-esteem. She got around, sat around, a bit like a bloke and had an awkward ambling gait that somehow made her even more gloriously femininely delicious to men. Her name was Martha and she was my haven. Back then, wherever Martha was, I felt safe, accepted. In hindsight, I guess I was her new pet project.

***

He was delicious. I was young, still only 19, still in my first year at college.

"Look what I brought home for you, Rosey."

Martha was smug. She knew she'd done good. He had been hitching to the coast from the main highway, and Martha was on her way home from wherever she'd been that day. She picked him up, and after they got talking, invited him to stay.

In those days, it didn't seem such a bizarre thing to do.

Andrew was from Surrey, south of London, and was a young man in his early 20s. His face held no guile. There was interest, amusement at being considered a plaything being brought home for me, but no smugness. No sleaze. He was open to his interest, at ease, and he saw through my feigning pleasant neutrality.

There was no way I could crack confidence looking at him. Especially back then. I'll have to describe him so you're on the same page. Please forgive the clichés. He was tall, seemed very tall, must have been more than six foot. His skin glowed, golden, olive golden. Defined, lean muscles, black tightly curled hair -- ringlets when it's wet -- aquiline profile, green eyes, British accent, one that comes from generations of wealth with generations of underplayed pretension. He had just finished his undergraduate degree at Cambridge, earth sciences,

and was on his grand tour, a gift from his parents for finishing, he said. ¶
¶
I took him to the islands. Took him camping out on Long Beach. Played in the water, played in the sand, played in my bed. Took him everywhere I went, actually. Life was simple. We didn't need to know too much about each other, it just worked, everything worked.¶
¶
Andrew stayed for almost a month. I took him into The Wall, into the wilderness end of Styx River Station, fairly near where it joins the National Park, and we camped out for a week. We didn't take anything with us. I said I'd show him a different way to live. It was the wet season, so we swam in from wall ridge to wall ridge, collecting bush food as we went.
I know it was confronting for him. After the first few hundred metres into The Wall, the atmosphere becomes cloying, the trees and ridges close in, sheathing your breath, steeping your thoughts. You become part of the rainforest. ¶
¶
The wet season makes it so much faster to reach the inner, secret pockets. He knew he was lost, disorientated, reliant on me not just to identify food, but also to return. He thought he had a good sense of direction. Andrew was, after all, a scientist. He thought he should be able to work it out, keep the route in his mind, but when he turned to look behind, he was disturbed. He said the channels had shifted. The walls had moved. Nothing looked as it had been. He was shocked, hadn't believed the folklore that told of people entering, never returning. Had scoffed at the locals. They were ridiculously superstitious, he had said. ¶
¶
The pocket I was aiming for first, Shakespeare's Pocket, was an hour or so in. We swam across a double-width passageway. The water was blood warm and still, and on the other side, the granite felt solid and gave us sure traction up onto the ridge. Wild tomatoes swarmed across the rise, tiny, ripe and sweet, far sweeter than he expected. Yellow, orange and red, all of equal sweetness but with very different flavours, and juicy, fragrant with wildness.¶
¶

Andrew said he had been absorbed by a Eugene von Guerard painting. Every brush stroke was there, colouring figs and palms and unrecognisable trees with mangrove-like aerial roots all offering or throwing down food for us to collect. Creatures watched us. We couldn't see them, but could smell their breath, feel their interest. Every now and then they called to one another. Every now and then, one family of birds would visit another, flapping massive wings, leisurely rising to skim a path they knew well. Andrew was worried about crocodiles, but I just laughed. They never came this far in. There were plenty back in the deeper, tidal reaches, but none where we were. No barramundi up here. No muddy banks. No need for them to venture so far in. At least I hoped so. ¶

¶
The last ridge before The Pocket rose up past a ring of Burdekin Plums. The trees created their own microclimate offering a place to rest, enticing us to sit for a while as they had for a century or two or three or four. Probably, far more. Grindstones still waited next to smoothed out rock hollows, the obvious spot to gather and to grind plum seed flesh to create tangy energy bars. Complete protein, my mother said, and sufficient vitamin C for the day. My grandfather always said you didn't need any recipes: the shadows told you what to eat. So we ate. ¶

¶
Our first view of Shakespeare's Pocket included hundreds of bridled nailtail wallabies. Andrew had no idea what he was looking at. To him they were mini kangaroos, amazing, but kangaroos. They are very small, even for a wallaby, with white markings on their faces, hence the "bridled" part of their name. And they have a black hairless tail-tip. That's the nailtail bit. This special tailtip is what makes them so fast at spinning and whipping away, my mother said. Their tips are their magical disappearing act, she said. ¶

¶
Neither Andrew nor I realised back then, that in front of us was a dying species, soon to be declared endangered, shrinking to a population fewer than 250, fading somewhere into the 100 or more pockets of the far inner Wall. We didn't know that in years to come, there would no longer be nailtails in Shakespeare's Pocket. ¶

¶
Back in the 1970s, the nailtails didn't move between pockets much, if at all. Their own pocket was their wet season habitat, their dry season habitat, their everything-they-could-possibly-want habitat, with ever-present pasture surrounded by prehistoric woven rainforest outcrops, sheltering permanent springs, offering permanent sustenance, permanent abundance of everything. Everything except diversity, the nailtail Achilles heel and their only exit need -- for seasonal lakeside courtship. ¶
¶
We stayed in The Wall for the week. We made shadows in the deepest reaches. Effortlessly. Then we returned to South Camp, but something of both of us remained. ¶
¶
We agreed to meet up in Guatemala in six months. That was when I had college holidays, and hopefully had saved enough money. But it didn't happen. Andrew found himself in hospital over there somewhere with para-typhoid, and was whisked home by his parents to a "proper" hospital. He has a rare blood type, AB-. No way were his parents taking the risk of leaving him there, maybe needing a blood transfusion, and the likelihood of no clean blood donor. They had warned him against third world countries. Too big a risk, for him, they said. ¶
¶
I was in hospital in Leichhardt for spinal surgery -- definitely more on the side of dodgy than "proper". Lucky I didn't have a rare blood type. ¶
¶
How did my back injury happen? The doctors asked. ¶
¶
"I don't know," I lied, "it just happened." ¶
¶
No one asked any more questions. Pain. Numbness, unstandable pain. It was months before I could walk again. And many more months for the infected gaping foot-long wound to heal. Nothing seemed to work. Back then no one spoke of golden staph infections. ¶
¶
Blue Nurses visited me at South Camp for weeks, running into months. Nothing seemed to fully control the infection. In the end, I had Martha stuff the

wound with paw paw. Ripe paw paw straight from the tree, all mushed up and held in its skin, then tipped up and slapped straight on the wound. Skin covering skin. It was virtually healed within a week.

***

Andrew did come back to get me.

He told me this much, much later, a long time later, far far too late later. He came back for me less than a week after he left me. Before my hospital horror. Before he got sick, before his hospital horror, he came back to tell me he couldn't leave me.

I wasn't home when he came back. Martha told him I had gone. She told him I was away camping in The Wall with my previous boyfriend. A double smack in the face for him. I wasn't. I was at college. She knew that. I have never seen that boyfriend again, after meeting Andrew.

She was my best friend! Why did she say that? Why didn't she let him know? Why didn't she let me know? Surely jealousy wouldn't make a person do that. But, jealousy of what? There is no self-gain in such behaviour, except the other person wouldn't have something good happen to them. I still don't really know why she did it.

***

North of my growing up house, around the first three headlands, the tidal bore insists on having its way every day, mostly twice, laughing at the estuary's attempt at insistence. My kayak is probably not an advisable mode of sight-seeing, but it does me, and I love to touch base with my old friend the estuary bore tide, who gives me hope in persistence.

I haven't always acted 100 per cent honourably. It's hard to admit one's own cheating ways, but I'm reminded of it every minute of every day, gladly.

Andrew and I met up again six years ago in early 1986, nine years after we first met. We kept it secret

from his wife and from my would-be soon husband. ¶
¶
We met in Brisbane in a coffee shop. He recognised me straight away. He said I hadn't changed at all. I had to look at him a long time to see him. He was there in part, and I slept with him for old time's sake, but he wasn't there in full. ¶
¶
We toured the Andy Warhol exhibition and I know he was bemused at my enjoyment and desire to linger past closing time. There are many galleries in London and Sydney, not so many in Brisbane, and even fewer in Lilian Bay and Leichhardt. Well they exist, but not in any comparable way. ¶
¶
He wasn't enough the same for my stupid memories and imagination to deal with. I told myself his stale breath sealed the deal, so I let him go. I wonder if he wants to rewrite those scenes? I certainly do. How fearful happiness is. How different my and Sophie's lives would have been if my sense of smell wasn't so keen. ¶

*** ¶

¶
We were very careless with friends back in the 1970s, even more so back then. Careless but needy -- a disastrous combination when we made so little effort to keep distance in check. Few of us had an address book, and even fewer of us had the phone on. Friendship ties could be tenuous, but imperative. We relied on the stepping-stone connection of a litany of peripheral friends, and friends' friends, and friends' friends' friends to haphazardly stay connected. Friends might have nothing in common with us except the connection to others. Some friends were out and out loopy, with no perceivable justification for connection, except they were young, fresh flesh and sleeping with your ex-one-or-two-sleep-over-occasion-boyfriend's trippy flatmate, Marz. ¶
¶

*** ¶

¶
Kara knew me from the 1970s. We reconnected just last year, at a pretty swanky party. She was paid to read our fortunes. ¶
¶

"Your mangrove eyes are still inscrutable," she said to me. "Let me concentrate, I'm going to have a good look. You're not giving me much. I'm feeling a strong barrier, self-protection," Kara said. She was so right.

"You don't remember me, do you?" she said. "I was Marz's girlfriend. Remember? Jerry's flatmate? You had a big black dog -- he didn't smile at anyone but you. I crashed at your place after a party once, and woke up with his face less than a centimetre away. I was spooked, but he didn't hurt me, didn't touch me. You still don't remember, do you?" Kara asked, but she knew I did.

It was early on in the South Camp days, I remember Jerry's house on a hill further south, low on furniture, high on drugs, massive sea view.

She laughed. "I miss all the tripping," she said. "I loved tripping. It helped me talk to the aliens. There's so many of them up there. They're all paedophiles you know. That's where the paedophiles come from. They don't like me; they know I don't like them. They're very wary of me."

I was getting pretty wary of her too.

"Do you remember Gina? Yeah? She died."

Gina. My Gina. Gina who had a face and body to die for and a life to match. She had the sort of life that makes you feel inadequate with your sad pathetic excuse of an upbringing. Back then, her family owned a newspaper and a printing company. They had the best house in the best street in the best old money part of town, and they had a beachy, beach house -- not flash, just sand between your toes, sun-bleached wood, beachy -- perched high up on a headland above a private cove on one side, and a strolling-distance-from-town beach on the other. She went to the local grammar school in Leichhardt, the most expensive one, and had an older sister who actually liked her. She had parents who also liked her, and who welcomed all her friends into their home. Even a half-caste illegitimate, penniless gin. They saw no race, were oblivious to social lack-of-status, and were generous without any expectation of payback.

Gina liked me. She was interested in me. But I was too intimidated by her gloriousness to give much back, especially as we grew into later teenage-hood. She asked me to a party at her place in town, her 17th birthday party, a big event. I'd only visited her beach house before, but should have realised. I turned up with no shoes. I didn't normally wear any if I could help it, and it didn't occur to me to put any on. As soon as I walked into the first room full of antiques, crystal, velvet, tapestries, ancient silk hand-knotted rugs, I knew my mistake. But Gina drew me in, was so attentive, generous. Her parents, too, were warm, so hospitable. But it was all the others. One hundred pairs of lifeless eyes. Contemptuous judging eyes. Some, remembering eyes. Jeering eyes. All resenting the time Gina spent with me, eyes. Ready to pounce as soon as I was left unprotected, eyes.

My birthday gift to her was a portrait I painted soon after I first met her, when we were 12. Her hair shone, her face glowed. It was the head thrown back laugh we shared every school holiday and long weekend as we were dumped by the waves. She said she loved it. She said it was her favourite birthday present.

"A soul kiss from the past," she said.

Then she showed me her second favourite. They were authentic ancient artefacts, she said. A friend of her dad had given them to her. Wuku artefacts the friend had "found".

"Dreamtime magic," she said he said.

My body gasped, shrank back as she held them out to show me: a stone axe, a nulla nulla, a carved bowl and something wrapped in bark held with intricately woven string, the most sacred of sacred, a mummified head of a precious child stolen from life or an elder preserved for her wisdom. Someone significant to the family group, a sacred soul at rest, preserved for eternity, or should have been.

They were scavenged from a sacred place, an ancient place, a place sacred to Wuku women. They were stolen from the shadows.

She was so pleased, so excited at "owning" something from my heritage. I'm talking about the 1970s. She didn't realise the sacrilege. She didn't realise Dreamtime magic for us was black magic for her. She didn't realise she should have refused the gift. She didn't realise she was doomed. And I didn't have the guts or kindness to tell her.

I should have stayed. I should have told her. I should have helped her return them to the shadows. I should have helped her say she was sorry, helped her apologise to the shadows. I should have. I couldn't. When her attention was taken, I melted away, evaporated from their lives. I should have repaid their kindness. But I didn't. I didn't feel worthy enough.

***

I think what's happened to Sophie, her disability, is because of Gina. All the other bad things too -- to me and to anyone creeping close to me. Gina's death is a sign; it answers everything. I should have intervened and insisted she reject those birthday "gifts". I should have made sure they were all returned to Wuku country. So many lives destroyed. I caused so much suffering. I can't undo bad karma, but I can try to stop it regenerating.

Chapter 12

Rememory 54

It must have rained. It must have rained change. Soft sand flats transformed to slab grey pondage. Sludge grey. Oil grey weighing down, coating sand basins, creating a pondage system interlinked with lighter grey sludge. A day too grey for pleasure.

There are skeletons in the caves behind Red Fall's waterfalls. Skeletons that probably quite neatly add up to the number of people who dared to enter without a Wuku, the number of people evaporating from within The Wall. Of course, they could be animal bones, but that's not what the stories say.

Rememory 55

The jasmine is shouting hip hip hooray, it's going to be a good day.

Our whole school fitted on two buses, and everyone had to chant the times-tables all the way to Red Falls. No Christmas carols for Mr Stephens when there was a times-table to be had. We had to do hand signals too.

"Brain gym," he said. "Helps us remember," he said.

Like, really, Mr Stephens, how old do you think we are? Some of us are almost adults now! Will be next year, some of us—me, anyway. But hey, it was such fun.

It was my moment, at my place, for the school break-up party. My chair fitted in the luggage hold, but it was of no use today.

Red Falls waterfall and lagoon skirts The Wall's southern basalt fringe. While it's really our private property—part of a freehold block of Styx River Cattle Station—townspeople have always been welcome to visit.

It's hard enough to get there from the Lilian Bay side, but from the western Mango Downs State School side, it takes almost two hours. In wet weather, you need a proper four-wheel-drive. That's no doubt why it has never become a major tourist destination. Red Falls is mostly just for locals, who see it as a pilgrimage to their sacred land.

There are certainly enough dead beer tins and Bundy rum bottles to support that theory.

From the western approach, the road to Red Falls has three quarters of an hour of reasonable bitumen, twenty minutes of reasonable rutty dirt, then off the main road the rest is thirty to forty minutes of bone-smashing bulldust and rocks in the dry, and up to an hour of bone-crunching, slipping and slathering in the wet. And buses have to be extra careful, even in the dry, even four-wheel-drive buses. No vehicle returns with its body unscathed. No person returns with their thoughts unshrouded. Even the dead beer tin and Bundy rum bottle owners.

Sometimes, about three or four times a year, The Wall flips a car or two. It has never been happy that the locals built the road so close to its outer wall, so every so often, ever so slightly, the basalt rises just a little, just enough, to flip cars curving onto that final track. It's usually four-wheel-drives that it flips, four-wheel-drives with mag wheels, bull-bars and spotlights. They take the bend too casually, not always too fast, but always in a manner too familiar, then—flip. They never see it coming, but as they wait for help to arrive, they hear the stormbirds laughing.

This final track to the falls, shared by all road approaches, is vivid red. You are sheathed in either dripping-blood mud or billowed with blood dust. Every single time it's shocking. You know it's coming, but every single time you turn down that last piece of track, thwack! A million years of history hits you in the face, bloods your windscreen and you know you're in real Dreamtime land. The red of the outback is never believed in paintings or even in photos. It's hard for the uninitiated to conceive, out of their frame of reference. That last stretch around Red Falls' bend opens your mind to a world, a culture, a people, an essence of another reality. You enter Wuku time.

Rememory 56

Walking from the carpark—and I use that term very loosely—Red Falls seduces your unease into a sense of complacency. Gus offered to carry me down the steps and along the riverbed to the falls, but Mr Stephens insisted on doing it. An insurance thing he said. I think it was more to do with Gus being too close to my bobbling breasts and those sorts of body bits. I didn't care. As long as it wasn't Sharon, it was a win for me.

Rock steps lead you down four stories of cliff-face. Even the most frail and timid seem to step with confidence to the white river-sand below that cushions, cradles your feet—not mine of course. It strips people of their shoes, refreshing, cooling, as they step through grey-green paperbarks. Reams of white paper litter the trunks, fluttering, somehow unshredded by teenage boys, unmarked by teenage lovers. This has to be a kind place. This has to be a haven. Silly, romantic notions of a kind land. Sure, it's a magnificent, unique land, but not a kind one; not to interlopers, never to those who do not belong. As the bones attest.

Pizza isn't usually my favourite food, but usually I wouldn't complain anyway. This pizza was different—all of them were different. All the mothers had made pizzas for lunch.

"They are for everyone to share," Mrs Stephens said.

Just as well for me, hey.

Mr Stephens had board shorts on.

"You goin' swimmin', sir, hey," Gus said. (In Queensland, questions are often statements, and statements often sound like questions.)

"Yes, Gus," Mr Stephens said. "I'm going in with Sophie—that's right, isn't it, Sophie?"

I back-of-hand to mouth swatted in reply. Mr Stephens wasn't worried about a bit of drool. Red Falls falls would take care of that. I had my sports uniform on as bathers. No one thought to pack anything else. Sharon didn't do the swimming in public thing, and hadn't packed my bathers in case that meant she had to. But I didn't care. Swimming is a sport, hey.

Mr Stephens walked with me in his arms towards the lagoon, and stood for a moment looking up. He looked stunned. Everyone does on their first visit. On their every visit, actually. The waterfall gushes diamonds down and throughout the bloody rock face—happy water, abundant water, pure clean spring water, pouring five stories from the river flats above. It looks like one gigantic Henry Moore reclining figure turned into a water feature with the humanist elements worn away by time. It taunts you to explore further into The Wall's interior, to follow the water's source. Locals bring house guests and picnics, just for the day, just to the edge. Groups of naturalists visit, smitten with the springs, wistful for what could lie beyond, within The Wall, but they settle for staying wistful. Developers drool, salivate, do their sums, daydream with architects, but they too have so far stuck to the drooling. Until now, no one has ever seriously plotted to mess with the place. Too many unexplained disappearances, too many spooky rumours, too many people showing real fear at the idea of entering Wuku territory. Only my father and his cronies have the gall to ignore fifty thousand years of warnings.

Mr Stephens waded into the diamonds carrying me, and when he was waist deep, let me float. Gus came over with his boogie board to rest the top half of me on, and together they held my arms. Country boys off properties, when they are good, are exceptional. They step in wordlessly to help in whatever way needs the helping. Gus was one of these. A good bloke to have around in an emergency—or when you take a cripple swimming at Red Falls.

The water was blood warm and quickly reached their armpits. Each held me by one of my arms on either side of the board, so I was sort of free. We followed the other kids and kicked off towards the waterfall.

Red Falls' pool was made for seventy-three kids and twenty-two adults. There was plenty of room, but not too much. The water kept coming and coming and coming, pouring and pouring and pouring out of the rockface. From where we were, at least seven different portholes flowed down towards us. They were fed by the springs above. That bit was reasonably obvious, but where did it all go? There was no surface runoff, and it kept the same level always, unless it rained—then it flooded.

Every outing is an education opportunity for Mrs Stephens, too.

"Filtration," Mrs Stephens said, "the water seeps through the sand to join underground streams."

So kind of it to oblige. Fortunately, it filters the pee too.

I didn't see my father arrive. In time for lunch, of course, minus pizza. At first, he walked his slow strut, more of an amble really, feet marching in opposite directions, chest puffed, shirt-sleeves rucked up above his elbows. Then he infinitesimally paused, stretched up a little just like the wallabies do when they see something that needs watching. All his senses were on duty, and he started running, slow motion at first in the sand, then powering into full charge. I could see the sweat spreading, turning his shirt from eucalyptus to mud. I could smell it too—in my mind only; he was still a fair way away. Even my olfactory senses aren't that good.

Mr Stephens didn't see him. He was wedged on the rock wall behind one of the smaller falls to hold the board from going too far under. The water falling stings if you go too far in. All the other kids just dived down to avoid its whip. Gus had his beanpole legs braced against the rocks and held the board with both hands. He had grown into a lanky giant with carthorse hands, so we were pretty stable with him holding one of my arms on the board, and Mr Stephens's arm hooked through one of the porthole rock type of things, with his other hand holding my other arm on the board. Sounds complicated, but they had it sorted. I so love floating in water. Pain I wasn't aware of melted, and I squealed, laughing. Gus was laughing too—not really squealing—but he laughed right into my eyes.

"Sophie!" My father was screaming my name. Crazy-man screaming. It was so embarrassing.

Mr Stephens whipped around. "She's fine," he yelled. "We've got her. She's safe." His voice was loud, but a bit strangled.

Mrs Stephens had my father by the arm and seemed to be talking to him, but he wasn't looking at her. At first, I thought he was angry at me. Or at Gus. Or at both of us. Or at all of us, including Mr Stephens. But he wasn't angry, he was scared. Worried. About me. His face, that crushed velvet face, crushed into the weirdest smelly underpants shape. I'll never forget seeing it all scrunched up, crushed into love. For this moment at least, life was good.

Chapter 13

Rememory 57

Today the sea is eager for full tide. The water is clean, washing all before it, and fast. It's having a good time, certainly not paying too much attention to peripherals such as flotsam, crabs, dogs or me.

Wuku find interactions with others difficult. So much of what they know and feel is never articulated—what most people would see as a cross between intuition and clairvoyance. Wuku don't see the need for close proximity in order to communicate and learn. Knowledge and wisdom seep in, direct from some other unexplained source. This is skin sense. Shadow talk.

I'd know, I feel I would know The Wall, even if I'd never been all over it many times, strapped to my mother's body as she clambered up and down the basalt ridges. While I was very little it was pretty easy for her to carry me with her any season, but when I grew taller, we tended to wander our country during the wet season when she could float me most of the way.

I have always loved the water. My mother swam from granite outcrop to outcrop towing me along. She laughed at my squealing and splashing that made it ten times harder, but so much more fun. It was a time to savour. I savour it still. Why didn't we stay there? How could we have moved so far from there? It eats at me that she could have, should have done that. We could have just disappeared together, just me and her, into The Wall. No one would ever find us. No one would probably look, not for us. Maybe. There are hundreds of kilometres of tunnels and caverns, most of them no one will ever find. Hopefully. My mother thought about it, I know. She talked about it.

"But what if you get sick, Soph?" she said. "What if the Rett Syndrome does even more torturous things that we don't know about already? What about the epilepsy? I am too cowardly," she said.

She gave in. By not escaping with me, she gave me up. Why didn't she fight harder for custody? She didn't win, so she couldn't have fought hard enough. The badness, the horror, the fear—I felt her fear. Or maybe she just forgot me.

Rememory 58

I can hear the sea now, trying to blow in, trying to help me heal. Telling me to keep going, telling me there's hope. The shadows whisper to me that there's hope.

It's so hard to keep a sense of self, with my father's self-importance sucking all available oxygen. My shadow songs tell me to soar. Reason tells me I have no chance, but these Wuku voices laugh and say "you wait". Maybe my mother should have killed him, but if they didn't let her have me, or if she went to jail, then I'd have no one. Is no one better than him? I'm not sure.

All education has done for me is uncover a more detailed analysis of my crippled body, my impotence, my cowardice. This retreat into negativity and self-hatred is selfish. It's allowing me to wallow in the mire and comfort of masochism. The more energy I expend in self-hatred, the more I can take refuge from the agony of pleasure. Pleasure brings guilt. Pleasure brings unbearable fear that the pleasure might end. But pleasure also brings a wider focus, opportunities, options, the chance for me to be able to do something, to maybe one day find her. That has to overpower my fear. I must create a life, a viable, positive existence. The mire beckons so temptingly with death. Life is so hard to imagine, especially for someone like me.

Rememory 59

Whiffs of coral spawn meet me as they drift up from the beach. The sand dunes look soft and white, but underfoot, under the woman and her dogs' feet, the sand is hard.

He has formally applied for the "eco" tourist development. "In harmony with and accentuating Indigenous interests," I heard my father read out.

I wonder what's happened about the nailtails? I care, but I'm not sure I can do anything. I can email someone maybe, but if I let them know I care, someone—he—will shut me down Internet-wise. Doing nothing so adds to my shame.

The worst part of my shame is being seen as someone whose mother abandoned her. "Just a worthless scrap of rag." Gus's mother called me that. She was serving in the school tuckshop, and I'd been taken downstairs early, so Sharon could "change" me before the classes broke for lunch. While Sharon was disposing of the evidence, she parked me under the building, just near the tuckshop. Mrs Gus knew I was there. Sharon had asked her to keep an eye on me for the moment or two she was at the bin. Maybe it didn't register with Mrs Gus that I could hear and understand. Maybe it did.

"She's just a scrap of rag," I overheard her say. "A home would be far better. It's cruel, her mother abandoning her," she said. "Couldn't cope with the disability."

Mrs Gus knew no restraint.

"Gus is obsessed with her, you know," Mrs Gus said to the other tuckshop mother.

"Why can't he find one with arms and legs that work, at least one that can talk?"

Shame Mrs Gus can. But she wasn't finished. She liked to twist the knife hard.

"That Rose knew no shame, you know. Just up and left. And with all he gave her, just up and left him. Puff! *Gorn*. Abandoned the child. Never heard of again."

She did the hand movements to go with it all. There she was, in full crescendo of nasty, conducting her orchestra of teeth with an eggy knife and a flap of buttery bread.

If Mrs Gus stopped to think, surely she could ferret out just one note of compassion for my mother. Surely, on some level, she must understand how the ruthless, the narcissistic, the Machiavellian personality types stop at nothing to have their own way. But then, most don't ask or want to know, so most have no idea.

Most Murris don't need to ask. They automatically know. Exploitation, bullying, being cast aside like a piece of garbage, expendable, is all so many of them—us, I suppose—know. Anything different, now that'd be something to crow about.

It hurts that so few people are interested enough in me to ask about my mother's whereabouts. It hurts that she isn't of any interest past a judgement. It hurts so, so much, and it's such a relief to be able to box that piece of pain up and only at times have to confront it.

Rememory 60

The woman with the dogs has thrown herself into the sea. She took all her clothes off first. All of them. Xavier and Harry don't care, and she doesn't know I am still parked on the verandah watching. It is pitch black apart from the full moon shining on her and the phosphorescence. I wonder if the guy up the road from her, who spends an inordinate amount of time behind his telescope, is watching.

My father had been on the phone for hours. I heard him crack more than a few tinnies, and I think he'd forgotten Sharon was out—on a date, go figure. If she can find someone, maybe there's even hope for me.

I was a bit hungry and thirsty, and had risen a few centimetres on two episodes of splodge, but it wasn't cold, and the wind was keeping the mozzies and sandflies away.

I could vaguely hear him croaking on about approvals and inspections and meetings and all that sort of thing.

"I'm the most knowledgeable about the place," he was sprouting. He would have been finger hair-raking. "They should be asking me, not some city twits who don't know their way out of a university. They don't know anything about the place."

He was slurring a bit. It was more than a dozen full-strength designer beers talking. What an idiot. He didn't know anything about The Wall. He'd hardly been in there except to check cattle, and then only the outer pockets, and every time he had Mum or me with him; always used to be both.

Dodgy Dom, I think, was on the other end of the phone, trying to settle him down by the sounds of things, but tolerance of his drunken friends isn't one of Dominic's fortes. My father had no more audience.

"Okay, talk to you 'morra," my father said, probably to a beep, beep, beeping phone.

Good job it was a mild night, because he didn't talk to me till 'morra either.

The night air took me closer to the shadows and I thought of my mother's worry.

What if she's forgotten everything? My mother worried that I wouldn't remember her stories, our trips, The Wall, the Wuku, our shadows.

How could she remember? He won't tell her, my mother wrote. She was always worried in case she was no longer around to care for me, or to keep things, knowledge things, cultural things, fresh for me. She worried that so much local knowledge would die, shrivelled in her wake.

"Don't worry, I remember," I told the shadows. "I remember everything. All what my father called mumbo jumbo, all the stories, all those times being carted on her back, all over, everywhere, I remember it all. I remember the waterfall cave and the can't-go-back bush, and especially I remember my nailtails."

To try not to get scared all night out on the verandah, I think about The Wall and my wallabies. I want to warn my mother about the development. I want her to help me save it all: our country, our creatures. I want to save it all for her. One part of me says, no way I can do anything, I'll never be able to use it anyway. The other part of me, the part that comes from that determination she showed in getting me to school, that part of me insists I keep it all for her. I can't see I'm in a position to do anything to stop them. I can't see that any environmental study is going to be able to give the full picture of my nailtails. Someone is going to pay someone off. No one seems to have taken it on as a cause in any real way. No one would care. No one would dare. But maybe I can.

Rememory 61

In the middle of the night, out on the verandah, I realise how loud the sea is from my place. It's a white noise roar. For me it's a pleasing white noise roar. It grounds me and I feel safe, in the right place. It's lapping quite gently now.

You never forget your first love. It doesn't matter how young you are, how old you are, how perfect you are, how disabled you are. Your first love, it saturates your life in tiny droplets. Every person you meet is measured against the memory and inevitably falls short. At times loneliness can trick your mind, but something always brings you to your senses. A touch too rough, not lingering when it should. Words unspoken—by me, always too many words unspoken—when a glance should do. For me, it was the smell, for too long ignored, rationalised, normalised, that wreaks havoc twisting into unexplainable angst. Simply no one else passes the sniff test. He is the one I choose to remember, my mind-love.

> You were my only sweet morning smell
> I smell you in
>   his wet dog smell
> I smell you in
>   his car drive stink
> I smell you in
>   his stale old-man-house
> I smell you now, alone.

Rememory 62

It's a new day and it's all pretty. Pretty fluffy sea, pretty pastel sand. Fresh and pretty.

He felt so guilty this morning. So, so guilty, and I felt pleasure in his guilt. The sun decided to open the door to rain. It wasn't a mist of rain. It was sudden, definite in its intent. And the sky brightened. It knew the world would stop to watch this gift and delight. It's surely far too poignant to be called anything so prosaic as a sun shower.

He's taking me to Sunday afternoon volleyball. It is partly guilt that motivates him, but in this world, I'm his entree to the house of local Greens Party member, Freda "Freddy" Fitzwilliam. Freddy and her partner Claudia Renton extend a standing and open invitation every Sunday at four pm for backyard volleyball, except it's in the front yard. They would never turn me away; they are far too decent. My father has no shame and is happy to exploit this. He is looking to suck up a bit of green credentials. It won't work. These people are polite, but not stupid, and Claudia, especially, doesn't need his validation of her social worth and place in the world. Her family are old money, and her bank balance sits heavily under this weight.

From reading her diary, I know my mother sort of knew Freddy back in the old, old days at South Camp. Freddy came to the odd party, smoked a lot of dope, my mother wrote. She still does by the smell of things. Before the divorce, Mum and I would always go to the Sunday afternoon gatherings. But we'd go on dusk, after the volleyball finished. Mum actually hated playing volleyball.

"It's too violent," she said, "but I love the company, and sitting around playing music, and drinking tea and sharing yummy food afterwards."

I did too.

This time my father was keen to show his physical prowess, so this time we went earlier.

He parked me under a mango tree beside the volleyball "court". The volleyball net was made by our local permaculture guru. It's actually a fishing net reshaped to hang between two skinny unhewn tree poles. Ropes, anchored by rocks, hold the poles in place.

You're probably getting the picture that it's all fairly organic. The house grew from the ground twisting and turning to co-exist with more mango trees, umbrella trees, and uncountable other trees. Last time my mother took me, it was for a party. It was night time, and a row of about a dozen kids of all sizes were perched on the roof welcoming the guests with laughter and gusto. A row of possums it looked like, and of course no one fell off, or got hurt.

The Fitzwilliam-Rentons throw themselves into life with open arms, embracing all they encounter with love. Claud is loud, in your face and usually shrieking with delight. Freddy is friendly and knows the words of every 1960s and '70s song. She doesn't need written music. She just grabs any old guitar she can reach (or mandolin, or ukulele or probably harp if she could get her hands on one) and plays song after song after song really well.

Back in the 1980s in London, they were individually part of a share house. Claudia is tall and buxom. Freddy is short and weedy. Claud said she wasn't attracted to Freddy, but at some stage they slept together. It wasn't just a one-off, but a casual, convenient thing. A comfort. Then Claudia got pregnant to a mutual friend. A man, obviously. None of the three of them were in any way a couple, so Claud had a bit of a dilemma. She thought of having an abortion.

She'd had heaps before, but no, this time she wasn't going to. She would raise the baby.

Freddy said, "Well it's going to be my baby too, I'm in on it too. If I was a man, it could have been mine, so it's unfair to leave me out of this. Count me in."

Twenty-two years and two kids, a dog, bird, horse and chooks later, they're probably the most secure partnership around. They have to work at it. On Fridays, Claudia always organises or does something special, romantic, for Freddy. It usually involves sex. On Tuesdays, it's Freddy's turn for Claudia. It usually involves food.

So, volleyball this afternoon. My father will spend an hour in the beachfront Coffee Club first, me parked in a corner, while he has a beer or three with the creepy cronies. They'll be plotting and planning about nailtails, and engineering a favourable enviro report, and he'll be getting some greenie psycho-manipulating technique tips from Psycho Silas.

Rememory 63

The beach looks lovely as we drive the coast road home after volleyball. The moon chats to a fresh covering of shells that lie in dense waves of big shells, tiny shells, no shells.

If I'm not asleep, drives home offer good rumination time. My father often has the Cruiser windows open, and his cigarette ash fireworks up in the wind whooshing through the car. He's silent, ruminating too, probably.

I've been thinking about my father and The Styx a lot lately, why he wasn't like other fathers, other husbands, thinking about how it all happened, why it all happened, how he—or my mother—could have avoided everything that happened, if he and/or she could have avoided it. As you grow up, you have to revisit all of this sort of stuff. To repark it in the new holding bays your older mind has on offer.

Cattle dynasties no longer attract the wealth, lifestyle or respect they once did. Forty years ago, even twenty years ago, having a cattle station meant something, not just financially, but also socially. These days, graziers are seen as a bunch of down-at-heel hicks, and are only legends in their own rapidly decreasing circles. By the time

I was sixteen, he no longer had status, buying-power or, in his eyes, a reason for existence. In the dark recesses of his self-esteem, he had become a non-person, ordinary, and that wasn't something he could live with.

So, something had to change, and Styx River Station, with its twenty kilometres of beaches and close offshore islands so suited to tourism, was an obvious winner to propel him into developer superstar status. Winning custody meant he was no longer head-butting my mother in turning the place into eco-Disneyland. With her gone, everything was all set to go, except for one small obstacle: the nailtails.

Some years the wallabies don't appear for dating sessions at Styx Lake at all. Those years it's generally been really dry and the lake is smelly. This year, there may have been just enough rain to keep things fresh, not enough to break the drought properly, but enough run-off into the lake to keep it fresh. So nailtails might well appear, all things being equal. Which is good, theoretically. As long as nailtails are officially sighted on Styx River Station, there will be no straightforward development approvals. As long as the shooters don't find them first.

Chapter 14

Rememory 64

Shards of light break the sky just before dawn, and I can hear rumbling from within The Wall. The air is still. It has stopped to take stock of what's going on.

The sandflies were out when we arrived home from the Fitzwilliam-Renton's, so he parked me in the office. It is the only air-conditioned room in the main homestead, and it's really quite nice as far as offices go. My mother designed it to be really airy, with massive windows, roof-high, overlooking the cliff to the north-east, and looking out towards Pearl Bay in the far distance.

He had calls to make.

"Stan, me man, how goes it?"

My father does the lean back in the chair, feet on the desk, beer in one hand, cigarette in the other, phone crooked between shoulder and neck, make the dregs of society feel like they're your best mate, thing well.

"Stan, maaaayyytte, I need some roos culled again. They're taking over the place. Yep. Yep." I didn't count the "yeps", but there were a few.

"You've got permits?" he said between "yeps". "Yep. Yep. As long as you've got some, enough to cover your arse in case the shit hits the fan." He listened to the other end, pretended he was interested, and at the same time dragged on his fag and poured himself a glass of port.

"Yep, yep. Just give me the tail-tips, hey, burn the rest. No trace, you got it?" my father said between his teeth and the durry he was sucking on.

"Yep, I'll add a cash bonus for each black tip. Ten bucks a black tip. … Yep, just the tips. I need the job done clean, hey. No mess. Fast and clean. You got it? … Good. When can you do it? … Can't do it any sooner, hey? … Okay, yep, that'll have to do. Let me know when you're done."

There's no way roo shooters would burn anything, no way. There's heaps of money in roo meat for pet food, and in the skins for tanning.

No way will they burn bank notes. But it's a sure thing they'll be keeping any nailtail meat quiet. They won't be blabbing anything to anyone. They won't be leaving any evidence. Ten bucks a tail-tip, holy crap, that's got to be a record. My poor nailtails.

He's good at that sort of thing. Getting people to do what he wants without them having any idea they've been manipulated, controlled, used. I don't think he needed Psycho Silas to tell him how to do this one.

Email to: Federal Minister for Environment

Dear Minister

I am writing to you to worn you about an enviromental violation that is happening as I write, and every year for as long as I can remember — at least five years. Our native bridled nailtail wallabies are being slortered every time they emerge from The Wall to pick on the new lakside grass. The murderers are quietly (apart from the gunshots) and painstackingly eliminating all emerging breeding groups to further the culpret's evil intention of developeing Styx River into an eco-tourism resort. Ironic isn't it? But they are well awear that the proven existence of nailtails will eliminate this area from any developer's plan. I gravely urge you to act on this information before our local nailtails are extint.

Yours very truly and extremely sinserely

A very concernd local.

Rememory 65

The sky fell for one brief minute, then packed up and moved on. I think it took one look at us and decided torture was more fitting.

Crony number one told me it was all his idea, my father becoming Mr Wuku by getting rid of my mother, Rose.

It was late afternoon and Psycho Silas was "watching" me while my father met some buyers at the cattle yards. Silas was not a positive influence in meetings with buyers. He didn't fit in, and almost seemed to intentionally sabotage discussions. So now my father always excluded him from any pure face-to-face cattle buyer business.

Payback time. Silas couldn't just "watch" me by ignoring me like he normally did. He was gleeful, no, that's not the right word, there was a smutty yuck factor in his glee. He was talking to me, very one-sidedly, more of a blurt really, and he kept fiddling with his crotch in a sub-conscious, stimulated way, as if no one else was there.

"Your mother just couldn't help herself, could she? She couldn't simply play the game. Rose never did know when she was well off. Just couldn't keep out of things, without always having to have her say, stick her bib in."

He was animated in his telling me, and opened Dad's best bottle of red that he keeps on the shelf to show off with. He glug-glug-poured a glass full, closed the office doors and turned on the air-conditioning. He lit a cigar.

"She just couldn't go along with things, could she?"

His face was closer to mine now. He blew smoke into my face. He loved that sort of cruelty, seeing people squirm, seeing their sensibility snap-freeze. No doubt he chose psychiatry for a profession just as many paedophiles choose education or the church.

He told me how they had been scheming some sort of scam for years, as soon as he met my father, before I was born.

"But, oh, no, she couldn't just go along with things, could she? Oh no, had to big-note herself. Marry her, I told him, and you'll be Mr Wuku." He laughed. No, it wasn't a laugh. It can only be described as a cackle. Such an ugly word, and so fitting.

Silas was obsessed, couldn't leave it alone. He was wandering around the office, picking things up, moving them somewhere else, hiding some things at the back of cupboards, in drawers.

"It was me, me, who first mooted the idea, the plan," Silas said, poking himself hard, several stabby times, in his own chest.

"I, me," poking again, "I made him get rid of her. It was me who made it happen." He stab, stab, stabbed his chest. Must have been getting pretty bruised by now.

He was so proud of himself. He wasn't happy to leave his manipulation gymnastics as a bit of fantasy amusement, a bit of sick fantasy. His jollies came out of making it actually happen.

"She had to big-note herself with everything," he said, and turned his gaze on me again. "With all her infantile save-The-Wall ideas and this ridiculous school business. Alienated all their friends." He poured another full glass of red. "It was all her doing, all her fault, really. She always took things too far. Never knew when to shut up."

"A redhead Scots-Irish convict stock Mr Wuku." Silas cackled again, a sentence of cackles, obviously thoroughly amused. He puffed on the cigar a few times in quick succession, leaning back in my father's chair.

"Classic brilliance, if I do say so myself. Capitalise on the bleeding hearts, my man, I said," Silas said.

"She had to go. Job done. Almost."

His attention snapped to me; he dragged my chair over in front of his chair, between his legs, and he looked right at me. I could smell his too much aftershave and the red wine, and breathed in his cigar breath.

Needless to say, my hand slapping and drooling were in overdrive. I felt bare in my too-small nightie and soggy nappy.

He'd never really talked to me before, and he hadn't sought me out this time. I was delivered. It was condoned. My father was responsible, Silas would reason, for his being alone with me. My father's choice, his fault. Endorsed.

The light is muted in the late afternoon as shadows creep through the house. I was feeling super creeped out too, as you might have guessed. Yucked. His eyes lingered on me, trailed down me, then back up, taking in my frantic hand slapping, my mouth juices, then his gaze trickled down again to my nappy showing through the wet of my nightie.

His eyes narrowed, pondering the possibility of me. Was I ripe? Yet?

Rememory 66

A journalist came to school today. Anthony White, a local conceptual artist, brought him. Anthony works at a nearby coal mine, but comes as a volunteer to our school one morning every month and teaches us art. He teaches me how to mind-paint, he calls it, by using my eyes to draw on my computer.

"I'm going to put on an exhibition for you one day, Soph," Anthony says just about every time he visits.

It will never happen, but it's nice to be a contender, even if it's only in our minds.

Anyway, the journo, he's from New York in the USA. His name's, Calliope. Go figure! We've got a town near here called Calliope! I love his accent. He gave us a talk on newspapers and about being a journalist. He is billed as part of our ongoing careers talk-fest. They certainly have an uphill job with me. But this guy did spend most of the time with me, learning about Rett Syndrome. He was really interested in how I worked my computer. If I could talk, I'd definitely be a journalist.

Rememory 67

Thank God my jasmine is back. I suck in lungfuls, let it soak through my insides, my outsides. It feeds me.

The creepy cronies are over for the weekend. All three of them. I could hear most of what they were going on about. My father'd put me in front of some recordings of *90210*. My video player still wasn't fixed, but he had pinched the one from the staff quarters for me. How chuffed I felt. Blessed. To attract video player precedence. *90210* had been my favourite when I was probably too young for it. These days he vacillates between *90210* and *SeaChange* Season Two videos. It's the best thing Sharon ever did for me, introducing *SeaChange* episodes into my life, because now I have an intellectual crush on the main heart-throb, Max Connors. He's probably ancient now, but in our *SeaChange* videos, he looks quite young and dishy. However, lately, it's been *90210* ad nauseam. Stands to reason: the *90210* video's already in the player, *SeaChange* Season Two is on the bookshelf. Jesus Christ, there's nothing wrong with my memory, dickhead! The two hundred thousandth time is perhaps a bit over the top, even for you.

So anyway, I was listening to their plotting 'n' planning; three-quarter time listening probably.

"We have to go legit on this," Dodgy Dom said. "Anything else won't cover you. These guys are a respected research group, connected to the uni. You remember Ian?"

My father ran his fingers through his wisps.

"Remind me again …," he said.

"He's Kittie's brother-in-law [Dodgy Dom's wife K-Kittie, OT

K-Kittie], a partner with Diamond Partners—they're valuers and environmental researchers—so we do have a bit of an in. He said he'd send out two youngish researchers—fully qualified; they have to be—but young, fresh out of uni. One's still studying there actually. Both female, and maybe, just maybe, perhaps susceptible to influence …" His voice sing-songed sleazy cute (if there is such a thing).

They all laughed. I couldn't see anything amusing. Legends in their own minds, this lot.

Psycho Silas knew his role as master manipulator. "Give them a good time, the full works, drive them around for hours, do the billy tea, newspaper-wrapped sandwiches thing. Maybe even get a couple of good-looking ringers to ride into The Wall a bit with them," Silas said.

Rabbit Warren liked to contribute his gems of wisdom too. "Do a couple of half loops of The Wall. Avoid the pockets of course, but a few hours in the ute, lunch at the creek, a few more hours in the saddle will probably cover things pretty well."

Dodgy Dominic was not going to be outshone. "For Christ's sake, make sure there's no fuckin' roos anywhere though."

Chapter 15

Rememory 68

The sea is right in view, just over the road, through the pandanus.

Yet, while I'm parked at the cafe waiting for them to have another cronyising beer or three, I'd rather take some sort of perverse pleasure in searching out, making up, others' vulnerabilities. It's good research for my new creative writing obsession. I found a great website where everyone posts their stories. I'm tending towards modern romance writing, so I'm going to use a pseudonym: Sophie Rose, I think. My web friends have no idea I'm a legless, armless, voiceless girl-wonder though, so it's good.

This story-writing is a bit cathartic for me I guess, channelling my mother's shadows, dreaming happiness into a life for her. My shadows still remain silent about what happened to her. They still aren't talking, so I'm creating my own Wuku Rose shadows, projecting her voice, her writing onto my stories. I'm wanting her to have a life, even if it's a fictional fiction writer's life. But if this is to be her life, I can't help thinking, "How could she forget me?"

Very confusing, hey, if you think too much about it, so I won't. Rose is my muse, and I will happily cop the emotional baggage that comes with that. I'm using this first story for an English assignment as well. It's supposed to be a 450-word written soliloquy vignette in present tense. I tell ya, grade eleven stacks on the guff. But I quite like working it all out. I'll ask the websiters what they reckon. But of course, there's no way I'll actually submit anything to school as an assignment—losing my invisibility cloak of dumbness, now that would be stressful.

writersunite.group

"The Cyclist"

by Sophie Rose

I did it again. I can't believe it, just walked on by, back to my world of me, clear steering from you. So used to holding on to aloneness, that any other option is simply foreign, unrecognisable even when it's smack in my face. The comfort of emptiness frozen into stepping past hope, stepping over chance.

You were perfect, are perfect, quietly walking by, quietly leading your bike. $5,000+ bike, maybe $15,000 (have no idea really, but it looked expensive — titanium, black). Not that that's relevant, but it emphasised your quiet, non-showoffyness. Street clothes, Melbourne clothes in Lilian Bay. Quiet clothes, quiet colours, close clipped hair, even closer clipped beard growth. Understated, tall.

You looked up just a fraction, chest rose a fraction, chin tilted a fraction, steps paused, interest piqued. I knew even before my eyes had focused, even as I cruised into the car parking space, before I could see, I saw, drawn. I became perky, doing confident, acting content.

As I stepped into the chemist, we glanced at each other, timing synchronised. You followed me in.

Chemmart's selection of age defying creams proved fascinating for you. Quietly looking at nothing, trying to appear engaged. Unsuccessfully. Successfully, to anyone watching, except me (it should have been).

I knew, you knew, we knew.

I think what I liked most, apart from the obvious, was the nonchalance of the Macro recycled hessian shopping bag folded over the crossbar of the incredibly expensive road bike. Neatly attached, somehow.

You said "hello" to me.

I can still hear that voice in my ear quietly, deeply soaking in, colouring my world smudgy greys, smudgy whites, such a deep voice.

I want to smell your voice slowly for a long time. I want to follow it down to its source, your naked voice to a quiet place. I want you to touch my face, drink my breath, swallow my heart, whole. I want you to do it slowly, quietly, smudge our thoughts, our lives at least once, at least twice, at least more.

I want you to come full moon walking with us up Bluff Point tonight. I want you to jog along Pandanus Beach before sunrise, with me and no one else. I want to go cycling with you, anywhere, together.

I want to go away, way up north, stay at the Styx River Hotel, the pub with paper-thin walls, for the weekend, with you. I want to watch the tidal bore together, on sandstone cliffs, holding hands.

So many things I could have said. "How do you tie your bag onto your bike?" "Are you from out of town?" Even, "Cyclin' are you?"

But none of that happened.

"Hello," I said and walked on by.

Rememory 69

The sea seems super clean today, fresh. Twitchers are out in force with impossibly long lenses and tripods. Skinny men, large women, all khaki clad with droopy hats and serious boots, dragging serious gear over not particularly serious sand dunes.

Xav, Harry and the woman slipped past them, her bare feet shouting their disparate habits. There's an elitist air wafting at the woman and the dogs, as they pass. Pride and exclusion create cohesion and vibrancy. These twitchers could actually be voyeurs. The equipment's the same, but I've no doubt they're twitchers. There's far too much sincerity in their focus, too much of a look of nothing to hide. I envy their fellowship.

I knew all those endless viewings of *SeaChange* Season Two would come to something. This next story I've written is inspired by my intellectual crush, Max Connors. But I'm not using his name of course. I'm no groupy fantasiser. I reckon Gus is a bit like Max, but nicer. It's a sequel to the last story—just so's it's got a happy ending, hey.

writersunite.group

Note to readers: Please substitute your heart-throb of choice. Someone I know would choose Idris Elba, aka Gabriel from *The Inspector Lynley Mysteries* on TV. She's swooning, I'm sure, just by my typing his name …

"My Date with [heart-throb of choice]"

By Sophie Rose

I met [heart-throb of choice] online at PerfectPerson.com, the Internet dating site for the modern young woman and man (for pathetic losers). I knew it was him even though he didn't post a picture or a name.

Green Cordial was his online name. Vintage. Appreciation of earlier, more simple, times. Unassuming.

6'4" — he said on his profile — *[age of choice]-years-old, average build, no children. University education, works in the [job of choice] industry.*

Looking for someone within 25km of [location of choice]. The clincher — him for sure.

Interests include reading the newspaper and other things, he said on his profile, *writing, most things arty — all, if done by a family member or friend. Walking the dog, watching the neighbours grow old in an affectionate way, Dean Martin songs, Snow White statues, bear hugs (from people)* — bears too probably, but possibly has little opportunity. *Likes pets, single.*

Almost humour, almost kindliness, always poignant. So obviously him.

Looking for someone quiet, humane, independent and a bit bookish, he said on his profile.

Handy (but of course, not essential) if you like bike riding, hiking, swimming in the sea and music." Transparently him ([Heart-throb of choice] went [activity of choice] a lot).

He sent me a kiss: "I'd like to get to know you, would you be interested?"

I sent him one back: "Yes".

He sent me another: "I would like to send you an email. Would you like to receive one from me?"

I sent him one back: "Yes".

He sent me an email.

Patricia Holland

It was a very stressful time for me; this whole Internet meeting place. No one could ever know it was me. No picture, no distinguishing giveaways. Change the town, change the age, change the height, the hair colour. No mention of a job, university or even industry.

After each time I replied, I emptied all trace of PerfectPerson.com from my computer (even though no one else ever uses it). Every time after we corresponded, every cache, every file, folder, cookie, crumb, every web trace, every trash tin — banished.

Otherwise, someone might find out, someone could guess it was me. The shame, the humiliation that I would be so needy, so lonely.

We corresponded for weeks, then months.

"I'd like to meet you, soon," he said.

I logged off quickly. After every reply, I instantly logged off in fear of discovery. This time, again I froze, escaped, fled, before I replied.

But it was so good as it was. Gentle banter about nothing important or revealing. The gentle lost art of correspondence — wasn't that enough? That was plenty. For me. More than I had had before.

"Would you like to meet?" I saw he said again a week later when I finally logged back on.

He was patient, quietly persistent; amused, quietly amused (just like [heart-throb of choice]).

"We could meet at an art exhibition over a painting or two, a glass of wine or two, amongst a crowd to make it easier, more natural, less confronting," he said.

A bit less. Maybe. For me.

It was to be in Melbourne of course. The me in my profile lived in East Melbourne. I didn't, nowhere near, 2000km nowhere near.

"Yes, ok, I will. I'll wear black," I said (so he could recognise me).

"So will I," he said (so I could recognise him). "How about we meet in front of painting number seven in the catalogue," he said, "whichever that is."

"Ok," I said. My feet felt cold, I didn't want to go anywhere, just wanted to stay home with me alone, with the front door shut, and the sprinkler on right in front, sprinkling over the gate so no one would want to come in, without getting wet.

He chose the exhibition — "The Cyclist".

How could I resist? I'd heard about it. Anatomically exposed manic paintings of the beautiful people of inner Melbourne, naked; on their cool colour-coordinated fixies, naked; on rag and bone fixies (beautifully maintained of course), naked; on their weekend alternative, multi-thousand-dollar road-bikes, naked. Naked beautiful people on beautiful bikes — more naked than naked — totally exposed, their innards showing: bones, organs, muscles, sinews, in action, riding bikes.

How could anyone resist staring into the inner workings of so many beautiful people cyclists viewed by the artist over the past two years in Fitzroy and Port Melbourne and Carlton (the cool part) and East Melbourne? Affluent, carefully unpretentious hipsters cycling to breakfast in Port Melbourne, touring through Williamstown, working as young professionals (some not so young, but still groovy): academics, lawyers, actors, artists, doctors at inner city hospitals. Pure voyeuristic heaven for cyclists and anyone else. Pure vicarious slurping.

The paintings are a by-product of the artist's real career. She's a medical student funding six years of study and a hipster lifestyle with art. She sits in cafes, snaps people riding by, and paints them. Two-by-three metre canvases smashing you in the face with beautiful people riding beautiful bikes. She calls herself sapiophilestudio.com and exhibits in a swanky flash Fitzroy gallery (and in New York) (and in Paris) (and in Hamburg).

Fitzroy, home of the beautiful people — and the slightly tatty. Home of the trendy young things — and older ones too. Home of the metrosexual professionals — and substance abusers (sometimes both) (quite often in fact). Home of the cashed-up hipsters in lofts and terraces — and poor non-hipsters from the council high-rises. Home of the successful artists and performers — and hangers-on who have to bus in from the suburbs.

The paintings, they all sell for lots of money, fast.

"If there's no painting number seven," he said, "we'll meet in front of the seventh one on the left as you walk in."

All eventualities catered for.

I said, "Ok".

There was no problem with what to wear. I only had one outfit for that sort of thing: jeans and black knitted dress-top bought from Jay Jays four years ago. It made me look like one of Charlie's Angels, cool, retro, slim-ish. Buttons were missing from one of the cuffs, but no one would notice. No one would know I'd worn it every Friday night outing for the past two months (three actually).

I washed my hair, plucked chin hairs, shaved my legs, and pits. Just in case.

I put lipstick on in the taxi to the airport, on the plane, in the taxi to the gallery twice. Then wiped it off just a bit. Then put it back on just a bit, to look natural, to look as if I hadn't put special effort into it.

They all came to the exhibition, hundreds packed in, spilling out on the street, all with a glass in hand to see themselves hopefully painted, to buy themselves painted — a testament to their being someone who matters to people they don't know, but would like to; to each other.

The taxi cost $42.50, and he dropped me off around the corner.

The gallery had seemed like a low stress meeting place, except when I got there, except for feeling awkward, except when they looked at me accidentally, when their eyes flicked me, dismissed me. Except for glowing with self-consciousness with a frozen mind. Except for being the only one not part of the inner Melbourne outer inner suburbs beautiful inner circle, the only non-contender (a loser, in their eyes) (in mine too). Except for that, I blent in.

Don't make eye contact, blend. Channel I am important to them, if they only knew me. But I am so important and talented I don't need to be known: I have a date with [heart-throb of choice]. Have a quest — match the paintings to the punters.

I thought I would recognise him, just inside the entrance looking intently (and very intelligently) at number seven in the catalogue, wearing black.

He would be standing so nonchalantly, showing no interest in the eye contact dance of, "Hello, lovely to see you," move on, "Hello, lovely to see you," move on, "Hello, lovely to see you," move on, "Hello, lovely to see you," move on, and on and on. Oozing he is so important and talented he doesn't need to be known by everyone, even though he knows he is (but not in too much of a showoffy way).

He wasn't there. Standing in front of painting number seven (in the catalogue), it wasn't him, red stained wine glass in hand, eating a dripping pork spring roll, black stove pipe pants too tight, far too tight, too black studded belt, black hair too long, too shiny-black uniformly. Black beard attached to a black moustache too long, too pointy, too black uniformly, too everything, too nothing. Black eyes looking into every female's naughty bits, licking their skin, tasting the inner workings of their private parts, violating with his eyes, his thoughts, violently.

And he wasn't 6'4". Nowhere near.

I steered to the right. Hard right, behind the crowd, flattened to non-existence, skimming the wall, brushing past the air between, face-on to the paintings, sliding sideways urgently, casually. Silently screaming in fear of recognition by the [heart-throb of choice] personality impersonator (who had no idea what I looked like), or by anyone.

I slithered to the back, farthest back of the room where no one of any hipster note wanted to be. Then I saw him. Not [heart-throb of choice] (the real one), not [heart-throb of choice] (the PerfectPerson.com personality impersonator). It was him. Him. Him.

He didn't have his Macro hessian shopping bag (or his black bike). He didn't have to. I knew him from the shape of his back, I knew him from the nape of his neck, I knew him before he turned around. I saw him before I saw him.

The cyclist, my cyclist from Lilian Bay's Chemmart Pharmacy age-defying cream section. I knew he was from Melbourne. I knew. He knew. I knew he knew.

He turned. He knew I knew.

"Hello," he said.

Chapter 16

Rememory 70

A grey sea promises far more to me than a blue one.

Sometimes I forget who I am when I'm on the 'Net. Everyone treats me like a whole person, no different from anyone else, and I start believing it. I'm so glad I've got this, but it's so, so much scarier, what I've not got when I log off. Becoming one of everyone else gives me the perspective to acknowledge the deep, deep sadness of who I am. What about everyone else like me, those who don't have the Internet? I'm so scared, so sad for them.

The Internet has also given me guilt. I'm not totally without aptitude anymore, so I can't sit here and ignore the threat to my nailtails. Every day I don't do something to help them, my guilt grows. That must mean the Internet has made me less vulnerable. More options, more rights, more pain, more sadness.

Speaking of which, another big thing is the boy thing. I need to excise entertaining the would-love-to of having a boyfriend. I don't even want to go there in terms of the poor-old-me who-would-want-me. I wouldn't want anyone I care for, to want me. It is so totally unacceptable to lay that on anyone. A zillion times more unacceptable to do that to someone I liked. I have to permanently excise that thought option from my brain. Inside I weep.

Rememory 71

I want to frolic with Xav and Harry in the sea, but I can't, so I'll just mind-wallow.

There are these things called blogs. It's like a river of your thoughts flowing throughout the world for everyone to sip, to taste. I'm not sure how everyone gets to know that individual bloggers exist. Raylene might know. People write blogs for whatever reason they want to. Most times no one even knows who they are—even if they live right next door, you wouldn't know. I might be able to become a proper person cyber-wise. Maybe I'll be able to say whatever I like, to whoever I like. Maybe I'll be able to get support for my nailtails. Maybe I'll be able to tell people what he does to me. Maybe they'll make him stop. Maybe this is all just crap.

www.silentscream.blogyourblog.com

Silent Scream

The future and lives of Lilian Bay's unique and sacred neighbouring residents, the bridled nailtail wallabies are under dire threat of extinction because of the greedy and the corrupt.

More than 50,000 plus years of our history, heritage and honour are about to be wiped out if some local developers have their way. They say there's no more nailtails. They claim their environmental impact study will prove the breed is now extinct except for the few poor souls incarcerated in captivity, and the stuffed one sitting next to our only thylacine. Sounds convincing? Nailtail shit!

Number one, the study is to be carried out on the very outer, northern edge of The Great Basalt Wall, now ex-nailtail territory. It's not even close to the area that is home to today's nailtails.

Number two, they didn't mention the shoot-out last wet season to eradicate every single nailtail in sight. March before last, 200 nailtails lay dead on the ground. Then they were skinned, tail-tips removed, and the flesh tagged and sold with the goodwill of government 'roo shooting permits.

Don't believe me? Come and do your own stakeout this November. Camp on Styx Lake. Be part of history, save the last few nailtails by keeping them away from this season's shooters. Or if we're really lucky, photograph the last few families left. Don't worry about the isolation or about all the rumours of The Wall swallowing expeditions of explorers — you won't be alone — the developers' marksmen will be hovering, trying to clean up any poor little creatures remaining.

Please help me make my screams heard.

SS

Chapter 17

Rememory 72

I haven't told you about the sea in much detail lately. It's changed. Bull sharks have been spotted up and down the coast. No one sees it in the same light anymore. I do of course. I love it. I love that nature is rallying its protest against exploitation. Go you blackest black bull shark sea. Do your damnedest.

Remember Anthony White, our local conceptual artist, mine dump-truck driver, visiting art teacher, would-be politician (I didn't mention that bit), Internet art seller, and cat owner (not those bits either)? Well he's posted a letter on his website—www.anthonywhite.net—that he wrote to a corporation of mercenaries, Blackstone Mercenaries International (no relation to our own outback town Blackstone). Blackstone MI offer their protective services for people and property in the most dangerous places in the world. Amongst other contracts, they operate extensively in Iraq protecting servicemen and women. The US government is paying them—paying Blackstone MI, I mean.

Anyway, this artist, Anthony, wrote to Blackstone asking for a quote to protect the whales in Australian waters. Blackstone MI may have to burn or sink one or two Japanese ships, but apart from that, it's a fairly straightforward protection job, and far less challenging than their normal gigs.

Our coastal surveillance officers capture, arrest and burn the boats of Indonesian fishermen who sneak into our waters to fish. So, apart from politics and the wealth of Japan, it's no different in doing the same with the Japanese whaling boats—unless poverty and desperation attract a greater penalty than affluence and greed. Anthony's still waiting for a reply to his letter. I put a message on his blog, asking him to write another one to save my nailtails. He won't know it's me of course.

Anthony's artwork is beyond most locals. They only understand landscapes, flowers and portraits of people, dogs, horses and cattle. The Anthony White Money Series is so foreign to their consciousness. If it's within spitting distance, they get angry about its very existence, fearing ridicule I think.

Fortunately for Ant, international art collectors see things differently, so sales are pretty hot overseas. His string of exhibitions in Switzerland, France, USA, England, and Canada keep him busy enough to mostly get over the local rejection.

Anthony is smart and quirky, very big picture, but can also be extremely small-town. He obsessively avoids crab holes when he drives along the beach to our local surfing spot—so he doesn't hurt the crabs, he says. And he loves his cat, Beyonce.

Rememory 73

It's spooky. The tide is right out, but everything's different. There's debris strewn across the beaches—exposed roots from sand-dune creepers, shells from faraway sea beds, a whole mangrove tree on its side, two to three metres long, leafless, with twisted roots half its length long, reaching out, begging for help. And the feeder creek to The Causeway has moved. Again. It's shot right across half the length of the beach and winds back around, copying a real river, a micro river secure in its windingness, with islands, hairpin bends; an old-establishment ecosystem.

But that's not the really spooky bit. Way past the sand flats, probably half a kilometre out to the edge of the receding tide, there looks to be a wall of water. Nobody else seems to have noticed it—nobody in this case is one person and her dogs exploring way out along the creek towards the sea, towards this wall of water. They are far braver than I would be. She's pretty nonchalant if she did notice it, but wait—she's turned back now. It's just so odd, sitting here, and just below me, where there should be sand or sea, is a hedge of water, foamy waves going nowhere, marking time, waiting. It's all got to be an optical illusion. The woman and her dogs are leaving now. Quickly. As quickly as the boggy sand and dignity allow.

Straight after school today, my father bundled me into the Land-Cruiser. Before he strapped me in, he extracted the dead sandwich crusts marinated in dried vomit. We must be going to town, I thought. He even changed me out of my uniform and dressed me in purple patterned leggings and a blue differently patterned corduroy dress on top of a "Welcome to Leichhardt" t-shirt. It's not actually my t-shirt. It was left behind by one of my father's "friends"; I forget her name, something starting with L, I think. My father left my hair in its lop-sided plaits. One half of my hair, well only a quarter really, is missing, ripped clean out. A casualty of my last "episode". I look decidedly post-modernist, I reckon.

As we raced to town at a hundred and twenty ks per hour, my father talked on his mobile to Psycho Silas.

"Yep, we're on the road now," my father said. "We should hit Leichhardt at sixish, Lilian Bay six thirtyish, so we'll head straight to the gallery. Will be there, six forty-five at the latest. Yep, should be a good turnout, see you soon." Plonk.

He threw the phone on the dashboard, lit a cigarette and cracked another beer. We both settled in for the cannonball drive to the coast.

We were attending Anthony's latest Lilian Bay art exhibition. It was, as usual, a flop. All his friends turned up, also as usual, including three or four or six ex-girlfriends. He can't remember exactly all the specific acts themselves, and for one, whether it happened at all. Hopefully they can't remember too many details either.

"Could have been seven of them possibly. Maybe eight," he said to Silas later in the night. Silas shrank at the news, belittled, I reckon. The pores on his face hollowed and he contracted a little all over. Beaten at his own game, probably. His midnight-blue (it looks purple) velvet smoking jacket and silk cravat looked all of a sudden a little shabby, cheap. He'll never catch up to Ant, and certainly nowhere near as nonchalantly. Anthony is minimalist in terms of bragging, saves it for the most deserving.

Now, a word of caution. It's an art exhibition, remember. Lots of people and names you may not know. Just run with it, hey. Don't stress if you don't remember who's who. Most of them don't either.

Standing in the same arterarti group as Ant and Silas was Liam, Anthony's ace "wingman" for picking up women. By Liam's side was the local GP, Bill Weston. He's a big fish in a small pond art collector and *bon vivant*, and was magnetted to his very plain but very nice, if not very adventurous, new wife, Jane. Around the circle, beside Jane, was Richard, the over-stuffed local easy-case lawyer—yes, sadly, yet another one—with Lulu his partner, ex designer-shoe shop manager and newly qualified public relations graduate. Richard and Lulu weren't magnetted. She gushed and he pompoussed, so they balanced each other well, and didn't need the security of magnets.

The full complement of gallery attendees could be further detailed, but it does get a bit boring if you don't know, and will probably never meet, them all, and are not particularly enthralled with middle class would-be arty types. Trust me, the list goes on and on and on.

We were all there, even me. I was parked under a Peter Drexel nude on the mezzanine floor overlooking and overhearing the entire exhibition. Yes, I formally admit it, focused hearing—benefit numero uno of Rett Syndrome. The nude above me was very big, but certainly not Peter's best work. Most of his drawings and paintings that were stock-piled in the gallery only sold out when Peter started to get sick. As soon as word of his ill health was circulated in the gallery newsletter, his work was snapped up, gobbled up.

"He's definitely not your healthy, bounce back, type, so undoubtedly a good investment," Psycho Silas said during one art gallery gathering, and Dodgy Dominic concurred, I'm not sure with what authority. Silas is a doctor so he should know, I suppose most people thought.

Back to this exhibition. Stretching a little to one side, I could see my father looking a little covetously at one of Anthony's dump truck paintings.

"Really, enough's enough," I silently screamed at him. You could tell because my legs were going nineteen to the dozen, flapping in my chair. "Our walls are all already well enough littered with Anthony White art. How about a new bed for my room?" my legs said.

My father finds it difficult, impossible, to resist a "sure thing". He bought three Drexels when he heard Peter was in hospital. No idea where he's going to find wall space if Anthony gets sick.

"G'day, g'day, how goes it?" my father said after he wandered over to the Bill and Jane group. He slapped Bill on the back in a show of unwelcome familiarity, and kissed Jane enthusiastically to make up for her plainness. Silas wheeled over to the drinks table and collected a glass of champagne. It was Yellow sparkling, the pink variety, to add pizzazz to the occasion, and always a safer bet than the cardboard red and white, according to everyone's lemon suckin' lips. We must have missed the Veuve Clicquot one bottle starter that Hugh Ashton, the gallery runnerer, always provides in a show of we-are-part-of-the-high-flyers-glittering-arterarti-beautiful-people.

"Mayyyte, mayyyyte," Hugh said, joining the group and reverting to outback talk in welcoming my father. "Welcome, welcome," he followed up with. Repetition adds pizzazz pizzazz too.

Jane half smiled, accepting another cheek-slurp, this time a chicken peck on both cheeks, from Hugh. So cosmopolitan. Jane had veered forward slightly to show belonging, then magnetised back to place, reverted to her half smile, sipped her pink Yellow and sucked her teeth. Her music-box winder had wound out, but I was thinking that she looked quite nice. She had blow-dried her hair, I think.

Anthony floated back over, lighting the group up like only the belle of the ball can. Silas took the floor. "Ant, my dear chap, what an achievement, an excellent turnout, my man." Patronising arsehole.

Silas saw himself as head arty type of his cronies, above even Bill. Bill was just a GP after all. Silas splattered anyone else's attempts at the Head Arty Type title by out-buying them. He had ten Anthony Whites: six number threes in the "Money" series, namely a $3, US$3, £3, €3; four number thirty-threes: a $33, US$33, £33, €33; a "Moon Franchise Agreement" painting of a duck (the owner has the exclusive rights to sell all official Anthony White artwork between 0–10 degrees north latitude and 0–10 degrees east longitude on the Moon's surface); one green and gold "Dump Truck"; one "Eulogy for a Whale" (number three); and "Coal Sculpture Number Three". Anthony always keeps number one of everything except for "Coal Sculpture Number One". He gave it to me the second time he met me at my school.

I could see the folds of Silas's face plumping, etching out "got one, got one, got one". He's bought something, I bet. It'll help him get over Anthony's scoring prowess. I bet there's a red sticker on some painting featuring the numeral three. He once bought the almost identical painting in the concurrent international exhibition at a hundred times the price. I guess it depends where the number three in the series is. It would be just like Anthony to make sure they are all in the international exhibitions. He thinks Silas's a complete tosser too.

"My fans didn't let me down," Anthony said. He's three-quarters serious, and the more he sells, the higher the self-belief fraction rises. "New York is chockas. We're live-streaming."

Anthony looked up to the ceiling screen showing, in real-time, his concurrent New York exhibition in NY Gallery. NY is "the" gallery in New York City for quirk and conceptual art, and it had recently snapped up Ant to join its stable.

When Anthony has an exhibition overseas that he doesn't attend, he always simultaneously holds a Lilian Bay exhibition. He insists that invitations give the option for either event, on the off chance anyone feels like popping over from the US or Europe to Lilian Bay, or vice versa of course.

It's four am in New York, but that's not an issue, Anthony assures anyone who will listen.

"The place is still packed," he says. "NY Gallery is three times the size of this place [Lilian Bay Fine Art Gallery] and also has a mezzanine gallery floor. In both galleries, we suspend the dump truck paintings throughout the air space." Anthony gestures wildly up to the ceiling space. "We string them up at differing viewing angles, right up to the ceiling."

"Yeah, Ant, not stating the obvious a bit, hey?" I mind-say looking up at dive-bombing dump trucks.

NY's ultra-early morning opening-night time of four am only adds cachet to 24-hour New Yorkers, Anthony reckons. In New York, the video feed of the Lilian Bay exhibition is billed as an installation, and NY punters can put on head phones to listen to the Lilian Bay Gallery attendees' conversations. There are pick-up mics all over the place in the Lilian Bay Gallery. And vice versa the bugging device from NY.

Ant put the NY audio headphones on me for a bit. The New Yorkers "laaarrrve the Arrrzy accents," every single one of them says several times (except any Australian punters at the New York show).

"Twenty-three have already sold at NY," Anthony said to the Bill and Jane group of fans. He was salivating a bit and his eyes were ultra-bright. Not drug ultra-bright, but excitement laced with incredulity ultra-bright sparkling eyes, backed up with a fair bit of figurative hand rubbing. I don't know why he's surprised. His international market is rocketing.

"How many are sold here, Ant?" Bill asked. There's a cruel streak in Bill.

Anthony's eyes stopped shining for a moment and breath escaped from his every pore. Regardless of being fabulously wealthy and selling masses of art, world-wide, Ant is a sensitive soul. "Three," he said, "but the night's still young." He regained his cushion of air, and floated to another group of fans.

Not many paintings sell in Lilian Bay, despite the much cheaper price tags. Plenty of people come to drink Ant's wine, but few to buy his art. The irony of his lack of hometown support never fails to both tickle and irk him. He kind of likes the reverse snobbery of being just one of the locals, who, apart from a few of us, wouldn't know better, but he is no end irked by the local art "experts" who should know better, and fail to give him his due. No one locally really knows his exact sell rate, but without doubt, he's the region's most prolific selling, and highest grossing, artist. Each year throughout the world—mostly over the Internet—Anthony sells more than two hundred paintings, averaging twenty thousand dollars each. Yet his local exhibitions, showing virtually the same paintings at his "hometown discount rate"—one per cent of the international price tag, so averaging around two hundred dollars—rarely sell more than a few.

The pricing structure looks quite complex, but it's simple really. All paintings exhibited in Australia are sold at their face value. For example, with the "Money" series, the $5 painting costs five dollars, the €5, five euros. In the "Eulogy for a Whale" series, number sixty costs 60 of the currency of the nation's waters in which the whale was killed. The prices of all paintings exhibited internationally are simply one hundred times the face value.

"They have to pay for international exposure," Ant says. Whatever that means.

All prices are inclusive of freight anywhere in the world.

That very few of his local friends take financial advantage of his Australian prices by reselling internationally reflects on the quirky type of individuals they are. They are all so different, some are quite poor financially, yet they are swollen in their loyalty and ethics.

Occasionally some of Anthony's international "fans" turn up in Lilian Bay. They can pay for their holiday by buying a painting at a Lilian Bay exhibition. Anthony will even freight it home for them. "It's all part of the price," he says. He says his fans add culture and dollars to the local tourism industry.

"This is Lars, one of my Swiss fans," he'd say, or, "Meet Ana and Karl, fans from Germany."

Ant is very into the "fan" thing and administers his own fan blog complete with an option of being sent complimentary autographed photographs of himself—that's complimentary as in free, hey; they're definitely not flattering photos. I ordered one and had it delivered to my school, so I know.

This latest exhibition of Anthony's is a follow-up to his "Eulogy for a Whale" series. It is called "Slayed in Japan" and features harpoon spears. Each painting looks identical except for different coloured backgrounds, consecutive numbers on each spearhead, and unique blood spatters. Ant paints a new harpoon spear painting in memory of, and to honour, each whale murdered by Japanese pseudo-research whaling ships. We'd all like him to reach the end of this series.

Every exhibition Anthony holds, anywhere in the world, includes works from his previous exhibitions, such as paintings from his "Money" series, from his "Moon Rights" series, and his "Dump Truck" and "Coal" series.

"It is important to offer new and old fans the opportunity to widen their collections," Anthony says.

Bizarrely, and pretty much everything about him is bizarre, Ant has a full-time job driving trucks out in the mines. He earns four million dollars every year with his art, yet he works seven-days-on, seven-off, four hours' drive west, driving dump trucks. He reasons that if he drives the dump trucks slowly, he's doing something positive for reducing greenhouse gases.

After every week-long shift, with every trip home to the coast, Anthony brings back chunks of coal—legally. They are his free allocation. True story! An 1890s statutory entitlement allows each employee of the mine a weekly allocation, presumably for home heating purposes.

"White's numbered coal carvings, carved by his dump truck,"

Ant's web site blurb reads, "have been sound sellers for the past two years."

One lump of coal fetches $5000 (including freight) on the international market. Each is numbered, named and photographed and featured on the website with purchaser details. He does this with all his art—unless he doesn't know who bought it, or if the new owner requests anonymity. I did. His two metre by three metre dump truck paintings sell for $70,000 and he can't—or won't—keep up with demand. He can't really, because he only paints one for each month he works there. His family still think he should get a proper job and go back to stockbroking.

Rememory 74

There's a reason for my telling you about Anthony and this latest "Slayed in Japan" exhibition: his guest list. Ant's invitation list always includes the leader of every country he has sold art to, and arts writers from these countries' most prestigious publications—*The New York Times*, England's *The Times*, *The Singapore Times*, Switzerland's *Tages-Anzeiger*, the list is long. That's how Calliope Tsutsis, arts writer and blogger for *New York Reporter*, came to be in Australia to visit my school and for the Lilian Bay exhibition.

"And why did youse guys come here, hey?" Lilian Bay local weekly newspaper, *Lilian Bay Local*, sent out their gun—and only—reporter. Her business card also lists "advertising executive" as her title.

"Youse coming for Beef, hey?" the gun reporter asked Calliope. Leichhardt and environs are very proud of the biannual Beef Expo.

"No, I'm here to interview Anthony," Calliope replied.

"Ant? This Ant?" She looked genuinely surprised.

"Yes, Anthony White—this Anthony." Calliope was amused.

"Why?" she asked. "Oh, about the mine downturn, hey?"

"About his art," Calliope said.

"You call that art?" she said. "You've got to be joking. It's all a joke really. We all think it's a big joke, youse guys calling it art. Youse've been sucked in, hey. Me kids did better at kindergarten. No one ever buys anything, hey. Maybe his family buy one or two. Tell you the truth, we all feel a bit sorry for him."

Calliope was loving it, and taking it all down for his blog.

"But you haven't wasted your time, hey?" gun reporter continued. "I'll give you a couple of heads up. No dramas. I'm not competitive. The real stories around here are the Beef Expo coming up again next year, and there's a new international resort in the pipeline. It's very early days of course. They're still waiting for approval, but the Council here is right behind it, and inside sources reckon it's a sure thing," she said tapping the side of her nose.

"So fingers crossed it'll be a goer. That's if those greenie wankers pull their fingers out and let our town develop. It's not the blackfellas this time who're the hold up, hey? Having that spastic kid who's part black—and I'm talking about a spit of piss black—makes him, the father who's the main developer, hey, as good as black too, so that's no problem. No, it's the bloody wanker greenies crying over a few lousy roos. They's runty roos at that, hey. I dunno how they get away with making such a drama about a few roos when there's millions out there and they're all pests, hey."

Calliope gleamed. His face and physique are frugal on flesh, and his eyes simply bulge brains. He is New York understated, New York underestimated. So the gleaming was all within his crow-black eyeballs. My heart rushed. He had smelt a real story.

Rememory 75

The sea is angry. The gallery spotlights stream out onto the sea, but only its surface glows. Beneath that, it's pissed off. The once soft waves have become tools of hatred, ripping gullies, slashing sea beds. We've never had rips here before; nothing you'd count as a rip. But we have now. And they're fast and mean. Calm shafts entice the unwary, then—brooking no argument—snatch them, shooting them out past where they want to go. This place has changed.

"What do you mean, 'as good as black'?" Calliope asked the young woman.

Guilelessly, the "journo" from our local rag explained the deal about me. "The spastic kid's the only one left from that tribe on the place. Stupid, I know, but her mother's legged it. She used to be the elder—or la de dah 'custodian', she called herself."

Each time the young journalist repeated key words, she raised her first and second fingers of each hand for quotation marks.

"Now the mother's gorn, the kid's the 'custodian'. They have to consult her about sacred women's sites, or some nonsense. Ridiculous, hey, sure is. Since land rights rubbish, yer land's no longer ya land, hey? Ya've been on ya place generations. Some've been there two hundred years, five generations, then some Abo who's never spent a brass razoo on the place, gets some say. Anyway, 'cause the kid's spastic, the father's her 'legal guardian'. He only has to 'consult' himself for 'consultation', hey."

"You've got to be kidding me," Calliope said. "There's no way. I think I've already met this kid. Where's the mother?"

When the question was asked, I shrank further into my invisibility cloak. Sitting alone up on the mezzanine gallery, shrinking back into my chair, trying to shrink inside dead Peter Drexel's nude.

"She ran off to Aurukun and got done in by some blackfella she was bangin'," the young woman said. "She was a soak anyway, hey, didn't give a stuff about the kid. Loved the booze. Loved the dope. No one never heard of her again, hey. They're like that around here. Blackfellas. Go walkabout at the drop of a hat. Booze is their number one family member."

I slunk, faded even further into the back crook of my chair, melting into the dead egg sandwich crusts, smearing myself into the milk mushed into crevices, sinking willingly into the contents of my nappy. She hadn't known my mother or me back then, but it didn't seem to matter. They're all so judgemental, so quick to believe or make up the worst. They have no idea. No one rang us asking about my mother. No one tried to speak to me. No one tried to find out what went on, why she left, or even if she did. He could have killed her for all they knew, for all I know. He probably did. I guess he did. As good as, at best—worse, most likely. Even the blackfellas didn't look. They're so used to being no one that when someone really does become no one, no one thinks to look.

Rememory 76

The sea is roaring. It hasn't rained for a million years until the recent downpour. I'm lying in my cot bed and I can hear the sea quite stirred up, whooshing in gushes towards The Causeway.

Anthony is at it again.

Email to: Blackstone Mercenaries International

Mr Erik Prince
Academi (Blackstone Mercenaries International)
Security Management Services
Arlington, Virginia, USA

Dear Mr Prince

I would like to invite you to quote on protecting the remaining population of one of Australia's endangered species, the bridled nailtail wallaby.

The entire nailtail population is located in one fairly remote geographical area, approximately 700km north of Brisbane. These creatures are protected under Australian Federal Law, but are still being slaughtered, probably by local kangaroo shooters enabled by landowners.

This protection contract is privately funded and separate from any official government agency. The contract is ongoing, and I offer cash payment.

Yours sincerely
Anthony White
http://www.anthonywhite.net

And Calliope, the reporter from New York, has gone public with what he learned from the chatter at the exhibition.

NEW YORK REPORTER

Arts Beat

White Hot Oz at NY

By arts writer and blogger Calliope Tsutsis

NY Gallery's latest fad in the conceptual art scene, Australian artist Anthony White, is no hero in his Central Queensland hometown of Lilian Bay. He's just plain weird. Here in New York, plenty of his work is being snapped up for $20,000–50,000 a piece, but locals in Lilian Bay (population 13,000) won't even buy his art with two zeros knocked off. His friends have purchased one or two for friendship's sake, but the local art lovers say, "Really, you can't be serious. He's actually a bit of an embarrassment. We just come along for the wine."

Fortunately for White, everyone else in the world seems to agree with New York. In Europe, White's "Number" series is super-hot property, with buyers devouring millions of dollars' worth annually. And now NY Gallery has added him to their prestigious stable, White's future looks even brighter; luminous, white hot.

But back in Down Under Lilian Bay, even in fine art circles, White is so ho-hum. The regional gallery only took his work — donated — because White's doctor friend threatened to kick up a stink if they didn't. Never mind that White is the largest selling artist in the region — both in terms of volume and dollars. Never mind that he's edgy, leaning to Warhol-level quirk. In his hometown, Ant is just Ant. Ant the ex-stockbroker (hence the "Money" series), the big odd bloke who lives in a tumbledown 1950s block of apartments, drives a clapped-out Jeep, and for a job, drives a dump truck at a coal mine 200km out west, seven days on, seven days off.

The coal mine is the inspiration and source, literally, for another recent collection of his work, the "Coal" series. An 1890s statutory law allows each mine employee to take home up to 5lb of coal weekly; back then for heating the house; these days, in White's case, to make art — literally. White sells numbered lumps of coal, "carved by his dump truck" he says. The mine humours him. As long as the dump truck gets filled, this eccentricity is irrelevant. They mustn't know about his eco warrior driving. White says if he drives his coal dump truck slowly, he's reducing fossil fuel production.

After each 12-hour shift, White works on 10' x 12' canvases, lately some of harpoon spears and some of dump trucks. He's just finished a portrait of the yellow and brown dump truck with a blue cab door that he drives, and another of the new, very shiny, sun-gold yellow one that's just arrived, and yet another of the green and rust one a co-worker drives. There are several more in existence — all sold. He has now completed a total of 23 dump truck paintings — one for each month he's worked at the mine. No more, no less, White says.

As I write, NY Gallery is red-stickering 43 coal sculptures (Weeks 50–92), 45 paintings of harpoon spears from the "Slayed in Japan" series (all virtually identical and numbered "for each whale slaughtered in the name of Japanese science"), and four dump truck canvases. In both the NY and Lilian Bay exhibitions, the dump truck paintings float in the air, hanging from the ceiling like oversized Tonka toys, a likeness of which White is very proud.

"I'm glad you've seen my point," White said. "The difference between the two is purely scale — scale of rock capacity, scale of commercial value, scale of benefit to the community and scale of boys playing with toys. They're the perfect gift for that billionaire who has everything — a billionaire sized Tonka — especially if he has shares in a mining company. How sublime."

If White's success grows proportionally from the many hundreds of his 12" x 12" number series that average $20,000 each, to this 6ft x 10ft dump truck series, the outcome for him will be indeed sublime.

Also soon to be on show at NY Gallery is a preview selection of White's new series, "Wallaby Wipeout", which highlights his region's endangered bridled nailtail wallabies. White is donating his share of the profits to their preservation.

White donated his share of the profits from the "Slayed in Japan" series, and the earlier "Eulogy for a Whale" series, to Sea Shepherd Conservation Society.

Anthony White's art can be viewed at www.anthonywhite.net.

Rememory 77

The sea and sky have merged. It's all one big puff cloud.

"Will you write me into it?" Anthony typed. "Mention my artwork. That way I can surf on your best sellerism."

It was Anthony's monthly art visit again at our school. He was taking turns typing with me on my computer. It was like a real conversation. Ant always took it for granted I was normal, mind-wise.

"Hey, Gus, come over here," he said as Gus came up the stairs.

"Won't be a mo'," Gus said.

"Nooooooo!!!!" I typed, "My f cant no."

"No worries," Anthony said. He minimised the Word document, and turned as Gus bounced into the room.

"Hey mate, how's your sculpture going? If you start working on it, I'll come down in a sec and have a squiz, after I have a look at what Soph's doing," Anthony said.

"Sure thing, thanks." Gus jumped down the stairs three or four at a time and flipped himself over the rail at the bottom.

After Gus left, Anthony re-opened the Word document we were using.

"What's going on?" Anthony quietly asked.

"If my father knows I can think, he might stop me using the computer," I typed. "I can't risk it."

"I'm not sure hiding things from him is a good idea," Anthony said.

My face said it all, and Anthony changed his mind.

"Okay, I won't do anything you're not comfortable with. Writing some sort of journal is a good idea, though," he said.

"Write in it whatever you want — fiction, non-fiction, a mix, faction, a post-modernist factional memoir. A memoir would be amazing. Go for broke. But write me in, hey. That would be so cool."

"If I write it, I'll write you in," I typed back. It was good to be considered a contender even if he was only minisculely serious.

I didn't tell him I'd already started writing. That would be far too threatening, for me. Far too confronting. Bringing the possibility, probability, of failure into reality. I had been writing fiction and some diary note stuff. I hadn't had the confidence to give it a more impressive genre name. He suggested I write a memoir. The old no-one-will-believe-it's-true angle. He didn't know the whole story, but knew more than most. He was surprisingly discreet. I wanted to write a tribute to my mother. I didn't want anyone to forget her. I didn't know many people who had known her, but I didn't want her memory to fade. I wanted it to grow.

My mother used to talk to me about writing. She said it could be my way of having a career. She said she wanted me to become famous. Internationally.

"I want Barbie dolls to be made of you, Soph," she said. "Barbies in wheelchairs. I want you to be on the front pages of magazines. I want you to be a poster girl for the disabled. I want you to be Superhero Soph."

And I so wanted it too, because she did. I've read it's part of the grieving process. Craving immortality for a loved one. In this case, through her dreams for me. It's all part of not accepting the finality of loss. Not fully accepting the loss. Nowhere near! No way was I going even close to accepting her gone. I wanted to write about her life with me. I might not, probably not, get a chance to finish it, but I was feeling a tiny bit more at peace, now that I started.

"Did you read the article about my exhibition?" Anthony asked. "I emailed it to you."

"Yes, I read it," I eye-typed. "Yes, you shone like a beacon of success. Yes, everyone should show you due respect and reverence. No, it won't happen. Leichhardt Art Gallery will not buy your work. Have you framed it, the story I mean?" I loved our banter.

"I've chosen the frame," Ant said, "but I haven't printed a proper copy yet."

It didn't really follow anything in the conversation. I just blurted: "I need $10 for a URL name. But you can't tell anyone, ever. Please, will you be my benefactor? Call it an advance, I'll pay you back from book sales."

Anthony laughed and typed, "I would be honoured to be your benefactor. Think of me as your silent partner."

He paused to open his wallet, then typed in his credit card number, expiry date, and three digit code. "Go for broke, Soph. I'll keep it between us. My money is your money. Use it whenever you need or want to. I'll make sure it's kept topped up."

"Are you going to write everything, the whole truth?" he asked.

People always think something's all true, but it never is. There's no such thing as absolute truth—even pure reason will never get you there. Anyway, the truth's not all finished yet.

"I'll tell enough," I typed.

NEW YORK REPORTER

Arts Beat

White hot on the tail of Oz wallabies

By Calliope Tsutsis

It's a puzzling story and one that is certainly not yet all told. I was floating around Down Under's Central Queensland again, covering yet another few million dollars in the making at the Oz opening of Australian conceptual artist, Anthony White's, latest series, Wallaby Wipe-out. His previous NY Gallery exhibition, "Slayed in Japan" and the "Coal" series, sold out, returning almost $1 million in less than one month.

White has become a commercial phenomenon in the art world, and is easily the highest grossing living conceptual artist in Australia. With each series, White has transformed his life. He was a stockbroker during his "Money" series, then coal mine dump truck driver for his "Coal" series. Now he's an environmental crusader, and is about to launch his latest series, highlighting the plight of Australia's virtually extinct bridled nailtail wallabies.

He's also running for Federal Parliament and "eyeing off the environmental portfolio", White says.

There are so many angles to this I hardly know where to start.

Number one, that White feels the need for a job.

Number two, that his current job is driving dump trucks at an open coal mine in the remote outback.

Number three, that embroiled within the issue of the disappearing wallabies are stories of their ongoing massacre, a multi-million dollar eco resort, and quite possibly Indigenous exploitation of the highest and most sordid nature.

I'm going to be hanging around in Oz for a while, I can see.

Arts Beat

Embarrassed confession

By Calliope Tsutsis

I must confess.

I purchased artist Anthony White's *Wallaby Wipe-out 39*. I feel rather sheepish because at the exhibition's Queensland opening, my painting cost $39 — and that's Australian dollars!

If I had purchased the virtually identical *Wallaby Wipe-out 40* at the New York version of the opening, I would have paid $4,000.

And by identical, I mean identical. Identical in size, same greenish brown tones, same basic splatter on canvas. I'm told the ten paintings exhibited in Queensland were randomly chosen from the concurrent series exhibited in New York's NY Gallery. All, to all intents and purposes, identical, except for the thousands of dollars difference in price tag.

And, of course, except for their individualised blood spatters. I hope Customs and Border Protection let it into the US. Rumour has it, the splatters have real wallaby blood in the paint.

White, however, denies the rumour. "It's my blood," he said.

Chapter 18

www.silentscream.com.au

Silent Scream

What the hell are you doing, everyone out there? He's annihilating your history, your culture, your kids' futures. The last of the nailtails will be emerging from The Wall soon for their seasonal romp. Last time they appeared, the shooters obliterated every living creature in a one-hour genocidal slaughter. This is the last chance we have.

Miss this one, and the only nailtail will be the stuffed one up there next to the Thylacine in the endangered/extinct section of our National Gallery.

Get off your arses, camp by Styx Lake in Central Queensland and stand in their way – literally. Link arms and form a human wall of salvation. I'll let you know the date and time.

Please help me make my screams heard.

SS

Rememory 78

Oh dear, the sea, the sea, soak me up.

"It's that fuckin' bitch Rose!"

The cronies—and I—were at Dodgy Dom and K-Kittie's beach house, chewing the fat, trying to get to the bottom of who could be behind the blog, *Silent Scream*. I was parked on the verandah overlooking a pub and Lilian Bay's Main Beach.

Creative beach names in Lilian Bay, hey: Main Beach, Rocky Point, Fisherman's Beach. Lady's Beach is a little more interesting. Maybe named in the late 1800s, early 1900s because of its total seclusion from any surrounding land. I bet lots of fishermen found good fishing spots just offshore.

Dominic is always slightly too vehement in his hostility towards my mother. Could have something to do with her once laughing at his declaration of love. I think, at the time, she actually thought he was joking in a "Rose, I-love you and really-support-you-as-a-human-being" kind of declaration. But he wasn't. It was in an

"I'm-a-greasy-sleazy-best-friend-of-your-husband-who-wants-to-shag-you" way.

"It could be one of those enviro wanker tree huggers, Freddy or Gus or someone in that crew," Psycho Silas said, ignoring Dominic. "But how could they know all this stuff?"

"One of them will have a friend who has a wife who has a brother-in-law in Council or the Enviro Department or somewhere," my father said.

We certainly all know our own tricks best.

"It's got to be Rose," Dominic said.

"I reckon it's gotta be," Rabbit Warren agreed.

Silas was silent, his eyes fixed on nothing, looking nowhere.

"It's not Rose." My father said it quietly, but for some reason, from the tone of his voice, some subtle intonation, Dominic and Warren believed him.

And they were not appalled by the fact that they did.

Chapter 19

Rememory 79

Cyclone Thea is teasing the coast just north. It's a king tide tomorrow. A lot of people are worried. Pandanus beach is serene, wildly serene. It's excited, looking forward to the big chance of a return to its ancient shoreline before Council bulldozers and dredgers set in.

Almost ten years ago, they dredged a new channel into The Causeway to stop nature reclaiming its own. High tides were slurping at the thin bitumen strip of road that was pathetically protecting piles of bricks and asbestos. Everyone—at least the local everyones—knew that this beach moved with the wind. It vacillated between being a beach with a single tidal estuary-fed lake, and being a beach with two tidal estuaries spilling over The Causeway and filling the inner reaches. Sometimes it is one massive boiling expanse of water, swooping on the entire coastline and flooding way beyond The Causeway's "lake", collecting goodness manufactured by millions of mangroves kilometres inland, and delivering it back to the ocean's plants and creatures. You can't tame this beach, well not for long, not when time is measured in tens of thousands of years, and life force surges along a floodplain sent from the earth's core.

In Lilian Bay, today, you can't buy a battery radio, masking tape, torch or a generator. Even the grocery shelves looked depleted when my father dragged me into town, just after lunch, for a last minute half-arsed cyclone supply shopping expedition and crony meeting at the coffee shop.

There's quite a few of them gathering. There's cronies number one and two, Psycho Silas and Dodgy Dominic; the talk-the-leg-off-the-chair ginormously obese local mayor; and two matching on the way to bulbous real estate agents. My father and I got to the coffee shop first, and sat outside, just around the corner and mostly just out of the blast of Thea. My father parked me closest to the sea, next to the window just behind him. The wind whooshed around the corner whooshing my hearing with it.

None of the others acknowledged me when they took turns to arrive. They didn't notice me, and I was happy to keep it that way. All of them, except my father and me, were in suits. The number of office-hours suits this coffee shop must see. There are cappuccino suits any time from early morning (which means from ten am) until just after lunch at three-thirty. After "lunch", the suits gather for oversized glasses quarter filled with wine or full of imported beer. I can't quite hear what they're up to because of the whooshing, but it's got to be "the development". I can smell it.

It's a wonder they haven't renamed "the development" something exotic, eco-touristy already. I mean surely that would be the first thing they'd change. "Styx River" is hardly the name for an Australian destination of more than twenty kilometres of pristine deserted beaches, thirty kilometres of unique prehistoric mazes, waterfalls, pure spring-water pools, vast expanses of virgin tropical wilderness to explore, fifty thousand years of untampered Indigenous history.

If my mother had any idea this was on the cards, no way would she stay away. She'd do something to stop it. In her diary she wrote of regular conflict with my father over touristising The Wall:

```
I can't believe it. He's on about it again, turning
this place into some sort of tourist resort. ¶
¶
"Come outback. Morning tea with a real Wuku, then
ride dirt bikes through the basalt maze. Plenty of
bush to explore. Lunch under centuries-old Burdekin
plums. Try out the ancient grindstone. Make some cave
art. Explore underwater caverns -- dynamited for your
convenience." ¶
¶
What the fuck! No way. No way am I going to let
him turn this place into some indigy-dude ranch.
My family's cultural heritage is not a tourist
attraction. ¶
¶
"There are sacred sites, women's sacred sites right
through this place," I told him. ¶
¶
"I won't let you," I told him. ¶
¶
"I will block you," I told him. ¶
```

I can't imagine my father would have been too happy being told what he couldn't do with his own land.

If I prayed, I'd pray. If I thought it'd work, I'd do it anyway. By the stream of blog comments, *Silent Scream* seems to be having some effect, but I can't see these guys backing off. Not while they've got the whiff of two thousand strata title managed apartments to sell. The underground caves could be their ready-made sewer. I can't think of a lot that I can do to help, but I'll try. I've got to at least try.

Rememory 80

Today the beach disappeared. Swallowed by the sea, by Cyclone Thea. All gone.

People were everywhere, out looking for disasters, out looking for something to gasp at. I was out too, with my father attending a meeting to try to save the nailtails. My father asked to attend the local Greens' meeting to "put his case forward" for his "eco" resort. You've got to give it to him for gall, for thick skin, for his sense of European white male entitlement; frankly, for courage.

We met at the Fitzwilliam-Renton's. All the hippies were there: the enviro-academics, the right-wing left-wing greenies, the left-wing right-wing greenies, the plain old greenies, the twilight dwellers, and us. If I was a real person, I'd definitely fit one of those groups, probably a couple of them.

A warm hug greeted me. Several, in fact. Claudia was animated, and gushed.

"It's soooooo lovely to see you. How absolutely fabulous you came. You must sit down. How about here, this is the comfiest. Shall I help you out of your chair? Would you like a chai?"

"Don't worry, she can stay in her wheelchair," my father said. None of the greetings had been directed towards him, but he happily accepted them as if they were. "I'd love a chai," he said, and sat in the comfiest chair.

At the Fitzwilliam-Renton's, the chairs are all different. There are wonky wooden ones, curvy backs, straight backs, chipped metal, seen-better-days bentwood; most dump-rescued or donated.

I could tell by the reaction of each sitter-downer they were Alice in Wonderland chairs that didn't feel as they looked. The comfy cushion-swamped day bed is deceptively hard. Cushions are compulsory to avoid spring bite on the formal wood and vinyl 1960s green couch-settee. The two identical green chairs have completely different personalities. One is soft and spongy. One is hard as gravel. My father sat on the wicker-rocker flagship of chairs, and was instantly hugged too, but by patchwork, embroidered, knitted, appliquéd and crocheted blankets and cushions, each recording the hobbies of Audrey, Freddy's mother. Just as well the blankets and cushions welcomed him, there was no way Claudia was going to hug him—or talk to him, or even look him in the face.

Freddy convened the meeting.

"We have special guests today, Sophie and her father,"—Freddy gestured to me, then to my father—"who has come along to talk to us about his proposed development. Welcome, we are very happy to listen to what you have to say."

The people were gracious. Most looked at him and half smiled. Everyone looked at me and beamed.

"After this address, we will go into a closed members' session to discuss party matters."

In other words, my father had to leave. It all sounded very official, but the dogs and incense coils somehow softened the formality.

My father droned on and on and on and on. Claudia sat next to me and helped me sip warm milky soy chai. It was delicious. Plenty of honey and freshly mortar-and-pestled spices that sang through your olfactory receptors and taste buds. She read me a cartoon book of Shakespeare's plays, and started with the witches' scene in *Macbeth*. I laughed and giggled at her rendition of "Double, double toil and trouble, Fire burn, and cauldron bubble …"

My father was getting irritated with Claud and me, but kept to his spiel. It was a tough crowd and I think there was mutual relief when he finally finished.

"Are there any questions?" Freddy asked.

Silence, except for Claud continuing to read to me. "Fair is foul, and foul is fair; Hover through the fog and filthy air." She did the witchy face expressions including spittle spitting, and I was cacking myself.

"Well, I have another meeting to go to," my father said. "So I thank you for your time and we'll be on our way."

"Leave Sophie with us while you go to your meeting, and pick her up on your way back home," Freddy said.

"We'll be up for ages, and would love to have her. She's used to us. She used to come here all the time," Freddy said.

"With Rose," Claud said to Freddy, still not looking at, or directing her words to, my father.

My father was about to refuse, then looked at Freddy, then at Claudia. I could see him thinking, "She's a doctor, the other one's a teacher."

Or, come to think of it, more likely he was thinking, "It could help with the development."

"Okay, if you're sure," he said. "Sophie will be happier here than going to another meeting with me. Thanks. I'll pick her up in about two hours."

None of this was directed at me, but Claudia looked into my face and said, "Sophie, would you like that?"

She looked at me for ten seconds more, and said the only words she directed at my father. "Sophie says yes, she'd like to stay."

Almost without a pause, she flicked to the cartoons of Shakespeare's *Merchant of Venice*, and started reading Portia's "quality of mercy" speech.

After my father left, there was more chai all round, and the meeting resumed.

"Well, what are we going to do about the nailtails?" Freddy asked. She continued as if my father had never been there.

"We need international recognition," Richard, the bloated solicitor from Anthony's art exhibition said.

"We need to find a pressure point. An angle that bleeding hearts will haemorrhage from."

Claud started whispering me a running commentary of the background to everything going on.

"Our Dickie-boy, he's a right-wing left-wing greenie. He's always run with the bad boys, but never actually takes part. He wanks to the concept of rebellion, but draws the line at, in any way, risking consequences. First-hand knowledge, Soph," Claudia whispered. "The consequence bit, I mean, not the wanking."

I was cackling big time, and my legs and arms were flapping. She wasn't fazed by the drool. She said it was good hand-cream. That made me cackle more.

Claud continued her backgrounding of Richard.

"About thirty-five years ago, at four am in the morning, the night after our high-school graduation dinner, with no sleep, too much energy and a rising anti-climax, he didn't sully his hands. There were three of us: me, Dickie and Andre. Just like Andre and me, Dickie didn't go to bed. Just like us, he did lots of plotting. Just like us he decided to Vegemite the toilet seats at the school; they were all black toilet seats in those days. Just like us, he decided to honey the banisters and hoist Andre's knickers up the flagpole—in fact it was all his idea. Yes, he drove the getaway car, his dad's computer dashboard Volvo—and this was in 1977! Yes, he too saluted, as Andre's underpants ascended. But he didn't touch the honey, didn't open the Vegemite jar, didn't do any smearing, and didn't do anything he couldn't argue away with, 'I tried to talk them out of it,' and, 'I got them to leave as soon as I could'. That's Dickie-boy Richard. Exit stage risk-free. He is the self-serving king, but ridiculously smart."

My legs and arms flapped and I squealed. Claud enjoyed my enjoyment and fed me her own home-made vanilla slice with the chai.

"Lovely mix of metaphors there, Richard. Great idea, but any real ideas?" Gus always knows how to say things that bite but don't sting. It's the same Gus from school. He's into enviro things, big time.

His mother, Mrs Gus, hates it. "It's not natural," I heard her say, missing her own wit. "It's not natural, a grazier running with the greens."

Gus is so opposite to Richard in virtually every way. He's fit, slim, sincere, honest, humble, healthy, nil level of shiftiness—Gus is, I mean, not Richard.

"Moving on," Gus continued. "I don't know if you're at all familiar with the blog, *Silent Scream*. Anyone here have any idea who's behind it?"

Gus was looking at Freddy, who was looking a bit surprised, not quite sure, as was Claudia.

Fortunately, no one noticed my shrivelling a bit behind my chai dribble and vanilla-slice crumbs.

"We thought it was yours," Claud said, directing her comment towards Gus.

There was a bit of toing and froing until both sides seemed to accept—at least superficially—that perhaps there was someone else behind it.

"Could it be Ant?" Gus asked. "But so unlike him to avoid taking the credit."

"Who cares who wrote it, we need to get behind it, that's all," Freddy said. "A sit-in on Styx Lake could well be a goer. Who's interested? Claud and I'll be there."

Most people indicated their eagerness to attend.

Freddy continued. "How about we have Folk Club out there to swell numbers? We could have an evening of seventies protest songs or something. People will turn up for a Dylan, Joni Mitchell revival, or just enviro protest songs generally. That'd span generations and give us more scope. Maybe the Country Music Club will be in on it too?"

Rememory 81

Cyclone Thea damaged my beach as well as all the others. The sea has rusted out. Blood and decay from all the poor dead creatures that drowned in the floods, mixed with heavy metal solvents, fertilisers, sewage, and masses of other revolting stuff, have raced down the river from redneck Leichhardt and beyond, rushing to smother all and any life-form in Lilian Bay. Including my beach. It will be a long time before the sea-water will stop bleeding.

Dropping me off at the Fitzwilliam-Renton's became a Sunday afternoon ritual. It suited my father to have a few hours free of me, but it was Claudia who actually suggested it when he picked me up after the Greens' meeting. Yes, she actually spoke to him directly again—still no eye contact though.

"Sophie said she'd like to come to volleyball and chai every Sunday," Claud said without making eye contact with him. "Four o'clockish to seven-thirtyish," she said.

"Okay," my father said. "Will do."

They're getting almost chatty.

For all the other greenies, however, there was a massive slosh of a cold war between them and my father. They were polite and tolerated each other, but sides had now been clearly established regarding the nailtails and their habitat. My father didn't stay for volleyball and chai any more, but having a convenient place to park me was another matter.

Small towns differ from cities in that way. Social groups often include people with disparate points of view, many times within the same family. Wherever possible, people compartmentalise their political, religious and other ideological points of view in the interests of community life.

"Sophie! We love you! You're here! Which side do you want to go on?" Claud bellowed out, as Freddy and I approached the volleyball court. My father had handed me and my chair over to Freddy with barely a word.

"About seven-thirty, then," my father had said.

"No dramas," Freddy had replied.

Since my father started leaving me there, Claud insisted I be part of the game. Totally ridiculous and quite dangerous for everyone, especially me, but I didn't ever get hurt. I've been bumped around a bit, but not hurt. One of them nearly virtually always leaps in when the ball comes my way. One of them stands next to my chair and does the serving when it is my turn to serve.

Freddy answered for me, "Which side is winning?"

"Our side of course," Gus and Claud said.

"Sophie wants to be on your team then, hey Soph?" Freddy said and parked me within their team next to Gus.

"Hey, Soph," Gus said.

"Hey," my legs flapped.

I made six each side, not that hippie volleyball was in any way stuck on traditional side numbers, or traditional rules at all, for that matter. Anthony was the topic of conversation.

"Ant got in, he fuckin' got in." Richard had just arrived and said it as a statement of disbelief rather than of new information.

"A fucking Member of Parliament. Unbelievable. He reckons he's right in with the enviro minister—he's heir apparent, he says."

Richard couldn't leave it alone. "Unbe-fucking-lievable. He said he'd do it. Couldn't get a guernsey in Council—three times he lost,

THE STYX 163

hey, or was it four? Then first time he tries for the Feds ... Wonder what paintings will come from this?"

"Yes, but there's more," Freddy said. "Bloody Ant. You know he's one sick puppy. As a backup plan for the Styx Lake sit-in, just to make sure in case the shooters start shooting, 'as a private individual',"—Freddy did the finger actions as she spoke—"Ant's commissioned all the local roo shooters to take photos of every nailtail they see, dead or alive."

"He told them it was for his artwork, another wallaby series," Gus continued. "Hundred bucks a nailtail photo, he's offered, and he even supplied them with cameras, complete with date stamp. He says he is categorically against such genocide, but it will be sufficient evidence to halt any development."

"I tell you, with him helping run the country, how can we go wrong?" Freddy said.

Rememory 82

There's a ship perched on the reef just outside my place. It's parked there, stuck, bleeding oil. I woke up, peered out at my sea, and there it was.

I've got a new bed. A proper one, much bigger and it's higher. I had to scrunch my legs in the old cot bed, or lie on the diagonal, to fit. I kept getting a leg stuck, twisted between the bars. This new one's got sides, skinny bars, and I can see through them to the sea. It's not against the back wall anymore. My new bed's across one set of the French doors opening onto the front verandah. As soon as I wake up, I can see the sea. The doors open outwards, so he leaves them open; for airflow, he says. Hopefully he'll shut them in winter.

At first the ship looked like it was floating along the horizon, strayed from the shipping channels, heading north. But then I realised it didn't move. It was stuck.

Our home computer babysat me again this morning. No one was around, so I logged online, via the dial-up. I see Styx River's development is in the news again. The application is becoming a big issue in this region, and the cronies have set their PR machine into action. I'm afraid that between them, anything is possible.

I think I've mentioned that my mother knew Psycho Silas from before her marriage, in fact she introduced him into the circle, well before she married my father.

She wrote about it in her diary, that she met him when she was about twenty years old at a party. She said she was intimidated by his literary and historical big-noting. He was in his internship year, after he'd finished his medical degree, and was pretty, totally, full of himself. It was soon after Andrew left, and my mother was lonely, she said.

```
That's the only justification I can offer -- I
know it's pretty lame. The night of this party, I
went home with Roland, the big-noter's friend, a
solicitor, who incidentally was a complete dud in
bed. ¶
¶
A few weeks later I met Silas again, when I was in
hospital with my first back operation. The surgery
had not gone well. Apparently, the orthopaedic
surgeon had panicked because he couldn't get me to
stop bleeding, and he had been drinking before the
operation. He didn't know if he'd taken out all of
the ruptured disc -- or any, in fact -- he later
confessed to Silas, his squash partner. He said he
panicked, just sewed me back up. Very late that night
after a few more drinks, he'd rung Silas to offload. ¶
¶
"He was pathetic," Silas told me, "half-pissed and
blubbering down the phone." ¶
¶
"She started bleeding excessively, and I panicked,"
the surgeon told Silas, "I don't know if she'll make
it. I don't know what state I left her in." ¶
¶
"You'll just have to reopen," Silas said. "Clean
things up. I'll assist." Silas had only had 1/3 of a
bottle of port. ¶
¶
Silas called in to see me the next day. And the next
day. And the next day. He wasn't my doctor officially,
he said, just an interested party, a friend. Yeah,
that's why he inserted my catheter. That's why he
wrote me up for pethidine, heaps of it. ¶
¶
```

I could tell he was intrigued with me. I knew he saw me as his little "coloured" sojourn to the other side of the tracks. He was too touchy, feely, creepy; he seemed to think I'd be flattered. I was repelled initially, but after a few weeks in hospital, bed-ridden and unable to sit up, I became hungry for visitors. There were no mobile phones in the 1970s. I was lonely and craved attention, any attention, even his attention. Loneliness is dangerous like that.

He started to visit me two to three times every day. He'd bring me flowers, gifts, wrote me poetry, courted me. One letter referred to me as his "Boudicca". I felt smothered, but flattered, grateful. Wanted.

We were an item I suppose for a few months, quite a few really, almost a year actually, until my chance meeting with someone else changed just about everything. Silas said he understood. He said he wished me well. He said there were no hard feelings. He even became friends with my new companion. Best of friends. Enmeshed you could say.

Rememory 83

The ship's gone now, towed somewhere else, to another reef, waiting for the argument to be resolved over who will foot the enviro clean-up bill.

The clean-up. Yeah, right. I have visions of lots of environmentalists employed to clean each grain of sand on my beach, gently, thoroughly wiping each grain with soft, sterilised tea towels in hand. Others in the clean-up crew travel out to sea, breaking the news to each creature's family and community, offering sincere regret and financial compensation for the loss of innocent lives. Then there would be high-level executives calling on all the human residents along the coast, offering sincere regret for the trauma caused and loss of lifestyle, lost days of peace and pleasure.

All I've heard is that the ship's coal cargo will be unloaded to allow the ship to be towed back to China.

Today the nailtails are celebrities. They've gone national and are on the front page of *The Weekend Federation*.

THE WEEKEND FEDERATION

Nailtails nailed?

By Janine Parlow, environmental writer

Another pristine chunk of Australia is undergoing a tug-of-war between environmentalists and developers, with a proposed 2000-unit eco-development provisionally approved by Central Queensland's Lilian Bay Shire Council. The development must also pass environmental scrutiny, with an independent environmental impact study to start late this year.

Environmental group spokesperson, Gus Bishop, said there were a number of environmental concerns with the development, including unmonitored access to the pristine environment, waste and sewage disposal and other pollution issues, and significantly, disturbance to the endangered bridled nailtail wallaby.

"This place is like no other. It's prehistoric," Mr Bishop said. "It's untouched and the only true home of the bridled nailtail wallaby anywhere in the world. At best, there are only a few hundred of this endangered species left."

Continued on Page 6.

streuth.com.au

Nailtails or no nailtails, that is the question.

By visiting New York writer and blogger Calliope Tsutsis

Deep in Central Queensland, where the size of your exhaust pipes and hairstyles named after fish are status symbols, one cog in our planet's rich tapestry of biodiversity is about to disappear. The runty, easy to miss and critically endangered bridled nailtail wallaby has very few numbers left, fewer than 300, or simply none, depending on who you ask.

The wallaby species is endemic to the extremely remote subtropical Basalt Wall Region, and is at even graver risk due to a proposed tourism development. The existence of the species – or not – is a pivotal factor in environmental approvals for the gazillion dollar "eco-tourism" development application, submitted by a local landowner-led consortium.

The landowner claims the species is kaput, died out over the past 50 years due to drought and changing environmental conditions. But a recently "viral" anonymous blog, *Silent Scream*, and Basalt Environmental Group (BEG), led by Greens candidate Dr Freda Fitzwilliam, claim there are a few hundred left, but that they are being systematically slaughtered each breeding season by professional contract shooters. Both *Silent Scream* and BEG claim the landowner is behind the slaughter, and accuse him of systematically cleansing the region of nailtails, over the past ten years at least.

A spokesperson for the landowner said the property regularly culled "roos" using contract shooters.

"They are all legal culls," he said. "And of course they don't touch any endangered species. We engage professional roo shooters and the shooters receive training in species identification and are specifically instructed not to shoot endangered wallabies."

At the risk of generalising, roo shooters are not usually well-read, knowledgeable, enviro-conscious types. Even if they did know the difference between a nailtail and some other wallaby, they certainly wouldn't care.

For those of you not in the know, kangaroo shooters operate out of their utes in the middle of the night using spotlights, and shoot from distances averaging 200m. To roo shooters, a roo is a roo is a roo, whether it's a kangaroo, wallaby or wallaroo, endangered or whatever. There are small roos and big ones. Shoot first, ask no questions. The most precious roo is a dead one.

Good luck, nailtails. Make sure you wave the tips of your tails up into the spotties so the shooters won't aim at you. Maybe dip them in fluorescent paint. Make sure the little white markings on your face are easy to spot and don't look like targets.

But the nailtails are not fighting alone. *Silent Scream* has recently gone viral with more than one million followers worldwide already this year – a massive number in environmental blogging terms. The site is calling for community protective action in the form of an onsite sit-in, to photograph nailtails, hamper shooters, and witness any slaughter.

Let's hope it is successful. To give them support, or find out more, go to silentscream.com.au

THE WEEKEND FEDERATION

Nailtails protected

By Janine Parlow, environmental writer

If bridled nailtail wallabies exist, they are safe, according to recently appointed Federal Member for Basalt, Anthony White.

"Legislation clearly protects all endangered flora and fauna, and the bridled nailtail wallaby falls into that category," Mr White said yesterday. Mr White was responding to claims that the endangered wallabies were being systematically slaughtered.

"Land owners have a responsibility to manage their land, including culling feral animals, such as wild pigs, foxes and rabbits; and culling native animals in pest proportions, such as dingos and kangaroos. But current legislation is very clear that no endangered species may be culled."

Mr White said contractors had to obtain permits to operate as contract dingo and kangaroo shooters.

"These are professional shooters," he said. "They are highly skilled and are aware of the very hefty penalties for breaching this legislation."

"All legitimate claims of any breaches are handled by our environmental protection officers, who have direct powers to prosecute where appropriate."

"In the case of repeated, serious breaches, gaol terms can be the result of successful prosecution," Mr White said.

Mr White said an environmental impact study into the status of nailtail wallabies was to be carried out later this year to provide up-to-date information on current numbers of the species.

Rememory 84

There's a rainbow glowing now the ship has gone. A real rainbow, none of this metaphorical stuff.

I'm parked at Lilian Bay's grooviest coffee shop, The Coffee Club. I know I've talked about it before. It's very popular. It was the first one to be opened on the beachfront. So much for the no-one-would-come. All the professional whingers said: "it's too windy", "too far away from the main street", "too hot to sit outside", lots and lots of toos. Small town Queensland syndrome. I love lots of things about this place being a small town, just not the lack of appreciation of its environmental aesthetics.

It's late afternoon, after school, and the weather is about to change from warm and sunny and bright, to rain and wind. A sub-tropical storm is moving in from the sea. Everyone's mood is just that bit more hyper. Everyone is racing around doing whatever the change brings for them. My father is yakking "business" with some business types. I'm just sitting—no change—just sitting, looking, thinking. This morning at school, I saw that Anthony had posted some links on *Silent Scream*. The links are to copies of emails he's put on his own blog, as well as to some articles.

Email to: seven.com.au/sunrise/phase2-contactus (Sunrise Team)

Hi Kochie

Yesterday on Sunrise during your chat about Japanese whaling in Australian waters, you joked that we should get the pirates who are taking ships hostage, to stop the whaling ships.

I have been concerned with this very same issue for quite a while, and some time ago was moved to take just this type of action to tackle the problem of the Japanese illegal whaling. I wrote to Blackstone, the US company that is contracted to protect US citizens and dangerous operations in the most extreme situations in Iraq, and I asked them to quote on protecting whales being hunted in Australian waters.

I envisaged that Blackstone would organise a highly trained, specialist contingent to travel to the southern waters to bring a halt to the Japanese whale poachers.

This issue also got me thinking about land-living endangered species, and specifically the bridled nailtail wallabies, of which, at most, only a few hundred survive. So, I again wrote to Blackstone asking them to also quote on protecting the remaining nailtail population in Central Queensland.

A media release and copy of all relevant correspondence can be viewed, along with other information and my artwork, on my website www.anthonywhite.net. I am an Australian conceptual artist, selling my art internationally across almost a dozen countries, with exhibitions in New York, London, Paris, Zurich and Lilian Bay. I drive dump trucks at a local coal mine, ironically and totally coincidentally near Blackstone, Central Queensland. I was recently elected as Member for Basalt in Australia's Federal Parliament; however, I write this email as a private citizen.

Kind regards
Anthony White
Lilian Bay, Central Queensland
http://www.anthonywhite.net

Email to: Blackstone Mercenaries

Mr Erik Prince
Academi (Blackstone Mercenaries International)
Security Management Services
Arlington, Virginia, USA

Dear Mr Prince

I recently wrote to you inviting you to quote on protecting the remaining population of Australia's bridled nailtail wallabies. Unfortunately, I haven't heard back from you. In case you didn't receive my initial letter, I'm repeating my invitation for you to quote on your protection services.

This endangered species requiring protection is located in one fairly remote geographical area, approximately 700km north of Brisbane, and they are protected under Australian Federal Law. However, the wallabies are still being slaughtered, probably by local kangaroo shooters, enabled by landowners.

While I am an elected member of Australia's Federal Parliament, this protection contract is privately funded, and is separate from any official government agency request. The contract is ongoing, and I offer cash payment.

Yours sincerely
Anthony White

anthony@anthonywhite.net
http://www.anthonywhite.net

SPAN NEWSWIRE

Private Military to End Japanese Whaling?

AUSTRALIAN Federal Member and conceptual artist, Anthony White, is working on an extreme and controversial solution to end Japanese whaling activities in Australian waters and to protect endangered wallabies in Central Queensland.

Mr White has written — as a private citizen, he states — to Blackstone Mercenaries International for their assistance in sinking illegally operating Japanese whaling ships, and in providing armed protection for the remaining critically endangered bridled nailtail wallaby populations.

Blackstone Mercenaries International is an international security provider, currently contracted by the United States government to provide security services in Iraq.

Mr White said that to his knowledge, this would be the first time a private military company had been used to protect whales and wallabies.

"I simply can't sit back and see our protected wildlife, our supposed to be protected wildlife, continually slaughtered in our waters and outback," Mr White said.

"I want the situation sorted out once and for all, so that our vulnerable creatures are protected.

"I am sure many people will say that this is extreme behaviour, but these Japanese ships and kangaroo shooters are operating illegally, and are blatantly flouting our country's laws."

"While we could send the navy after the whaling ships, Blackstone are actually better equipped and trained to deal with the larger Japanese ships operating in the harsh conditions of the Antarctic waters," Mr White said.

"As far as the wallaby protection goes, surely silencing a few gun-toting cowboy shooters is child's play for Blackstone," he said. "And to save public money, I'm funding this myself."

Mr White is a Queensland-based artist producing controversial work, and is often likened to US artist Andy Warhol. He was recently elected as Member for Basalt in Australia's Federal Parliament. As a private citizen, Mr White wrote to Blackstone in December last year regarding the whales, and in February this year and again this month, requesting a quote for wallaby protection.

Mr White said he was currently awaiting a response from Blackstone.

Rememory 85

The sea is moving. There's a stealthiness about it. It's creeping back to where it was before the channel was dredged.

"How about the nailtails getting front page of *The Weekend Federation*, how good is that?" Freddy, while priding herself on her non-confomist non-wearing of shoes and many other alternative lifestyle habits, is always especially impressed by media attention.

It was Sunday afternoon volleyball. I'd been expecting my father to have a hissy-fit and not take me to the Fitzwilliam-Renton's anymore, because of the nailtail campaign, but let's face it, there's no way he's going to ditch his FOC Sunday arvo freedom.

"Have you heard any more about it?" Richard asked. "Gus must be pleased."

"He's stoked," Freddy said. "It's all come about because of that blog, *Silent Scream*. I thought Gus wrote it, but he said he didn't. Then I thought it was the sort of thing Ant would do, but he said he didn't, and, as Gus said, it's not like our Ant to deny credit for something. So, dunno, no idea." Freddy's shoulders momentarily looked dislocated.

Richard looked at Freddy and Claud in turn, one eye askew.

"It's not us," Freddy said, shaking her head. "Your serve, Dickie-boy."

There was a flurry of volleys, Claud leaping to my defence every time the ball came anywhere near me. I was giggling uncontrollably, and my back-of-hand mouth-swatting flipped into overdrive.

"It's worth having the game just to hear you laugh, Sophie," Freddy said. "Must be chai time, hey?"

Richard rolled up the fishing net and stowed it in the purpose-built shed, constructed by Freddy and Claudia's fourteen-year-old daughter, Marigold.

We processioned through the garden's winding paths to the house, where wafts of cloves and star anise told everyone to merge into their favourite chair. Marigold wheeled me in next to her, and took up her ukulele. Her fingers wandered through snippets of The Beatles, Bob Dylan and Joni Mitchell. They must have been practising protest songs for the sit-in.

"Is it all on for the shoot-out?" Richard asked.

"We prefer to refer to it as the sit-in," Claudia said. She has never really warmed to Richard.

"Folk Club and the country music crew have agreed to a combined gig by Styx Lake," Freddy said, picking up her guitar and floating sound waves over to Marigold. "Hope the country music people don't mistake which side they're supposed to be on, and bring guns."

Rememory 86

A woman slipped in the sludge left by the storm-surge as she collected beach pumice for her cockatiels. I'm sure it must have been cockatiels; she didn't look the budgie type. A younger woman, just a girl really, helped her up, and indicated to the safe-passage ground-cover bordering the track.

We used to have cockatiels. My mother let them out every day to flit around the plants in the atrium. We used to collect pumice and cuttlefish for them too. The shop stuff was just not the same, Mum said.

Shells bit the cockatiel woman's feet as she walked to the sea.

Ant posted that Blackstone hadn't replied yet.

"It's early days," he wrote, not very convincingly.

Chapter 20

www.silentscream.com.au

Silent Scream

Let's hope the nailtails will show their pretty striped faces next month.

Word has it that the developer has commissioned an "independent" environmental report on the state of things, bridled nailtail wallaby-wise. Let's hope the fact-finders are not nipping out bush simply to wave their magic wand of approval over Styx River and all within – blindness in the name of progress.

Word has it that the developers have made sure the environmental scientists being sent in to report are both female, white of course, and in their 20s. Let's hope these young women don't get sucked in by the cowboys, rumoured to be contracted to beguile the "little ladies".

Two fit young bucks complete with cowboy boots, hats and spanking big shiny belt buckles, have been engaged to sweet talk, soft soak and in short, leave the little ladies simpering.

Let's face it, few city girls can resist a red-blooded ridgy-didge cowboy, even if his name is Dud.

Let's hope for the sake of our nailtails, the women are up to such tomfoolery, and are not short of a good time back home.

Let's hope this is not a perfumed flick of a feather duster to bypass government environmental protection application requirements.

Let's hope they really do some real research, and realise you can't judge the nailtail life story by a single cursory glance of no nailtail.

Surely our women of today will be made of more steely substance, not simpering sycophancy.

My money is on the women, but I wouldn't ever underestimate these developers, so it's no sure bet.

Yours in fear and foreboding

Please help me make my screams heard.

SS

www.silentscream.com.au

Silent Scream

How the mighty have risen. Styx River developers travelled hand-in-hand along a dirty pathway to success. In the early days, a certain developer and some public service consultant cronies plotted and schemed their way into positioning themselves into prime manipulating positions.

There's the developer who had a minor (for him) custody issue and uncooperative ex-wife in his way of gaining cultural heritage control over his eco-tourism development.

Then where do we start with the State Government consultant psychiatrist, who incidentally, is the lone signature on the damning custody case affidavit in which he said the soon to be ex-wife had serious mental health issues, drug and alcohol abuse history, a history of sexual abuse and promiscuity. If she's still alive after all that, she is obviously too self-absorbed to be a good mother.

That he was a one-time live-in boyfriend of the developer's ex-wife, the crazy one in question, he of course denies. The relationship was platonic, he said. He felt sorry for her and wanted to give support, in the form of an expensive ring that looks suspiciously engagementish, and in the form of numerous embarrassing flowery love letters including at least one reference to "my Boudicca". Perhaps his main evidence of the wife being mentally deranged and emotionally unsound, was evidenced by her rejection of him (*au contraire* I would have thought).

It was also this same said psychiatrist who offered friendly professional under-the-counter advice on how to manipulate the judge in this same custody battle. He is continuing to offer constructive manipulative advice in greasing the passage of the Styx River development application, of which he is a major shareholder.

Some of the conversations went like this, word for word, fly on the wall, fly in their ointment:

Crony One (years and years ago):

> I'll write a report saying she's an unfit mother. She won't get custody. She won't have time to get anything to combat it. It's very difficult, near impossible in the short term, to prove you're sane.

Crony Two:

> They won't have a chance to hear any detailed evidence, but no judicial registrar will be able to ignore it. They'll offer the safe option: you, the family firm and the nanny. It'll be enough to make sure you get interim custody. It's hard to recover from that, especially as she won't have ongoing financial resources.

Crony Three:

> No one's going to give a penniless, drug crazed boong custody

over you, pillar of society with four generations of credibility behind you.

Crony Two:

You've got Rothstein as the judge. He's smitten with squattocracy.

Crony One:

Treat him like he's one of you, and he'll eat out of your hand.

Developer Himself (yesterday)

I've been thinking about these scientists and the inspection.

Scenario One: They go in with me. I can wander them around for hours and hours in the wilderness nowhere near nailtail country. We could even end up in Shakespeare's Pocket. That'd be okay. There's no nailtails there anymore.

Scenario Two: They insist on going in on their own. Without a Wuku or someone who's been there, it's virtually impossible for anyone to find their way in to the inner Wall where the caves and the other falls and the nailtails are. They'll wander around in the wilderness for hours and hours and they'd be very unlikely to even find Shakespeare's Pocket. They'll get lost in the outer Wall, then won't come back when they're supposed to. Then the SES will do the normal aerial search. They'll find nothing. You can't see anything from the air, no entrances, nothing. Then they're bound to ask me and/or bring in tracker dogs. They can't possibly search it all, and I can wind them off track. I'll lay a drag scent. We'll spend a lot of time looking, but just on the peripherals, dozens of us. With all that going on, there won't be a nailtail in sight. We may eventually find the scientists, but the publicity around the search will add cachet. If we don't, which is most likely, it'll be our own version of Picnic at Hanging Rock. International media coverage. They'll make a movie out of it. That's got to be the ultra-best outcome.

I reckon we've just got to make sure they go in without us. How do we do that?

Crony One:

Describe who we're talking about, the envio-scientists. Who are they?

Crony Two:

They're young, female and ambitious, but not with much experience.

Crony One:

Elementary, dear chap [he's such a pretentious wanker]. Might be best to cover your bases, though. If you can get them in and out nailtail-less, surely that's the best way. The cleanest way. Have a couple of good looking young bucks there in case they're susceptible to flattery. You can drive them all over the place for hours, on the homestead side of The Wall. Have the boys ride out with them for another few hours. Nowhere near the nailtails of course.

Or if that doesn't seem to be their fancy, if they're a couple of butch know-it-alls, tell them it's tricky country. Tell them they need your guidance. There's no way they'll bow to that. They'll be mentally spitting at you, automatic reaction. They will insist on going it alone. Either scenario, home and hosed. It's a win-win.

You get the picture. Don't let those women go into The Wall by themselves. The shadows warn it won't end well.

Please make my screams heard.

SS

Rememory 87

Oh dear, I fear I've swum into a rip.

"How the fuck?! Who's been blabbing? Have you read that fucking blog?"

I guessed it was Dodgy Dominic my father was talking to. Dom is always the first call for sounding off, and a safe bet for mutual outraging. Dom is especially outraged when his ethics are called into question. Even when he knows he's been doing something dodgy. How dare anyone question him, a man of his standing? Even when it's true.

I was sitting on the couch in front of another *90210* rerun. The laze-about slob "nanny" Sharon was away for the weekend. So was everyone else. What was I thinking? Of course they'd suspect me. There was no one other than them who was there to know all this stuff, only me. My hand–mouth swatting became more agitated, but I had no control over it. The skin on the back of my hand was wrinkled, getting sorer, even the scarring was saturated. And the drool drooled to my nightie, wetting my entire front, showing through to my breasts, showing through to my sodden nappy. Still my mouth swatting continued, out of control.

The office door was open so my father could at least appear to keep his eye on me while he was on the phone. I concentrated on blocking out *90210*. It's a skill.

"It's neither of us, obviously," my father said. "I can't see it being Silas. No, I can't see him shooting his mouth off that much."

There was silence from our end—apart from *90210*.

"It's that fucker Warren, it's got to be. He's a fuckin' soak, can't keep his fuckin' mouth shut," my father said. "He's always fuckin' big-noting himself, but I didn't think he'd lose it that much."

"Who else could it be? That slag Sharon was away, wasn't she? There was no one else there. Both times. Maybe we're bugged?"

Silence. There was silence and I could feel my father's eyes looking at me out through the door. More silence.

"She can't talk," my father said quietly.

"Nup, no way. ... Yep. ... Yep, she uses a computer at school with an aid. She's a fuckin' retard for Christ's sake." He was defensive, so I judged him almost kindly.

More silence.

"Get real, man! How could it be? Okay, I'll find out what's going on at school. Silas has just arrived. I'll see what he says."

I didn't hear the normal crash down onto the phone cradle, but felt him approach, felt the air slowly change. He stood next to me, watching my hand repeatedly smack my mouth, the dribble cushioning the blow a little. He was silent, watching, longer than just a moment. I was slumped on the couch, slipping to the side, towards the edge, but still I focused on *90210*. I was so good at focusing my eyes, regardless of what the rest of me was doing.

He sat me more upright and went to meet crony number one.

They talked a few beers' worth, out of my hearing, but I could hear the sss-pfsst of the stubbies opening.

I smelt crony number one coming towards me. It's a dapper smell, of someone who values himself highly. It's an ugly smell, and the back of my flappin' hand flapped the whiff into my mouth. It makes me feel sick. His face, so close to my face, as he squatted down beside me, and looked into my face. Stared at me. My whole face was absorbing his beer breath, three Corona stubbies' worth and he doesn't floss much. His eyes on my breasts lingering there, chilling them, making them even more obvious, my nightie more see-through. My hand was frantic, flappin' back and forth to my mouth flat out. Oodles more drool drooled. Blood dripped from the scar on my hand, colouring the drool orange, then darker to red. I could taste rust and I could hear my heart escaping from my chest. His eyes were still on my breasts, circling, circling, then slowly gliding down to my nappy, they paused. I was so, so scared. I felt so small.

"Get out of her face! Now! Leave her alone." My father had been over at the main bar, fetching another six-pack of Coronas, and his voice was angry.

"Don't be ridiculous, it's not her." He was uncomfortable with the creep's scrutiny of me, of him being so close. He was protective. I loved him for that. It doesn't seem like much, but it was huge at the time. For me.

"Leave her alone I said, you fuckin' idiot." My father picked me up and put me into my bed away from Silas's sight.

But they never cronyised in front of me again—well, at least not for a while.

Chapter 21

Rememory 88

Sunday, early morning

The day starts with a crisp welcome, then stormbirds warn that perhaps the day is not as pure as first light promised. The air whips wafts of bush jasmine with wattle undertones.

I was hungry, but everyone was busy, out of routine. So, I lay, waiting. The survey for the environmental report was happening today.

The ringers Jack and Dudley arrived at daylight. Sitting in the breezeway, they sipped tea and chomped on the bacon and eggs Sharon willingly supplied.

"Have you got Soph up yet?" my father called out to Sharon. "She'll need changing, and breakfast."

Sharon eventually dragged herself—and her eyes—away from the belt buckles to see to me. Nappy, clothes, cursory teeth-cleaning, hair-doing. Dried food cleaned off my wheelchair for the first time that month.

I was being trotted out (figuratively speaking of course) to play the sympathy card. I wondered if these women would bow to revulsion. Men are desperate to avoid confrontation with pathetics. Women, especially these types of women who have persevered to overcome bullying male entitlement, have learnt to face the face of adversity face on.

Sure enough, these passive aggressors didn't flinch. They related as equals to those so obviously less than equal, knowing only too well the one-size-fits-all mire of non-entitlement. They arrived earlier than expected and were great.

"Hello, Sophie, pleased to meet you." She said her name was Emily, and she smelt nice. Full eye contact. No gushing.

"This is Laura and we are here to learn about your country and your bridled nailtail wallabies. I don't know if you know about our role here. Pivotal Consortium, which your father heads, has applied for rezoning approval for the eco-tourism development. We can't approve it if it in any way impinges on the viability of nailtails. But your father advises us Styx River is no longer a habitat for them. So we're here to investigate and report on that situation."

All this was spoken directly to me. My hand to mouth swatting became more frantic, but they couldn't read the language. My father appeared and I could see him squirm with discomfort, then "hail fellow well met" butted in with cheesy sleazy bonhomie.

"Sophie's not interested in all this business. She can't talk at all. Sharon ..." He stopped mid-sentence, then called her name more sharply. "Sharon!"

Sharon was still mooning over the ringers. We heard another car pull up out the front. An olive-green Range Rover with electronic sunroof. The latest model. No dings. Andrew Martin stepped out and walked through the gate, up to the front of the homestead. Holy shit!

My father looked taken aback and was mightily pissed off, I could tell. Surely everyone could tell. But they didn't seem to. My father snapped out of it, and did his normal teeth-clenched smiley thing.

"Andrew, welcome," he teeth-clenched. "We didn't know you were coming."

"I thought I'd come along as an observer," Andrew said. "Sorry for no notice—I rang last night, but got the message bank. Left a message. Yes, thank you, I know Laura and Emily. We spoke last night. We've worked together before."

My father introduced Andrew around the ringers and Sharon, but missed me.

Andrew walked over to me. "Good morning, Sophie," Andrew said. "You've grown a great deal since I met you last. Do you remember me? I'm Andrew Martin." He shook my hand, which was just as slobbery as last time.

"Sharon, take Sophie to her room for a rest while we take Andrew and the ladies for a little ride in the countryside," my father said. He does condescending quite well. "There's a great view from Mangrove Mountain, it's on our way. We'll give you the full tour."

I shrieked and flailed. It was all I could do. I wanted to scream, "Have you read *Silent Scream*? Don't be sucked in by these sleazebags."

I wasn't there to see my father laugh that patronising amused-by-the-little-lady laugh. But I knew it was coming. I knew it so well, and I could still hear them after I was plopped back into my bed.

"No, it's no trouble, we're very happy to take you," my father gushed. "It's a big country out there. Five minutes in, and the bush all looks the same, hard to navigate, easy to get lost. And that's not even counting the actual Wall. We don't want you ladies disappearing. Jacko, just swap their gear into our ute."

I thought he'd overplayed his Psycho Silas double blind—maybe triple—manipulating thing, but alas, not.

Laura's voice was crisp, her message clear. "Thank you, but we would rather be independent. Andrew expressed interest in joining us on the study as an independent observer, so we were just waiting for him. Now we'll get going. We came prepared. We have a four-wheel-drive, aerial maps, satellite phones, an EPIRB and, if all else fails, flares. Very kind of you to be concerned, but no need. I come from Cunnamulla and Andrew's been here before, a long time ago, but still … We'll drive up beside Styx River as far as we can go, then walk in."

Andrew. Been here before! Andrew! Whaaat! Surely not my mother's Andrew? It couldn't be. But it fit. His green eyes, his face, his hair, his voice, his interest, his him. It all fit.

No one noticed my father's confusion over the comment regarding Andrew's previous visit. It was fleeting, and my father let it go, not having time to properly process any possible, and highly unlikely, implications. He simply let matters rest; after all he'd got what he wanted. He gave in so easily. But they didn't notice.

Rememory 89

Styx River estuary on our southern side has a tidal bore. The tide is super-fast, rising twenty metres in less than an hour. You have to be careful not to be caught as it all rushes in. You can hear it coming. First it seeps grey-brown water, swirling, creating white foamy caps. Then it flows cathartic volumes, a wave spreading across the breadth and length, rising invisibly until suddenly you realise it has consumed everything and is still going. The banks up that end of the estuary slope inwards, and crumble. There's no way to climb up to safety.

A few have surfed the wave in on a king tide, when it's at its highest, and rode all the way to the inner mangrove swamps. Crazy business. Most who watch the bore tide for the first time find it shocking: its power, its insistence, its instantaneity. For some people, in the early days, it was oblivion.

Intertwining the estuary, the basalt wall greets the ocean with a forest of mangroves. It's not people-friendly because of the roots and knotting branches, not to mention stonefish: deadly to step on. The mangroves look like the setting for a Peter Weir movie, and peering into this section in bright daylight, it is twilight. At night, it's black. No exception. Full moons never penetrate. People rarely penetrate. When the tide is out, the estuary looks like it might be a safe, guided way into The Wall, but it's not. It's a one-way trip to Lethe. Even the Wuku rarely risked slighting the estuary tides for anything but the briefest excursion.

Rememory 90

Sunday, mid-morning

I know which way they'll be going. They'll follow the track this side of the estuary to where the trees start to meet overhead. They'll wind around a few bends, and will take the track north, through the gate that skirts a wide arc in the river. They'll drive up the sandstone rise as far as the vehicle track allows, and walk through the first hacked-back clump of can't-go-back-bush. It will seem relatively easy to start with.

"What's all this garbage about people walking into The Wall and never walking out?" the women will think.

They'll get complacent, enjoying whiffs of chamomile and eucalyptus, questioning the memories that hover with the smells, but not quite catching them. The cement rise over the first basalt outcrop will lull them and lure them through the first shock of wall-to-wall basalt.

It will seem very different to Andrew. Wet season hasn't properly hit yet—if it comes—and the passageways won't be flooded.

When you're walking along through the maze, the walls don't seem that high. It's a bit of an optical illusion, they're way too high to see over. They're too high to clamber over too, especially as the walls slope in towards each other as they go higher. It must be from being worn away during the wet season when they're flooded. Their surface is rough, pumice rough—no, even rougher than that—a macro caricature of pumice, and they suck your skin in. You often bump into them, slightly off balance, and you bleed easily. The ground is grassy, a naturally mown pathway bordered by smooth stones and rocks, inviting you to take the next turn, and the next, then the next.

The shadows are telling me where they are. They've been walking for two to three hours now. Andrew must have remembered the way this far into the maze, because so far they haven't made any wrong moves. Very soon, just off to the side, they'll pause, drawn to, wondering at, the sinkhole. It's only about five metres across but looks endlessly deep and is surrounded by a circle of smooth rocks. When I was little, we called it the fairy circle. It was our wishing well.

The fairy circle dried out once and it was less than a metre deep. A perfect circle of perfect grass and perfect stones. Then next summer, after the wet season, it was a pond, endlessly deep again. My mother told anyone who noticed that it was a different circle, and it was easy to get confused, to turn a different way; but I know it was the same place. She didn't want to have to deal with whitefella logic. It was just easier that way.

If Andrew remembers well, they'll go on twisting and turning for a couple of hours more, turning suddenly into the first pocket. Even with Andrew, they may be too in awe to work out a proper landmark for their return exit point. They'll be seduced. Weird prehistoric-looking birds with extra-long flappy wings will rise slowly from one weird-looking tree, to hover, then settle on the next. The birds are in no hurry; they call out languidly, and other creatures reply. The trees interlink at odd angles and their leaves seem over-large. Nothing seems familiar. Water seeping from the ground knows where it's going, winding through lush grass, healthy grass, native grass, through trees, rocks, boulders, around basalt outcrops, disappearing back into the earth to reappear in another pocket, further on into the maze.

Maybe this far's okay, maybe. Maybe if they methodically walk the perimeter of this pocket, they'll find where they came in—if they left a marker. It's a bit dodgy, because there's a lot of options and they all sort of look the same, and some aim to tempt. The shadows are cat shadows, they play with their prey. But Andrew is very canny. Possibly, maybe, the first pocket's okay, but go further than that—they'll be cactus.

Your thoughts aren't your own if you go further. They belong to the Wuku. To the shadows. Your logic goes, your mind goes loopy. You can't judge what's what anymore. You can't find where you came in, so you panic, to find a way out, any way, but not the right way. The Wuku say they read the shadows. The shadows hold all of history, all the present, and all the future—everything. Things change, pathways close, others open, but the shadows put you right they say. The shadows tell you which way to go—this time. The direction changes each time. The shadows say that's why whitefellas get lost. They always want things to stay the same.

I hope Andrew doesn't remember the way further into The Wall. I hope the shadows leave him alone. Surely seeing the first pocket will be enough. No nailtails—time to turn back. Logic will tell them that the four-plus hours they've walked in will bring them to the homestead at twilight, if they turn now. But that's whitefella logic—doesn't count here.

If they cross to the other side, on the way they'll pause at the few posts left from the cattle yards, from old Shakespeare's times, when he built the yards. They're skinny rock-hard posts now, fossilised almost. A couple of uprights and a few rails are pretty much all that's left. If they keep walking, and somehow Andrew remembers the right path into the basalt on the other side, they'll walk on for another hour, two maybe, becoming oblivious to the folds of time passing, and then they'll rest. They'll be sitting under the great-grandmother tree, Burdekin plums lying around in various states of undress, and then they'll notice the stone and the grindstones. He will recognise this place.

Generations of Wuku have sat in that same spot, high above the path, but still cradled by four walls of basalt. There's an airiness about it, a freshness, a sense of safety. A lounge room, a wait-a-while room, where time is not an issue. The stone is large, flat and concave in the middle from years, possibly tens of thousands of years, of strong hands grinding fresh seeds and grain. I can see the hands: very dark, very skinny fingers with light stripes seemingly worn from millions of grab and push, grab and push. The grindstones, a darker, harder stone, were always left there. I wonder if they're still there, surely they will be after this lot go through.

Now they're this far, they'll venture further, wondering how much further they'll need to go. Turning right after the Burdekins would, could, wind them back here, but they'll feel drawn to turn left. By now, surely they'll be wondering what they're doing in there, disoriented, the shadows playing with their thoughts, distracting them.

Surely they'll remember the stories of those who ventured in but didn't venture out. They'll be reluctant to be the first to speak of their unease. It couldn't happen to me, they'll all think, but somewhere deep inside, they'll know it could. If they have turned right, they'll find the estuary, they'll be way up past the bridge, but relief will flood into their minds. Darkness will be not that far off falling. They'll come home then. I wish. But I know they'll turn left.

Rememory 91

I'm not describing things well, I know. But I'm trying to give you the feeling I get every time I fold back into my country, in my mind, following the shadows. I love shadow talk, my shadow love. But I fear them too, for them.

In The Wall, there are food plants everywhere, growing in every crevice, taking up room wherever they wish to. Some plants have dropped from the sky, and so we call them the new plants—tiny tomatoes, prolific, orangey-gold, covering short fat creeping fingers bursting with tight clumps of leaves displaying the sweetest, sweetest fruit. It's a place of abundance for us. That it has been a place of utter despair for some is hard for me to understand on one level, but on another I totally get not belonging: exclusion.

Fortunately, hopefully, this lot had a definite end point of no-go-past—the first pocket. Surely Andrew will have thought to mark the exit point. Surely this lot will experience the spookiness, the warning, and will turn around in time—surely, hopefully. They have to listen, they have to. Please. The Wall won't adapt to our contemporary over-inflated sense of self-importance.

There would be, of course, no nailtails to be seen—well of course they were there, somewhere deep inside—but not to be seen, just watching, peering through the shadows.

Chapter 22

Rememory 92

Sunday

Styx Lake looks shocked. It has transformed from a wilderness expanse of lilac waterlilies and black swans, to a backdrop for the early years of Maleny Folk Festival.

My father drove through the bush tracks skirting The Wall, down past the paperbarks and over to the lake. On the southwestern side, eco-friendly looking people gathered in several groups of ten, twenty, fifty to more than a hundred, playing sundry recognisable and unrecognisable musical instruments. Some sang songs of protest from the seventies, some with a country music twang, others contemporary indie-rock with bodies dancing, gyrating, weaving their souls together.

More cars turned up. They weren't dated, scruffy vehicles of the disadvantaged socio-economic world. The stringed-off paddock car park was filling with predominantly shiny late-model vehicles, mostly the four-wheel or all-wheel drives of the professional middle classes.

My father pulled up in our LandCruiser, and then parked me in my chair under a bloodwood, not that far from the closest group. He smiled his nodding parallel-white-lips smile, and the nearest group of musicians and spliff smokers basically ignored him as he approached, so he veered off to the right, swanking over to a group of young women. He has no shame, you know. They're all doing the protest sit-in because of him. If he is ever caught at a weak moment and finds that shame could be about to descend, most of it just beads off him; the rest he carries with pride.

Gus came over to me. "Hi, Soph, want me to wheel you over to our tree?" My legs and arms flapped, which he took for a yes.

He introduced me to Calliope, who said he remembered me from school and Anthony's exhibition. I was surprised. I'm always surprised when people recognise me. I don't feel as if I exist in people's minds in any permanent way. I feel ephemeral.

Gus knelt down in front of me and gently held both of my hands.

He looked into my eyes and smiled. "Hey, Soph," he said. It was a whisper of a "Hey, Soph".

"You like the ukulele?" he asked, standing back up, and struck a few notes of a song I didn't recognise. It was a nice, tinkling sound, very pretty. I was pleased for the attention, the interest. Gus is the perfect person, always has been.

"Good turn-up, Gus." Calliope was typically understated. "*Silent Scream* seems like it's sent a pretty loud message."

Gus looked quickly at the journalist. "It's not me, you know. I haven't written it. Is it you? Freddy and Ant swear neither of them is behind it."

Calliope laughed, shaking his head. "Nope, not me," he said.

Freddy joined us. "Hi, Sophie. Marigold, Nima and Petra are over with Claud. She sent me over to tell you all the chai is ready."

We wandered, Gus pushing my chair, over to the little gas stove with a steaming ginormous enamel kettle. A group of people softly played seventies songs and they were all wearing identical t-shirts with confronting artwork of a bridled nailtail wallaby in perfect skeletal form, but with a pretty bridled face and black leathery tail-tip. The artwork, crowned by the words "Silent Scream", was both beautiful and harrowing at the same time.

"Cool shirts, guys," Calliope said. "Where can I get one?"

"We got them made especially," Claud said. "Sapiophilestudio dot com created them for us."

Sapiophile Studio is the artist I wrote about in my story "My Date with [heart-throb of choice]", who had "The Cyclist" exhibition in Melbourne. She's actually real, a real artist—you can check on her website if you don't believe me. She's amazing. As well as painting obsessively anatomically correct people and creatures' innards, she also paints things from a cellular level. Some of them are massive canvases with amazing shapes and colours. My favourite is a two by three metre canvas called "The chemical compound of chai". It is just sooooo beautiful—hundreds and hundreds of different stunningly beautiful cell structures of all the different spices—like a canvas of olfactory sensations. She uses the Sapiophile Studio name because she's actually a doctor now, so she likes to remain anonymous. I like her especially, because she has a sister who has Rett Syndrome too. Had a sister.

"Ant bought the original nailtail drawing. It's massive, bigger than real life—it's one by two metres," Claudia said. "He said it was, 'an important addition to his environmental collection'." Claudia did the quotation two-finger gestures.

"He reckons it's all tax deductible. Not sure how the chai one is tax deductible. He bought that one too."

Claud passed me over a shirt. "Here you go, Soph, this is yours. I think it'll fit okay. Want to try it on?"

My legs said yes, but Freddy said no.

"Claud, no. Her father won't like it. It's not fair."

"I'm sorry to say this, Soph," Claud said, "but your father gives me the shits. I'll hang onto it for you, but in the meantime, you can out-of-body-experience wear it, and I'll whip it away when the old bastard stomps over."

I giggled. Freddy shook her head, "Claud, that is just not okay."

"Crap, Soph agrees with me, don't you, Soph?" My legs and arms flailed "yes", and I giggled again.

"It's just not fair. Don't." Freddy sounded quite upset, seriously stern, then continued her conversation with Calliope.

"You can tell us, mate, we know it's your site, *Silent Scream*."

"No, it's not me," Calliope half laughed, holding his hands, fingertips up in front of him, palms out, wrist-twisting a few times. "Can't detect any New York accent in the blogs. Definitely an Aussie twang, I'd say. But we don't really need to know, as long as they keep coming. Bit like Banksy of cyberspace. All adds to its power. No nailtails yet?"

"They won't come out while we're here," Gus said, with his left hand holding a warm cup of chai to my lips for me to sip, while, with his other hand, he drank his own. "Hopefully the shooters will get sick of us hanging around too. They're camped just over towards the other side of the lake, and I think they were getting pretty pissed off with us all, until Petra and Nima wandered over with some peanut butter munchies as a peace offering. The shooters weren't sure how to take them—both Petra and Nima, and the cookies. I was worried they were hash cookies, but apparently not. Petra and Nima said the shooters stank of dead meat and cow shit. Bit of a culture clash, hey. The shooters ate the munchies, but."

"The enviro report lot have gone in," Freddy said.

"They must have gone in on their own, hey, Soph?" Gus said. "That's why your dad's here, hey?"

"Ant said he spoke to the officers," Freddy continued. "Two women, smart and very professional."

"Yeah right," Gus said, "that's why they're working for that company. It's going to be a white-wash. They should know the nailtails are far too timid to allow themselves to be seen in the outer wall. They'll all be hanging around in the caves waiting for the invasion to leave—us and them."

"Ant said they admitted that could well be the case," Freddy said. "The researchers are part of the uni—it's academically affiliated." Freddy had her hopeful voice on.

"They said they had to compile an independent report. They admitted that not seeing any wouldn't mean there were conclusively no nailtails. I got the impression from Anthony that they were under a lot of pressure to produce something meaningful that will stand up to scrutiny from all parties—that means us too. I think they're a bit defensive of being ridiculed, of being seen as ineffectual," Freddy said.

"Ant had to interfere of course. He tried to organise for his enviro consultant Andrew Martin to go in too," Freddy said.

"Ant means well," Gus said, "but he's kind of getting off on being a pollie. Who knows which way he'll jump next?"

Freddy was stubbornly optimistic. "It could be great for us—I mean Andrew is incorruptible I'm told," she said.

"What's his background?" Calliope asked.

"I don't know anything about him ... I don't think ... not specifically ... I don't think ... only that he's got a reputation for not getting pushed around ..." Freddy was fairly stoned now, so it was an effort, this remembering thing, and her sentences weren't finishing with full stops.

"Andrew Martin?" Gus's brain went click click click. "He's an enviro legal consultant for the Feds. Well respected all round. Feared by some. Originally from England. Travelled up this way years ago, he said, when he was hitching around after uni. Eventually married an Aussie from Sydney, met her in London, came back over here, retrained as a lawyer, and specialised in environmental law. I've run into him from time to time. Nice bloke."

"Ant said he couldn't track him down ... in time ... but he left messages ... so wasn't sure ... if he'd be there ..." Freddy's voice was drifting even further, in case you didn't notice.

"I'm hoping he just turns up here ... or there ... you haven't ... heard anything ... hey Gus?"

Gus turned away from Freddy and Calliope, holding his phone up high. "There's no mobile coverage here, so we're a bit shut off from everything."

"I've got satellite coverage," Calliope said. "Hang on; I'm just about to check. But there won't be any *Silent Scream* messages over the weekend."

Gus looked at him. "What's the weekend got to do with it? You do know who's behind it, don't you?"

Calliope looked slightly uncomfortable, but laughed it off. "I just noticed the posts are all uploaded on week days. I've got a phone message, hang on, I need to call in."

Chapter 23

Rememory 93

Sunday, midday

The shadows, my shadows, they taunt and they tease, they know what you know, they toy and torment, and sometimes they tell me all. Andrew channelled the shadows, and enough of Rose stayed with him for the shadows to be intrigued, to play with him for a while.

"Did you go further in than this, Andrew?" Laura asked.

"It was a long time ago," Andrew said, "And I was with a friend, a Wuku, but yes we went over the next few walls into the next few pockets. But it was wet season—and I had absolutely no idea where I was, or how to get out. Really the Burdekin plums are as far as we should go; we definitely need to turn back now. It gets very confusing."

They were sitting on the ridge with the grindstones, using the base stone as a table for their water bottles and lunch containers.

"But the second pocket is probably where they'll be, hey?" Emily said, standing up, ready to move off. "Let's just go a little further. I'll keep note of the turns. Which way do we go?"

"Left?" Laura suggested. "It's the widest."

Andrew looked down the corridor, walking slowly, reluctant to enter. "I really have no idea. We were swimming across and I wasn't thinking in terms of right and left. But really, this is as far as I want to go."

"If you want, you can wait back there," Emily said, "and we'll just go a little further, then pick you up on our way back."

"If we sit up there quietly, the wallabies may come through down there for the shade. They might not notice us at first, and we'll be able to get some pictures." Andrew was running out of arguments. He wasn't even convincing himself.

"They know we're here already," Laura said, twisting her head to speak over her shoulder and to check the other two were still following, as she kept walking. "Have done since we first started.

Remember the birds we disturbed? Even if you don't believe the shadows stories, logic has to tell you all the other creatures would notice squawking birds. With us and Styx Lake campers, I'd say there's no chance of any actual sightings this year."

"Anyway, it doesn't matter if we don't see them," Emily said. "We don't actually need to see them."

"What do you mean? Don't we need some photographic evidence or something for the report?" Andrew was big on tangible proof.

"Yes, but probably the scats will be enough," Emily said.

"The scats?" He looked at her as if she was a little loopy.

"Yes, the poo," she said. "We know this is the nailtail ecological niche, so we just have to find their scats. We can identify them by their scats, their poo. That's evidence enough without an actual specimen sighting, sufficient evidence for us, I mean, to identify their current occupation. We can get DNA from the scats too, for verification. The National Museum has given us permission to take DNA from their stuffed nailtail, so that's our backup plan."

"That's what they don't understand," Laura said. "All this shooting business—apart from being abhorrent, it's just ridiculous and meaningless scientifically."

She trudged forward, but made sure the others were within listening distance. She was on a roll. "If there's fresh scats in this ecological niche, we can exclude any other species because nailtails have a very narrow diet. The scats are like a dietary list of everything they eat. Nailtails are very specific in their food, that's why they're disappearing. They are so selective, and in such a fine ecological balance, that any encroachment on their habitat endangers their existence."

Laura paused, just long enough for the other two to keep pace. Andrew was entranced; Emily, proud of their project, was happy to listen to Laura indefinitely.

"Fresh scats will give us clear evidence of a current population of bridled nailtail wallaby. Proof enough for us. Proof enough legally. There's a heap of work to do with the samples when we get back, and we need to collate supporting evidence. But if these things all align—and I think they will—the chance of it not being fresh nailtail poo is virtually zero. Emily did her PhD and post-doc on it—identifying rare and endangered species of wallabies from scats and ecological niche."

"And these here are scats," Emily said, right on cue, bending down. "The right size too."

Emily photographed the scats, and took a video with a 360-degree-pan. Laura took out a brown paper bag, wrote on it the time, date, and location, and handed it to Emily who bagged the poo.

Laura tried to get a GPS reading, but the screen said "no signal". "Whaaat, that's weird," she said, "There's no signal. Maybe the batteries are just low." She replaced them with new ones from her backpack, but there was still no signal. "The GPS has packed it in," she said.

"It's the magnetic field," Andrew said quietly. "Somehow it interferes with the satellite signal. That's why we really need to go back."

"Yes, I know, but ideally, I'd like to get a few more samples in different locations," Emily said, walking ahead, focusing on the ground. "If we can find the sort of place they like to sleep—if we can't find evidence of them camping in the grassy areas just inside the next pocket, maybe we can find some in the caves on the other side. Isn't there supposed to be a big waterhole, Blood Falls, and caves, then another pocket? Let's keep going just a little further."

"Really, that's not wise," Andrew said, "Let's take what we have, turn around now." But he knew there was no chance they would. The Wall's magnetism had them.

Around the next turn was another, then another, and another—all choices that they didn't realise they had taken because the L-junctions weren't always L-junctions. When you got right to the end, sometimes they were T-junctions, or X-junctions. Some were dead ends.

"It's further than you think," Laura said. "Maybe we should turn around. At least we have some samples; enough to work on." She was starting to sound nervous.

They made three, four turns back—the only logical turns to take, they were sure. But the walls seemed to have moved.

Their pace picked up, a few more turns. The Burdekin plum trees had disappeared.

"I think we're lost." Emily sounded shocked.

"Yes, we've been lost for a while," Andrew said.

"How embarrassing." Laura was the one from Cunnamulla.

Losing oneself happens quietly. Panic brought in the shadows, and a coolness descended.

"Does the satellite phone work?" Laura asked.

"Yes, I think so," Emily said.

"It won't," Andrew said.

"Do you want to give them a ring, Em, and tell them we'll keep walking until dark, then if we don't get anywhere we recognise, we'll set off the EPIRB? We probably should keep the flares for when it gets really dark, or if we hear any rescuers." Her voice was a little too crisp, her throat constricted.

Sadly, when Emily looked, there were no signal bars. The Wall doesn't allow mobile phones. Unfortunately—or maybe fortunately, to allow fear a few hours' grace—they didn't know that EPIRBs weren't allowed either. The signal they had one chance of sending would merely sing through the shadows. And the flares, so dazzling from the ground, would fizzle in the shadow air, dampening any distant sighting in the night sky.

Chapter 24

Rememory 94

Sunday, late afternoon

There's no change at the campsite. Music's playing, food's being eaten, some people are bonding, others not so much. It is going to be an endless night.

Calliope had been on his satellite phone.

"Is Anthony coming out here?" Gus asked.

"No, he's at Styx River," Calliope said. "I don't think he wants to leave the power centre before he has to. He thinks they may have a problem with the research team. They haven't come out."

The night dropped in, and my father and I left them to it. As we drove back to the homestead, Styx Lake seemed to rise closer, bringing with it an intimacy with the bush and The Wall behind. Birds broke the normal rules, and well into the darktime, screeched their protest of invasion. My father whistled a jaunty tune between his teeth.

Chapter 25

Rememory 95

Sunday late afternoon

I can hear the shadows screaming.
If the researchers have fallen to temptation, I know the shadows will lure them in. They'll keep walking, pretending to be confident, but knowing they are up shit creek.
Andrew will feel fear first, but he'll mask it well.

There was somehow something fitting, inevitable, about this, Andrew thought, as if the shadows had lured him back. There was peace in acceptance. Where had the confident, edgy and sought-after environmental lawyer gone? He didn't really exist anymore. Not properly. Not all of him. At least it would make it easier for the women, if he was calm.

The pathway that chose them took them very close, temptingly close, to the Burdekin plums. Andrew thought he could smell them, but put it down to his mind playing tricks. The maze drops at an angle where the trees are no longer visible—quite close, but not visible unless you climb the wall. At this stage of getting lost, no one does, they just walk faster.

The researchers wound deeper into the labyrinth, far away from the open spaces of the pockets where rescue helicopters would have been able to land. The shadows had them heading towards an inner set of falls, Blood Falls. As the crow flies, it's not really that far from the locals' spot of Red Falls, only a few kilometres northwest. These inner falls are the real red falls, the Wuku's Blood Falls, because of so many lives claimed, my mother said. The water runs red, an optical illusion of light and the blood-coloured stone beneath.

For Andrew and the women, the falls spoke of safety. Unfortunately, it wasn't Wuku they were listening to.

"At least we won't die of thirst," Laura said.

They don't realise the water is salty.

Rememory 96

Sunday late afternoon

The women have guts; you have to give it to them. There were no tears. No complaining. No learned helplessness. Just quiet determination and learned self-reliance.

Blood Falls has the same Henry Moore reclining figure rock face and the same cascading water as Red Falls, but Blood Falls are almost twice as high, and the black ink lagoon below lies deep within a basalt crater. From where Andrew, Laura and Emily are standing, looking down into the crater, the lagoon's surface lies tens of metres below their feet, and the water itself is more than a hundred metres deep, flooding as it sinks into endless screaming cavern mouths.

Behind Blood Falls, there's a track around the rock face that inclines steeply up, walkable-steeply though. It looks to climb around and up onto the ridge above, to a flat area that promises to open up. The track is actually two different tracks, their dead ends hidden by pinky red-tipped can't-go-back bushes and pandanus and cabbage tree palms. You can reach the caves from the track this side, but you can't access the higher track. The can't-go-back bushes face in the opposite direction after the caves, and even if you could push through, the tracks miss by vertical metres. From below, standing on the crater rim, it all looks planted, orderly. You'd swear it couldn't have happened by chance. Wuku would say it didn't. Wuku say their dream shadows knitted the can't-go-back bush for protection.

Can't-go-back bush is endemic to the basalt wall region and looks harmless enough. It looks positively anodyne in comparison to its close cousin, the obviously prickly wait-a-while vine. You can brush past the can't-go-back bush and feel angora-tickled or gently stroked by its tips. As you walk through, you breathe deeply its jasmine-like scent. But try to turn around or back out, then you're stung, wasp-like and physically grabbed by double hooked barbs that turn bright red and start smelling like cats' piss. If you fight against the barbs, the branches don't snap off, they wrap around and cling to you like the worst Velcro nightmare. But continue on your way through within a shortish time, then it's instant release and the stinging stops, soothed by jasmine and chamomile wafts. Those who named the can't-go-back weren't joking. You physically cannot go back. If you stay fighting too long, poison from the stings burns your skin. It's more painful than the stings of Irukandji jellyfish, and most people start producing an allergic reaction, leading to anaphylaxis. If you survive that, the pain makes you wish you hadn't.

The researchers were keen to climb to the top of Blood Falls to set off the flares on dark, so didn't falter pushing through the bushes up to the caves. Andrew followed the women, and as he felt the shadows cool his body, his mind paused his steps just long enough to remember the stories and smell a faint whiff of cats' piss. He moved on and smelt jasmine with a hint of chamomile. He wished for all his life that he could hear the shadows talk.

Chapter 26

Rememory 97

Monday, early morning

Styx Lake rises with the sun. Mist congregates just above the water-lilies, then stretches skyward, tightening, tightening, until suddenly releasing its hold to uncover translucence and a blue sky. The fish slink down, well into the lake, but the swans stay to watch the pantomime.

My father had me up early, and when Gordon Parker, the local State Emergency Services big-wig arrived, we drove the outer perimeters of the north-eastern edge of The Wall, as far as the track allowed. We, of course, found nothing. The ringers, Jack and Dud, in the Toyota ute, continued to search the north-western edges. There were five or six other SES and search vehicles roaming all over the place. It was a heaven-made, bush-bashin' four-wheel-drive jamboree. They were having the time of their lives. We dropped Gordon back at his vehicle so he could continue the search by SES helicopter. Fat chance.

As we drove around Styx Lake to the campsite, steaming honeyed chai tea, accompanied by strains of a lone mandolin, wafted through our LandCruiser window. Freddy had all she needed: family, friends, music, hot chai, and a cause. She glanced at our car but kept singing.

My father parked and walked over to a windmill on the lake. It pumped to a tank that fed cattle troughs in the next paddock.

I sat in my seat and swatted my mouth with the back of my hand. Calliope drove up just ahead of our LandCruiser and walked towards the music.

"Hey, Calliope," Claud said, "heard from Ant this morning? Did they make it back okay?"

"He sounds very worried," Calliope said. "They were supposed to let off the flares and EPIRB last night, but nothing's been seen or heard of them. He's called in the SES to search. Do you think we should go in this end, to meet up?"

Gus walked over from his tent.

"No way! All that will do is add more problems," Gus said. "I can't believe they let them go in alone."

Freddy's fingers hadn't stopped strumming, but her song choice switched to The Beatles' "Yesterday". Freddy sometimes has trouble empathising.

Gus was thoughtful, quietly sipping his chai.

"What are you thinking, Gus?" Calliope asked.

Gus spoke slowly, almost reluctantly. "The SES will search for one, maybe two days, maybe longer, maybe weeks. It'll go global, especially with Andrew originally from the UK. Unbelievable publicity for the developers. They might even apply to bring bulldozers in, but it won't happen. It's never happened before. I think we've played right into their hands. And not a nailtail in sight the whole time. The *Scream* predicted it exactly."

Everyone was silent, even Freddy. Even the constant background of birdcalls seemed to pause.

"We've got to find them," Calliope said. "Who knows this place?"

Rememory 98

Monday morning

Jasminum polyanthum, trachelospermum and cestrum nocturnum are going crazy shooting perfume everywhere, all the time. The sea is boiling.

All the creepy cronies had gathered back at the homestead that morning.

"I'm not a monster," my father said. "I did not want this to happen."

"Yes you did," Psycho Silas said, munching on crispy bacon. He wasn't particularly fazed. Dodgy Dominic wasn't commenting.

"I did not," my father said. "I really thought they'd get out."

"You said it would add cachet," Silas said. He crunched and spoke simultaneously with his mouth open. Hard thing to master. Must have had plenty of practice.

"We've got to do something," Dominic said. "This isn't good for us. It taints us. We'll be held up forever." When the going gets tough, Dominic has no spine.

"Maybe they'll let us bring bulldozers in to look for them, rip the place apart," Rabbit Warren said hopefully.

"That won't happen," Dominic said. "It's never happened. They'll just keep looking on the ground, and with choppers."

"Anyway, no way would bulldozers be a match for the basalt walls," Warren said. There was a reverence in his tone.

"You could take the SES in, right in," Silas said to my father.

"I can't," my father said.

"Won't," Silas said.

"No, can't," my father said, "not without Rose. Ten to one, the researchers'll end up in the inner caves. I've never been in. No way would I go in there without her. The caves are like a magnet, and if you go in, there's no way out. Unless a Wuku wants you to."

"We've gotta do something. Doesn't look good doing nothing. How about we ask *Silent Scream*," Dominic said. "At least it'll look like we're trying to do something."

"It's some fuckin' greenie wanker writing it. What will they know?" my father said. "But if it'll make you happy, I'll ask them. And I'll keep driving around. Then it'll look like I've done all I can."

Rememory 99

The world is still: the sea, the land, my heart.

I didn't get a chance to get back to *Silent Scream* until later that day. My father's blog comment was not the first by any means, but perhaps held the most significance for me. There was a frantic note in its wording. Even a hint at helplessness. Pleading for assistance.

There was simplicity, a calmness, in my reply.

Rememory 100

Monday early afternoon

I know they are in the caves. The shadows sheepishly told me.

www.silentscream.com.au

Silent Scream

On behalf of the present, past and future population of bridled nailtail wallabies, I will help you.

The researchers are in the caves behind Blood Falls. Rescue instructions follow.

Our screams have been heard.

SS

Silent Scream

The shadows have told me the way in for tomorrow. It needs to be someone fit and quite slim. Someone brave. And it has to be done tomorrow afternoon, starting after 2pm, but you must be back before 3pm. You cannot go today, or tomorrow morning. These instructions will not work any other time, any other day except tomorrow between 2-3pm. Trust me on this. It's a tide thing: no other time.

There is a hole in The Wall above the homestead at the top of the estuary. Massive desert bloodwoods grow in a circle. A few are missing, but young ones grow in their place. There's heaps of trees all over the place, but if you look up, you can see the bloodwood circle.

In the exact middle of the circle is the hole, the way in. You need to be careful. It's not marked and there's long grass all around. You'll need some sort of knotted rope or ladder, 584 metres long including stretch. Any less, and you may not survive the drop without serious injury; any more and there's not enough ker-splash.

Take a torch with you and secure it well to your head or body, preferably both. You don't really need it, but it will make it all a little less scary – for all of you.

At the end of the rope or ladder, you'll drop into a pool. It's very deep, so don't worry about hitting the bottom, but it'll be a longish drop, 10 metres. Don't swing if you can help it, just drop straight down. You can't take tanks, you'll be too heavy in the drop, and they won't fit later on. Don't worry, you won't be coming back this way.

You need to air-drop a full 10 metres so you can sink deep enough through the water to the passageway. It's a fair bit under the surface – about 8-10 metres under. After you drop, as soon as you stop descending into the pool, start to swim underwater north-west. You must drop down between 2pm and 2.30pm tomorrow. The current on this tide, tomorrow, will take you to the right cave tunnel. Work out the direction to swim before you drop. A compass won't work down there. You can tell where north is by the slight breeze. At that time, tomorrow, it will come from due-north.

Swim into the passage the current pushes you towards, and let it pull you through, head first, arms ahead. It's narrow, I know, but it's ok.

Keep your hands on the top of the tunnel to feel for an opening above your head. Don't take the first. It'll try to suck you up, but push yourself past it, and wait for the second one. Whatever you do, do not take that first opening – it narrows and narrows. It's way too narrow to turn around and the current makes it hard, probably impossible, to back, back down.

Let yourself pop up the second passage. The pressure will pop you up through 15 metres of water, into a cave with fresh air, but it's very dark. The time it should take you from drop to cave is not that long, so your breath should last okay. Just stay calm.

In the cave, hold onto the side of the rock to get your breath. Don't let the current take you further until you're ready.

The next part is a bit tricky ...

Rememory 101

Monday afternoon

"It's far too risky. Could be some sort of crazy crackpot. It's loopy, far too dangerous." Freddy was normally all for crackpot loopy ideas, but I guess this crossed even her line.

About half the people had left the campsite before sundown on Sunday, but the stalwarts were staying for the week.

My father had picked me up from the school bus, and we went home via Styx Lake. He left Sharon and me under a tree, in the Cruiser with the air-con running. So, he did the responsible thing.

There was panic in everyone's voice, everyone's except Gus's. Gus was set on going. Thank God it was going to be him and not Ant. Ant would get stuck.

Then Mrs Gus drove up. She had a baby-shit yellow nylon scarf over her hair, with two plastic curlers in her fringe, poking out from the scarf. She must have been very stressed.

"Gus, I need to talk to you. You need to come home now."

"Want a cup of chai, Mum?" Gus asked. He never got angry with his mother, regardless of how ridiculous she was.

"I've heard what's going on. You are not going," Mrs Gus said, her bobble-headed curlers bobbling.

"Go home, Mum." He said it kindly. "I'll have Calliope ring you as soon as I'm out. I'm going, so please go home."

Mrs Gus turned on my father, and spat words at him.

"It's your fault. You have no right dumping HER on the school, expecting Gus to fetch and carry after HER. It's not right. There's special schools for those sorts of children. They've no place taking up resources normal children are entitled to. It's got to stop now. He's not going."

"Eileen, he's eighteen. He's a man," my father said almost kindly. "He knows his own mind. Gus always has."

"You go, then," Mrs Gus spat. "It's your place, you go. No, I didn't think so. You're a coward." Well, she had a point.

"Eileen, I can't. I'm too fat," my father said, quite rightly too. Thank goodness. He would definitely get stuck, and would take a long time to rot out.

The direct appeal didn't work, so Mrs Gus switched to the tears option.

"I'm being mean," she wailed. "I don't want to be like this. Gus, you can't do it. Pleeeeeeassssse."

Mrs Gus was in for the long wail, and really, you couldn't blame her. The instructions did sound very dodgy. She was desperate, beside herself with worry—with good reason. She had a good understanding of The Wall honeycomb, above and below ground.

Just up north a bit, and a fair bit inland, there's another set of lava tubes from the same volcanic flow as The Great Basalt Wall, but a smaller outcrop on a touristy cattle station kind of place.

There, you can safely wander the caves, and stay the night in pretty flash railway carriages. The opening of these caves feeds clearly into other tunnels that all link up, and most of them are dry. It's way, way more compact, and a drier land and cave-scape, and there's no surface spring water. They have cave dives in what water there is, and they've enlarged any small holes—with dynamite—to cater for larger people. It's quite a way inland—no tidal shift—and there's set guided tours, with pathways and handrails and uplights, so no one can get lost.

That isn't Wuku land. It's another mob, who are a lot more adaptive, and a lot of them have jobs on the station, giving extra cultural flavour to the experience. They've actually done a good job if you don't mind touristy places. But they're not Wuku, and there're no nailtails there, and our maze is ginormously more extensive, tidal, overgrown, and difficult to access.

Everyone around here has been to those touristy lava tubes, even me. So, everyone has a micro frame of reference of what's down there under and around us. She was right to be scared. I was scared too.

Chapter 27

Rememory 102

Tuesday morning

Just like every other day, the tide comes in, and the tide goes out. The sea sparkles and the sky shines.

My father forgot to make sure Sharon woke in time to take me to school.

Too late, he stomped over to the staff quarters, pushing my chair and me ahead of him. He thumped on the door of the "honeymoon suite", the double room with ensuite where Sharon lived. Of course he didn't wait for an answer, and banged the door open, wafting out sour air.

Over the years, there's been a fair bit of action and shenanigans in the quarters and guest rooms of Styx River Station, but even my father's face turned inside out at the sight of Sharon's white cauliflower buttocks, overcooked, astride one of the ringers. I wasn't sure, at first, which one.

My father tried to block my view, bless him, but it didn't work. I peered around his legs to see two feet in mismatched woollen socks stuck out the bottom of the wrought-iron bed, and a silver belt buckle inscribed with the word "Dud" hanging on the end post, dangling off a pair of stiff blue jeans. A bit of a clue as to who it was, but by no means definitive.

I was screaming and flailing, back-of-hand slapping, in almost a blur. I think my "distress" egged my father on. He didn't realise I was choking with laughter.

"Get up. Now. Both of you. You, Dudley, are driving Sharon and Sophie to school. You can feed her on the way, now get going. Make sure you wash your hands well, both of you. With soap."

That was me sorted, thank Christ—for both of us. I was desperate to get to the computer to see what was happening. I always quite liked Dud. He was totally kind and respectful to me. He noticed I existed, which was more than most people did.

As Dud (smelling of soap) scooped me up to put me in the car, and

Sharon (hopefully also smelling of soap) made peanut butter sandwiches, I could hear my father yabbering on the phone to Dominic.

"Get over here. Now," was the last I heard.

Rememory 103

Tuesday, midday

Anthony said it was his day at school, even though it was lunchtime and he normally comes first thing in the mornings, and it was Tuesday and he always comes on Mondays. And it was definitely not his week. He found me in the computer room.

"Hey, Ray; hey, Soph. What's going down?"

God, he must have been stressed. He is normally a crazy fountain of energy and bubbles.

"Ray, if you like, I'll do some one-on-one with Soph, while you have a break. I bet you haven't had lunch. I brought heaps of KFC—it's in the staffroom. Go for your life, I've had mine."

"You don't want any, do you, Soph? She hates it. That's right, hey Soph?"

He was trying to be normal and Ray bought it. Maybe she was just smellderised by the cloud of KFC fumes.

"Okay, Soph," he spoke quietly. No one was around to overhear, so he didn't waste time typing his words.

"What do you think? It's your site, isn't it? Gus wants to go. Is it safe? We can't let him come to any harm. There's no way you would, is there? Maybe I should go instead."

I opened a Word document, but he didn't give me a chance to focus my eyes. He hammered more questions at me. My back-of-hand to mouth flapping fired up. My hands were mouth-swatting, stuttering, they were going so fast. I couldn't make my eyes work. I couldn't see through the tears.

"Do you know for sure?" Ant said without giving me a chance to answer. "I mean, it's not just indigy-didg, mumbo-jumbo, is it? I mean, how do you know it'll work?"

My hand-swatting was erratic. Blood was trickling blood-orange through the drool. My mind was swelling in my head. It was blistering fear. "No one knew. No one knew. Once you tell something, you can't untell it."

My eyes started stuttering gibberish on the screen. I could see Anthony was scared. Scared for Gus, scared in case I was behind *Silent Scream*, scared in case I wasn't. I was scared of escaping my bubble, my invisibility cloak of spastic retard.

Then the taste of blood turned sweet. I was no longer a non-entity living only in the shadows. I could change the course of others' lives. I had broken through—I had become a person.

My breath calmed, and I typed without pause and virtually without mistake. "Gus needs to follow the instructions. Yes, it's my site. Yes, Gus can do it. Safely. No, I won't let harm come to him. You can't go, Ant, no way, you're too fa big, you'll get stuck. I know because I've been. Heaps of times. With my mother. Heaps of times every year, all of my life until she left. She carried me on her back, dragged me through."

Anthony read every letter, every space, every word I eye-typed. (Hopefully he skipped the "fa" bit.) Then he sat back and looked at me. He carefully wiped the drool from my face and my uniform. He blotted the blood on my hands. His voice was quiet, and kind of defeated—relieved defeated, but strong. I think I mean resolved.

"Okay," he said. "Okay. Gus will go."

He went to walk away, then turned and looked at me. "Thank you, Sophie. Thank you for this."

As he walked away, tears re-joined the drool and blood as I went back to my back-of-hand mouth-swatting.

Chapter 28

Rememory 104

Tuesday, early afternoon

I know Gus is safe. The shadows keep me posted on his progress.

"Holy shit, I'm packin' it," Gus thought. The shadows could smell his fear.

SES Lisa drove as far as she could towards the group squatting in the bloodwood circle. One of the station hands had brush-cuttered around the hole, and it looked ridiculously insignificant compared to the high-rise wall of pock-faced basalt, just a little way further up the slope.

"*Silent Scream* has it right so far," Gus thought.

"Hi, Leese, let me give you a hand with that." Some of the others came over and together they all lifted the rescue gear—including a ginormous rainbow serpent ladder—out of her truck and laid it on the ground in a pathway to the cave hole. The ladder was of dinosaur-proportions to reach the 584 metres below ground, and was made up of a coloured medley of ropes and cable ladders—equipment hastily collected from the district's many SES groups. While this cave is certainly not the deepest in the world, it is by far the deepest in Australia, reaching down about two hundred stories, twice the height of Melbourne's Eureka Tower.

"Thanks for that, looks like we're all set," Gus said, stepping over the ladder while he checked all the joins.

There were seven people hovering with Gus.

My father was there. He was in a fair bit of bluster. His shirt clung to his body and his acrylic flares were damp in the crotch area. You could see it from the back.

Anthony stood quite still, a bit out of breath after the exertion. He was silent. Didn't mention his fans once.

Calliope was taking photos and video footage. He's really one sick puppy. It'd make great blogging material, regardless of which way it all went. His concession was that he was quiet too. Just mainly the whirring of his motor-drive spoke what he had to say.

Dudley was the brush-cutterer, and he was leaning against a bloodwood along with his whipper-snipper, a little way from the group, rolling a smoke. Workplace Health and Safety was having a day off.

Lisa, still fresh-smelling, was fully SES-dressed in orange overalls, steel-capped boots, and belt with dangly Swiss army knife, spare rope, two-way and GPS. She looked a bit Guantanamo Bay, but her posture hadn't made the connection.

Freddy, also looking fresh, but in a more relaxed way, had left her mandolin in the car. This was obviously a momentous occasion. She had that spacey-eye, loose-lipped sort of look that always followed a group walk and sweet waft of smoke behind some bush.

Gordon the regional SES director squatted nearest the hole. He had silently overseen the equipment unloading, but looked a little irritated.

"I'm not sure you should be doing this," he said several times.

"I can't approve it on an operational basis," he also said several times.

But he maintained his position closest to the hole until Gus walked over.

Gus wore his surfing wetsuit, a sort of long-legged singlet all-in-one, and he allowed Lisa to fit the headlamp to his head. She clipped its safety lead securely through his wetsuit shoulder strap. I think she spent longer than was absolutely necessary fiddling and farting around Gus, but no one seemed to notice.

Gus unzipped the suit and shoved another torch down the front. Any other time it would have caused ongoing ribaldry. Today it caused more silence.

Three more people stood together, a few metres away, almost tripodding each other. They shone with fear. Laura's parents had driven and flown and driven through the day and night and day from Charleville to get there. Emily's mother looked shrunken. She was cleaning lady thin. Emily was her only child, her bright mutation of intellect. The three parents bonded tightly. Fear and grief dissolve social and economic status.

Lisa anchored the ropes and steel cable ladders with two side-by-side purple climbing ropes to the nearest large bloodwood tree. To make quadruply sure, she also locked on steel cables and tethered them to two ancient, and even bigger, bloodwood trees—just in case one fell over, I think. The SES are ultra-careful. Stormbirds shrieked in the distance as Lisa attached a final knotted red and black rope to the drop end of the ladder. She looked at Gordon, then Gus, for significant lengths of time. Short, but significant. Then her eyes swept the others in a look that said "handover".

Gus stepped over and a group of them helped to winch-feed the ropes and ladder down the hole. The ladder rungs really only just fitted sitting sideways. One by one they fed it down the 584-metre pitch. The ladder and rope length had been measured twice—making allowance for stretch—once by Lisa, and again by Gordon, to officially sign off that part of the job.

Lisa couldn't help herself. She shone the SES-sized torch lamp down the hole, onto the ladder and rope, the light bleeding into nothingness. Nothingness reached down into nowhere. She dropped a rock down the hole. A sizeable rock, bigger than a brick size. Nothing. Not a plop, not a splat, not a thud, nothing. The shadows wouldn't even make that concession.

"You don't have to go, you know," Gordon said. "No one would blame you. No one would think any less of you. It's a fool's errand."

"Thanks, Gordon," Gus said, "for your kind last words."

"It's time." Bloodwood shadows fluttered a salute as Gus disappeared from sight.

Rememory 105

Tuesday afternoon

"Holy fuck!" Gus gasped for air and dug his fingers into the edge of the pool wall. The headlamp dangled down his back after the 554-metre climb down, the 30-metre shimmy, the 10-metre drop, the drift swim northwest, and the 15-metre pop up into the cave from the second ceiling hole. It is very difficult to put on a headlamp with one hand, but not impossible.

Gus's thoughts are as significant as his splutterings, probably more. The shadows know both, so I'm going to give you both. Probably a mix of both.

Wall shadows flickered dappled water on the basalt cave sides. Gus looked around. "It's like falling into a time warp," he thought. "Fuck! And that wasn't the tricky bit!"

He could feel the rhythm of the current in different levels of insistence urging him to move.

"Take your time," he thought, still recovering his breath.

It could have been shock, fear, incredulity, I'm not sure, but the only thinking Gus had control over were the words of *Silent Scream*.

"You'll feel the ebb and flow of the current and you'll notice that it rises and falls a fair bit on each surge. If you've still got your torch, shine it on the basalt wall that the current points to. You'll see a number of openings at different levels. It looks like some kid has gone wild with a hole-puncher. Don't worry if you've lost the torch, you can still find the right passage. The tide will tell you. The current runs in sets of seven. Count the strongest as the seventh. Use the seventh as your bounce down."

Remembering the words helped him slow his breathing, and he focused on counting two full rounds of seven. He felt the rise and fall of the pond as each surge came, and made his way over to the hole-punch wall. The seventh surge came the highest up the wall.

"One, two, three, four." On the next round Gus sucked in the last of the cave air he would breath and bounced down on seven. Underwater, he held onto the pool's sides to try to prevent himself from surfacing.

"One, two, three—let go." The current chose which hole to send him through, and hands and head first, he travelatered in, picking up pace as the current strengthened, sucking him along.

He could feel, rather than see, other underground watercourses joining the main current. Different temperatures and different flow-rates stroked his face, his hands and his shoulders and his feet. After about ten seconds, he knew there was no way back. The current was just too strong.

Along the roof of the flow, Gus felt his first air pocket, and with his mouth touching the rock ceiling, he gasped in honeyed air, grabbing the rock to slow himself down as he sucked in one whole lungful, then the current insisted he move on.

Two more pockets, two more lungfuls, then he tasted salt.

"Holy fuck, should have drunk water back there in the pond," he thought. Panic leaked in.

"Keep calm, trust the process." The words of *Silent Scream* were a comfort.

"Brave young man," the shadows thought.

As he flowed through the basalt tube, Gus concentrated his hands on the roof. The water was cold, so he couldn't feel his skin rasped raw, but he knew it was. He felt his blood flowing, leaking from him, joining the tide. But he didn't care. He felt the ceiling disappear. With his whole might, and extra help from the shadows, he dug his fingers, his nails, his whole future into the chute above, and star jumped his legs to each side of the passage for purchase, just like *Silent Scream* instructed. His legs dragged forward and his lungs screamed, but the third current surge pushed him upward, projecting him into the chute. As half of his body lifted above the main channel, he was sucked up, and popped into the world's sweetest cave air. The water was still salty, but he didn't care. The air was so, so sweet to swallow.

Gus's headlamp didn't reach the cave walls, but there was a crack of brightness deep in the distance. He scrambled out of the pool, and walked towards the light.

Rememory 106

Tuesday afternoon

Silent Scream said the hardest thing might be talking them all into following him, and it was right. But the shadows helped Gus convince them.

"Holy crap, Gus, where did you come from? But am I glad to see you. Do you have any water?" Andrew stared, his brain having to recalibrate.

"Is there a way out through there? I couldn't find one. Is it far? Are others coming? Do you have any water? It's all salty here." Laura's questions staccatoed at Gus.

"Do you guys know each other?" Andrew was back on track. His manners didn't let him down for long. "Laura, Emily, meet Gus, our saviour. Gus, Laura and Emily. We are forever in your debt." Andrew's social graces were a comfort to them all, even the shadows.

"We are so, so glad to see you, Gus, you have no idea," Laura said. "We've run out of water. There's only salt in the caves. For some reason, we can't find a path back. It's so weird."

Laura spewed her quotient of words, and wasn't waiting for answers. "You didn't bring water? How far is it out that way? Thank God you've got a torch. Ours are going flat. And the GPS isn't working. Or the satellite phone. But I guess the EPIRB must've, or was it the flare? We set one off both nights. Is that how you found us? I am so thirsty. Is it quicker that way, or back the way we came?"

Gus fished his spare torch out of his wetsuit and handed it to Laura. She didn't bat an eyelid at where he'd had it stored. The comfort another bright light gave them all was disproportionate to its actual total lack of use on the swim out.

"Are the others meeting us here, or are they waiting at the bottom of the falls?" Emily asked, calmer now, more authoritative.

These were not women who let a rescue happen without their input.

"We couldn't get back through the scrub," Laura said. "It sort of closed up. We couldn't find the track back down."

Gus took a deep breath. "There's no one else coming, guys. You've just got me," he said. "And it's a rather unusual way out. Underwater through a cave tunnel system. It's the only way out we know."

"How did you know we were here?" Andrew asked.

"*Silent Scream. Silent Scream* posted the rescue plan. Told us how to get you out," Gus said. He was getting a bit wary, but couldn't keep his mouth shut. The shadows were telling him it was time to move. The tide would soon turn.

"You've got to be fuckin' kidding," Laura said. "No way am I going out in any cave tunnel, underwater. I'm too claustrophobic. I'll wait till the others get here."

Gus looked at them all silently. He rotated eye contact between them, and slowly spoke.

"You have to trust me. It is two forty-five pm. We have to catch the tide out before three pm. I will be leaving in the next five minutes. You can either come with me, or you will die. No one else is coming. No one else can come. This is it. Do as I say, and I'm sure we'll be fine. After all, the directions got me in here. I found you with the directions. Getting out is comparatively easy. I will give you three minutes to think, then we have to go, before the tide turns."

Andrew knew Gus from environmental meetings and the odd conference, and had never known him to speak without thinking clearly first.

"We will follow you, Gus," Andrew said. "Thank you for doing this for us."

Laura went to speak, but Andrew didn't hold back.

"For fuck's sake, Laur, we have no fresh water. We have no way out. And if Gus says no one else is coming, I believe him."

It was easier for Andrew because he had the advantage of previously experiencing shadow talk. He more easily trusted the untrustable.

"No way, I'm not going." Laura's face was not sitting straight. Her mind wasn't either.

Emily's voice was gentle. "Come on, Laur, we'll help you. I'm going. You have to. You can do this."

"Have you got a zip-lock bag? We can't let the scats get wet," Emily's empathy didn't override her research. "And another for the memory cards."

Control was not something Laura was comfortable giving to others. But she adjusted, and passed Emily two zip-lock bags.

Rememory 107

Tuesday, later afternoon

A little sheepishly, the shadows flickered goodbye as The Wall sucked them out into the current, which was even stronger now. The nailtails watching all took a sigh of relief too.

Gus went first, Emily second, then Laura, then Andrew. Gus had his headlight shining, which, at the start, made it all a little less frightening. They stood above the exit chute and Gus detailed the instructions.

"We go in head first. Arms above your head, and aim straight down. The current will pick you up; just go with it. Make sure you're head first. I'll slow down as much as I can, but there's a limit to what I can do. Basically, once you're in, the only tricky bit is making sure you go down the right-hand passage when it forks. I'll try to wait there, but I'm not sure I'll be able to. You've got to hold your breath for quite a long time, but there's an air pocket soon after you get into the right-hand passage. Big enough to take a full breath. It's not far after that."

Gus didn't tell them how worried he was in case they didn't take the right passage. The alternative had no air pockets in a cave system that, at its shortest route, was ten kilometres to the estuary. The out-flows at the end were many, kazillions in fact, but all were too narrow for a body. The tide would turn soon and would drop the water level, but the air might not be fresh and even if it were, it would be too late for them.

As he dived in, Gus mantra-ed to himself *Silent Scream*'s final instructions. Or it might have been the shadows putting the words into his head. Same thing really, so either way, it doesn't matter.

"It has to be this specific day. If you go the next day, the directions would be different. The tides change daily and they are never the same the next day, the next year, ever. Different tides, different currents, passageways close, others open. No tide in relation to the last is ever the same. But the next tide will come."

Rememory 108

Tuesday, later afternoon

Just before the tide turns, deep in the caverns under The Basalt Wall, the shadows have a field day arguing the subtleties of water depth and flow. It's like an everyday family squabble over the cooking and washing up, but here, deep in the labyrinth, the stakes are deadly.

Gus's sweat of fear was the first tweak to be taken into consideration. He didn't like going first, because he wanted to make sure they all left—but, crucially, he wanted to try to make sure they took the right-hand tunnel. So his body displaced the first sluice of water—and his fear-sweat adjusted the tidal calculation.

Emily still had the courage of youth, so it was easy for the shadows to send her body down the right-hand tunnel. Her finger tips touched Gus's toes as they both swept towards the way out.

Unfortunately, Laura stalled one second too long before diving in.

She hesitated, such a small tiny second, hardly more than the shortest pause, an entirely understandable mini falter, but it was just enough of a backward smile, and at that time Laura was not thinking of the plight of others. So often the unwitting actions of some repay the kindness of others with a dismissal of their worth. But, fortunately, Andrew didn't know anything about this when he dived in, because any extra extrusion of fear-sweat on his part may have stuffed things up—tidal calculation-wise—for Laura too.

The water took Laura's breath as it sucked her body down and into the main current, which was in its last rush to freedom before the tide turned. This section of the cavern wall is smooth, and the contrast from the gnarled basalt leading to the cave opened her eyes. She forgot to be afraid, and zero visibility became a caress, a respite from reality. She traced the side wall with her right-side fingers and toes, Braille-reading a connection the shadows enjoyed, and neatly swept her into the right-hand tunnel. She didn't realise she'd made the choice, had no thought for the bullet she'd dodged. The shadows ticked her off as a job well done.

Andrew, however, was another story. He was alone as he dived into the tunnel, and the current treated him differently from the others. It was spent after the madness of the outgoing bore tide, and took a moment to breathe. Andrew didn't know this. Years of Bronte Beach surfing made short work of this comparative lull in flow. But when the current slows, the shadows descend and the water level drops. His fingers and toes traced the side wall on the right side, but in his tracing of its smoothness, he missed the entrance, which was now quite a way above, and he strongly and neatly swam into the left-hand tunnel.

Chapter 29

Rememory 109

Tuesday afternoon

SES Lisa made sure her resuscitation equipment was orderlyly positioned beside the cave pool. SES Director Gordon was, of course, in charge, and comprehensively oversaw her due diligence as he sucked on his umpteenth roll-your-own of the day. On a reasonably regular basis, he discreetly spat and picked strings of tobacco off his tongue.

My father had dragged me along for the grand finale rescue operation, as Sharon had disappeared from the homestead after she'd dumped me when we got home from school. She wasn't even in the honeymoon suite. Dad and I looked.

Calliope was in full camera flash mode, as was Anthony.

Anthony had a tiny Leica camera that cost almost as much as Calliope's ginormous whirling gurling Nikon.

"I have an up-to-date first aid certificate," Anthony said to SES Lisa in between clicks. Most of his Leica clicking took place in quite close proximity to SES Lisa.

There were several "so have I"s after he announced his first aid qualifications, so we were well equipped. Only thing was, if they all got out, we might not have had enough car seats for everyone. They didn't think of that, hey. Dud had his tray back though, and I know Calliope would love to ride "outback" back in that.

SES Lisa had flood-lit the cave so it was star sparkling full moon and midday sunlight all in one. We had all driven up to the end of the estuary, and walked in up to the edge of the basalt wall, helping SES Lisa carry all the gear. (Minus rainbow serpent ladder, of course. And I didn't do any walking or carrying.) We were instructed by *Silent Scream* to wait beside the pond in the most outer, outer basalt wall cave. The cave is actually a lava tube that didn't collapse when it cooled a millennium or so ago. Yesterday, the shadows wouldn't have let our motley crew find its entrance. Today, it loudly laughs at us, calling to us, only half hidden by rainforest trees and vines. It actually has a walkway of wild jasmine leading to its mouth—but most people would never notice, except for sniffing the sweet puffs of air. Wild jasmine is not a show-offy shrub.

We all knew this cave pond was there—by all I mean me, Mum and Dad—but only Mum and I had ever swum in or out of the tunnel deep, deep in the pond. This was where the shadows told me Gus and the research team would surface. My hand slapping made orange foam, I was so nervous.

SES Director Gordon sat on his haunches, lighting another roll-your-own and spouted forth, in-between discreet spits, on the need to respect and work with nature. It was a peaceful background sound for everyone waiting.

Emily's and Laura's parents had pride of place right beside the pond, but sitting on a basalt shelf, off to the side a bit, so as not to get in the way of SES Lisa and the rescue and resus equipment.

Then Gus popped up.

Just like that. One second he wasn't there, the next he was. And his headlight was still on, but it was hard to tell it was on, because of the blasting spotlights. SES Lisa was right there, on the job, and she without pause jumped up to help him out. But in one neat whoosh, he pulled himself out of the pool and sat on the side, heavily breathing.

Then Emily popped up too.

I heard a gasping sob from Emily's mother. It was bigger than she was. Anthony ushered her forward, making it clear she had positioning priority.

Mrs Gus arrived right on time for Gus's popping. Thank the Lord she wasn't there earlier, else I may have completely disintegrated under her stare.

Mrs Gus didn't need Anthony's help in positioning priority. Her elbows made short work of anyone foolish enough to be in her way, and she wrapped herself around Gus, weeping over him, and wailing at my father, all at the same time. I was just glad Gus was safe. My hand slapping slowed down a bit.

It was only a minute, if that, before Laura appeared. Her parents quietly wept as they hugged her. Anthony didn't need to give them positioning rights either, but they didn't need their elbows. Everyone automatically offered them room.

Another minute passed, then another and another and another. Everyone had moved from joyous elation to shuffling discomfort. Gus was the first to speak.

"Laura, Andrew was coming straight after you, wasn't he," Gus said. "I mean, he didn't change his mind or anything."

"No, he was ready to dive straight after me," Laura replied. "He said he'd try to stay right with me to make sure I took the right passage. He was definitely coming …"

Rememory 110

Tuesday, late afternoon

Andrew knew he was cactus when his breath ran out and his lungs started to shrivel. The tide had turned and was dragging him back the way he came. His brain and lungs spiralled out of control and he used all his strength desperately, desperately fighting the tide, not realising he was in the wrong tunnel, and not realising he was actually fighting against the shadows that were trying desperately, desperately to save him. Fortunately, as his breath and mind spiralled to nothing, he blacked out and let the incoming tidal bore sweep him along into the arms of shadow-love.

As the left-hand passage welcomed the incoming tide, the right-hand passage was still floating betwixt the two.

The shadows cradled Andrew's body, ignoring the screams of the threatening tidal bore. They ignored the bickering currents, flicking them aside again and again, and floated him along the right-hand passage, along and up into the cave. If it hadn't been Andrew, the shadows admit, they probably wouldn't have bothered.

Andrew's body was lifeless when Gus and Laura and Anthony and SES Lisa dragged him onto the basalt floor. Fortunately, the SES resuscitation equipment was orderlyly positioned right near them, so Lisa worked her magic. Anthony was keen to utilise his skills, but SES Director Gordon cordoned everyone back with Jesus-on-the-cross arms and an authoritative voice. He managed all this despite having to bark through his roll-your-own stub of a durry. He was also offering clear advice to SES Lisa, for which I'm sure she was grateful.

I suppose I should tell you that Andrew was okay. The green brine he vomited on Lisa's orange overalls was a joy for all to see. In relief, all the shadows breathed out, and cooling breezes with a hint of jasmine calamine wafted through the cave.

Part III
Power Wars – 2004

When lenity and cruelty play for a kingdom,
the gentler gamester is the soonest winner.

William Shakespeare, *Henry V,* **III.vi.46**

Chapter 30

Assessment report into the bridled nailtail wallaby population in or near The Great Basalt Wall, north-east of Leichhardt, Central Queensland.

Commissioned for the Environmental Impact Statement in relation to The Styx River Eco-resort Development Proposal

Diamond Partners
Valuers and Environmental Researchers
Affiliated with East Australia University
PO Box 1099
Leichhardt Central Mail Centre Qld 4970

1   SUMMARY

1.1   INTRODUCTION

This Assessment Report (AR) prepared by Diamond Partners, independent valuers and environmental researchers, assesses the current existence of populations of bridled nailtail wallaby within The Great Basalt Wall near the proposed development on Styx River Cattle Station, via Leichhardt, Central Queensland, and the likely impact of the development on such populations.

The development proposes 2000 strata title units, a caravan park, hiking, four-wheel drive, mountain bike and motor-bike safaris, and other listed outdoor adventure activities. The development will include access tracks and roads in and around Styx River Cattle Station's section of The Great Basalt Wall (Appendix A).

Detailed information on the proposed development is contained in the proponent's Environmental Impact Statement (EIS) (Appendix B), public comments and submissions on the EIS (Appendix C), and responses to these submissions in the proponent's Response Document (RD) Appendices. This report also relies on information, comments and advice provided by relevant Queensland and Federal Government agencies and additional information provided by the proponent (Appendix D).

1.2 SUMMARY OF FINDINGS

A research team located and collected fresh scat evidence within the proposed development site.

a) Evidence of a current population of bridled nailtail wallaby was found in the form of:

   i. Scat and environmental niche analysis.

   ii. DNA sampling of collected scats compared to existing recognised species exhibit (National Museum).

b) Any development and disturbance of the bridled nailtail wallaby habitat will severely threaten the viability of current numbers, which are recognised as endangered.

c) Styx River and the adjoining Great Basalt Wall is established as a recognised habitat of the endangered bridled nailtail wallaby.

…

Chapter 31

Rememory III

This morning the sun rose without the help of a cloud.

School was uneventful, but I knew something was wrong. When he picked us up from the bus stop, my father's face was tangled into a fist, and his lips were white. Sharon was quite chatty, despite him not saying a word in response to anything she—or my legs—had to say.

Eventually, after we got home and unpacked me, my father spoke. "Leave Soph with me," he said to Sharon. "You have a break till dinner time. There'll be a few extra for tonight, three extra. Just the usual rooms, thanks."

Dodgy Dominic was the first to arrive. "Hey mate," he said. He sounded a bit scrunched too.

I was parked on the front verandah, just in sight of the squatter's chairs. My father handed Dominic a piece of paper.

"One fucking page, the bitch," my father said. "You'd think she'd have the guts to ring me, but no, just a one-page letter. Doesn't even have our names on it. She didn't even have the decency to personalise it. I thought she was a mate, a friend."

Taking into consideration his tone of incredulity, one of his "friends", I'd say.

"Friends and money don't generally mix, you know that," Dominic said.

He didn't seem to notice the irony in this.

"Well we're fucked. I'm fucked. This was the get out of drought card."

My father's voice was getting a little pointy.

"The drought's done me in."

So has the verandah *Country Life*-ing and the Mt Kilimanjaro-ing, the new LandCruiser Wagon-ing, and the Chamrousse skiing, I thought.

"I'll have to sell. Five generations, and I'll have to sell."

The gods of due privilege were definitely against him.

"This'll be Warren," Dominic said, seeing the dust swarm arrive.

He sounded quite eager for the company. "He's bringing Silas and some prawns. Let's have them in the bar."

"You go over, I'll just get Soph sorted with the computer. I'll be over directly," he said. He stayed sitting in his squatter's chair, legs on its swing-out legs, arms mingled with the coffee stains on its arms, finishing the dregs of his beer and another cigarette. Then came over and undid my wheelchair brake.

"How about some computer games, Soph?" He was trying to be chirpy, and I felt a little sorry for him with his hiked-up shirt-sleeves and his cricket-glove hands. His nails were extra chewed, moist and bleeding at the edges.

The jasmine was especially strong that afternoon, wafting in and out of our nostrils, playing with us, oblivious to his pain, or, on second thoughts, revelling in it. And the sea sent up a rather pleasant breeze.

"There you go, Soph. Will be back soon."

I won't hold my breath, I thought.

He'd left the letter open on his desk, adding to the paper history of months of The Styx postal service. Some, many, envelopes remained unopened. Some, I'd say, from their brown coffee rings and cigarette ash, were of many, many mail deliveries ago vintage. ANZ bank statements, overdue telephone bills, two different credit card statements, both maxed out, an American Express second notice, and on top of all this, the letter in question. There is no dignity in exposing one's inner financial workings.

And there was no dignity in the letter.

Rural Advance Australia
Development Finance
2994 Pitt St
Sydney NSW 2000

Managing Director
Pivotal Consortium
C/- Styx River Station
Via Leichhardt QLD 4702

Dear Sirs

Re: Pivotal Consortium – Line of credit for rural tourism development – Styx River

We regret to inform you that your application for a Line of Credit for the above rural tourism development has been declined, and we cannot provide you with any finance at this time.

    Even though your Stage 1 request for $2.3 million falls within our Rural Advance Scheme, the recent Environmental Protection Agency Report on Styx River poses a significant impediment in the implementation of your development.

    Should the situation significantly alter after 12 months, you are free to pursue another application. If you have any questions or queries about this matter, please contact me.

Sincerely
Ms Laurine Palfry
General Manager
Rural Development Finance

Chapter 32

Rememory 112

My mother's jasmine is not always kind. That early evening, every jasmine plant, all together, laughed and laughed as my father walked over to the main station bar, forcing him to at least subconsciously, in his despair, acknowledge my mother.

There was no one near to hear the ping, pong, ping, tring, pring, ling of the dial-up Internet, so I checked my emails. My account is password protected, so I'm not too worried he'll read anything, and anyway my father wouldn't have a clue how to access it.

There was an email from Anthony.

anthonywhite@anthonywhite.net

Hi Sophie

I'm not sure if you are aware of the outcome of the environmental report. Laura and Emily did a fabulous job. They did their science magic thing, and whooshhh, Abracadabra, nailtail proof.

This means the Environmental Protection Agency has put the kibosh on the resort "until adequate and satisfactory provision is made for the ongoing safety and security of the current and future populations of bridled nailtail wallabies."

That means it's all a no go — 2000 units, caravan park, mountain and motor bike safaris are just not an option.

So heyyyyy, you did it!!!! Celebrations are in order. Just wanted you to know. Good luck for the remainder of your last year of school. I'll be away for a while, but will definitely be out for your school formal. Looking forward to it.

Best
Ant.

I replied.

ss@silentscream.com.au

Hey Ant,

Thanks for thinking of me and letting me know. That's great for the nailtails. Laura and Emily are amazing women. And Andrew is amazing too. So is Gus – and you too of course!

Only one problem. My father says he has to sell. He was banking on the development bailing him out financially. Silas's financial backing has also mysteriously shrunk, making it totally kaput. I'm worried who'll buy the place, and what they might do.

Could you let Andrew know, please? Just so he can maybe keep an eye on the nailtails if I suddenly disappear, and Silent Scream suddenly disappears. In case I end up computerless. I mean Andrew doesn't know SS is me. Only you know, so please, it's best to keep it that way. I want you to keep it that way.

Sophie

Anthony replied immediately.

anthonywhite@anthonywhite.net

Hi Sophie

I'm sorry about your farm finances. That's a pretty huge blow for both of you, and for the nailtails, and for The Wall. Who will the shadows have to talk to, if you go?

Leave it with me.

Ant

Ant was on the job, big time.

anthonywhite@anthonywhite.net

Hi Andrew

Just heard Styx River may soon be sold – financial problems. Seems the development was the bailout option. Can we get together to talk about the situation?

Best

Anthony White
Member for Basalt

Rememory 113

It was fairly late afternoon when Andrew and Ant sat in the lee of The Wall's shadows, talking. They were out in the middle of nowhere, sucking on a couple of stubbies of craft beer. Ant is into craft beer, especially Tasmanian organic craft beer. And he'd chosen a little English-style pale ale number with Andrew in mind.

There were certain things that couldn't be said, but certain things they both understood. Andrew wouldn't do anything unethical or illegal. Anthony couldn't be seen doing anything unethical or illegal. Only The Wall's shadows were listening in.

Both men pretty well understood the situation. Both understood the dire consequences looming over Sophie, the nailtails and Styx River. Later—years, years later—Anthony filled me in with the overall gist of their conversation, but the shadows told me it all first.

"I did a mortgage search," Andrew said. "It's close to two mill owing. Far too much for him to service in the present drought. Even if it rains tomorrow, it'll be years for him to catch up with the breeding cycle to have fat bullocks or even export heifers. Even if the grass appeared tomorrow, he doesn't have the breeders left to breed his way out. He'll have to buy in more than half his normal herd of breeding cows and bulls. That's another two mill he'd have to borrow just to breed himself fully stocked. If it rains tomorrow, I mean really rains, spaced out over the next three months, he needs that two mill to just be in a position to be fully operational; plus another four years at least until he's anywhere near full stocking and operational capacity. His breeders have to get pregnant, calve, and the calves grow one or two years for export heifers—if the market's still there—and three to four for steers. He'd need another mill or two, just for operational costs to get to that full working state, and that's if it keeps raining for those years."

"Since when did you know so much about cattle?" Anthony asked.

"My family has cattle and coffee places in Jamaica," Andrew said.

Anthony sucked a few mouthfuls of his beer to let everything sink in.

"No, you're right, it's just not going to happen," Anthony said. "No way he can service something like five mill. He's going down. He's right, you know, the development would have stood a good chance of saving him. The ten, fifteen years of drought we've had has knocked them all around, so many have had to sell out. Mind you, he does have a pretty cushy jet-setting lifestyle. But generally, the only ones left have sacrificed everything and everyone for the sake of saving the property, all with no surety of success. If you're a betting man, I'd say the odds are million to one against it. It's madness to gamble on the vagaries of nature. These guys have a whole different mindset from the rest of us. Only the really tough nuts have survived. They are prepared to go down with the ship, and he'll take Sophie with him. What's going to happen to her, if he goes broke?"

"If it's a forced sale, some tougher nut will sniff out his situation, and will squeeze his nuts dry; buy it at fire sale rates," Andrew said.

"What'll happen to Sophie then?" It was more rhetoric than question.

For a big bloke, emotions aren't always expected to show. Anthony's head was bowed, waving over his beer, and his voice wobbly. Even the shadows wobbled for a moment.

"There's something I'm not sure you're aware of," Andrew said, his voice a little reticent. "When I did the mortgage search, the property's not in his name."

Anthony looked at Andrew, not sure which way this was going.

"It's all in Sophie's name," Andrew said quietly.

Rememory 114

The Wall of course, knew all this, but was happy to listen in.

"You're fuckin' kiddin'. You've got to be fuckin' jokin'." Anthony's private school education slipped in the emotion of the moment.

"Yep, she owns it all, lock, stock and barrel, Styx River, the cattle, everything," Andrew said.

"It goes way back. Sophie's great-grandfather, William Northampton, when he died in '72, left everything to his firstborn—and, as it turned out, only—child," Andrew said. "So, Northampton's daughter, Agnes, aided by her accountant husband, inherited the lot.

"They managed things pretty well it seems. She was a powerhouse and ran the cattle operation. Ben was, some would say, ruthlessly good with money. He died well before Agnes, and they only had the two children—two sons, Sophie's father and his brother Alex. When Agnes died, she left the whole lot to her granddaughters—there are three of them. The property opposite Styx River—it's called Hillsong—went to her younger son Alex's two daughters, and Styx River—worth ten times more than Hillsong—went to Sophie. The freehold title deeds and leases of Styx River are all in Sophie's name."

Anthony sat back letting the information process. "Pretty tough thing to do to her sons. I wonder if they knew? Before their mother died, I mean."

"She mustn't have trusted them. Interesting. Wow, there must have been something she saw in them, or recognised," Anthony said.

"It's said that she loved Sophie without limit, and was extremely protective of her. She loved all her granddaughters, but was especially protective of Sophie. Agnes died when Sophie was five, around about the time Sophie's mother, Rose, left slash disappeared," Andrew said.

"Now where does that leave us?" Anthony asked.

Andrew sipped his beer. "As I see it, we've got a couple of best possible scenarios. One, that the place is safeguarded for the wallabies. Two, that Sophie is secure," Andrew said.

"The other way 'round I reckon, and add to the new Scenario One, that Sophie has continued and guaranteed access to an enabled computer," Anthony said.

Andrew was sightly perplexed at the imperative of the latter, but moved on.

"Compulsory acquisition of the property will cover them all. Ant, it's in your power to push for that and, I'm judging, get it passed. I'm thinking you turn the place into a habitat reserve for bridled nailtail wallabies, to be held and managed in perpetuity for and by Wuku custodians."

"That will mean the wallabies are safe, and as Sophie's almost eighteen, we can set up a trust fund with the money. She's the Wuku custodian, and if she were able, she'd be able to call the shots for the reserve. That's the weak point in all of this. Sophie's father will push for himself to call the shots, and we'll be back to square one. At least she won't be any worse off than she is now though, and, with close scrutiny by enviro groups, the nailtails will be relatively safe."

"I can see it, with really good safeguards, probably working fine for the wallabies, but won't he still have control over her money?" Anthony said. "But I guess there won't be that much left after all the debt is cleaned up."

"Well, no on both counts," Andrew said. "Well, maybe so in terms of controlling the money, but we can try to safeguard that too, hopefully." Andrew had maintained the clipped formal tones of a lawyer, and dealt with them as they were sequentially in his mind, the most straightforward response first.

"One, in terms of compulsory acquisition, the Federal Government can't be seen as taking advantage of the property owner. In this case because of the drought situation, you, the Federal Government, would have argument to recompense at the price it would attract in good times and in good condition." Andrew took a breath.

"Two, it is automatic that when a minor who is considered not able to manage their own affairs—such as with someone with an intellectual disability—turns eighteen, a guardian is appointed, often two or three people, to manage the care of the person and if required, an administrator—can be the same person/people—to oversee their financial affairs."

"So yes, perhaps he could continue to treat the asset or financial resource as his own, but not if we push for at least one independent party being part of the administrator-guardianship group, then it would be a lot harder for him, and he certainly wouldn't have a free rein. The danger of course is that they will argue for the father and his two friends being the advocates. On paper, they sound pretty good: the father, a doctor and a lawyer. That would certainly be an issue we'd have to overcome."

Anthony was quiet and didn't respond immediately. Andrew let him have time to think, to adjust to what he'd said.

Silently, with only a clink or two, and a shwoosh of ice, Anthony took another two stubbies out of the esky he was sitting on. Both men took synchronised swigs of this fresh beer. Both sets of eyes scanned the bush, taking in without seeing: the shadows, the basalt wall. It felt intimate, faintly cloying.

"There's something you probably need to know, that might affect things considerably," Anthony said, taking a deep breath. "I'm not comfortable telling you. I'm really breaking a confidence, but I think you have to know."

Andrew looked at Anthony, screwing his eyes against the sun's glare that ricocheted off the basalt wall, striking his eyes, almost stunning him—warning him.

"Sophie is not intellectually impaired," Ant said looking directly at Andrew. "She is extremely smart, and intellectually fully capable."

You wouldn't say Andrew was sceptical. In fact, he didn't seem that surprised, but he could foresee one major issue.

"That may well be the case, but we need to find a way of proving it, because her father will have no trouble arguing the case of disability."

"Sophie's behind *Silent Scream*. It's her site. She started it all on her own. Is that enough proof?" Anthony's voice wavered a little. It wasn't in his nature to break confidences.

"You're kidding. How do you know? Holy fuck, you're kidding." Andrew's English public school education slipped a little too.

"Nope, she did. Totally. True." Anthony nodded his head, a bit like a bobblehead toy, but serious, more dignified, I reckon.

"Yep, too true," he noddingly continued. "She used my credit card to pay for her domain name. She actually asked me for it, had it all worked out totally on her own. Once she had the eye-reading program, she didn't have an aide helping her on the computer. The site started after she got the eye-reading program. And when she asked me, she eye-pointed typed. I was sitting right next to her. She answered my specific verbal questions. There was no one else anywhere near. It was her. Sophie is intellectually normal. Very bright in fact."

Andrew started bobblehead nodding too. But in an even more serious and dignified way.

"Well, that changes things totally," Andrew said.

Rememory 115

The notice of intention was ridiculously short in relation to the impact it had on the lives of the people affected. Three main passages repeated in my father's mind. He read the passages again and again, word for word, out loud several times, and down the phone to Dodgy Dominic several more:

> Compliant with *The Lands Acquisition Act 1989* the following leasehold, freehold and stock route titles will be compulsorily acquired by the Federal Government to make provision for a fauna reserve for the endangered bridled nailtail wallaby. This reserve will be held and managed in perpetuity for and by Wuku Wuku people, who are cultural custodians, and will continue regardless of changes in the endangered status.
>
> The current Wuku custodian will retain residential rights to the Styx River homestead under a lease agreement.
>
> Due compensation will be paid to the land owner/lessee preferably on a negotiated basis where recognised conditions are taken into consideration. Acquisition by negotiated agreement involves the owner/lessee and the Commonwealth agreeing to the terms of the agreement and the amount of compensation.
>
> Objections to this acquisition may be made within 28 days stating reasons for objections in relation to the Act.

"It's the whole fucking place," my father said.

His voice was like I had never before heard. Weak. Every word lost tone and almost cracked. He was almost crying.

"The whole place," he said.

"Don't worry, we can object," Dominic said. "You're in shock, mate. Leave it with me. We can keep the objections going for years, decades probably. It's on so many different titles of freehold, leasehold, stock routes. And we can block it based on Indigenous interests, Indigenous ownership, Sophie as owner."

I bet Dodgy Dom was nodding and shaking his head at the same time. He always does when he gives legal advice. They must teach it in lawyer school; too tricky to be natural.

"One thing though," Dominic continued, "with Sophie, she's turning eighteen soon, we need to apply to be legal administrators. You, me and Si, we should get approval as administrators and guardians. That way at least you'll get to stay there. It's okay, mate, happens every day."

I wonder if anyone fully believes Dominic's bullshit.

"It's a fishing expedition on their part to see how difficult you're going to make it for them," Dominic continued. "They hate taking this sort of thing to court, especially with Sophie's condition and cultural heritage issues. We've got to get that administrator-guardianship appointment in place though."

"We'll get the bastards. Fucking greenies." Dominic was going almost full throttle now.

"Four generations on the land, five if you count Sophie. Don't worry, mate, we just need to get that advocate agreement. That's the deal breaker."

My father replaced the receiver softly. I didn't actually hear it land.

Chapter 33

Rememory 116

The air is asleep, but still the jasmine has snuck into the homestead.

They seemed to have given up hiding things from me. Psycho Silas was paying me more and more attention, especially when my father wasn't watching. He started bringing me little gifts—Kinder Surprises, choc marshmallow snowballs, and packets of Iced VoVos. Now if he brought vanilla slices, he might be in the ball-park. I'm joking, but kindergarten sugar isn't my bag.

I just knew it wasn't my happiness he was thinking about. I felt a bit like a farm dog he's making friends with, being nice to, getting chummy and familiar with, grooming. I made sure I was in full drool production mode when he was stuffing Iced VoVos into my mouth.

His kind always go in for the kill when they sniff something wounded. My father was definitely not working on all cylinders at the time.

Silas the sleaze has been in my room again. Sharon had already put me to bed and was in the honeymoon suite humping Dud or Jack, maybe both. Mr Sleaze was sitting on the side of my bed, stroking my hair—the side that isn't pulled out. He was leaning over and sort of half lying next to me. I was squawking and spitting big time, and flailing and kicking, almost disjointing my shoulders and hips. But Silas wasn't paying any attention. He was intent on his quarry, i.e. me, and was in caress mode, his hand stroking, chucking my cheek like you do a kitten's neck, or a hampster's, or something else a hundred per cent vulnerable that you think should be grateful—and is so, so not. Drool production was at an all-time high; so was my panic.

My drooling puts Silas off though. A bit. He hates being flicked with snot-laced pink drool, and it has become my specialty. I know it stains his shirts, and they are, he has said innumerable times, of the finest Bangkok raw silks, white, cream and the palest silver. Can't bleach 'em. Made to measure.

My father was preoccupied. Major understatement. He knew his generational status was about to slip away. He kept catching glimpses of himself as the careless one who let it all happen. His body and neck shrank each time he caught a glimpse, but his face stayed bulbous.

However, he mustn't have been as preoccupied as I thought.

"Silas!" My father had silently walked into my room, making his voice sound even more abrupt, fringing on admonishment. "We need help with this wording. In the office. Mate."

The "mate" didn't belong, and was more chafing because it was added after a full stop.

My father's presence pushed Silas out of the room. They did the circling dog thing, swapping places. Without another word or puff on the cigarette in his mouth, my father picked me up, put me on the couch, and turned on *SeaChange* Season 2 episode 26, my favourite. He sweated discomfort. Not like ringers musterin' in summer sweat. More like a cheese sweats, discretely beading all over. He'd be positively ringer musterin' stinkin' wet, if he saw all of Silas's attentions towards me.

Silas of course understood my father's discomfort. Retribution naps, never dies, and I think Silas's main source of jollies was my father's aversion to facing, vocalising, that he, Silas, his maaayyte, could be such an unsavoury threat towards me, Sophie, his disabled daughter. Silas teased, tortured, my father's sense of mateship, of trust. For Silas, I would be just a quirky bonus in his smiling-assassin game of pleasure and retribution—I'm not sure which had first priority.

Neither Silas nor I, however, factored in my father's inheritance of four-generations-on-the-land-ness.

"Silas, mate," my father said, stubbing his cigarette butt in a dead maidenhair fern. "Give me a help with the espresso machine. Mate. Coffees all round, hey?"

They walked towards the kitchen. From the couch he plonked me on, three sets of French doors line up and you can clearly see through into the kitchen. I had a clear view. I think my father knew that.

Silas, the knowledgeable one in all things cultured, reached across the espresso machine's silver spouty thing, to grab the coffee holder thing.

My father twisted a knob and …

THE STYX 241

"Fuck!" It was a bit more little girl's scream than just a "fuck", but you get the gist.

An extremely high-pitched, squeaky, "Fuck!" A full of surprise and horror, "Fuck!" A brief shot of steam had seared the back of his hand. Branded his hand.

Dud, complete with silver "Dud" belt buckle, cowboy hat, boots and spurs, was ride-on-mowing the lawn out the front, so the others—Dodgy Dom and Rabbit Warren—couldn't hear Silas's "Fuck" and little girl's scream. It must have been Jack who was bouncing around under Shazza. My brain is helpful in calibrating useless information such as this last bit.

Silas was in a bit of shock. He squashed himself into the kitchen bench corner, holding his hand to his neck—his balls were his other auto-option, but his neck won out. He couldn't move. Not that he tried to move. My father's bulk blocked his way. My father lit another cigarette, this time with the stove burning-churning-gas clicky lighter thing. He left the clicky thing on, burning, churning gas, as he took his first fag drag, a long, lung-searing drag, a shit-in-the-face-of-cancer drag.

"I'm going to be blunt," my father said, cigarette in one hand, stove lighter clicky thing burning, churning, in the other, and looking Silas straight in the face. "You're me mate and I love ya, man, but Sophie's off limits."

"I shouldn't have to say this," my father said. He sadly shook his head, and the burning, churning, stove lighter clicky thing waved in sympathy. "You shouldn't make me do this, man."

His eyes seared Silas. Silas was shitting himself.

"If you touch her, mate, I will kill you. It's that simple. That's a promise, not a threat. At some stage, I will know, and you will die. I want to be very clear about that. I want you to be very clear about that," my father said, very clearly.

"My good chap," Silas actually spluttered. He knew about the four-generation thing in theory, but being pussy-whipped in the face with it was something else.

My heart grew. I felt safe. Well, safer.

"Who's up for a coffee?" My father's voice was almost chirpy. He was obviously cultured enough to operate an espresso machine.

My hand slappin' was doing a jitterbug, but Silas spun on his heel towards the office, and became totally focused on the notice of intent letter, his burnt hand behind his back. I could taste blood, but it was sweet.

Rememory 117

This morning, the sea spun silk and left it on the beach.

Dodgy Dom didn't mess around. When he gravelled to a stop at the front gate, he stomped across the lawn, still in his cloud of arrival dust, and headed, head and neck first, to join my father who had emerged from the office. Dominic was flapping a wad of papers in his hand. He had the application for my guardianship and administration order wrapped up in triplicate.

"You just need to sign it and I'll lodge it today," Dominic said. No hellos, no how ya goin', no how's ya father, definitely no how are ya, Soph.

He continued without pause. "We need two people to witness who are not parties to the application. Warren, you can be one, and who else?"

"Take it over to Sharon," my father said. "She can sign it too."

Stomp stomp stomp, chatter chatter chatter, stomp stomp stomp back.

"All done," Dominic said, totally ignoring the need for Sharon to actually witness my father's signing, and totally oblivious to the more formal atmosphere between my father and Silas.

"We'll get this show on the road. I've started drafting both appeals—for the acquisition, and for the enviro report. We'll hit them with both." Dominic at last breathed out.

My father snapped off the caps of four Coronas. "How much is this going to cost me, Dom? I'm not in a position to be outlaying any more on this."

"Maaaayyyte," Dom said. "No dramas, mates' rates. Trust me. We'll see you through this."

"Yes, but I'm the only one here with his arse on the line," my father said. "I'm the one who'll have to walk away with nothing. It's an issue for me. I've got Sophie to think of. I just can't spend a dollar more."

"You don't have to fork out for anything straight up, don't worry," Dominic said. "There's no cost to appeal."

"There's legal costs," my father said.

"Yeyhhh, but ... Maaaayyyte, I'll keep it down." Dominic was virtually altruistic. "You've got to do this. Hey, Si? There's no other way, hey?"

Silas spluttered a bit, which Dom took as an agreement.

"Trust us, mayyyte. We'll stand with you every step of the way, hey Si?"

Warren didn't seem surprised he wasn't consulted in this. He was just happy to be there.

I'm sure my father was not convinced.

Rememory 118

My sea has left me. Every king tide has a corresponding low, low tide.

Andrew emailed me his—my—response to the cronies' guardianship and administration advocate order application. It had lots of "pursuant to"s in it. Even blind Freddy could see the cronies had no chance. Even blind Freddy could see I was up shit creek.

No way was Dodgy Dominic a patch on Andrew. Nowhere near as many "pursuant to"s in Dominic's original application. Basically, Andrew's—my—response dismissed the cronies' application on the grounds that I was capable of making my own decisions. I was the sole and independent creator and author of the well-known environmental blog, *Silent Scream*, it said.

That was sufficient validation and verification of my abilities and mental capacity, apparently.

The "response" continued:

> Sophia Beatrice Noorgoo Wukuburri is seeking to appoint her own administration facilitator, lawyer Andrew Braitling Martin, with limited functions: to advise and or implement financial and legal aspects of her decision-making, as and when she wishes and instructs.

Holy shit, I was fucked.

Rememory 119

I can feel the sea spray. Way, way up here on my verandah, the sea spray pleads forgiveness.

I can tell you, I was not happy that Anthony told Andrew about *Silent Scream*. I was at school reading my emails, and was totally not happy.

"You promised, Ant. How could you do this to me? How could you betray me, Judas me?" I screamed my reply email through my eyes. It was very difficult eye-pointing the letters with tears, and my back-of-hand swatting going nineteen-to-the-dozen, and my legs helicoptering off my body.

"YOU FUCKING JUDAS." I typed this in capitals. Once you capitalise the first letter, it's actually easier to type it all in capitals. But it looked more upset. It looked more angry.

I was panic-scared and I felt sorry for my father. Bizarre, I know. But this rebuttal Andrew prepared was so big-city lawyer. It was so rubbing salt into my father's gaping wound of losing The Styx, even though, it seems, it was never his in the first place.

Who'd have thought my grandmother would think of everything? Could foresee the need to bypass her son—her sons. Who would have thought she was hard-nosed enough to continue, even from her grave, to effect what my father and his brother would see as her ultimate rejection of them? How could you do that to your child, strip them of all rights, all money, basically all heritage? And make them powerless to act.

Mmmmm.

Anthony's response to my email was immediate, and remained calm. A little sad between the lines perhaps, but calm. No full word capitals. He apologised for not telling me in person. Time had been of the essence, he said.

"But Sophie, it will mean you'll have a say; they'll have to listen. Sophie, you have to let us do this. Actually, I'm sorry, but we are doing this."

"FUCK YOU!!!!!!!!!!!!!!!!!!!!!!!!!" I typed and sent.

You promised you wouldn't tell.

Rememory 120

As soon as I wake, I hear my favourite stormbird, and another's haunting response. The Wall shadows enjoy the lack of inhibition in lone voices, and allow them to echo unhindered through The Wall's labyrinth.

My father and his cronies will receive the administrator-guardianship application response today, by email at least. The mail service hard copy to The Styx might be a week away, but no doubt it'll be the email that chucks the shit at the fan.

Hopefully, I'll be at school when he reads it—when they read it. I'm very worried. Change requires more courage than I think I have.

"Sharon." My father's voice sounded pre-reading-of-administrator-guardianship-application-response sing-songy and over-cheerful. Financial disaster was at least a few weeks away, so he was practising for his public face. I decided to draw on his courage.

"Sharon. I'll drive you all the way to school today. I'm heading over to Diamond for the sale. I'll pick you up on the way back through, so don't worry about catching the bus home. I shouldn't be late."

"Yeah, right," I thought to the last bit.

That's at least six hours' respite, I was thinking. He'd be out of mobile phone range for most of the time, and even if he remembered to take the phone, he wouldn't hear it ring or ping in the glove box over his country and western she-done-him-wrong songs.

I'd be back here, probably alone, when he found out. That would not be good. The back-of-hand swatting was working overtime. Again.

At school, most of the day was yet another practice for our senior formal graduation ceremony, so I didn't have much computer time. Just barely enough to check my emails.

Andrew had cc'd me into his application response. There it was, and there was my father's email address, and Dominic's and Silas's, alongside the qcat.gov address, all four of them neatly displayed next to the "to" bit.

It had already been sent. There was no going back.

Rememory 121

I wished the dust storm announcing their imminent arrival would float me away with it.

I could hear two cars. It's an approaching sonic boom like the der-dum-der-dum-der-dum-der-dum galloping scenes in *Gunfight at the OK Corral*. The first car had to be Dodgy Dominic's station-wagon, and the second, chewing dust, was Psycho Silas's penis car. Rabbit Warren and his belt buckle were no doubt with Silas. I could hear a two-person bottom-out on the house paddock grid.

My father was rattling around in his office, but hadn't checked his emails. He isn't the incessant check-social-media type. He was leaning back in his chair, smoking a cigarette, a half-drunk beer beside him, and he was half singing one of the Styx Lake protest songs, Bob Dylan's "Blowin' in the wind".

He looked kind of happy. I felt kind of guilty.

"Looks like we have some visitors, Soph," he said.

Sharon's face appeared at the door.

"Tea time for Soph, is it? Thanks, Shazza," my father said.

Shazza, you beauty! I was joyously grateful to her for once. This even trumped bringing *SeaChange* Series Two into my life. Thank The Wall shadows! I wouldn't be alone when they dumped the latest on him.

"Why the fuck don't you answer your phone?" Dominic said as pleasant greeting, stomping across the lawn and stomping down the verandah.

I could easily hear them all from the kitchen. Sharon was reading *That's Life* magazine while alternately spooning piles of orange and green muck into my mouth, also triple alternating with chunks of half-cooked fish fingers. Nothing they were saying was registering on her face.

Silas wasn't quite so bombastic as Dominic. "Have you read the email?"

"No idea what you're talking about," my father said. His voice had lost its smiley sound.

"That fucking Andrew Martin," Dominic said. "Fucking interfering ... for fuck's sake. I tell you, he's got a lot to answer for."

"He does seem to have overstepped the mark," Silas said. His voice fluttered a little in his vowels.

"Not so sure of yourself now, are you, Si," I thought as I mangled a still-frozen-in-the-middle fish finger.

"Here's a hard copy." Silas must have handed my father the email to read. The silence made me sick. Even more so than Sharon's "cooking".

"We'll fuckin' appeal, the fuckin' arsehole," Dominic said. "What fuckin' right has he got to interfere?"

"We can supply contradictory evidence." Silas is even scarier when his voice has this quiet, tempered quality.

"I can write a report as an expert witness based on my observations of her intellectual capacity over the last eighteen years. I think we can quash this rubbish."

From the kitchen window, I saw my father walking towards me. Sharon had parked me in my chair while she went to run the bath, and I was mighty nervous. He stood in the doorway looking down at me. My back-of-hand to mouth swatting had changed into gooey pink drool splattering down my front. He gently, but ineffectually, wiped my drool, dabbing me with a tea towel, then he just stood there, looking into space right at me, staring, but not really seeing.

In the background, the cronies were still ranting on about an appeal.

"Fuckin' this, fuckin' that." But my father was ignoring them, still just standing there, staring at the air around me.

"We'll start drafting the appeal," Dominic called, poking his head out from the office, ignoring me, aiming at my father's back.

"No," my father said, looking me in the eyes for the first time I can remember.

"There will be no appeal."

Chapter 34

Rememory 122

He pretty well straight away put me into a care facility—didn't even let me finish the last bit of school. It is called "assisted housing"—which is government- and everybody-else-speak for "put in a home for retards". There was no discussion, of course. I had a feeling something was up. There were gazillions of phone calls backwards and forwards, and he kept the office door shut.

Anthony kept me in the loop with all the other goings on, cc'ing me in all the correspondence and emailing the rest of the paperwork, so I kind of knew he knew I knew what was going on. I'm not sure if I totally believed it was all happening. A bit like you know it's true, but don't internally believe it.

The day before I was packed up and shunted off, we had our grade twelve graduation lunch at school. You don't actually have to pass everything to "graduate". Attendance is elegant sufficiency in most Queensland schools to attend "graduation" ceremonies, and definitely was at ours. No one at Mango Downs would willingly miss their "graduation" lunch. My father drove Sharon and me in, and he stayed for the ceremony. His eyes hardly ever wavered from my face, except to flicker towards Gus, who was always by my side or pushing my chair. Gus looked so hot in his ultra-white shirt, still with the new-shirt creases, and his father's second-best RM Williams wool tie. Gus'd even cleaned his boots.

Everyone at our school ends up winning a prize for something, and Gus wheeled me out front for us to collect ours—one each. Mine was for "Overcoming Adversity". Gus's was for "Community Service". I guess that meant me.

Yeah, Gus, you only got it because of me. Just kidding. But we're pretty much in sync, because as soon as he was handed his trophy, he waved it in the air, and said quite loudly enough for everyone to hear, "Thanks, Soph, you won this for me too, hey?"

Mr Stephens gave him a stern look, and his mother sniffed, clearly miffed that I was stealing her son's individualised thunder. Gus just threw his head back, gave a "yippee" and an awful whistle, and raced us back to our places, doing a handstand on my chair for the last roll up the aisle. Gus is very fit.

Mrs Stephens had something in her eyes and was wiping them, but I could see she was leaking a smile, and patted both Gus and I on our backs. Mr Stephens gave Gus a stormy look. He never gave me stormy looks. He gave Mrs Stephens a stormy look too, for smiling. So did Gus's mother, but in her case, more of a thunderstormy look.

We had a "formal" lunch in the open air under the school building. The grade eights to elevens waited on us and our parents. The students had decorated the table with mis-matched tablecloths, flowers from our school yard, and green and gold paper serviettes—our school colours.

I sat between my father and Gus, and Gus's mother and father sat on the other side of him. Thank the lordy lord Mrs Gus didn't sit this side of him, but I think she was being ultra-careful of the spittle, seeing as she was wearing her best beige linen. I think she said it was "mushroom" in colour, but it looked beige to me. She was wearing pearls, and she didn't have any bobbleheaded rollers in her hair.

Gus fed me my lunch.

His mother said, "Gus, for heaven's sake, her father can do that. You attend to yourself." Mrs Gus never uses my name.

But Gus just laughed, kissed her cheek and kept spooning me gravy squashed into mashed spuds, pumpkin and peas. We had beef of course. No one eats lamb, pork, seafood or chicken in public in cattle country. Definitely no tofu either, hey.

Anthony was there as promised, as unofficial art teacher. He sat opposite me and chatted to Mrs Stephens for ages. She looked really happy and so much younger, almost animated. I think she was wearing blusher. Ant chatted to Gus and me too, but there was no opportunity to have a real face-to-face chat on my computer. I still hadn't got over his betraying me. I kind of knew he had to do it, though.

Anthony and my father totally ignored each other. My father didn't even try to con him, charm him, seduce him or bash him. Very restrained.

My father was ultra-quiet, but nice. He stayed with me and made sure I was where I should be. Not that he really needed to, Gus was totally used to doing that.

Sharon was there too. She was sitting down towards the other end of the table with the brother of Cara, another girl "graduating" that year. Cara's brother was a ringer with a big silver belt buckle. It had gold highlights, so she must have been super impressed. I admit he was very good-looking back then. Now he's gone to seed and has a red face and huge gut. But back then he was a hunk. As if he would go for someone like her, except for a quick fuck.

Everyone was talking about what they were doing the next year. There wasn't schoolies because of the drought, and the daytime lunch "formal" wasn't really what anyone else'd call formal, but everyone looked nice, country nice. There weren't cleavages and fake tans out at Mango Downs State School, in dry-as-a-bone 2004.

A few people applied for uni—all girls. Two boys, including Gus, were going to agricultural college. The rest would be working locally in town, or on their family properties. Mr Stephens was proud of achieving his 100% earn or learn target for graduating seniors. That included me too. How cool is that! Who would have thought it, hey?

The day before our formal, Anthony had emailed me and told me he was applying for uni for me.

"No argument, Soph. What'll it be? Law? History? Medicine? Vet Science?"

"Very funny, Ant," I emailed back. "Is there somewhere I could do creative writing online? Something you only need a portfolio for, not a high school certificate?"

"Absolutely," he said. "Count yourself in."

Computer access might be a major problem, but we were all on a high, and I was caught up in the being-excited-about-the-future too.

Rememory 123

The sea is crying and the jasmine is drooping.

"Sharon, please pack Sophie's clothes. Everything that currently fits. Not her school uniform obviously. Just the things you think she'll like to take with her."

Sharon was too dumb to ask too much about what was going on, and started packing my stuff in his suitcase. I didn't have one of my own. Fortunately, I hadn't learnt to expect a choice of clothes, because there was no way she was going to be comprehensive in her packing.

As she wheeled me to the car, my legs and back-of-hand flapping were all going like whirly whirly tumbleweeds. I noticed the jasmine had no petals. I was scared.

Rememory 124

Raylene later told me my father rang her, and asked for her help.

They met at the new Mac shop in Leichhardt, she said.

"Go for broke, Ray, I want the best," she said my father said.

"How would you like to pay for this? Cash or credit?" the young shop assistant said.

"Credit, thanks. Visa," Ray said my father said.

"Certainly, that's a total of $7,792," the young shop assistant said.

"No dramas," Ray said my father said.

Rememory 125

That next day after our school graduation, only about forty hours after he knew about me and *Silent Scream*, my father drove me to Lilian Bay's Pro-independence Unit for Kinship and Enterprise—PUKE. They really don't think things through, do they?

It's a Christian aged care facility that also takes retards like me. I'm the only one under seventy, literally. But I've really come to like the other people here. Some of them are lonely, some skite about how many times their family takes them out, how flash the restaurant was, how many people were there, that sort of thing. It's a bit cruel really, because some people never have visitors, never go anywhere.

Generally, though, I like the other inmates. On the whole, they are very kind to me and funny. The ones with dementia don't remember that I can't talk, or that there's anything wrong with me, and chat on about stuff in their past, repeatedly. It's really interesting because they often throw in something new—old new, and I like that they see me as normal, as one of them.

We all have our own rooms, with our stuff put in furniture that our family can supply. I've only got the centre's furniture, but it works fine. It's fine for me.

My father drove me there that first day, wheeled me and my bag (his bag really) to my new room, then started to empty the suitcase.

His phone rang, and I could hear Gus's voice screaming down the other end, maniacally distraught, and showing far more than casual concern.

"Where is she?" Gus screamed. "What have you done? How could you do this? You're fuckin' evil, you fucker. You can't just dump her in some home just because you're sick of looking after her. You fucking low life fucker."

Gus hadn't read the advocate application response, so he still had no idea about me and *Silent Scream*.

My father wasn't getting any chance to speak. "Gus," he tried to say, "Gus—" But every time, he tried to speak, Gus interrupted him. It was going on and on, and must have been getting very annoying.

"Where the fuck have you taken her? How do I contact her?" When Gus paused a nanosecond to breathe, my father quietly said two words to him.

"Silent Scream," my father said, and hung up.

Part IV
Surrender – 2014-2016

And if you wrong us, shall we not revenge?
If we are like you in the rest, we will resemble you in that.

William Shakespeare, *Merchant of Venice*, III.i.60–62

Chapter 35

Rememory 126

I've moved rooms. This one is right at the back, really big, with a verandah, facing east, overlooking Main Beach and the Lilian Bay Islands, and in the distance to the north, I can see The Styx. The door is usually open, and someone is always watching me, in a good way.

"Hey, Soph. How's the study goin'?"

Gus breezed in, told one carer her hair looked stunning, hugged Alva who has the room next door to me and was in her wheelchair parked just inside my room, and in one flounce, he lay full length on my new couch.

"Great, thanks, how's the cows?" My Mac computer spoke aloud. I've got the latest, you-beaut, vocalisation feature set up on my computer. I've chosen a really cultured English accent—a perfect match, I reckon—not. The computer screen is massive, I can eye-type from my bed, from the couch, and from my favourite lounge chair that Gus made for me.

"Wanna go out for lunch?" Gus asked.

"Cool bananas," my computer said, which means yes.

"Dad emailed and said he'll be in about three, so I'd like to be back by then," my computer said.

"No dramas. You want to come too, Alva?" Gus asked.

Alva nodded, and shook her head and smiled, then drifted back into the past. "We'll bring you something back, then," he said. "Gingernuts?"

Alva smiled to people in her past, and patted Gus's arm. "Lovely boy," she said. She's pretty spot on, hey?

Gus reached over and opened my full-length windows facing the sea. Wafts of jasmine flounced in. He was very proud of his plantings and loved to remind me whenever possible.

"Mmmmmm, lovely, thanks, Gus," my Mac duly said.

"Anthony said he'd like to do a trip into The Wall again soon. You up for it?" my Mac asked.

"Fantastic. Love to." Gus rolled onto his back. He looked happy.

My eye-typing continued. "He's got a film crew who want to do a documentary on the nailtails, so he wants to check what it's like going in, in the wet season. We can all stay up at the house for the weekend."

"Don't suppose I can bring Mary?" Gus asked. Mary was his new rescue dog, and Gus hated leaving her alone. She hated it too.

"Of course. I'll call her my assist dog, so sure thing. Ant won't care. The rules are only there for when you need them, remember." I used my sing-songy voice app for the last bit. It was one of Anthony's favourite sayings.

"You ready to go?" Gus asked.

"Hang on, I'll just go to the loo first, so you don't have to take me when we're out." I always like to make him uncomfortable. Keeps him on his toes.

Gus was reading Calliope's arts blog when a carer wheeled me back.

"Calliope still at it?" I asked.

"Sure is," Gus said. "I was chatting to him on Skype last night. Ready to go? I'll grab your laptop. There's something I want to talk to you about, Soph. There's new research, Rett research."

"What do you mean?" my Mac said. I felt cold. Scared. My hand-swatting started up. I couldn't look at him.

"Calliope told me about it. Findings from a research hospital in the US. They've been looking into Rett. They think they might be onto something.

"Soph, even being able to control one finger would make such a difference," Gus said.

Chapter 36

Rememory 127

You normally only get two guest tickets at a uni graduation, but I wangled four. I pulled the disabled card, and told them I needed my two carers to come as well as my two guests. And I requested entry for my assist dog, Mary, too. Of course everything was granted. There's got to be some bonus, hey?

East Australia Uni is very spread out and you have to walk kilometres to get to the Great Hall, which is a dedication to the creative talent of accountants. Lucky for me I had my chair, so Gus, Anthony, Andrew, my father and Mary did all the walking. Another bonus of Rett.

Anthony and my father led the way, closely followed by me, with Gus and Mary walking next to my chair on one side, and Andrew on the other.

I told the "authorities" that I needed Gus and my assist dog to accompany me up to the stage for the degree handover and handshake. I'm evil, I know, but I told you I'd think of some benefits of having Rett.

I chose a poppy-red dress to really stand out against the black graduation gown. And it matched the red around the floppy Harry Potter hat that they assured me was not a joke.

The hall was packed and everyone was really happy.

"Doctor of Philosophy Creative Writing Sophia Beatrice Noorgoo Wukuburri," the Vice Chancellor read out.

I was just about racing Gus up the ramp. He even had to jog a couple of steps when he got left behind, gawping at everyone. Mary trotted obediently beside my chair, never deviating. She was wearing her new red harness to match my dress. She knew how to play the game.

The applause and caterwauling was deafening. I didn't know so many people knew me or who I was. The Vice-Chancellor carefully shook my chicken-bone hand, and smiled right into my eyes. My eyes smiled back, and she tucked the degree cylinder on the chair beside me. I tweaked my chair's joy-stick to set me off down the ramp in a sedate and dignified fashion. Mary trotted beside me, equally dignified.

Then whooooosssshhh, before we even got half-way down the ramp, Gus grabbed the two side armrests, kicked off into the air, hurtling us down the central ramp and red carpet, hand-standing on my chair all the way to the back of the hall. Mary leapt around crazily, tongue hanging out, racing ahead and barking. Not at all like an assist dog.

Rememory 128

After the ceremony, Gus drove Mary, my chair and me home to my PUKE room, and we sat on the front verandah overlooking the sea. The jasmine-wafting sea wind was enough conversation for all of us at that moment.

From a bashed and battered thermos, Gus poured mugs of chai he'd made earlier in the day. Chai only gets better after a few hours' steeping. He placed mine on the table within a straw's reach, and picked up his ukulele, interweaving a tune with the jasmine breeze. He played his slightly adapted version of Paul Simon's "The Sound of Silence"—adapted for me. Mary very gently nosed her head onto my lap as the words lilted through me.

I wept, but this time, not alone. And this time, the silence had a voice.

Epilogue

January 2016

To: sbnw@silentscream.com.au

From: ctsutsis@nyr.com

Hello Dr Sophia Beatrice Noorgoo Wukuburri,

Congratulations, Sophie!!! You are a marvel. I am so proud of you.

Anthony told me that you had your graduation ceremony last Friday. I wish I was there to congratulate you in person. He also told me you are doing really well living in your new place. You must be, to have achieved so much.

Creative writing huh? Any chance of you telling your story? WOW! THE most amazing success story against the most incredible odds in the whole world. If you do, or want to publish any sort of writing, let me know if I can help.

My wife, Janine, is actually a literary agent now — she's a partner in her agency — and incidentally, earns far more than me! I'm still with the New York Reporter, in a very cushy role, editing the Arts Blog site, but I still have my weekly column.

You may have heard from Ant, I have two kids now. Noora is six, and Styx is four — yes named for you and Styx River!

If ever you can come to New York, it goes without saying, you must stay with us.

Again, congratulations to you, my dear Sophie, and may your pathway smooth to glass.

Much love and admiration,

Calliope

To: ctsutsis@nyr.com

From: sbnw@silentscream.com.au

Hello Calliope

Thank you for your email and for your gorgeous flowers — you remembered jasmine is my very, very most favourite! Finishing the doctorate was such an amazing feeling — well worth the years of agony I put my poor eyes through.

You said in your email that if I wanted to tell my story, to let you know. Well I do want to, but not just as a story of success against all odds. I know that it may be seen as that, and I'm happy for it to be so, but my real purpose in writing this story is for justice — or is it revenge? Definitely some of both — wild justice, I'd say.

Rache ist süß. Reconciliation opens the door to the sweetest kind of revenge — not one of happy families and of forgive and forget, not one of anger and hatred, but a revenge that results in justice. By simply shining the light on the bastards at rest, shining a light, allowing the truth to air. I will take such sweet, sweet pleasure in watching them self-combust. Let the reader be the judge, jury and executioner.

I want to lay my story spreadeagled on the ground. I want everyone in it to be judged, to be made accountable. I want people to fry in their own septic souls. People in power over those who are vulnerable need to be held accountable for their decisions and actions — good or bad, good and bad. They need to know that at some stage, everything they do, everyone will know. Let them be judged by their actions, let the truth commend or condemn. Through this, let justice, revenge and reconciliation all lay their claims to each other.

I wrote my story as a memoir for my PhD, and it is attached. This story is my story, and this story is my mother's story. I have written it to give both of us a voice and to give air to whatever stench was buried when she left or disappeared. My mother melted into her Wuku invisibility cloak, and even the shadows aren't talking. My story will speak for both of us. It will bring us together, one way or another. When I find my mother, or what happened to her, then I will feel I will have made a place for myself in this world.

My memoir contains my memories: the memories of a young girl, the memories of a young woman. When I was very young, every day I kept mental rememories of my life: my life with my mother and then my life without her. It was how I held on to her. I told myself the stories over and over again, and merged them with The Wall shadows. When I first had access to a computer, I typed them all up, and kept them going — and still do.

I've left the story basically as I wrote it each time, adult tidied and extrapolated, but still adorned with the skin and garments only youth and young adulthood can own, can display. Our memories and perceptions warp when viewed from the horizon, far better to allow them to speak from the shadows close to their source. The shadows have kept me on track, and do still, because remember, as you once told me, truth is rarely written in ink. It lies in nature.

I know if my great grandfather Shakespeare was around to offer advice, he would have quoted his namesake and told me to "Tell the truth and shame the devil." I have laid bare as much truth as I know, and hope against hope that others pick it up, and dress it with their truth, and seek more truth waiting to be found.

Of course, I've filled in a few gaps, I have read her diaries, and have brought my adult understanding to the unfathomable, and I've listened to The Wall and let her speak for herself.

I know that telling my story may not end well, but please allow me at last to speak.

You are the only one I can trust with this.

Author's notes

I wrote *The Styx* because I wanted my daughter Sophie to be a hero. In real life, she didn't need this book to be a hero, but in her memory, I wanted my Sophie to have a voice. I wanted her to be a voice for other girls also severely disabled—especially for those who, unlike her, don't have parents who love them or family who love them. *The Styx* is an entirely fictional narrative, the Sophie in this story is a fictional character, but perhaps, for someone with Rett Syndrome, for someone young and vulnerable, for someone Indigenous, for someone living in a remote location, it could all be true.

The Great Basalt Wall in the story is loosely based on Northwestern Queensland's incredible Great Basalt Wall, but transposed to the fictional Central Queensland region of Lilian Bay. Red Falls is a real place within the Great Basalt Wall, but slightly adjusted for the story. Nigger's Bounce is also a real place in the same region of Northwestern Queensland, but to the south of the Great Basalt Wall. Black Gin Creek is an actual creek north of Rockhampton in Central Queensland. In Australia, there is a Styx River that runs through Ogmore, just north of Rockhampton; and another located in the Northern Tablelands district of New South Wales, east of Armidale. While the Styx River in this story is fictional, all three regions are unique wilderness areas and share the same ethereal, eerie quality.

The towns of Lilian Bay, Leichhardt, Pandanus Beach, other minor towns and Styx River Station are all fictional locations, all inspired by Central and Northern Queensland towns and other places I have visited or read about. People in Yeppoon and surrounds may experience some geographic wafts of familiarity from time to time.

I used to live on a cattle property north of Charters Towers and beside The Great Basalt Wall. While this geographic location inspired the setting of the story, none of the people from up there inspired any characters in the story.

The only exception is that, on the property, there is evidence of a past Indigenous population—but I was unable to find any remaining family members or even a name for the group of people. One man said his father knew of some people way back who came from the region, but they were all gone now, he said. The Wuku Wuku people of the story are fictional, but written in acknowledgement of a people no longer talked about or known. The Darumbal people are the traditional owners of the Yeppoon region in Central Queensland, where my story is loosely and fictionally located and on whose country much of this story was written. However, *The Styx* is not about the Darumbal, nor are the fictional Wuku meant to represent them in any way, except in one aspect: my story is a white migrant Australian's acknowledgement of and apology for the treatment—past and ongoing—of our Indigenous people past, present and future.

Having said that, I need to admit that two of the characters in *The Styx* are based on real people, using their real names and their actual website addresses.

The first such one I need to acknowledge is Anthony White. *The Styx* Anthony White is the real Anthony White, conceptual artist, ex-stockbroker, currently dump-truck driver, who owns an amazing property where he lives alone in his mansion on a hill overlooking a bay. Approximately thirty per cent of what I say about Anthony is true—maybe fifty per cent depending on your definition of truth. The remainder is fiction. You'll have to work out which bits are true for yourself, as I imagine even Anthony and I will disagree over which is which.

Anthony has not read the manuscript before going to print. He is, however, happy to be included in the story—in fact he kind of insisted.

"Make sure you write me in," he said.

"Like, use your real name?" I said.

"Everyone likes to be seen as a real person," he said.

Reality sometimes is a little unsettling and after a moment's thought, he added, "Should I read it first, or just trust you?"

"Neither," I replied.

"Fair enough," he said, and we both happily left it at that.

There is another Anthony White artist, the Australian-born, Paris-based Anthony J White. Best not confuse the two.

The other real person is the artist Sapiophile, who is also a real artist and, just like in *The Styx*, is also a doctor. She has agreed to be named via her website sapiophilestudio.com and is the sister of the real Sophie.

All other characters and names, apart from very well-known public figures, are entirely fictional.

I was inspired by an article on the Boston Children's Hospital science and innovation blog—see <https://vector.childrenshospital.org/2014/03/rett-syndrome-sees-glimmer-of-hope-in-phase-i-trial/>—for recent research regarding Rett Syndrome, but *The Styx* novel does not represent or reflect this research or findings.

The endangered bridled nailtail wallaby is indeed endangered and is in reality endemic to Central Queensland. For general bridled nailtail wallaby information, I accessed the site <https://www.ehp.qld.gov.au/wildlife/threatened-species/endangered/endangered-animals/bridled_nailtail_wallaby.html>, but I have extended the known facts of this species in *The Styx*. (I have probably a bit more than "extended" the known facts in pursuit of the nailtail's fictional stardom.) For information about the wallabies' scat, I used the following reference: B Triggs, *Tracks, Scats and Other Traces: A Field Guide to Australian Mammals* (Oxford University Press, Melbourne, 1997).

Some other places and historical events have been slightly adjusted to fit the story. The location of the Queensland Education Department has been transposed onto the Department of Primary Industries building in Ann Street, Brisbane. The Queensland pilots' strike was actually in 1989, not the early 1990s. Cyclone David happened in January 1976 but Cyclone Thea is fictional.

One line in the "Shadows of the Wuku" was inspired by the line "Drink the wild air's salubrity" in Ralph Waldo Emerson's poem, "Merlin's Song". In the Epilogue, the words "truth is rarely written in ink. It lies in nature" are adapted from words of Martin H Fischer.

Acknowledgements

Thank you to my specialist scientific, environmental and Indigenous issues advisors for your information, clarification and recommendations. I am so grateful for your support and input. All errors are mine alone.

Thank you to Linda Nix and Chris Mitchell of Lacuna Publishing for choosing my manuscript and for supporting my writing.

Thank you to Queensland Writers' Centre Hachette Manuscript Development Project for including this manuscript in your 2015 program, and thank you to Hachette editor Kate Stevens and author Kim Wilkin for your input as a result of this program.

Thank you to my sister, reader and mentor Valerie Cameron, without whom writing would be a far lesser—and less informed—pleasure.

Thank you to Indigenous writer John Wenitong (author of *The Fethafoot Chronicles* under the pen-name Pemulwuy Weeatunga) and scientist Flavia Santa Maria for your advice and support.

Thank you to Diversy River Writers (2015 QWC/Hachette Manuscript Development Program group), Kali Napier, Victoria Carless, Imbi Neeme, Sue Pearson, Wendy Davies, Susi Fox, Angella Whitton, and Mary-Ellen Stringer for your manuscript feedback, peer mentorship and support. An extra thank you to Kali Napier for going so far beyond the call of duty with your time and knowledge.

Thank you to academic Stephen Butler, artists Sari Beasley, Caroline Huf and Anthony White, and writer Bruce Honeywill for your support in the very early stages when I needed support, "permission" really, to continue on my own writing pathway. Thank you to Meredith Gray for your brilliance.

Thank you to academics Lynda Hawryluk and the late Liz Huf for year after year organising and hosting Kanome Writers writing workshops at the beautiful North Keppel Island Environmental Education Centre.

Thank you to the Sunday afternoon hippie volleyball and chai crew who make such inspiring and generous friends.

Patricia Holland, July 2017

About the author

Patricia Holland was born in Liverpool, England, but has lived in Australia since the age of five, in Melbourne and on farms and cattle stations in Central and North Queensland. She now teaches at a secondary college and lives in a coastal town near Yeppoon in Central Queensland.

Patricia's publications include:
- journalism articles in magazines and newspapers, including *Queensland Country Life*, *Outback Magazine*, *National Farmer*, *Townsville Bulletin*, *The Morning Bulletin* (Rockhampton), and *The Northern Miner* (Charters Towers);
- short stories in *Idiom 23 Literary Magazine*; and
- a children's book, *Patch the Australian Cattle Dog* (1999), which won a regional education award.

Patricia Holland
photograph by Glenn Adamus

The Styx is Patricia's first novel, and is dedicated to the memory of her eldest daughter, Sophie, who suffered from Rett Syndrome and died when she was seven years old. Earlier drafts of the manuscript were selected for Hachette's Manuscript Development Program in 2015 and Legend Press's Luke Bitmead Bursary in which it placed third in 2016.

Readers can find out more about *The Styx* and Patricia through her website:

www.patriciaholland.com.au

Lightning Source UK Ltd.
Milton Keynes UK
UKOW01f2214050318
318931UK00001B/365/P